"... .... his daughter ...."

THE

PEER AND BEGGAR;

A DOMESTIC TALE

LONDON

THOMAS WHITE PRINTER AND PUBLISHER,

59 WYCH STREET STRAND

THE

PEER AND BEGGAR·

𝔄 𝔗𝔞𝔩𝔢 𝔬𝔣 𝔖𝔢𝔳𝔢𝔫𝔱𝔶 𝔜𝔢𝔞𝔯𝔰 𝔰𝔦𝔫𝔠𝔢.

CHAPTER I

LATE on a fine summer evening a travelling carriage disturbed the solitudes of a dreary waste called Hedgemoor on its way to Minhurst, the seat of a viscount of that name   The expensive attention paid to comfort and elegance announced the travellers to be of distinction   The postillion who was now convinced that he had mistaken the road but had not sufficient courage to avow his error was pondering in great anxiety on ' What her ladyship would say   so much so that he entirely forgot that every turn of the wheels increased the difficulty of his situation   This anxiety, however, was soon shared by others of the party

Behind the carriage rode Mr Robert and Ma amselle Eugenie both very excellent persons in their several capacities of valet and lady s maid

' Ven vill ve be dere ?   enquired the loquacious Frenchwoman

The man shook his head

I was at Minhurst once, said he " it is a long time since, however and the country may have undergone many changes   As yet we have passed no object I can remember

Only von time Monsieur Robert ! and you have been fifteen years vid de family ' Your young gentleman not often make visite to his papa den ?

Mr Ronald, replied Robert, addressing himself to Ma amselle and placing much stress on the last four words, " does not *often visit his father*

' Piay vat for he no visit his fader, Mistare Robert ?"

' Can t tell

'Oh mon Dieu! Mistare Robert you are not von polite man   Your vords say you cannot tell, and your manniere assure me you know very vell   Dere must be some motif —

" I know no motive except that my lady is too fond of her grandson to part with him

A graver conversation was in the mean time carried on between the inside travellers   A tall youth, of great personal attractions lounged back in the carriage and listened with much interest to the discourse of an elderly lady beside him   The latter had reached the age when all pretensions to beauty ought to have been long renounced yet her regular features left traces of the past that went far to justify the desire to please manifest in her careful and elegant costume

'What, in heaven's name, is the matter?   enquired Ronald as he jumped from the carriage

He found an answer in the scene of confusion before him   At some distance ahead he perceived by the moonlight the postillion engaged in mastering the leading horses who, frightened at the sudden confusion, had broken their races and darted off in full speed   Nearer stood Robert endeavouring to ascertain the extent of the injury, while an indistinct figure, a few paces behind rising slowly from the grass and smoothing down her dress, appeared Ma amselle Eugenie in the greatest trepidation

What is the matter   Eugenie?   enquired Lady Minhurst with really great composure considering her age and situation   " were you thrown off?

'Oh mi ladi are you not hurt?   Ah mon Dieu ! vat vas my fright for fear mi ladi vas killed !

" I am more frightened than hurt   Eugenie

By this time Ronald returned to the carriage

Is there no getting forward?   was the first question addressed by Lady Minhurst to her grandson

'The carriage must undergo repair before it can be moved   replied he

'What is to be done?   By the lateness of the hour we must be near Minhurst   do you think we can reach it on foot?

The blockhead of a postillion tells me he has mistaken the road we may be twenty miles from our destination   I have sent him off to procure a chaise and a guide from the first house   You must try to dose away the time till the fellow returns for I fear this is the only chance we have of a nap before day break

With these words the young man resumed his seat and Robert having closed the door on his master assisted Ma amselle Eugenie to return to her place on the dickey   This time the valet's good nature made him polite, for he not only enquired if his fair companion had escaped with whole bones but he even carefully wrapped her in a plentiful stock of shawls, cloaks and great coats

Though the accident had in some degree dispelled the soporific effect of a previous political lecture of his grandmother Ronald found no difficulty in relapsing into repose after the fatigue of a long day's journey

His companion was more restless The habits of an active mind and the incidents of a busy life seldom allowed Lady Minhurst the indulgence of slumber until the demands of exhausted nature became too loud for denial The object of her present journey furnished thought for a night's vigil and most entirely did she yield to the disposition to meditate that gradually stole over her

The nature of those meditations our task, as the narrator of events, hardly warrants us to disclose they might have borne a character of affection and delight—for a mother was hastening to see her son, a grand mother to present a grandchild to his father but humanity has produced some specimens devoid of their cheif ornaments, and the reader must be referred to the actions of this Dowager Viscountess for their true cha racter Whatever was the nature of those meditations they were as troublesome as absorbing Many an attempt was made to give them a different train but oppressive thoughts are foes not easily driven from the heart when they have once found their way thither Her Ladyship let down the sash and sought a balm for the mind in the fresh Midsum mer night air and the moon lit landscape without

It would have been difficult to have made choice of a spot or an hour better adapted for the purpose The situation was strangely still remote even from the baying of a watch dog They were at the extremity of a vast heath, of great elevation and the rough, unfrequented road led by a rapid descent into a valley of singular beauty

The carriage stood beneath a clump of beeches on one side of this tract (for it scarcely deserved the name of road) while opposite, the sil very foliage of a few aspen trees marked the opening of an extended copse Trees, hedges meadows were dressed in the rich luxuriance of high summer and bathed in a flood of gentlest moonshine

Lady Minhurst was not proof against the influence of the scene Such beauties were not new to her but long, weary agitated years had inter vened since she had taken delight in them She hung spell bound from the carriage window and gazed slowly around The deep silence and soothingly suppressed light brought relief to her spirits not unsimilar to the relaxation afforded by a bath to the jaded frame That moonlight that silence, seemed to her strange and novel—such as they might appear to one who observed them for the first time and yet were as familiar and refreshing in their influence as the caresses of old and valued friends They gave rise however to a painful recollection The restoratives of nature had been neglected for expensive pleasures that had harassed in pursuit and palled on enjoyment

The beautifully thrown lights, deep mysterious shadows, fantastic and even perplexing in their outline amused for a time but the eye of the spectator at last became rivetted on the row of aspen trees Pale and sil very their restless leaves shivered in the still air except on the side front ing the thick copse at the entrance of which they stood In that direction the trees assumed a warmer tint and while their paler neighbours were constant as the moonlight that produced them these glared red and vividly and then seemed to die away at frequent though irregular intervals A moment or two sufficed to convince her Ladyship that this phenomenon was occasioned by a fire kindled in the neighbouring copse, and with some alarm, she suspected their vicinity to a gypsy gang She instantly seized her grandson by the arm

'See said she as Ronald stretched and yawned 'the red glare cast upon those trees! There must be a fire near us in yonder copse

Before the young man could reply the voice of her Ladyship s maid became audible Mistare Robert! mistare Robert! Fire! Robbers! Oh vat vill be our fate! Mon Dieu!

To jump out of the carriage, and enjoin silence was the first movement of Ronald then calling his valet, he consulted with him on the steps to be taken in case of danger

Robert, though a faithful, honest servant, had not the stoutest heart in an emergency of the kind he therefore recommended patience and silence We may then escape notice, till Townsend comes back, said he

Yes! yes! mi dear young gentelhomme shrieked out Ma amselle Eugenie who from her elevated post overheard the council of war dat is vat ve should all do Grand silence! As you do say in English be tronquil as de leetle mouses

Don t be hooting there, like an owl!' cried out Robert trembling all over at the elevated tones of his fellow servant

An owl! vat is an owl? vat for you call me an owl? Monsieur Ronald, do you hear? He say insults he call me an owl! Impertinent! continued the loquacious Frenchwoman grande impertinence!

Ronald again insisted on silence and looked wistfully towards the trees which now glimmered brighter than ever in the reflection of the flames Lady Minhurst read the wish expressed in his looks, and felt that it was suppressed for her sake

I understand you, Roland you would learn at once the extent of our danger but are restrained by your regard for me I am of your opinion friends or foes, the persons who have kindled these flames must be confronted

What face the robbers, my lady? enquired the valet trembling from head to foot at the proposition

'Who told you they are robbers? continued the Viscountess firmly

I suspect after all our alarm has been excited by a harmless gang of gypsies at their midnight carouse In that case if we confront them, our appearance will most probably inspire respect did they, on the contrary surprise us in the carriage I have no doubt but cupidity would be the strongest feeling and we should not escape unmolested So persuaded am I of the course I recommend, that I purpose sharing the dangers of the expedition

Vat a vonderful voman! exclaimed the maid

Wonderful woman! responded Robert

The astonishment of both, however was uttered in an under tone, while Ronald was making an attempt to dissuade his grandmother from her intention to accompany him

I go Ronald, she replied ' we will leave Ma amselle under the protection of Robert I am sure we shall suffice for our own defence

It was a wonderful relief to the terrified valet to hear the post assigned him nor was Ma'amselle Eugenie less gratified with a plan which left her a companion

Preceded by her grandson Lady Minhurst made her way into the dewy copse They advanced with great difficulty over deep cart ruts, the trunks of trees and trodden branches now and then guided by a burst of brilliance from the fire, and again groping through the thick shadows of the underwood In this way they passed about a hundred yards when the strong smell of smoke and the vivid light that assailed them at a turning of the road, proved they were near the cause of their curiosity

Each paused and listened anxiously The wind scarcely moved the trees neither sounds of merriment nor suppressed whispers reached them yet they distinguished the cracking of the green wood as its fresh ness yielded to the force of the flames

This is no night carouse, said Ronald, turning towards her ladyship

' Hush listen ' exclaimed the latter in an under tone placing at the same time her hand on his ' hear you not ?

Sounds were now to be heard, and seemed like the deep drawn breathing of an aged man in a sound slumber A gentle breathing as though of a younger slumberer accompanied that they had first heard but so low that it would easily have escaped the notice of any one less interested than our travellers

Ronald looked at his grandmother when they had made this discovery even then he was far from being sure they were not exposing themselves to danger and he wished to deter her from her project

We have nothing to fear from what we have yet discovered said the intrepid lady, noticing the expression of the young man s counte nance

' Who would sleep unguarded in a place and hour like this ? he ven tured to enquire

The lady smiled ' These persons enjoy too sound repose to be guarded while they sleep Let us on I am impatient for the result of our expedition

A few more paces brought them to the small open space of sward on which the fire blazed Ronald tore up some and held back others of the brambles that impeded approach, and he and lady Minhurst advanced into the midst of a circle surrounded by trees illuminated with the re flection of the fire cracking and roaring in the centre They were too dazzled by the light to discern, for the first few seconds, the character of the scene and the company they intruded on Some cause natural or artificial had checked the luxuriance of nature and fresh green grass covered the ground instead of entangled underwood forming a wide circle of verdure bounded by young trees In the middle of this ring the wayfarers had piled the produce of their depredations on the neigh bouring thicket and there the supply still warmed them as they slept Far above the wreath of smoke might be seen the pure still heaven, where the waning moon contended with the first rays of a summer morning and the silent twinkling of its attendant star A rivulet could not be far distant for the murmur of a stream over its bed of pebbles made the ceaseless music of the spot. The ground rose gradually towards the trees and formed, on the side opposite to that by which our travellers entered a smooth bank, whereon reposed two figures whose appearance excited great interest

Not far from the fire was an aged man in a sitting posture his head and hands alike resting on his raised knees an oil skin hat concealed worn and weather beaten features. Part of his person was buried in shade while the unsteady fire light lent an occasional and wild distinct ness to the outline on which it fell. A slender form with the round proportions of youth was stretched on the grass, a few feet from the old man whose luxuriant hair veiled the face and neck, and the arm on which the head reposed. The careless attitude of slumber lent an additional grace to a form moulded after the 'cunningest pattern of excelling nature, though wanting as yet the fulness of womanhood. It appeared from the posture of the sleepers that the elder had been overtaken by slumber as he sat watching the flames and his weary companion

The newcomers remained some time silent. There was a beauty in the place and a peculiarity in the circumstances of those who occupied it, which awoke a lively interest in the minds of the Viscountess and her grandson. It would have been an act of sacrilege to have raised a human voice at midnight in a spot that might have passed for fairies trysting place and next to inhuman, to have broken on the slumbers of two poor travellers whose destitution and fatigue converted a cold bank and brush wood fire into luxurious accommodation. Once or twice, however, the thoughts of the lookers on found utterance in broken sentences

How old and wretched! exclaimed Lady Minhurst

How young and lovely! responded her grandson, betrayed by sym pathy into the ejaculation though unaware of its great dissimilarity to the one that preceded it

Another pause ensued during which the lady approached the fire, and found its heat no unwelcome change after the chill air of the morning

I would stop here till Townsend returns said she, " did I not fear our presence might disturb these poor people, who have most certainly a right to enjoy their quarters unmolested

Let us remain, observed Ronald " they cannot have reckoned on much privacy at this short distance from the highway

I do not know they must be unfortunate, and are entitled to our respect, replied Lady Minhurst

And charity added the grandson if we go, we must not leave them without a solid proof of our presence

' The old man's wallet is by his side, rejoined the lady " if we could introduce some money unperceived

" I have a better plan interposed Ronald " The old man must be more acquainted with Fortune's whims than his young companion can be what if we give the maiden an instance of the blind lady's caprice?

Lady Minhurst assented, and the young man, carried away by his hasty and whimsical project sprung gently forward, and in less than a second deposited a well filled purse in the lap of the youngest sleeper. He then hastened back to the side of the Viscountess, and offered his arm to lead her to the carriage but an occurrence delayed their departure

The slumbers of the young and weary should be profound but slight indeed were those of the poor sleeper thus unexpectedly enriched either the situation was new to her or anxiety for the old man s welfare, kept her on the alert for no watch dog could have been more susceptible of the slightest sound The rustle occasioned by Ronald s feet in the long grass aroused her and as she sprung up in her seat, and looked anxiously towards her companion the purse fell unperceived, from her lap

These movements were not unnoticed by her benefactors To retire without attracting her attention was now impossible, and a polite fear of causing alarm led them to withdraw a step or two into the shade, where they were not likely to attract immediate notice This was not effected without causing a low sound, but it did not escape the quick ear of the girl In a moment she was on her feet, and assumed an attitude of deep attention Never was female more unconsciously guilty of being graceful yet her whole form thus suddenly exposed presented to the spectators an object worth a fortune to the skilful artist The effect her appear ance produced on either was suited to the characters of the two be holders the cold admiration of the lady became enthusiasm in the bosom of the young man As she stood in the fire light a gay smile as if derisive of her fears played over her handsome though almost infantine features a moment of reflection followed she drew her hand over her brow and looked sad, as if in painful thought Soon after she advanced on tip toe towards her sleeping father and here her panto mime took higher qualities than grace —a few gestures presented a moving drama of filial affection She first gently raised the man s hat and gazed fondly on his weather beaten face Satisfied that he slept she imprinted a kiss on his forehead covered his head with a kerchief taken from her own neck and then cautiously lowered his body into a recumbent posture better suited for repose This duty discharged, she stood a few minutes beside him, apparently grateful for an opportunity of administering comfort to a beloved protector

' Let us speak to this lovely creature said Ronald in a whisper some minutes after when she had disappeared in the part of the thicket whence the noise of a brook proceeded

I require no persuasion returned his grandmother, "especially as our gift buried in the grass, may escape her notice but let us chuse a a moment least calculated to give surprise

The re appearance of the maiden evidently fresh from her morning s wash suspended their conversation The fair stranger turned towards the spot where she had passed the night, and seated herself on the grass While her hands completed some portion of her dress her clear blue eyes were directed towards the heavens, that bright and cloudless scarcely differed from them in hue If one spot in the wide expanse had power to fix these lovely wanderers, it was that occupied by the morning star On this she gazed long and reverently with admiration and pleasure that amounted to worship and prevented Lady Minhurst and Ronald from abruptly intruding on her   At length an object seemed to attract her attention   she leant forward and looked earnestly at something on the ground   then rising   advanced towards it   she stooped and picked it up   —it was the purse

No treasure finder of an eastern tale could have experienced more sur prise   Little care had been bestowed on the fastening   and the haste with which she raised it   moving the slide   part of the precious store fell to the earth and studded the green sward   The maiden gazed on the treasure with an astounded air, and seemed to hesitate whether to gather it up or call her father   At length   the former course was decided on and kneeling down   she proceeded to restore the coin to its silken enve lope   The opportunity was too favourable to be lost   Lady Minhurst and Ronald left their concealment and advanced towards her   The gold produced more intense abstraction than her sleep had done, and they were at her side before she was aware of their presence   She started on observing the intruders, and with a faint cry of terror, bounded towards the other sleeper

" Strangers, father ! strangers ! cried she   attempting to awake him then   as if a thought suddenly occurred to her   she ran towards the Vis countess, and falling on her knees earnestly besought her   You will not harm him, a weak   poor man—do not   do not betray my poor father

' It is no part of our design   accident brought us here   we would rather assist him, if it is in our power, my pretty child,   said her Lady ship in a kind and conciliating tone

The maiden looked abashed   such kind words were unfamiliar to her and they excited her mistrust   After a moment s pause, as if for con sideration   she stretched out her hand   and displayed the purse

You are, perhaps, the owners of this money,   she observed   We did not steal it   he,   pointing to her father, " has not seen it   it was I that found the purse

We left it purposely in your way   and hoped that it would relieve your distress   Pray accept it,   interposed Ronald

The maiden s agitation had not as yet allowed her to notice the stran gers minutely   The benignant countenance of the Viscountess gave con fidence   but the more comely appearance of the tall and handsome Ronald again disconcerted her   Insensibly her eyes were   cast upon the ground and a deep crimson suffused her cheek

" Take it back   pray take it back ! she muttered in faultering accents " I dare not keep it

The young man looked astonished   for he was unable   to read in her confusion the painful recollections this incident conjured up   Lady Min hurst, either influenced   by more   penetration, or an   indefinite sympathy with the feelings of one of her own sex   took the purse   and mildly added

' To convince you that we have no   design   beyond your   benefit and that of this aged man   allow me to present him   with the sum we design for your mutual use

' Not to him ! for the love of heaven give it not to him ! said or rather shrieked the maiden, with an agitation that made Lady Minhurst share the surprise at first confined to her grandson

" Surely this sum would benefit your father '

The confusion of the maiden encreased

" Gold is no benefit to him, she continued " it makes my father cruel, wild, frantic He is a good kind father when poor, but the gold he changes for draughts of burning liquor Oh, give him no gold, no gold !

' It will, however, be useful to you, ' persisted Lady Minhurst " You are in want of raiment take this, my good child, and buy some In return you can replenish your fire We are detained on the road the night air is cold and I am glad to meet with means of procuring warmth

This was sufficient it required persuasion to reconcile the mendicant s daughter to accept money unsought from strangers, yet this appeal to her sympathy for assistance was readily attended to—she had too often experienced the bitterness of denial to allow any to seek her help in vain Lady Minhurst drew near to the fire, now in much need of fresh supplies, which the young hostess of the wood with fawn like step bounded off to obtain

Some moments only had elapsed, when a sound at once familiar, and rare, reached the ears of the Viscountess It was a name, a well known name, uttered by a strange voice she listened with drawn breath for its recurrence—attributing the sound to imagination

" Evine ! repeated the voice in a louder tone, in which anxiety and displeasure seemed to be mingled

The Viscountess looked first at her grandson and then in the direction from whence it proceeded Imagination had not deceived her it was the old man who spoke She was awe struck From strange lips she had heard a name pronounced, no voice save the powerful voice of conscience had for long years forced on her notice So great was the surprise occasioned by this incident, so powerful the effect it produced on her excited feelings, that heedless of the presence of Ronald, and the suspicious character of the waking man, she sprung towards him

" Who did you call ? she exclaimed

The man looked at her with a vacant stare then startled with surprise he made the wood ring, as he shouted in his loudest voice, " Evine ! Evine ! "

" For heaven s sake shrieked the Viscountess yielding to her agitation and following him, " who is it you call by *that* name ?

The man looked hard at the enquirer ' My child he replied in a sharp tone and then added with the air of one offended " but what is that to you ?

The reply of Ronald, who had watched the extraordinary emotions of his grandmother as may be imagined with no little surprise, was intercepted by the re appearance of the old man s child, who now emerged from the wood laden with fresh supplies of fuel for the fire

" Father ! exclaimed the girl, throwing down the burthen, and running towards the mendicant

My Evine ! my child ' ' cried the old man, embracing her tenderly why did you leave me ?

Lady Minhurst looked steadily on the girl in the arms of her fond

No 2

father   The fiown mantling on her brow revealed a thousand painful thoughts at work within   She seized the arm of her grandson   " To the carriage, Ronald ! to the carriage ' exclaimed she in a convulsive tone

She was obeyed   Lady Minhurst and Ronald walked rapidly away, unperceived by Evine and her father, who remained locked in each other s arms

---

CHAPTER II

No crowding, boisterous tenantry, no rustic pageant, welcomed Lady Minhurst to the mansion of which she had once been the proud mistress The unseasonable hour was an apology for this apparent neglect but the natural advantages under which the young heir beheld for the first time since infancy the seat of his ancestors, was to him an ample com pensation for the absence of rejoicing and congratulation

Minhurst park and mansion presented a magnificent spectacle as the carriage turned from the road, and passing through old and massive gates, drove up the principal avenue   The house was a spacious building of the Elizabethan age, with few pretensions to elegance and finery, but conveying ideas of stateliness and comfort to the beholder   It was situ ated in the centre of a well wooded park   and, viewed from a distance, appeared embowered in the gigantic timber which surrounded it

The sun had just risen above the highest trees when our travellers were able to command an uninterrupted view of the family seat   No one seemed stirring   no smoke arose from its countless chimnies, and the sunbeams were reflected from a hundred windows with the brilliance of burnished gold,   To contrast with this blaze of light were the long sha dows of oak and elm clad in all the richness of summer, thrown dark and fresh on the veidant sward   Even the giass sparkled with innumerable lights cast around by the myiiad dewdrops that studded its bright green A cloudless sky smiled over all   and, if to these visual attractions, we add the numerous and softened sounds of the morning, that rose in full chorus on the perfumed breeze, it will not be difficult to conceive that the young heart of Ronald craved no extorted welcome from vassal or tenant, as he drew near his home

" There is no one about, observed the Viscountess   " we shall be able to retire to our rooms unobserved

Though Ronald panted to see his fathei, a few hours delay was by no means displeasing to Lady Minhurst   A long standing feud had produced a considerable estrangement between herself and son, and there were conditions in their reconciliation of too mortifying a nature to her self, entirely to remove all embarrassment at meeting   Her cold and calculating nature struggled therefore with the feelings of a mother, and with a counterpoise so equal, that she longed for a few hours rest to determine on the deportment she should assume at the approaching meeting

This respite, however, was denied her a few more minutes united the long separated mother and son

A full hour before the wheels of the carriage broke on the stillness of Minhurst park, its owner was seated in a cool apartment annexed to his library, and opening on a small garden of choice plants arranged with great care He appeared about forty His handsome countenance was shaded by an expression of melancholy, devoid however of all harshness, though sad enough to gain the respect and sympathy of the stranger The general character of his physiognomy announced intellect and firmness a quick bright eye bespoke considerable mental activity yet there was something subdued in his demeanour, which solitude or suffering had evidently added to his natural character

Though at that early hour most of the inmates of Minhurst were soundly slumbering the apartment bore witness to an earlier visitor than Wilfred, Lord Minhurst his books and papers had all been neatly arranged, the French windows thrown open, and even the vases replenished with his favourite flowers, the very blossoms of which on the preceding evening had drawn forth his admiration as they hung on their graceful stems

To the uninterested observer these particulars might appear the result of a valued domestic s care, but the pleasure that beamed in the eye of the worthy nobleman as he glanced round his favourite retreat, plainly told that he recognised a more beloved hand in the detail of the arrangements

A common, undisciplined mind becomes by habit strangely unconscious of the every day blessings it enjoys it will not, therefore, be discovering the darkest shades in the nature of the new character we are introducing, to say that his heart, though long and constantly familiar with such displays of feeling, responded to them as readily and deeply as when they first surprised by their novelty, or soothed by their tenderness. To enter the room and look around him with the satisfaction of a well served master, was not his only part he had to suppress the overflowings of a thousand grateful emotions, and to dash away the tear that he surprised clinging to his eyelash

But we might have spared the reader this brief scene of pantomime, and made him acquainted with his lordship at the rising of the curtain, in this our second chapter, by a stage direction, such as, " Lord Minhurst discovered sitting in a pensive attitude, for in that position must we fix our actor before we can commence the business of the scene He had not been many minutes ensconced in a library chair before a young lady stole unperceived on his privacy With movements light as those of a sylph she glided forward, and reclining unperceived against the chair back, gazed affectionately on the person who filled it The two countenances thus brought side to side presented a strong resemblance and features that seemed handsome and dignified in the worn man, wore an aspect of surpassing loveliness in the half childish, half womanish countenance of seventeen

" Papa, said a voice whose music did no disparagement to the charming lips from whence it proceeded

It were useless to describe the action that followed Justice cannot be done to the fond spontaneous caresses of affection the child and parent who can recall (and who cannot!) the tenderest domonstrations of kindness they have received, will be able to bring before his mind, more vividly than we can describe it, the morning greeting of Lord Minhurst and his daughter Mira

The first enquiries of affection over,

" Shall we see Ronald to day ? ' enquired Mira

" I trust we shall, dearest I am unable to account for his not arriving last night

" And anxiety kept you awake I am sure of it, Papa you look so languid this morning '

' I confess I have not been free from anxiety

" It is very naughty of you to give way you know how easily a person may be detained in town a few hours later than he purposes I am sure we shall see him before the day is out He must be very much grown !'

" I am not so confident about it, Mira

" Why not, papa ? I am sure you would not deprive me of the pleasure the expectation affords without some cause

" Believe me, dearest, I would not," observed his Lordship pressing the young lady to his bosom, and looking in her countenance with a me lancholy expression

" Dear father, you alarm me Your manner is sad and mysterious

" I have long wished to admit you, Mira into my confidence on a subject closely connected with my peace I wished to make you ac quainted with my feelings before the arrival of your brother, but wanted resolution to do so This accidental delay affords me an opportunity I will not let pass Sit down, my love "

This language sounded strange to Mira Lord Minhurst had devoted ten years of solitude to the education of his daughter He had followed a system of training which tended to merge the relation of parent into that of friend and with so much success, that he became thoroughly acquainted with the heart and mind of his young pupil, who in turn never suspected that a secret existed in the bosom of her parent which required to be divulged in a formal act of confidence These words seemed at once to suspend the familiarity of friendship, and to leave room for anxious and painful conjecture It was therefore with a trembling hand and beating heart that she drew a low stool close to the chair in which he reclined, and seating herself, waited breathlessly for his narration

" You are my only treasure Mira, of two children, you seem to be the one allotted by Providence to engross your father s solicitude, and I trust to cheer the path of his declining days Rank wealth and a mind unambitious of distinction have not secured me from trouble Formed by nature to find satisfaction in domestic enjoyments, I have met with bitterness and suffering in my own house

' In your home, dear father—in our own quiet Minhurst ? Surely I —

' Patience, my child My unhappiness began long prior to your

birth that event has been its only mitigation To be brief in my story
At twenty one, I seemed in possession of all that can make life pleasur
able Young, handsome possessed of good parts improved by education,
and a peer by descent, I left college crowned with academical honours
to enter into the full enjoyment of all the privileges of rank and fortune
My mother was in ecstacies with my appearance and accomplishments,

and during my first season in public life I was the object of her idolatry
Excessive as her attachment appeared to some mothers of her rank, and
ridiculous as the unnatural custom of fashion led them to pronounce it
I had a heart capable not only of responding to the fondest yearnings of
maternal affection, but of finding the utmost pleasure, the very height of
my desires in her approbation Alas ' I was soon doomed to discover
that the best affections cannot escape the contamination of worldly
feelings do not shudder, Mira, beneath the fervent attachment of my
mother ran an under current of strong insatiable ambition I will not
enumerate the different stages by which this passion became manifest
neither can I attempt accurately to define its nature To this day I cannot
persuade myself that my beloved mother was originally or at any time
became, destitute of maternal feeling—maternal feeling in all its purity
and depth I cannot however deny, as you will soon learn, that to secure
distinction she has done more than place my peace of mind in peril To

reconcile the good feelings, whose existence I believe in, with the cruel treatment I have experienced I am forced to conclude that distinction and happiness are, in the opinion of my revered parent, inseparable, and that she conceives the true welfare of her son to be involved in his success in the world

I soon discovered that my mother s ambition made her careful to secure power   With the exception of Minhurst, which went with the title, all my father s property was secured, both enjoyment and reversion, by will to his widow   When a season or two had made evident my want of taste and capacity for the brilliant and hazardous career my mother wished me to pursue, I was plainly given to understand that my fortunes depended on the violence I did my own nature, and the subjection I manifested to her wishes   The best intentions can be nothing against incapacity   and my parent had recourse to another method to secure her desire   Her new plan was a matrimonial alliance   and, fascinated by the power of beauty, I fell into the snare   The lady fixed on was the daughter of a statesman   a man of great talent, extensive popularity but ruined in fortune   His child inherited her father s talent and her mother s beauty   and, united to these advantages, the experience, energy tact, and ambition of a family essentially political in all its branches   I cannot take upon me to say that she assumed the part of a diplomatist for the first time during our courtship, but I am certain that she then displayed the powers of a consummate actress   So thoroughly tranquil and humble were the tastes of my mind, that the appearance of wit, intrigue, and an inspiring disposition would have scared me   but these traits were carefully concealed   and I gave my hand and heart, as I thought to a young girl of great simplicity and exquisite loveliness

' My mother ' interrupted Mira, her eyes filling with involuntary tears, and her heart thrilling with the emotion that name must ever produce in a healthful mind

" The same dearest Mira   But be not apprehensive   I would not prejudice your mind against the sainted memory of a mother were it in my power   While my story requires a faithful portraiture of your parent s natural disposition, justice to her memory requires me to add that she engaged from a sense of duty in a glorious and successful struggle against sentiments and desires of dangerous splendours   When she found I could not soar with her Mira she limited her flight to mine If her nature debarred me from the enjoyment of sympathy, I esteem her living, and respect her dead

" To resume   I soon perceived   but not until it was too late   the real design of our union   At first it made me very unhappy   as I obtained an insight into my wife s character I dreaded the worst consequences but on better acquaintance I found that my mother had outshot the mark   My wife s aptitude for political life, her great abilities, and mo derate ambition   were more under subjection to right moral feeling than could be suspected, while no trial called for its exertion   Time, however, made us acquainted with our mutual tastes   when, each recognising the duties of the other   on each side such sacrifices were made as to ensure our mutual happiness   and your grandmother s hopes were for a time clouded   It was not to be expected that the projects and desires of a life would be abandoned by an ambitious, enterprising woman, while yet in her prime   Unable to make my wife the immediate instrument of her views, she succeeded in gaining an ascendancy over her that has given me an uneasiness which I fear, will only terminate with life

"Dearest father! exclaimed Mira, yielding to an emotion the last words excited

"Your patience a little longer   I became a father, and doated on my babes, Ronald and yourself   Forgive me Mira, if what I am about to assert, have the appearance of partiality   I have been severely punished for it   I said I doated on my children   but sympathy of sex, a lively prospective interest in the pursuits and fortunes of my son, closely bound my happiness with the welfare of your brother   On him I expended my solicitude   to his culture I devoted my energies, when a severe blow destroyed this, my fondest, my proudest scheme   Your mother Mira after a short illness died   You weep, Mira and my tears can flow with yours, though her last request has embittered for ever my existence'

"Oh, say not so! my dearest father

"Listen, Mira   The instigations of my mother accomplished what the dearest inclinations of my revered wife's bosom had never effected, while opposed to her duty   She inflamed the imagination of her sick daughter in law with gloomy views of the prospect that awaited her infant son, if placed under a guide calculated to rouse and cherish in his breast desires corresponding to his hopes   My incapacity was hinted at, dwelt on, reprobated   I was accused—I, a father—of inanity, indifference, when the welfare of my son was concerned

'You, my father! Alas, no faith could have been given to such statements ?

"They were whispered into dying ears Mira   sunk into a mind enervated by sickness, oppressed with solicitude, and, impressed with the brief space left for action, ready to obey the counsels of the first adviser I was summoned to the bed side of my wife, her death bed, Mira   Life was ebbing fast   she retained her loveliness in death, but so reduced, that the heart ached with pity at the sight

'My poor mother!

"Well my child, in that awful moment, when respect for the dying prevented denial   when sorrow for my own loss, and the loss of my children, almost suspended volition, a vow, a solemn vow, was extorted from me

Here the emotion of the speaker prevented utterance, and his youthful listener shed bitter tears from downcast eyes   He soon resumed

"It was a terrible oath, Mira and its fulfilment for a time seemed to deprive me of all motive and desire of life   Yet I must not repine   the request came from dying lips   and if sainted spirits observe with pleasure attention to their last desires, she may rejoice in my obedience

"But, dear father, this terrible oath —

"Required, my dear one, the extinction of a father's feelings towards the child on whom he doated   obliged me to resign the guardianship of a son to others—to confide him, body and soul, to my mother—must I say it, to my ambitious mother This explains all—the long absence of Ronald, your little intercourse with him, the cold tone of his letters My son has been no son to me God ! I thought my heart would have broken when they claimed the obedience of my promise, and parted us but heaven is merciful, and you were left me, you, my Mira, my own dearest daughter

The father clasped his child with tenderness and his warm tears be dewed her smooth white brow Heavy sobs, however, betrayed the bit terness of the recollection

" Dearest father, all may yet be well Ronald has attained the years of discretion, and they say he has a noble nature The son will return of his own accord to his father this voluntary visit looks well

" If he come, Mira if he come ! ' exclaimed the nobleman with energy May he not be the tool of my mother—the victim of her pernicious opinion that elevation and excitement are the only sources of happiness ? nay, is he not bound to her by a firmer bond ? On her he depends for fortune her displeasure can reduce him to beggary

" Oh, not so, while the reversion of the estate of Minhurst falls to him '

" It is nothing now, Mira, responded the father, " but a vain and expensive title Encumbered with mortgages, charged with a provision for your necessities, it will but burthen my poor son There is no hope ! no hope ! He cannot escape from the sway of Lady Minhurst '

" At any rate he will come to us, said the affectionate girl, with a tone of hopefulness " and then I am sure your fears will abate, my dear father

" I doubt it "

These last words, the language of deep dejection, had scarcely fallen from the lips of Lord Minhurst, when the sound of a carriage was heard Mira was the first to catch it and to run to the window and hasten back to her father were the movements of a moment

" Did I not say he would come ? ' she exclaimed

We refer our readers to the next chapter for the family meeting

---

CHAPTER III

A few words of further explanation are necessary to complete the description of the respective circumstances of the different members of the Minhurst family given in the dialogue between Mira and her father

The dowager Viscountess, despairing to realise the schemes of family aggrandisement through the instrumentality of her son, transferred to her grandchild Ronald, the expectations and solicitude previously cen tered in his father To prevent a second failure she persisted in main taining an entire controul over her new pupil a task of no great diffi culty after the promise extorted from Lord Minhurst by his expiring wife

During Ronald s childhood it required some firmness to resist the importunities of the bereaved parent, who constantly clamoured for permission to hold intercourse with his child but these attempts were as constantly met by refusal, and the perseverance of the applicant and the inflexibility of the refuser at last ended in perfect estrangement Among the first desires however, of the young man on being released from educational control was a strong yearning for intercourse with his father and sister The Viscountess could not stoop to combat his wishes by having recourse to slander, and dared not to support her objection by a sincere disclosure of her motives With reluctance then she made the long desired concession but to prevent the injury to her designs that might accrue from such indulgence, she determined to bear him company on the proposed visit

We have seen how their journey was accomplished, and it will easily be conceived, that under such circumstances the pleasure of meeting was embittered by the recollection of the past

Mira had scarcely announced the arrival of Ronald, than both father and daughter advanced to meet him

'My mother!' exclaimed Lord Minhurst with surprise, but losing, as he embraced her, every uncordial feeling

"Wilfred!' rejoined her Ladyship, in a tone of affection that was rather the result of tact than the effect of feelings suited to the occasion

"Welcome to Minhurst, my dear mother, this surprise is most agreeable, responded the son

"I am doubtless, an unexpected visitor, observed her ladyship

"Believe me not the less welcome Mira, my love, embrace your grandmother'

The whole attention of the young lady had been directed to her brother she had expected him with the interest of a warm, affectionate heart, and his appearance added admiration to her sisterly enjoyment Her mind, therefore experienced a sudden change of feeling as she obeyed her father and drew near to Lady Minhurst for what she had heard during the morning gave her no favourable opinion of her grandmother and she received her caresses with a shrinking, trembling heart Her ladyship kissed Mira with cordiality, and looking towards Lord Minhurst with an expression of admiration—

"You have concealed a treasure in the solitudes of Minhurst,' she observed

'Mira is an excellent child my great comfort, madam '

'No doubt! no doubt! We must become better acquainted, my pretty child Ah, Wilfred, how much is lost by family misunderstandings!

There was something in the tone of the speaker too much approaching ostentation, to gratify the Viscount he knew and feared his mother and an observation so unusual on her part, called for wariness on his The arrival of his son absorbed for the time every other feeling Locked in each other s arms, they abandoned themselves to the delight of the moment Lady Minhurst unused and little attached to demonstrations of feeling was the first to disturb their transports

No 3

" Your retreat is positively inaccessible, Viscount   and we have not
reached it without toil and adventures

The hint suspended further intercourse   Lady Minhurst withdrew
to her apartment

" Nay, my child, I do not require your attendance,' said she to Mira,
who offered to follow

" You must want rest, also, dear Ronald, observed the young lady,
while her father conducted his mother from the apartment

" I am too avaricious of enjoyment to take rest on a day like this, dear
Mira   Can I remember weariness when restored to such a father, such
a sister ?

Neither the solicitations of father nor sister could prevail on Ronald
to withdraw for a few hours repose   he had too many questions to ask,
too much to observe, to yield to their kind persuasions

Having quickly dispatched a hearty meal, and changed his dress, he
joined his delighted relatives in their favourite apartment, where a con
versation enlivened by interest and affection was soon carried on by the
happy trio

This was no moment for a formal enquiry into the nature and extent
of his son s studies   yet the countenance the figure, the manners, the
address the whole appearance of Ronald obtained the father s most
decided approbation, and by a strange similarity of thought, the physical
qualities most admired by his sister, were the immediate effects of the
mental qualities approved by the Viscount   Mira loved to look upon
her brother s noble open countenance, and admired his easy, unaffected
style   Neither was Ronald inattentive, or less pleased with the result
of his observations   In the Viscount s demeanour he discerned a
suavity that invited confidence, a dignity that ensured respect   and, if
any regret mingled with the pleasure of this introduction, it was caused
by the reflection that he had been long and cruelly deprived of inter
course with such a father   For the young Mira he felt both tenderness
and admiration   By turns, his rapture was transferred from her slight,
elegant, scarcely formed figure, to her beautiful countenance, whereon
the thoughtfulness of womanhood sat on features almost infantine and
then, to the brief simple sentences that escaping from time to time in
musical accents from her lips, disclosed a pure and elevated mind   A
short interview sufficed to make the little party delighted with each
other, and proved how justly Lady Minhurst had reason to dread the
effects of her pupil s visit to his nearest and dearest relations   But we
must intrude on the Dowager Viscountess, and notice the means she
employed to recover from the fatigue of her journey

It was high noon, and Lady Minhurst, just risen from the couch on
which she had endeavoured in vain to snatch a few hours slumber sat
before a toilette of no very modern construction, arrayed in a dressing
wrapper   Eugenie at her post, as renovater of nature, at the side of her
mistress

" Mi ladi nevere flatter herself—no, nevere ' ' commenced the atter
dant whose fingers, by some unexplained law of sympathy moved most
expertly to the accompaniment of her tongue   " after de peril, de danger
of de voyage, I very sure mi ladi look von vondare

'Your skill will soon put me to rights, observed her ladyship recovering her complacency as the process of renovation advanced, and grey hairs disappeared beneath the peruke and wrinkles under a tolerable layer of enamelling "Make haste, my good Eugenie this dressing is a terribly tedious business when I have no one to read to me

"Does mi ladi desire a morning dress ?

"No Eugenie I shall not leave my room before dinner, and will dress now Is Townsend returned ?' continued her Ladyship, growing more and more restless under the hands of her maid

'I vil ax mi ladi

'No matter finish what you are about You told them to let me know the instant he arrives ?

"Yes mi ladi I obey your orders

The business of the toilette now proceeded in silence—her ladyship growing more and more thoughtful and less able to endure the babble of her attendant, who with the enthusiasm of a skilful artiste, fell silent as her work approached its completion in order to contemplate more at leisure the effect of certain wonderful combinations of millinery and jewelry

"That will do Ma amselle, said the Dowager, after a very brief survey of the full length figure reflected from the glass "Stay, Eugenie you may enquire if Townsend is come back, and bring me word

The disappearance of the attendant leaves us at liberty to enquire what important affairs so far conquered the sex s vanity in Lady Minhurst, as to make her regardless of the transformation thus speedily produced on her rather antiquated person To effect this purpose more easily, we will venture to report a brief soliloquy that was scarcely audible to the wainscotted walls of the apartment in which it was delivered

"Townsend cannot have lost sight of them,' began the Viscountess when left to herself "when he came back with the chaise, they could not have advanced a mile on the way to P—— Then, *they* were on foot, and he was well mounted I furnished him with gold Their place of resort once ascertained, spies may easily be hired No ! no ' they cannot escape me now This anxiety may be foolish I will do them no harm, yet I cannot rest till they are in my power

These reflections evidently led to deeper thoughts on vague conjectures a vague plan was constructed Conjectures and plan, however, led to a tolerably distinct conclusion for her ladyship observed as she rose to inspect the well known apartment she occupied—

At any rate, if my fears are true, in the very worst event, the promise of a competence will easily induce persons of their penury to place some thousand leagues of ocean between us

So saying she proceeded with her inspection That apartment was but *too well* known to the Viscountess Minhurst

CHAPTER IV

Memory is a powerful source of emotion never do we prove higher pleasure never experience deeper regret than when it enables us to act over again some joyous or painful incident of our past lives Yet the influence of this faculty is not voluntary we cannot always summon to our aid a gay band of recreative souvenirs, nor can we always shun those recollections which are the inevitable precursors of regret or remorse The most common event the most insignificant sound—a well known scene a trifling word a casual glance are often the conduits of this vast reservoir—the open sesame by which the treasures of this mental cavern are disclosed

Our sympathy with the Viscountess Minhurst led us to these reflections Unconscious of the suffering she was about to inflict on herself that unhappy lady proceeded to the inspection of her apartment It comprised a suite of handsome rooms in former days reserved for uses of state and splendour and now set apart by the owner of Minhurst for those guests who had the first claim on his civility and respect Association apart, there was nothing in the rooms to inspire a modern mind with gaiety Respect for their antiquity or consideration for their value had induced the several owners to retain the original furniture and decorations From the elaborately gilded cornice of the painted ceiling still hung a ponderous tapestry of grotesque design, the fabric of some renowned Flanders loom till it met the heavy carving of an oaken wainscoat Ells of stiff brocade of a dark greenish hue floated before the windows and round the huge bedstead with its four fantastic posts that stood in the bed chamber Sofas fauteuils divans covered with the same material, abounded in the other rooms, with here and there an antique vase and table, or a guerdion whose marble slab was sustained by fantastical and gilded legs Occasionally mirrors in massive frames of silver, or candelabræ of the same metal relieved the monotonous colouring time had imparted to the walls To these necessary articles of furniture were added various ornaments, the produce of different ages and climates Among the most valuable were a clock from Italy once curious for the delicacy of its machinery and at the time we write of equally remarkable for its clumsiness a cabinet of ebony inlaid with ivory, and containing among other rarities an illuminated Romish missal of great beauty and one of the earliest copies of the Protestant Bible, reposed cheek by jole in perfect harmony In the boudoir a few contrivances of modern luxury had been introduced, and the most fastidious belle could not have lamented the absence of any requisite article of furniture from the dressing room

₩ ' Will these old portraits be kept for ever? muttered her Ladyship, as her eyes rested on two full length portraits professing to represent the first Viscount and Viscountess Minhurst, that in frames more cumbrous than elegant had been by an unaccountable caprice, appointed to adorn the walls of the small chamber appropriated to the duties of the toilette

Such pictures never existed' she continued 'You have not grown more amiable since we last met my good friends you frowned *then* as you frown now

She laid a stress on the word then for her mind referred to a moment when she had cowered before the stern immovable glance of the painted figures—when she had regarded them, inanimate and unconscious as they were as intruders on her lawless privacy as eloquent though dumb censurers of her guilt These words were uttered almost jestingly but the drafts made on the resources of memory are quickly honoured and before she had gazed two minutes on the faded canvass an aching heart made her avert her eyes in search of more agreeable objects The manœuvre was unsuccessful turning from the pictures they rested on the glass distinctly reflected her whole length figure as she stood in the broad light of the large window The rouge had been applied with so much judgment as scarcely to conceal her extreme paleness now strongly set off by the rich dark folds of her long velvet robe Her symmetrical commanding figure would under other circumstances, have still been an apology for vanity but beside the figure reflected from the glass *memory* ringed another and suggested comparisons that overcame every feeling of satisfaction In the form thus traced by memory the same features were visible but how different a colouring filled up the outline—how different an expression played on the same countenance There was no luxury of apparel but the hue of health was on the cheek the smile of contentment played around the lips the whole appearance denoted health and peace As Lady Minhurst continued to gaze on the Psyche memory continued its task The younger form suddenly assumed a splendid attire, but as the diamonds sparkled from her neck and the silken folds enveloped her person clouds collected round the brow the smile of health and innocence disappeared riches had been secured at the price of peace and honour and Viscountess Minhurst in her age and decay bewailed the hour when she exchanged the simplity of an humble maiden state for the honours of a splendid bridal

She drew her hand across her forehead, and paced the room with haste

'This will not do—this will not do' she exclaimed 'Regrets for the past are vain as wishes for the future It is forty years since I made the choice moralists may term foolish wicked I have not flinched nor will I Nature fitted me for greatness if to attain it I have done what would have staggered others it was but an effort to fulfil my fate—a sacrifice to destiny This emotion is weak and silly To a thousand women these rooms, after what has passed would be terrible the Viscountess Minhurst must, *will* survey them with composure

Accordingly she entered the sleeping room, and began an orderly inspection of the different objects More than once an expression of pain played over her features though immediately suppressed but with what effort her quivering lips and close drawn nostrils betrayed Her emotions at length got the mastery and perhaps no actor in the horrid scenes that room had witnessed would have so long endured the painful associations

'Here,' said she, drawing swiftly open the silken curtains of the bed,

' the poor wretch quivered with terror beneath the scorn of her spirited rival here on *her* nuptial couch and *mine* she assented to her own un doing she, the honoured wife, at my bidding—mine, the despised mis tress At this cabinet, she continued turning towards the piece of furniture, ' she signed her own ruin and my triumph Ha ' ha ' ha ' how the pale, weak thing writhed in agony as my hand guided her pen She writhed and writhed, yet her signature was there her signature at length as when it graced a love letter

Lady Minhurst now paused the sound of light music drew her from her abstraction it proceeded from the clock, that was furnished with chimes an invention first introduced about the time it was made The eyes of the Viscountess rested on the dial the hands pointed to the hour of one Her manner had already exceeded the bounds of moderation it now became an absolute phrensy

"One ! one ' she muttered Aye ' that was the hour —but at night in the deep dark night The poor wretch shrieked as those sounds announced that her last moment of grace was gone There she was borne off—there ' there '—through that passage

And the lady drew aside part of the arras with a frantic jerk, and open ing a concealed door gazed with strained eye balls down an obscure passage

'Tis as dark now as it was then but there were her moans—she could not shriek —no no we took care of that '—and her long white arms stretched out for mercy—that I could see in the darkness, till exultation blinded and deafened me, and left me no thought but of my triumph

A step was heard in the outer room the lady let fall the arras on the private door, and endeavoured to appear composed Ma amselle Eugenie entered

" Well, Eugenie '

" A letter for miladi

The Viscountess took the letter from off a salvei borne by a footman It was a dirty, ill scrawled, epistle bearing an impression that strongly resembled the top of a thimble This billet offensive to sight and to smell, was seized by her ladyship with as much gratification as if it had been adorned with the armorial bearings of the most powerful person in the realm Its contents were as follows —

'My onoied lady and missus this leaves i quite well and arty, as i opes it will find your laship, which is saying a good deel, all things con sidering a preshious scamper i had after Them there beggur fokes as your ladyship as took a fansi to but i diskivered their iding plais such a den as isent to be seen ani day i the weak Not forgiten Your direk tions, i as took mi login next dore to hem, No 4, Ditch alley, in the bowrs of P————, an i dosent meen to los site of hem kneether As your laship seamed ankshious, i thot it best to watch mi hone self, coz its more shoorer than to sit on anither in sich a konfounded tiklish biz nis, so hif your laship will rite word wat i is to do, ile be shoor to tend toat So i remanes your la ships dootiful sarvent,

' AARON TOWNSEND

" Poskrip —if i may make so bold to give your laship a word o avice them ere beggur fokes isent no gud an loges in a plais as isent reseptical, a rendy vows for all sorts of rifraf '

" The messenger is waiting a reply, said the servant, when he per ceived her ladyship had finished perusing the letter

" Give me writing materials mi amselle See the man be taken care of, while I write an answer

The servant withdrew, and Lady Minhurst took her seat at a writing table It was no easy task to answer Townsend s letter She had de spatched him in pursuit of the new acquaintances made the previous night in the wood, with strict injunctions to ascertain their abode, and on no account to lose sight of them al edging as a motive for this extraor dinary step that she desired to benefit the young female She was promptly obeyed Townsend was young and soon started on such a scent the nature of his errand could not fail to gratify a handsome fel low of two and twenty who had every disposition to fall in love with the first fair object that came in his way

Thus far the Viscountess had incuried no danger in employing such an agent the contents of his epistle satisfied her however that it would neither be proper nor safe to entrust him further with her designs and indecision retarded the reply she prepared to indite She was interrupted in her task by Ma amselle Eugenie

" Mon Dieu ' I has no bit of head at all pardon, miladi dis caid has been upon your toilette von leetle half hour '

' A card!' ejaculated Lady Minhurst

Oui, miladi vat you call a cart—von leetle monsieur did leave it—a leetle leetle sir, so droll miladi!

" Gregory Grasp Esq solicitor!' exclaimed her ladyship, reading the card and why was he not admitted? he is one of my best friends

" Oh dear me! a friend of miladi! It is certain de leetle gentleman had an air very distinguished but miladi, it was not possible for me to know de leetle gentilman de very big friend of miladi

' I hope he will call again How provokingly tiresome! The man above all others, muttered the Viscountess who could serve me just now! Did he appear desirous to see me? '

Eugenie looked at her mistress with one of those rapid glances which reveal the birth of a suspicion and at the same time are so transient as to escape notice in the heat of conversation

' Yes miladi!' she rejoined in a look and tone that implied she expected to confer pleasure ' he looked very impatient de leetle monsieur seemed to have a great big desire to see miladi I tell him miladi sleep after her *voyage* he tell me he vill come again before dinner

Ah, he will return this morning?

" Oh, he so desire to see miladi, I am certain he vill not fail to come!

' Well! very well! Mr Grasp was always zealous

' I am sure he shall come and mi ladi looks charming to day

The attendant uttered these words with as much expression as she dared venture to give them It was however lost on the Viscountess who seemed to have suddenly abandoned her intention of writing to Townsend

' Ring, Ma amselle, she said, tearing to pieces the sheet of paper on which she had written a few words " let them tell the messenger there will be no answer If Mr Grasp calls inform me for every one else I am engaged ' and she retired into the inner room, closing the door after her

Grasp—Gre go ry Gras p' soliloquised the Frenchwoman, taking up the card her mistress had left on the table mon Dieu! vat a nime! veery good name dat for de leetle droll Monsieur I laugh at him and he is de big friend de favourite Veery bad taste of mi ladi to love that nasty leetle man! Vell vell! she is English De ladies of mi country are more difficult A great ladi to love that leetle monstare! Oh dat is too bad! I shall be veery sad here no life in de men all no better than as many posts—heigho!

With these forebodings Ma amselle Eugenie executed the orders of her mistress and had scarcely ended a mental recapitulation of the personal charms of the handsome footman to whom she delivered her message than she was furnished with another source of wonder and amusement by the reappearance of Gregory Grasp, Esq, solicitor, &c, and magistrate of the town of P——

Gregory Grasp had learnt during a life of sixty years to allow nothing to escape his observation His little quick eyes of nondescript hue embraced objects with a rapidity only equalled by the velocity with which he gave a telegraphic motion to a pair of shrunken shanks, and scraggy arms He soon, therefore read in the deep, respectful and to a man of his impatient mood, interminable reverences of Ma amselle Eugenie that he had greatly risen in the consideration of that lady since he first paid his respects to her about three hours before As he was too sagacious a man to indulge in speculation it never occurred to him to enquire the exact position he held in her esteem or he might have trembled at the elevation to which the Frenchwoman s fertile imagination had raised him

" Your servante Mistare Grigy Gasp   I am delighted to see you

" Gregory Grasp Gregory Grasp ' squeaked out the little man in a quick tone with a correspondingly rapid movement of his very sharp nose and chin   ' Gregory Grasp is my name, if *you* please Maam

" Ah ' excuse me, Mistare Gregory   de pronunciation of de English is so veery difficult

" Is her ladyship to be seen ? interrupted the irascible gentleman elevating his prominent features into an authoritative altitude, to express how he disliked the ceremony of the waiting maid   " Is her ladyship to be seen ?

" Ah ' Monsieur Gasp, miladi is so impatient to look at you she is in von great fevare

' Fevare ' exclaimed the lawyer imitating the accent of the French woman   The devil ' Come to Minhurst to die ' Will not made per haps ' Doctor s opinion—serious eh ?

" No ' no ' no ' You have bad comprehend it is an error—a great big error—no maladie of de body a fevare of de heart—dat is all   and a most emphatic leer accompanied the remark

' A Frenchwoman ' growled Grasp, or rather squeaked in a low tone for no sound approaching a base note was within the compass of his vocal organs ' Ogles me dont like it never did Lady Minhurst got a fever of de heart ' He ' he ' he ' Poor viscountess ' squeamish in her old days ' her French maid thinks it sentiment just like the Parlez vous cant endure them never could Well, well Maam he added, addressing Eugenie " let your mistress know I am here I fancy I am the best doctor for her fevare

Away ran Miss Eugenie, enchanted at discovering something that bore the appearance of an intrigue, though both the parties concerned had numbered three score years leaving Gregory Grasp highly exaspe rated at what he termed the inconceivable impudence of the woman, and the disrespect of the menial It was curious to observe the mocking smile that curled the lips of the maid as she ushered him into the pre sence of her mistress

" Lady Minhurst delighted long absence—health—journey—reco vered from fatigue were the principal words audible among a long train of sentences delivered with great rapidity by the visitor, and accompanied by innumerable angular bendings of his slender person

Ah Mr Grasp my old friend !' said her ladyship extending her hand with a show of cordiality   You may leave us Ma amselle

Ma amselle would rather have been permitted to occupy a post of

No 4

observation in the room but the order to withdraw produced but little disappointment A lady s maid bent on obtaining information has always several resources at hand

Grasp and Lady Minhurst were in the boudoir by some accident the door communicating with the bed room had been left open and exposed to view the hangings of the bed As soon as the lawyer had taken his seat, and the first salutations were over, he made a rapid survey of the apartment It was not unobserved by her ladyship her eyes followed his, as they glanced round the room, and the smile of a fiend seemed to pass over the countenance of the man, while an involuntary shudder escaped from the lady

' Some time since we met, Lady Minhurst, said he, with a rub of the hands, and a malicious chuckle

' Years, ' faintly articulated the Viscountess, striving to dismiss some disagreeable recollections

' Long standing acquaintance our s, my lady old friends are glad to meet, it recals old times, makes them remember mutual services mutual services strengthen friendship '

His tone grew more sarcastic as he spoke and his countenance settled into a grin, as the last common place phrase escaped him

' Alas, what recollections ! responded the Viscountess

' Ah, I see you don t like recollections ' not always pleasant certainly and again he glanced round the apartment " cant bear them myself never did am grown indifferent now let them come, and let them go do the same ! '

" Grasp *you* were only an instrument but *I* '

' I don t forget our relation to each other it certainly makes all the difference You were the principal I an agent in common language By the bye, just the topic I came to speak about '

" To what do I owe the honour of this visit ? enquired her ladyship, as if wishing to direct the conversation into a different channel, and favoured in her desire by the last remark of her visitor

" Partly friendship partly business, rejoined the little man with some show of consequence " We have sailed through rough waters together, my dear lady always found me a sure friend in difficulty, eh ? a friend in*deed ?* Well, well ' comfortable to meet, talk over the past, and perhaps do a little something *for the present*, eh, my lady?

The tone of the sneerer became too bold for endurance Lady Minhurst frowned, and assuming a dignity well calculated to intimidate impertinence

' This is bartering Grasp, not friendship when did intimacy such as our s engender friendship ? What authorises you to indulge in sneers when you accost me ? I have employed you, and have not been niggardly in recompensing Remember your place, Sir I have at no time raised the hireling to a friend

Grasp s temper forsook him ' Yet the hireling, said he, " raised a neglected woman to the station and affluence of a fine lady !

' And in return for his services was enriched beyond his most sanguine expectations, ' sharply rejoined her ladyship

' Not quite ! not quite ! ' retorted the man Expectations are not easily measured never were never can be they are elastic have an expanding capacity my lady understands ?

"Perfectly and was not so imprudent as to hazard a visit to Min hurst, replied the Viscountess bitterly, "unprovided with supplies for the rapacious Mr Grasp

"So ! so ! we are still friends in*deed*, I see, observed the agent, his countenance brightening as he spoke "If you can do your part, our friendship shall be reciprocal nothing will be found wanting on mine hate quarrels among friends always did

"Let this seal our reconciliation ' added her ladyship coldly, giving him a note for a hundred pounds which had a most refreshing influence on the warm temperament of the obsequious solicitor He rose up glanced at the note, ascertained its amount, gazed wistfully round the room, then protruding his sharp face his eyes glistening with pleasure

"What is to be done ? said he in a whisper

"In the first place I want your opinion There is an individual in

the neighbourhood whom I wish to keep out of the way for a short time he is an old man the   her ladyship hesitated   " the tyrannical father of a young female whom I wish to benefit

' I understand rejoined the lawyer who had perceived the lady's hesitation, and had at once suspected that the Viscountess was concealing the true motives of her interference between the child and parent

Her ladyship resumed

He is tenacious of his parental authority nothing will separate them Could the omnipotence of the law be brought to my assistance Mr Grasp? I wish to know if an arrest or something of that sort could be effected and how far it would be dangerous, since there would be no grounds for it ?

' Is he rich or poor ? enquired Grasp

Oh poor extremely poor ' '

' The business will be all the easier   Let me see you would deprive him of liberty in order to—

' Have power uncontrolled power, to benefit his daughter

" Your ladyship is extremely benevolent said Grasp relapsing gradually into the sneering manner he had assumed at the commencement of their interview

" She is such a *sweet* creature!' added the Viscountess in her softest sleekest tone

Very charitable of you—very '

' And the father is *so* depraved—*so* thoroughly vagabond—gone beyond all recovery ' It is impossible for the child to rise, while they continue together

' Nothing can be more generous '

" Then you think you can assist me my dear Mr Grasp ?

' The man is very poor you say, quite destitute ? '

" From his appearance he must be a beggar a vagrant

" Good ' the moneyless are powerless the rich may insult slander, imprison beat them, and there is no redress ! It is more difficult to get the wealthy out of the way, my lady   And he glanced towards the bed

Again her ladyship appeared moved, and she asked in displeasure,

" Well, Sir, can this business be managed ?

' Certainly, my lady, certainly ! replied Mr Gregory, depositing with great care the note in his huge pocketbook then he added with deliberation, " but I must know all—every particular of the case

" You possess the leading facts, observed the lady, trying to avoid the question

" Humph ' a beggar girl—vagrant father—case of vagrancy—no difficulty   Then he added, in an under tone, " Benevolence ! stranger impossible no, no it cannot be '

" What do you say, Mr Grasp ?

' Plainly that I must be put in possession of all the facts of the case

" You have them

' Nay my lady old friends should have no secrets the face of the thing is improbable   What ' imprison a father to be charitable to the daughter? Impossible! The thing cant be I never thought it could

Her ladyship tried to read the countenance of her agent, but he never allowed any expression to settle long on his flexible features, and all attempts to learn the course his suspicions had taken proving fruitless she resolved to trust him further, as the only means of securing his indispensable services

' To be candid, Mr Grasp I have strong reasons for the kindness I wish to show this poor girl

" So I thought

" You will remember,' continued the Viscountess, evidently speaking with great effort, " a young female countenance we have both seen in *this* room reposing on *that* bed?

" Perfectly well, perfectly well ' and he grinned as he spoke

" You have heard her name?

" Yes yes, replied the lawyer, " I have it in writing '

" Grasp continued the Viscountess, " forty years are gone since then we have both grown old and yet, last night, I saw a young girl having the same features

' The thing occurs every day a striking resemblance always did, always will answered Grasp

" She was called by the same name

" What ! *Evine?* exclaimed Grasp

" Yes yes ! you see my reasons that beggar girl must be

" *Deprived of her protector* interrupted Grasp ' I see I see

Confidence was now completely restored between the confederates and a long interview ensued For its purport we refer the reader to the sequel of our story

---

CHAPTER V

" BAD girl ! bad girl ! were the first words uttered by the mendicant when Lady Minhurst and her son had retired But they were accompanied by a caressing tap on Evine s cheek, so gentle, that it might have been deemed a wondrous achievement on the part of so rough a hand

" Did I make you uneasy, father ?

' Bad child ! you should not leave my side while I slumber Though asleep I can defend you your lowest cry would waken me

' But there was no danger

" Who knows—who knows ? I don t

" Oh ! there could not be ! The poor lady spoke so kind, and looked so cold, it went to my heart and I could not rest without making up the fire

" Would she warm you, would she warm you ? You might starve first

Evine knew her father judged harshly, for the purse really and figuratively weighed heavily on her bosom, where she had placed it

" Are they gone ? said he, looking round

At that moment the wheels of a carriage were distinctly heard rum
bling over the adjacent road, and satisfied them of the departure of our
wealthier travellers

" Off! off!' burst forth the old man, with a vehemence that startled
Evine, accustomed as she was to the frequent outbreakings of her parent
" off! in a gaudy chariot, I warrant We must off, too on foot—on
barefoot! Yet she merits better, he added, looking with great tender
ness on his child, and taking her by the waist " she deserves a coach,
she does aye, a coach and four !

Evine smiled in return for this caress but she trembled in his em
brace Her father was a man of wild and ungoverned passions With
him the transition from dreadful fury to excessive kindness was sudden
and capricious She had, however, strong faith in his affection, and
learnt to endure his waywardness and violence by attributing them to an
uncontrollable nature

" Shall we start father ? she enquired, wishing to draw his mind from
the bitter companions the adventure of the night suggested

A nod was the reply and a wallet that contained the scanty wardrobe
of father and daughter the whole of their earthly possessions, was shoul
dered in a moment and they set forward on their journey

It was the morning twilight all the signs of tranquillity peculiar to
night were disappearing one by one the very breeze, gentle as a summer
wind, seemed to be invigorated with new freshness and gave a spirit
and elasticity to the motions of the wanderers Notwithstanding the
early hour, they had not proceeded far on the road before they were
startled by the sound of a horse s pace that seemed to overtake them

Evine s heart beat at the sound the night s adventure had made a
deep impression on her mind the forms of the strangers still floated in
her memory she wished, she knew not why to have further intercourse
with them and without considering the improbability of such a circum
stance, almost hoped the rider came from her new acquaintance The
sounds drew nearer, and nearer but the pace of the horse evidently
became slower as it approached and by the time the horseman came up
with our travellers it did not exceed their own

" Good morning old boy—good morning Miss said the rider at
the same time directing a scrutinising glance toward the mendicant and
his daughter which his frank salutation was intended to preserve from
notice

" Fine day returned the old man remarking the inquisitive regard,
and returning it without ceremony

" On tramp, old feller ?

" We have neither horse nor carriage, said the man on foot, con
tinuing his survey, and observing the gold laced livery hid by the upper
coat of the horseman

" Crusty, old chap ? Von t do, that, at no rate Bound for P——,
eh ? '

' May be so, may be not can t tell

A very lonesome road, this heie hif its agreeable we might keep one another kimpany a bit, vile ve goes one vay you know

' I reckon your master would not thank you for keeping our pace

" I calls no man master, ' rejoined the horseman, giving at the same time a twitch to the treacherous garment that had betrayed his livery

" I m appy to say, my time s my hone, and that s more than every man can sav '

" Then the less you give us of it the better muttered the mendicant

" Strike me lucky if you ain t civil you hill bred scum of the lower orders ! cried the other as he spurred his horse into a gallop   In a few minutes he was out of sight

" I hope he has his answer, said the mendicant in a tone of exultation

' You soon sent him off, father

" The better ! the better ! Who knows who he is ? who knows ? comes, perhaps, from those people, said he, laying stress upon the word those

" Do you think so ? Do you indeed think so, father ? '

" Cant tell   Who knows ?

For a moment the countenance of Evine brightened she looked thoughtful as she added,

" But why should they send after us, father ?

The usual answer, " Who knows, ' escaped from the man s lips, but, as if iecollecting himself, he stopped abruptly and placing his hard, bony wrinkled hands on both sides of Evine s smooth and lovely face, he held her at arms length and smiling with great delight as he gazed on her beautiful countenance, he continued,

' You have a treasure that you know not of, Evine   Desire of it will thaw the icicles of age, exhaust the ardour of youth, unbind the grasp of the miser, turn the brain of the wise, and shake the principles of the good ! Who knows ? who knows ? Because of this treasure men will fawn and caress you, my Evine women persecute and slander you, my child Who knows ? who knows ? It makes you most like an angel now, and may be your ruin hereafter Who knows, my child ? who knows ? '

The man continued to gaze on her with rapture but there was so much wildness in his glance that Evine shrunk from it   He perceived the movement, and withdrew his hold

" Poor child ! poor child ! he said, patting her gently on the shoulder Evine burst into tears

Reader, did the mendicant overrate the danger of beauty ?

Their journey was now pursued for some time in silence   The father sunk into deep abstraction Solicitude for his child s welfare, and schemes for her advancement in the world, occupied his mind   The object of so much anxiety had far other cares   Born to the poverty and wretchedness of a precarious and outcast mode of life, she suffered little from privation   Her sorrows were chiefly occasioned by the wild disposition of her parent —his frequent fits of abstraction the alarm he manifested for his and her safety, though he carefully concealed from her his reasons for apprehending danger, and the kind of danger he dreaded and these sorrows often weighed heavily on her young spirit for she had a heart capable of deep and strong affection   But there is in youth an elasticity that defies care and a readiness to find, and apply a balsam from without, to all the heart wounds that rankle within   The griefs that rack the youthful brain when it presses its pillow at night, are rarely found to await its waking on the morrow to the young every rising sun is a harbinger of hope   They leave to manhood the excitement of the wine cup of business, of ambition—the true waters of Lethe, in which men seek to engulf their woe   and find repose, consolation, oblivion, in their own spontaneous hopefulness, in that strong exhaustless faculty of enjoyment which finds beauty in every tree and luxuriates in the free air and warm sunlight of heaven

It was thus with Evine   the preceding night she had reposed a jaded frame on the hard, though literally the flowery couch of nature   and if the morning brought no change in her condition, no variation from the toil and anxiety of the day before, yet it broke in beauty and gladness The hues the perfume, the music of morning, found a response in the depths of her young heart   almost lonely in the world she had affinity with nature, and her bosom beat calmly hopefully and contentedly in that severest and most unsettled mode of human life, deep and unoccupied penury

The road to P——, the nearest town to Minhurst, was in a different though not exactly an opposite direction to that taken by the carriage of the Viscountess when confided to the care of a trustier guide it diverged from the heath of Wedgmoor, and traversed an undulating country, now beguiling the traveller with pleasant laughing valleys, adorned with comfortable, modest homesteads, and from time to time conducting him to heights that commanded extensive views of the surrounding country

As Evine and her father slowly ascended one of these hills, the attention of the former was diverted from the observation of other objects, to rest on the form of a young man reclining against a stile, placed in an opening of the hedge, near the summit   From that position he overlooked an extensive landscape   In the distance a faint outline of graceful hill seemed to melt into the grey of the morning sky   A smiling country of woody knolls and verdant meadows such as England exhibited as her greatest pride till the vast factory gloomed, and smoked, and laboured amidst their beauty filled up the wide tract between the spot he occupied and the horizon   A winding river formed a conspicuous feature in the scene, now lost behind a clump of trees, or hid by the mist still floating over its surface, and here and there glistening brightly, as if returning the salutation of the first sunbeams that played on its waters The residence of the Minhurst family was also a remarkable object Its broad, stately outline caught on its highest parts the early sunshine, and stood out prominent from the dark foliage of the majestic park   It was not surprising that a passenger should pause to admire the beauties of such a scene but the appearance of the young man denoted more than the interest of a lover of nature   His gaze rested intently on one object, and so great was his abstraction that Evine and her father reached, unperceived, the part of the road where he stood

As they drew near him he was attentively surveyed by the younger
of the travellers and he did, in fact, present an object such as one of
her age and sex could not fail to regard with pleasure His well made,
handsome person, owed nothing to a worn suit, in which the age of the
garment and the care of the owner seemed to contend for mastery This
defect was, however, partially concealed by the shade of a large tree and
abated in no degree the grace and comeliness of his figure, as reclining
on the stile, he gazed intently on the mansion of Viscount Minhurst
A nearer approach disclosed a countenance of great regularity, manli
ness and expression, but " exceeding sad A staff and bundle pro
claimed him a fellow traveller

For some time Evine had felt pained at her father s silence and looked
often in his face with those enquiring looks which so plainly reveal our
anxiety to know what is passing in the minds of those we love It was
easy to perceive that his reflections were of a moody cast, and to lead
him if possible to a happier train of thought

" Look, father, she cried as they passed the opening, look at yonder
great house A wealthy lord must live there

' Yes, child and what is scarcer a good hearted one Many a
poor wretch Evine, has turned from his gate with a lighter heart than
he approached it, replied the mendicant, stopping as he spoke to give a
hasty glance at the mansion

No 5

" Heaven bless him for it ' cried Evine

" It is as fine a place as any to be found within fifty miles of P——
added her companion, resuming his usual pace " But we must not
loiter we have a long journey before us '

" Did you notice him, father ? ' asked Evine, as they began to descend
the other side of the hill

" Who, child ?

" The young man who leant on the stile beneath the ash tree, said
Evine

" Aye, aye, child '

" How sad he looked, poor fellow '

' Who knows ? who knows ? Poor, perhaps '

" Then he looked so earnestly at the great house '

" Empty bellies know good larders

" Poor young man ! sighed Evine in a tone of compassion

' Why do you pity him ? asked the father

" He does not seem used to misery

" Who knows ?

" Oh, I am sure he is not ! How neat he looked no rags, no tat
tered finery It must be hard indeed for him to feel hunger, for he
cannot beg, I am sure

' God help him, poor lad ' ejaculated the man, and he relapsed into
silence

They now arrived at another hill of longer and deeper ascent At the
summit they halted for the double purpose of taking breath and admiring
the glories of the setting sun as it now rose proudly over the highest
parts of the country They had scarcely seated themselves on the rude
seat a felled tree afforded than Evine, with the curiosity of her age
turned her head to see if the young man was taking the same road with
themselves The eminence on which they were seated being the highest
in the neighbourhood, she could still discern him He retained the
same attitude, and continued to look towards Minhurst with the same
intenseness She considered him in silence his appearance bespoke
unhappiness and sympathy, that mystic interpreter between the unfor
tunate, awoke in her bosom a sudden and indefinable interest in the
fortunes of the stranger When she had observed him for a few minutes,
he started suddenly from his reclining posture, seized the bundle at his
feet, slung it on his shoulder, and hastened down the declivity that faced
them Hastily as this action was performed, it sufficed to throw some
light on the young man s circumstances he was, and so thought Evine
tearing himself with violence from scenes he dearly loved The whole
of her life had been past on the highway from infancy she had been
accustomed to see strangers come and go with indifference contrary to
her habit she felt a thrill of pleasure as she perceived the young man
taking their direction, and was betrayed into an involuntary exclamation

" He comes ! she cried

' Who ? enquired her father, roused from his abstraction by the
earnestness with which she spoke

Evine sunk down on the tree from whence she had risen to make her observations, and with a confusion and tingling of the cheek, by no means to be reckoned among her ordinary sensations, she replied,

" The poor young man

" Let him come the more the merrier, ' said the mendicant

This was novel language for her father to use He was a moody man, of solitary habits, rarely mixing even with persons of his fraternity more than was necessary to maintain a reputation of good fellowship Persons of another caste he invariably shunned, save when driven by destitution to solicit arms

" Will you speak to him then, father ? asked Evine in a tone of surprise

" And why not ? he rejoined " He bears no slave s badge his coat has not the freshness of the garments of your slave of wealth neither does he wear the golden livery of a slave of men Who knows ? who knows ? he may belong to us I looked as comely once yes, I, Evine !

All this was not very intelligible to his daughter His motives for shunning society were of two descriptions the one he withheld from a fear of giving his child more anxiety than she already underwent the other was suppressed because it was of a nature little likely to be under stood, or if understood, less likely to be appreciated at her early age He knew that beauty and virtue were regarded by many as commodities to be purchased and bartered for wealth, and with feelings only equalled by a miser s solicitude for his treasure he sought to shelter Evine from the effects of such sentiments Yet this parental jealousy knew how to discriminate he avoided a servant in livery, who might have been des patched to watch their movements by the wealthy young gentleman chance had thrown in their way during the night but he felt no reluct ance to hold intercourse with a youthful traveller, who, however comely his appearance, had the decent carriage that inspires confidence, and was moreover, in all probability, too burthened with care for his worldly advancement to waste either time or thought on an idle amour with the daughter of a wretched vagrant This distinction, however, was far beyond the attainment of Evine s understanding and she could only attribute the different treatment the foot traveller met, to that bestowed on the horseman, to the superior personal merit of the former

The young man drew near, and it was easy to perceive that, notwith standing his rapid pace, he was involved in deep abstraction Evine s father rose as the stranger came up to them

" A fine morning, mate," said he

The young man started to find himself in company but without in dulging in that evident inspection so common and natural to travellers at meeting, he replied

" Beautiful ! beautiful !'

As he manifested no intention to halt, the mendicant resumed his journey, and the three walked on in silence for some distance

The time was not lost either by the father or daughter Both sur veyed their fellow traveller from head to foot, and each came to a satis factory conclusion respecting his merits

' A worthy lad, thought the father

Evine had her thoughts too but we dare not translate them into words Her opinion of the stranger exalted as it was as it formed and grew in her " heart of hearts, was perfectly natural   in the conventicle terms of language it would appear exaggerated   Her sentiments on the subject will be best understood when we say that she was not seventeen—back ward for her sex—and beheld the most handsome form and countenance she had ever seen   But the young man was wholly unconscious of the favourable impression he produced, and walked on as one forgetful that he had companions

'We cannot keep your company long at this pace, my mate,' said the mendicant when almost out of breath

" Excuse me   replied the young man, with much natural courtesy   I was thinking, and had forgotten my company ' and he slackened his pace.

" That s it   so, we may manage to jog on together   that is, if you keep the road to P——

" What did you say ? enquired the stranger

Gone again ?   I asked if you were going to P——

To P——?   Oh further ! much further !

" You seem to have a good deal to think about, mate

' It is not easy to get through the world, was the reply

" You may say that with more truth some fifty years hence, rejoined the mendicant   ' but so young a man—fie on t '   I don t like to see young people looking so far forward, and they can have nothing to look back upon   Yet, who knows ? who knows ? '

The conversation seemed to have taken an attractive turn to the young man, for he put aside his thoughtfulness, and added—

' True   but the youngest heart must have ties he can look back upon with pleasure, and may fear to find no compensation for their loss when he glances into futurity "

He spoke with great sadness his tones went to Evine s heart

" Perhaps he has left a father? she whispered

It was a musical whisper to the stranger—for he caught it, though not intended for his hearing—musical for there were few voices sweeter than Evine s but chiefly so, because it had a response in his own breast one cause of his sorrow had been guessed, and he felt a harmony of heart with one who could so readily and easily sympathise with the secret sorrows of his bosom   Natural reserve was peculiar to Edward Vivyan, as it is to all in whom the sensibilities have too rapidly developed it led him to refrain from the expression of all strong emotions, when it was in his power and turning to the speaker,

" No ' a mother, he coolly replied

All the young and lovely affections of Evine were centred in her father His approbation, next to his well being, was her highest pleasure   Though he idolized his daughter, he was too great a stranger to moral contro', not to cause her at times much anxiety and poignant grief   Her mother she had never known, and associating as she did, every conceivable excellence with the name of parent, it is is no wonder that she regarded with the highest reverence that relative whose failings she had never known, and whose memory she had been encouraged by her father to cherish with enthusiastic fondness Edward became more interesting than ever in her estimation, since she knew he still possessed a mother

"You have a mother, then ? she exclaimed, in a tone that revealed both interest and pleasure

"Yes, God bless her ''

The ejaculation was scarcely audible yet it told a sad domestic story, though one of every day occurrence

"And you are obliged to leave her ?' she added, her heart growing sad as she spoke

"It will be for her good ' said the youth, brightening at the thought

"No doubt ! interposed the eldest of the party   Who knows ? Who knows? The poor soul is sad enough to lose you, no doubt, and may be,' he added, probably to change the subject, and cheer his com panion, "more than one pair of eyes have wept to part with you ? '

'How ?'

"Who knows ? Who knows ? But it strikes me you are not akin to any who dangle at the heels of the great

"I dont see your drift, my good friend, observed the young man

"Why, you dont look like the son of one of the upstart servants of the great house yonder To be sure who knows, but I look upon you as better born than that Well then, when a young man has just parted with his mother, and looks so earnestly at Minhurst Castle, when she dont live there, I look upon it that s a sign who knows ? who knows ?

there is a pretty housemaid in the way, or something of the sort

'A housemaid ! exclaimed Edward, reddening, and in a tone of pride that gratified and astonished Evine, though she could not account for either feeling

"My lady s maid then, may be but no matter what she is, young man take my advice, have none of them

"I am of your opinion on that point, replied Edward, with a firmness and severity that showed his displeasure at being considered capable of such an attachment

"Right, mate, right !" continued the mendicant "be free, lad, be free, and wive with the free

"Freedom is not always attended with comfort, said the the young man, inadvertently reflecting on his companion s condition, which he now began to view as the result of ill conceived notions of civil liberty

"I grant you that, I grant you that when a man depends on others for his comfort

"How do you mean ?

"I mean when a man lives by others, feeds on others, depends on others when he is bound down to one place, confined to the company of one class of his fellow creatures, at the risk of being despised, as though we were not all men, made by the same God, when he must sub mit to this or starve Is such a poor creature free ? Shame on such men !

'But these men have affluence, respectability, influence among their fellows

" Aye, aye ! who knows what ? But they have no freedom '

" I see, said Edward, " that you have scorned to procure their advan tages at what you imagine to be the sacrifice of freedom I do not so clearly see your gain

' Look you, replied the mendicant, fairly brought to a halt by the interest he took in the debate, and throwing his bundle to the ground, at the same time taking Evine by the hand " here is all my treasure, this child, those rags but I am free I go at no man s bidding I cower before no man s frown Your rich slave may never hunger, never feel weary who knows but he does not wake to a warmer sunshine, does not gaze on a finer world, does not breathe a purer air, than I do yet he must be chained through life to one narrow spot, because there grows his bread, while I can range the universe your slave of wealth dares not claim acquaintance with flesh and blood in better trimmings than himself, lest he meet with neglect and he shuns it when naked, lest the contact should degrade him but I——

" You, my friend, interrupted Edward, with a smile where sorrow and compassion were mingled " are shunned by the greater part of your race, and hunted up and down by the rest as they chase vermin from their habitations forgive me if my expressions appear uncouth but the penalty of the law, to which the mode of existence you defend, ex poses you——'

" Law ! cried Evine, in a tone of anguish " oh, do not talk of law ' my poor father ! is he in danger ? ' And she threw her arms round the mendicant s neck, and looked enquiringly into his countenance

The conversation had for some time been unintelligible to her the word " law she was familiar with, but with that kind of familiarity with which an infant regards the ghosts and hobgoblins forced on his imagination by a prating nurse The father pressed Evine to his arms, smiled on her, and then, with meaning at his new acquaintance——

" Fear not, my child,' said he " l am in no danger now none ' none ! Come, be calm, dearest.

" Thank God ! ' she exclaimed, recovering from her terror·

Edward yearned with pity for the young female—exposed not merely through her beauty, but through the principles and life of her father, to all the misery and degradation which almost inevitably attend her sex when in poverty and unprotected His experience of the world was slight, but a glance into futurity, connected with Evine, made him shudder A pause followed, but not of long duration, for the mendicant began to take that interest in his companion which often subjects the object of it to an unpleasant catechising

' Do you live in the neighbourhood of Minhurst Castle ? ' he en quired

" I was born on the estate,' replied Edward

" But you have not always lived on it ?

" I never was a score of miles from my native place '

' Yet you speak like a traveller'

" The distance you may walk in a summer day is the extent of my travels

"May be—may be but your head is no stay at home one   No! no!
a village clown don t talk as you do '

" I am, however, no better

" Who knows? who knows ?   But don t tell me you have not left
sleep for labour, and labour for sleep, all the years since you could scare
a crow, or bind a sheaf

" Not exactly my lot has been happier, much happier than that you
allude to

" Aye, aye, young man and you are no barren tree either   I am
an ignorant old man, but I have ears for a good argumentation

" If I am in any thing better than the lads of my condition, I owe it
to a dear, thinking mother, and a few old books

" Do books make people wise?' enquired Evine, who had listened
with much interest to all that passed

" Should they not ? rejoined Edward   " they are the repositories of
thought the savour of the sage s wisdom while he lives his legacy to
the world when he dies

" Who knows ? who knows ? I can t read not a letter! muttered
the old man

" Books,' continued the youth, yielding to his enthusiasm, are caskets
entrusted with the precious ornaments of wealth and genius, and sent
forth into the world to beautify and adorn others   From books we
obtain our knowledge of the past, our acquaintance with the present, our
hope for the future

" And she cannot read my poor child cannot read!' exclaimed the
father

' Will you not teach me ?' asked Evine, with the simplicity of a child,
looking at Edward and betraying by her countenance the pleasure the
idea inspired   " I will try very hard to learn   Could I learn in a
day ?

The extreme ignorance the last question betrayed, did something more
than excite a smile on the countenance of the youth it found a way to
the depths of a benevolent heart, and produced there dispositions of
kindness towards the enquirer, stronger perhaps than the brief intercourse
of the parties warranted

" A day would hardly suffice " was the answer   " and to morrow

" Aye, aye! interrupted the mendicant, finishing the sentence, ' we
shall be far apart   Who knows ? who knows ? Where are you bound,
mate ?

" To London! said the young man

" A brave place! have you friends there ?

" No friends   I hope to make acquaintances

" Who knows ? who knows ? Do you follow any trade ?

" I have left a humble employment for an uncertainty but London
is large

" Aye, aye! and the young have hope   Who knows ? who knows ?
a good scholar, no doubt quick with the pen, eh ?

'Tis the tool I am most accustomed to handle

" Well well! there is plenty of clerks and writers and such like in
London they ll give you work pity though, sad pity!

" What is? asked the youth

" To be such a fine, stout fellow, going to chain himself to a desk
to pine and waste, and grow double far from the sunshine and fresh
air! Who knows? who knows? You were never born to be such a
slave, lad your motions are too free your head too high shouldn t
go shouldn t go!'

" I love and admire nature not a jot less than yourself, considering
I have not been so long acquainted with her beauties as you have, and
I would not renounce the privileges you describe for the wealth of the
universe were it not that the comfort of a mother depends on my ex
ertions and success

" I understand your parents were once well to do, and are brought
low in the world?

No, no! thank heaven, fortune has dealt more kindly with us My
mother s condition never was better than it is now '

" And is she satisfied? '

" God bless her, yes! A more contented heart never praised her
Maker

" In seeking wealth in London, far, far away from this mother do
you hope to make her happier, young man?

Edward felt confused he knew he had his mother s happiness at
heart her consent, and her blessing authorised his journey yet he was
conscious that but for another motive powerful and deep rooted his
desire after a metropolitan life, its struggles and distinctions, had been
less ardent

" She will be pleased at my success, he faultered

' But would she purchase it by your absence? asked the mendicant,
unconsciously embracing his daughter

" You know a parent s heart, right well, ' continued the youth 'Dear,
dear mother! she would pay any price to secure my happiness

" And do you seek it in the possession of wealth?

' No, no! responded Edward

" I was sure not Of rank or importance, then?

" Still less! still less!

" Go back to her mate to your poor old mother comfort her age
who knows? who knows? the remembrance of it will be worth more
than all the great town can bestow

" Your words rack my heart for I must, I must be something be
distinguished

" Fool fool! said the mendicant mildly, and shaking his head
" poor fool!

" No, no! replied the young traveller " it is not foolish it is no
folly but, if it be so rank arrant folly still it is blessedness to acquire
the respect of those we love

' So, so! love is it? well well! I have known what that is, said
the father ' but, he continued, in a lower tone, " must so much

be done at the risk of your own happiness, young man, to gain the respect of her you love?'

So much! Oh! call it not much—no renown were too great, no eminence too high, to gain *her* respect To be distinguished by her from the common herd, what must I not become

"Poor lad! poor lad! She is then —

"She never can be mine, interrupted Edward in a tone of deep dejection, "but I may obtain her respect

Here the conversation was interrupted, for Evine wept aloud

' My child, my child!—what ails you?

' I dont know, I really dont know—I cannot help it, indeed I cannot, was the reply and she cried more bitterly

As Evine could not explain the cause of her grief it may be assuming too much to attempt to do so lest however the reader should deem this sudden display of sensibility wholly unaccountable, it is thought proper to observe, that Edward s manner during the above conversation, had become very energetic, and expressed in turn the elevated hopes of a sanguine temperament and the anguish of so unequal and probably an unrequited love Of his matter, his youthful auditor had but a vague comprehension yet sufficient to apprise her that the speaker suffered, and in no common degree His manner had a more sensible effect upon her She heard his voice grow tremulous with emotion she saw his countenance assume an expression of pain her heart was touched, and its sorrow found relief in copious tears

"Poor thing! poor thing! said the mendicant striving to console her sobbing "your story makes her weep Ah! if she knew all the poor and unfriended have to contend with in a city like London, her tears would not be so silly either—ah! who knows? who knows?

" I have what is better than fortune or patronage, said Edward, "a courageous and a hopeful heart But I have been drawn into a disclosure of my circumstances more ample than I intended making in return may I be allowed to learn something about the companions who have so pleasantly beguiled my first day s journey?"

"Aye, aye, mate! Tis a fair question but a poor man s tale, such as I am, is either too dull to be told or too long to be listened to My lot has rarely been better than you find it now, and as for my child here, and the speaker s voice took a tone of great melancholy " her worst misfortune is, I believe, to have known life, poor thing! poor thing! though it is a great comfort to have her, after all Who knows? who knows?

The travellers now came in sight of the town of P—— and we have merely given the substance of their conversation, and that part of it necessary to the developement of our story Noon was approaching It was a pretty town The buildings were well grouped, and formed a pleasing outline in the midst of a small and fertile plain When they reached the turnpike gate, the horseman who had already passed Evine and her father some hours before, stood dismounted near it. He again eyed them with the same furtive and searching glance, bestowing an extraordinary degree of his attention on Edward Vivyan The circum

No 6

stance did not however cause the party any surprise the keeper of the turnpike gate sold spirituous restoratives to the weary, and travellers will be inquisitive

"We had better part company," said the mendicant as they neared the town

"Yes—yes—you must not go with us," added Evine in sad and hurried accents

'I must however seek an humble lodging,' replied Edward

"Not such as ours —No! no! not such as ours — besides we may not pass the night in the town" continued Evine

"I certainly shall not the weather is warm, and I purpose resting till evening, and pursuing my journey to night

Well! well! a pleasant journey lad—and good success Who knows? who knows? You may be a greater man than you would wish to be one day perhaps, and remember that poor Wilfred Welbourne told you so — Who knows? who knows? God be with you, lad, God be with you"

Most sincerely did Evine join in her father's prayer, but she could not utter the supplication, and with a slight wave of the hand she followed the mendicant down a narrow lane leading to the poorer part of the town, leaving Edward to enter it by the principal street

'How strange!' said Evine to her father, as they stood at the door of the wretched abode frequented by wanderers of their caste, and were on the point of entering "there is the man who passed us on horseback!"

The mendicant looked up the narrow lane and beheld him walking his horse down it at a slow pace

"He will not find the best stabling for his horse hereabouts," said Welbourne, leading the way into their retreat and so thought Townsend, for he took the animal back to a second rate inn in the high street, before he fixed his quarters at a low public house, next door to that squalid scene of poverty and vice, a vagrant's home

Towards the close of the same day another horseman passed through the turnpike gate on the Minhurst side of P—— Though it was high summer a cravat covered his sharp chin, and the owner would gladly have disposed in a similar way had it been possible, of another prominent feature not far above Being himself a very curious man he would gladly have gone about in disguise, to avoid the curiosity of others A glance served to convince the turnpike keeper of the name, quality, and capacity of the rider

"There goes Lawyer Grasp again," said the man to his wife, as the horse's tread died away in the calm of the evening "I'll wager a pot, he has been to Minhurst to day —he passed through this morning

Yes, yes answered his wife coming out to gaze after the functionary, "and a nice thing he makes out of that family by all report —pretty pickings I warrant!"

CHAPTER VI

THE dinner bell rang before Mr Gregory Grasp took leave of the Viscountess   Their long interview had however its fruits   Lady Min hurst congratulated herself on having retained the services of so able an emissary, and lawyer Grasp rejoiced in the prospect of an ample re compense for services easily performed   It was therefore with more composure than she had felt for the last four and twenty hours, that her ladyship took her seat at the dining table   she found that the party was not confined to the members of the family

Though Lord Minhurst led a secluded life there were a few families in the neighbourhood whose acquaintance he cultivated for the sake of his daughter Mira   Limited to the society that part of the country afforded, he allowed himself in the pursuit of true worth to be allured by no meretricious attractions nor to be scared by any apparent eccen tricity   The dinner guests on the day in question frequently assembled at his board and were invited before he expected it would be graced by dearer and more welcome faces   He feared indeed they would be found very different to the society Lady Minhurst generally mixed with   but her sudden arrival admitted of no alteration in the arrangements of the day   The dowager viscountess was therefore doomed to meet some half dozen strangers of both sexes, of all ages between seventeen and fifty five but without one exception from the youngest to the oldest very homely old fashioned gentlemen and ladies   Nor was this the least inconvenience attending this unexpected conjunction of specimens of town and country breeding   ignorance of the world, and of fashion, does not always save men from affectation nor were the good hearted visitors of the noble Viscount free from this defect

Any society is welcome to those who fly from themselves and Lady Minhurst felt relieved by the presence of a portly baronet who sat next her

" To think that I should have the gratification of meeting your lady ship to day '   began the old gentleman   " It is so many years since we met   let me see   let me see   the last time we were together, you were my partner in a dance   That was not yesterday was it, my Lady ?

" I never recollect your meeting my mother, Sir Matthew Melter, interposed the viscount

" It was at your lordship's christening   I have often heard my brother mention the circumstance   replied Miss Clothilda Melter a spinster who strove most anxiously to conceal the decay of nature by a profuse employment of the succours of art

' Heard me mention it '   blustered out the fat gentleman   " Pre posterous, Clothilda, preposterous ' you were there yourself   you know you were

The vain Miss Clothilda Melter though not a great mathematician formed with rapidity the sum total of fifteen added to forty and irritated beyond measure at this seeming exposure of the length of her spinster ship, she furiously retorted

" Hold your tongue, Sir Matthew you don t know what you talk about—you never do ' I tell you it is quite impossible that I could have stood up in a dance at his lordship s christening which was forty years since—and I must know, I should think—so there s no occasion to say anything more about it

" I received most extraordinary news this morning my lord, said an extremely neat, and almost smart young gentleman at the opposite end of the table "most singular and extra or dinary '

' Pray let us hear it, Lord Sillton

" Do you know, my lord it is most wonderful—altogether remarkable —but my brother, Lord Vermont writes me word that the Member for the borough of P——, has positively and actually given up the ghost ' Now can you conceive anything more decidedly and unexpectedly out of the way ?

' An election for the borough of P——' broke out a bachelor at Mira s side " lucky little borough that always changing its represent ative Very difficult to guess the politics of the town, my lord, from the avowed sentiments of its Members in the House the last was an ultra Whig, the preceding one a high Tory, and the one before—

" Veered in the course of one session to all the points of the political compass,' said Lord Minhurst " and gave his constituents so much satisfaction, that a piece of plate was presented to him to mark the high sense entertained of his political integrity

" Ha ' ha ' ha ' simpered Sillton how very positively, severely and singularly good and cutting ' It really makes me laugh He ' he ' he ' '

' You should come forward Mr Fluentleigh, smilingly said the Viscount, addressing Mira s neighbour (for that was his name)

" Ah, do, Mr Fluentleigh do now come forward ' echoed Miss Clothilda

" May I rely on the countenance of our worthy and estimable host ' enquired Fluentleigh

" I make no doubt ' observed the Dowager Viscountess, while Mr Fluentleigh raised a cambric handkerchief of fine texture to wipe his mouth, well adapted by Nature for the very free emission of his over flow of soul " I make no doubt but my son is most disposed to favour your interest in all cases where it does not clash with his own you will allow that it is rather premature to solicit his interest which I believe is considerable in the borough, the moment he first hears of a vacancy

Mr Fluentleigh was effectually silenced by this rebuke Lady Min hurst looked at Ronald with an affection that at once made the Viscount aware of her swiftly conceived intentions The pride of the father got the better of his habitual shrinking from public life, and he determined to seize this occasion of bringing forward his son

The withdrawing of the ladies suspended the conversation

The Viscountess longed to hold intercourse with Mira courtesy, however required her to endure with patience the tittle tattle of the other visitors Mira and Miss Merriville, with all the eagerness of friends who meet about half a dozen times in the year, proposed a stroll through the grounds, to enjoy their little gossip in greater privacy

' What news have you to tell me dear Marian? began Mira as soon as they were beyond the possibility of being overheard " tis an age since we met

' Don t know we lead a strange dull life at Tranquil Dale I might as well live in a desert island

" Fie, Marian ' we hear of your visitors—there is Lord Silliton, and then the Honourable Francis Fraser Fluentleigh always there every day at Tranquil Dale

" Yes but my aunt thinks I believe, that matrimony is as fatal to my constitution as to her own, for she very affectionately keeps me from all intercourse with our male visitors at the risk of entertaining them herself Indeed, Mira, continued Marian ' I scarcely know how I should endure the solitude, did I not find amusement in attending to my little dumb animals in whose innocent playfulness I take much delight But pray, my dear girl, how are all your favourites ?

' If you mean my flowers they thrive admirably and I like botany better than ever Papa makes the study so interesting

" Ah ! how happy you must be ! But, continued Marian, " pray how is the other favourite ?

' My poney ? responded Mira

' No ! no ! no ! You know what I mean '

" Oh ! Ralph ! Papa s great dog ! He s very well I thank you

' No ! no ! not the dog the best favourite of all the rational the intellectual favourite—that repays your caresses with a sonnet, and is ready to return with a stanza every smile you give him —the pet poet— the poor sexton s son

' You laugh at me, Marian but never mind—Edward deserves to be a favourite He is so fond of his poor old parent, so kind to his young scholars and then, his verses are not contemptible—I am sure they are not

" Do you still receive his productions ? asked Miss Merriville

" How you talk, Marian ! To hear you, one would think the postman brought me an epist e in rhyme every morning I have very few of his verses two or three pieces at most

" No my love I had no ideas half so unpoetical In the first place I am aware that these verses come to you through the invisible agency of sylph or gnome, and are slyly placed in a conspicuous part of your favourite bower the very moment before you visit it

' You remind me, Marian, that you have not seen the alterations and with these words Mira led her companion to an ornamental building situated in a retired part of the grounds Intended for the favourite apartment of his beloved child the Viscount had fitted it up with every attention to comfort and elegance A marble bust of her mother a harp and a few volumes of the purest and pleasantest reading, formed the chief ornaments of Mira s retreat

' Bless me ! what noise is that ? exclaimed Marian, starting at a rustling sound

" Nothing love the waving of the acacia before the window Has not papa furnished this room delightfully ? is it not fairy like ?

"So much so, that I could almost sweai faiiies lurked here to receive us," replied her young friend, looking round as if suspecting the piesence of a third person "it is a very pretty place   such a study accounts for your attachment to botany

"I have better reasons for my attachment to that science in these flowers,' continued Mira, turning Marian s attention to a handsome vase "are not these flowers lovely?

"Pretty pets ! I never saw finer specimens of the kind   This nose gay of wild flowers might be matched with the choicest any garden pro duces   Where do you get them? asked the young lady

'The gardener procures them from some poor lad of the village, I believe   returned Mira

"He must ramble far to reach the dwelling of such lovely cieatuies, addea Marian, stooping to examine them more minutely

' Poor fellow ' how I envy him his rambles '' exclaimed Mira

"No doubt ' rejoined her friend, as she raised her head and looked attentively at Mira, at the same time biting her lips to suppress a laugh "Pray, Mira, have you noticed this nosegay before?

'No ' the flowers have been ienewed since I was last here

'So I thought foi I perceive among them a blossom I am sure you would not have consigned to the vase until you had ascertained the genus it belongs to'

A iare plant ! pray let me see it ''

Rare it *may* be common it certainly *is*,   said Miss Merriville putting back the gentle plants, and discovering a small note deeply em bedded among their leaves

Mira half blushed as she drew it out, and looked at her friend before she attempted to learn the contents

" Do not hesitate, my love   all specimens, you know, must be ad dressed to the botanist   Nay, if you are so long you will force me to assist you in the examination   and should it contain anything extraordi nary I shall put in my claim for a share in the discovery

' And so shall I ' added a voice, that made both the young ladies start   for, though familiar, it sounded close behind them

" Ronald ' cried Mira, turning round and beholding her brother

" How could you *do* so ' said Miss Merriville, in a tone and manner perfectly, though unconsciously, copied from her aunt

Like an impudent knight, I have sought the ladies in their bower, ' said Ronald

' It is too bad of you you have no business to—' continued Marian, looking first at the note and then at Mira, and inwardly deprecating what in her heart she began to fear was an untimely conjuncture

I am sorry if I have intruded at an improper time, observed Ronald but I can assure you I was dying with *ennui*   My best apology ' he continued, glancing in his turn inadvertently at the billet, " will perhaps be to withdraw

Oh no ' we will not condemn you to so terrible a punishment Sir Impudence ' ' said Mira, smiling   as lady of this bower, I am however entitled to inflict chastisement for the intrusion

' Speak, said Ronald, " and you are obeyed '

" Then I require you," added the lovely girl trembling, she knew not from what cause, as she spoke, " to favour us with a faithful and audible perusal of this mysterious epistle '

" I am honoured in my punishment, said Ronald, taking the paper

Marian regarded Mira with something like wonder, and the latter in her turn listened with deep attention as her brother read the following stanzas —

  ' May heaven guard thy gentle heart
   From ev ry early sorrow,
  Bestow amidst thy mirth to day
   A caution gainst the morrow
  For oh ' the woes are aye the worst
   That youth and gladness sever—
  That, tinging oft the course of life,
   Bequeath us gloom for ever '

  The early grief the direst is
   For gayest hours it saddens
  Bedims the sunlight of the smile
   When most that sunlight gladdens
  For love comes o er us in disguise
   Before the heart is shielded
  To bear away life s only joy
   The life a joy has yielded

Ah ! who can guard the trusting one
  From ties of love s own making !
Or bid her dread the gentle bond,
  As heaviest in breaking !
The youngest heart is young no more
  To whom alas ! tis given,
To doubt and shun the solemn vow
  Love makes in sight of heaven

Then heaven guard thy gentle heart
  From maiden s early sorrow—
Bestow amidst thy mirth to day
  A caution for the morrow !
And spare thy bosom ev ry pang,
  Hope ever leaves when blighted—
The loneness of the heart unloved,
  The anguish of the slighted

' Humph ! ' exclaimed Ronald as he finished

The pet poet again ? said Miss Merriville interrogatively

' Who ? asked Ronald

" To morrow my dear brother,' said Mira with some confusion, ' you shall perhaps see the author But they will want me at the house I am quite sure the coffee is served '

CHAPTER VII

' So, young man, you has got rid of your feller kimpanions, were the words with which Edward Vivyan was accosted, when, after a long saunter through the pretty, quiet, but intolerably dull streets of the town he entered a very humble inn, in a bye lane, whose appearance promised to suit the purse of a needy traveller. Our young friend immediately recognised the horseman he had passed at the turnpike

The man had a handsome, good humoured countenance, but with it an impudent swagger, already increased by some hasty draughts from a large ale jug, that was far from inviting the respect or attention of a stranger

" I left them at the entrance of the town, ' said Edward listlessly, as he took his seat on the settle

" Don t you be for telling me that a hold bird isn t to be caught with chaff Come, come, old feller you ain t going to make I believe you re such a hinnocent as all that, neither

Edward looked inclined to give the man a thrashing " What do you mean ? said he

' Oh, if you re after huffing a feller, I m your man any day of the week, mister But its prowoking to hear a chap profess to be so hinno cent of keeping bad kimpany, ven he talks vith em on the road, and lodges jist next door

" What ! are the old man and his daughter in the next house,' en quired Edward

"Jist as though you didn t know it now   Well ! I never   if you aint a good un strike me lucky   Yes yes, the old un and his darter are next door and so you may see if you likes to come to this vinder mister

Townsend was seated at a back window of the publichouse it was thrown open, and overlooked a yard that appeared common to that and the adjoining tenement   Through the dirty window of what seemed an outhouse but what was really the kitchen and refectory of the establishment next door the figure of the mendicant might be discerned among numerous other heads of every age equally neglected and shaggy

How strange ! that chance mere chance should place us near each other, exclaimed Edward

' Vell you are a good hand at a bouncer ! dash my buttons ! Do you mean to say as you knew nothing about the iding ole of them there people ?"

"Not I ! responded the young man

"You re a nice chap to swear black s vite   Did nt I see you, the old 'un, and his darter, like sisters and brothers all the vay along the cursed road from Minhurst, this here blessed dav !

"We were nevertheless strangers to each other up to this morning, and may never meet again

"You never seed each other afore ?

"Never ! '

"And you hasn t no hintentions of any kind somever to meet agin ?

' None at all

' Vat and no gammon ?

"I can assure you that is the case, though your questions seem to me —

"Werry himperent, no doubt, interrupted the fellow   "La ! bless you ! there s no harm in me   I m one as speaks his mind, that s all— and no mistake !   Come, don t be crabby, hold un   I must stop at this ere vinder till my currier, (i e *couriere*) as the French call em, comes back from the Wicount s at Minhurst

"Are you from Minhurst ? asked Edward, taking an interest in every thing connected with the spot

"Yes, yes, old boy ! Growing civil ? Vell I thought you would, blow me tignt ! when you found out who I vas   I m sent upon the devil s business, and don t half like it, I promise you   Take a swig, Mister ?

Edward accepted the offer—he would have done anything to hear of Minhurst   Mug after mug disappeared and Townsend having contrived to drink about four fifths of the ale consumed at Edward s expense, grew very communicative and friendly

"Look ee old un ! If I thought as you vere capacious enough to be trusted with a secret, he said in the height of his conviviality, ' I could tell you that as vould make you stare '

"Secrets are troublesome returned Edward "I have no wish to hear them '

"And it s all about them ere beggar folks—the hold un and his

No 7

darter,' continued the man taking no notice of Edward s disinclination to share his confidence "you needn t be ashamed of knowing your friends when Lady Minhurst takes notice of 'em

Lady Minhurst' ejaculated the young man

Aye Lady Minhurst ' Why you stares, old feller, as if a generous Wicountess was a wonder

'I am surprised to hear that her ladyship is at Minhurst, and not to learn her beneficence' remarked Edward

' You re not the only one as is We all come down togither yesterday —a queer move it was strike me funny ' In the midst of her gaiety— and a precious gay life she does lead in London to be sure pack up says her ladyship, and off she comes to this here dull place, which gives a man the orrors Here s a safe journey back to her ''

' Do you know the motive of this sudden visit? enquired Edward

Vy, to worry her son, perhaps dash me ' if I did nt always think her a wixen or may be to marry her grand children

Ah ' the young gentleman, or the young lady Miss ?

"Vy Miss Mira is likely to go first from vat they says about her and the Honourable Sylvester Silliton deuced nice chap it is such an amater of osses prime judge of cattle but what s the matter old boy ' Strike me dumb, if you doesn t look jist as if you were going to kick it '

Notning ! a slight affection of the head I am sometimes troubled with nothing more

Werry bad I must say to have haffections in the head, and for a young chap like you too Here s to your better ealth, Mister

Thank you, I am better already said Edward striving to regain his composure ' You were saying that Lady Minhurst was interested about obout Old Welbourne and his daughter he continued, anxious to hear of any thing that might improve the fortunes of his fellow travellers and unwilling to allow the conversation to return to a topic that gave him great pain

Vy, yes but vat s more she wishes to keep it a great secret so I m sent to this here place to keep a sharp look out, and I m not to lose sight on 'em

" Are they apprised of her ladyship s intentions ?

No, no ' vy dont you see ? the Wicountess has taken a fancy I m thinkin to the young girl and a pretty piece it is too, strike me lucky vants to take her into her own charge perhaps or something of that ere kind, you know But I thinks the old un vont consent, for I ve strict horders to be wery cautious, and not to let him suspect as I vatches him

Has her Ladyship known them long? asked Edward

Vell ! that you must know is the funniest part of the business they never saw each other in all their born days till last night ven, lo and behold ! all on a sudden my lady takes a fancy to this girl as come along side of her in the wood, and sends I off with horders to keep my eye upon 'em and not to say nothing to nobody

' Strange ' said Edward Vivyan and had he been sufficiently free from thought to occupy himself with the affairs of others he would have had full leisure to cogitate on the adventures of the day as his companion, yielding to the effects of the strong beer, as soon as the conversation flagged, fell into a heavy slumber but our young adventurer had his own cares, and was soon plunged into a deep reverie, in which a painful past and an uncertain future floated in turns before him For the former, his brief history had been chequered by but few events, but they were of that cast that leave a deep impression on the mind, and give it a direction from which during life it rarely wavers

Endowed with a strong poetic temperament he had passed impercep tibly from the training of nature, to the training of books in the former school he had learned to feel and enjoy in the latter he had acquired the power of expression For a long time his splendid and dangerous gift unnoticed, unencouraged, unsympathised with pained because it was unshared at last there came one to discern his genius to admire his productions, and to applaud his effort The heart of Edward was too grateful not to feel a strong attachment towards a patron of any kind but when his first and only poetical friend joined youth beauty sweetness of temper and nobleness of mind to a warm appreciation of his talent, it was impossible for a susceptible heart not to love the amiable patroness though in her he recognised Mira only daughter of Viscount Minhurst And when this passion unconsciously conceived and cherished began to display its inevitable symptoms, reason told him of his folly but bringing no remedy, left him in despair It was then that the young poet sunk into despondency his mind lost its fire, his frame its vigour There was one at hand to notice the change, to lament it to scheme and plan for his recovery—his mother With a bleeding heart she advised change of scene and a more active mode of life than his village school He listened to her suggestions, and with them occurred to his mind that dangerous hope to an energetic nature—the desire of distinction It was as impossible to overcome his love as to expect it would be returned but well earned distinction would command esteem, and esteem would be beyond price from her, who could not grant him her affection With the exception of an occasional imprudence in the shape of a copy of verses conveyed in a nosegay, and only looked on as the tribute of a poor poet to his lady patroness, Edward Vivyan started for the metro polis with his secret buried in his bosom, where it formed one of those powerful impulses which lead to renown or martyrdom

Such was his history, briefly told and such was the chief subject of his thoughts as the day closed over him and his snoring companion

It was already evening, and he rose to prepare for his departure when the landlady entered to arouse Lady Minhurst s very vigilant sentinel and spy It appeared he was wanted by no less a person than Gregory Grasp, Esq , who waited to confer with him in a small sanded parlour, six feet square fitted up with a round mahogany table, four oaken chairs two spittoons and a tea board the most sumptuous apartment at the " Cat and Gridiron Edward being left alone, thought more seriously of continuing his journey he loitered, however by the window that overlooked the quarters of the mendicant, and felt a strong desire to see once more his friends of the morning   A quarter of an hour passed away, when Townsend returned, ushering in the lawyer

' That ere s the feller I spoke to you about,   said he in Grasp s ear " he is a powerful chap   jist your sort   you can try the stuff he s made on, vile I sees to the rest

With these words the groom withdrew, and Gregory Grasp stalked into the apartment

" Fine evening, young man, said he

" Very, replied Edward

' Stay here to night ? ' continued Grasp

" No '

" Late to travel on foot   going far eh ?

Three questions in a breath make Edward think he had fallen into worse hands than ever   As he was determining how to silence the en quirer most effectually, the little lawyer rung the bell, and ordered spirits and water for two

" Can you take brandy, young man ?

" For me ? asked Edward starting with surprise   " Neither ! '

' Come, be sociable   I have some business on hand, important, con nected with the Minhursts   high family you know   in which you could serve me to your own advantage

" London is my destination, and I continue my journey to night, ' said Edward coolly, not being very much pleased with the appearance of the lawyer

It won t delay you two hours, continued Grasp   " a short space to earn a few pounds '

Too short I fear, for them to be earned honourably

" Young man ! impertinence insinuate honour   connected by monosyllables, lost in the rapidity of utterance, fell from the irritated little gentleman

" Excuse me, sir   I should be reluctant to offend you, but a proposition of the kind from a stranger, to give my services for an unusual recom pense

" Looks odd, ' interrupted Grasp   no doubt   honour   good thing right to be tenacious   good sign in young men !   But listen ! don t ask you to do anything blindfold   don t take you for a fool   far from it

" I am afraid, Sir, an explanation will be of little use   but since you urge it, I attend,   remarked Edward

" Came from Minhurst to day, I think ? '

" I did so, was the reply

" Had company on the road, eh ?

" An old man and his daughter

" Aye, aye ' an incorrigible vagrant   great nuisance to the overseers

" He may be so   I certainly judge him to be an unhappy man

" A fellow without a calling goes by a thousand aliases   What did he tell you his name was ?

Welbourne

" So, so ' Welbourne ' Thomas ? John ? ' eagerly asked Mr Grasp

' No ' Wilfred

" Humph ' *Wilfred* ' and the lawyer looking surprised, took out a portfolio and made a note ' Queer name his daughter s, pretty girl though added he

' Very beautiful,' replied the young traveller

' Aye, aye ' young men soon find out that long in her company, eh ? Anything transpire on the road beggars conversation curious no doubt ? continued the cunning man of law

Edward now began to suspect that the intentions of the enquirer were not altogether benevolent towards the persons in question

' You judge these poor people harshly, I perceive, said he in a severe tone "if you expect to find in me a person able or willing to support your suspicions, you are deceived There is much worth in this poor man a few hours intercourse sufficed to make me esteem him

" A worthy man who ruins his child, eh ? sarcastically observed Grasp

" I would stake my life on his affection for her, sternly replied Ed ward

" Devotes her to vagabondism don t look like love, that ?

" How can he do otherwise ? Is he not an outcast from society him self ?

" Pooh ! pooh ! Plenty to pity the child Lady Minhurst for in stance excellent woman that wishes to take her under her care but the parent won t part with her

Who would give up such a treasure ' Let her ladyship provide for both she is wealthy the burthen would not be great.

" Habits are not so easily overcome as plans are formed The old man is too far gone to settle down now Take my word for it, the young woman is lost, unless separated from him

" I cannot agree with you whatever his s tuation, a parent must be the best protector of his child

" His precarious mode of existence exposes him to danger, to impri sonment, and rarely leads to long life You must admit the very dis tressing situation of this very lovely girl most lamentable case to part them is most desirable

" From their attachment to each other I should consider it impos sible, rejoined Edward

Grasp paused took a long draught of the brandy and water, and then continued, looking slyly at his companion

" Physical force physical force scheming a little scheming---they will accomplish a good deal sometimes, hinted the pettifogger

' Surely the benevolence of Lady Minhurst has not so far got the possession of her judgment as to induce her to employ either in a case of this kind returned Edward looking round suddenly on Grasp and speaking in a tone at once so manly and full of censure as entirely to disconcert the lawyer

No ' not exactly fraud he replied, being thrown off his guard ' nor scheming neither Noble lady the Viscountess—no dirty work but the case of this poor girl is so unfortunate that —

Edward now lost all patience he began to conceive the nature of the task for which his services were required and colouring with indignation he said—

Pray sir is it for the furtherance of this most benevolent object the tearing asunder father and child, that you would employ me at a high remuneration ?

Grasp faultered he had seen much of the world, but was not in the habit of hearing himself haughtily questioned by the wearer of a seedy coat

Not ex exactly ' he stammered "precise purpose—unnecessary to mention, he continued, retreating to the door ' views dissimilar— no acting without unity Beg to take my leave—a good evening young man and he gained the passage As he passed the bar on his way into the street, he desired the landlady to send Townsend to him at his own house, as soon as he returned

' Let him make haste he added ' Tell him my plans are altered and no time is to be lost

" A plague upon him for an ass ' muttered the lawyer as he hastened through the town to his residence ' a thousand plagues upon him ' This young fool has got into Welbourne s confidence and might have drawn off his attention while I found means to secure the girl —or with his fine face, he might have decoyed her himself The fool refused my gold The ass ! what are the man and child to him ? Now must I go home and concoct another plan in the meanwhile perhaps they slip through my clutches D——n ' This matter managed successfully, were worth my own price my own price Yes ' yes ' Lady Minhurst is too prudent to refuse Gregory Grasp any reasonable sum for his important services What is to be done ? The law ? No ' no ' It may serve when there is time to plot and make out a good case This matter requires immediate action—a bold stroke—aye aye violence or fraud with this youngster s aid, might have deceived the beggar so well But that s all over, and only one course remains—violence, violence ! God send us safe out of it ? Pooh ' pooh ' nonsense, I work upon my own terms—a round turn egad ' Ha ! ha ' ha ! He ' he ' he '

And he rang an accompaniment to his shrill discordant laugh, on the bell of his own door

An hour had elapsed since the interview with Grasp, and Edward still sat at the open window The sun was verging fast towards the horizon, and the landlady began to hope the young man would remain her guest for the night He entertained however, no intention of postponing his journey to the next day and only delayed it in the hope of seeing the mendicant or Evine The hard lot of the latter, so obvious to every one had already made a deep and melancholy impression on Vivyan and it greatly increased by the few hints he had gathered from his conversation with the lawyer On these he pondered with much earnestness, but learnt nothing more upon reflection than what he had at first perceived He felt suspicious of the benevolence that did not hesitate to separate parent and child for to him, it could not be accompanied with an adequate compensation to either party Of the Viscountess Minhurst he knew but little, and though the suspicion occurred to him he dared not hastily attribute to her other and unjustifiable motives for taking such a step On one point alone he felt certain that Grasp was about to take active steps for the execution of this singular project, that a plot was actually in formation against his poor unprotected friends and would soon burst upon them, He longed to apprise them of his fears, but even that simple act of friendship could not easily be discharged

That morning he had experienced the pangs of separation in parting with his dear mother There was much to mitigate the severity of the trial *his* exile was voluntary and was considered by both as a line of conduct that would ultimately lead to good When he compared these circumstances with those of the poor wanderers and remembered that *they* were unconsciously exchanging filial and parental duties and caresses for the last time—that force and craft would be employed to draw them from each other s embrace and that, without leaving either a trace by which the cause of this outrage might be discovered or the destiny of the other be conjectured upon he rose with a shudder of indescribable agony and walked into the yard that was common to that and the adjoining house, hoping to meet Evine or her father

By this time the sun had set but it was not yet dark The shutters however of the vagrant rendezvous, were already closed Lights were required in the wretched hovel long before night closed in and to secure the inmates from the observation of those without, it became necessary to take that precaution None loitered about the premises from within came the sounds of conversation, conducted by many voices and occasionally varied by outbursts denoting both high jollity and warm disputation

Edward s anxiety to benefit his friends got the better of all the respect with which he was accustomed to regard the privacy of others and he drew near the dilapidated shutter which offered more than one chink to the eye of the curious A numerous group huddled round a large fire and almost concealed in dense smoke produced by a liberal use of the weed was all he could distinguish He waited, however with patience the smoke floated away to be rapidly renewed but in the interim he perceived the form of the mendicant To Edward it was a matter of surprise, to find the man whose conversation promised other habits in a state rapidly approaching intoxication Welbourne s weather beaten features were flushed with liquor his eyes glared wildly and his laugh rung like a loud roar above the noise of the sots that surrounded him There was another circumstance connected with this singular man that attracted the attention of Vivyan In the morning he had observed a few straggling flakes of grey hair escaping from beneath the mendicant s oil skin hat, and these, in conjunction with a stoop of the shoulders gave him an appearance of age that he seemed to have thrown aside in that hour of carousing The few locks that were now seen on his scanty brows were of the darkest hue his posture, though under the influence of drink was upright and the general description of sixty had given place to the vigour of the prime of life Evine s light form was to be seen hovering about the dark groups of rogues and beggars (for the company was of

no other description) like an angel's figure shuddering with disgust at
the revels of fiends   She made her way to her father's side and though
the noise prevented Edward from catching a word he perceived by her
gestures that she was endeavouring to induce the mendicant to leave the
scene of merriment   Her attempts were at first ineffectual but she at
length succeeded in gaining her father's attention

Edward had not much time to employ in further observations, for a
slight movement of the latch of an adjoining door announced the entrance
of another person into the yard   He withdrew from the window and
was on the point of entering the inn when he heard the voice of Evine

' This way, this way   said she in a hurried voice, at the same time
beckoning him to follow her   I have something to say —here we may
be overheard

She glided swiftly through an opening at the further end of the yard
and leading the way down a narrow lane, stopped on a rude bridge that
crossed a mill stream at the bottom   It was a little spot of great rural
beauty   The course of the water was serpentine, and being bordered by
thickly planted willows, shut out the view on either side   The roof of a
neighbouring water mill was perceptible above the trees, and the noise of
the water as it dashed over the wheel came to the ear in softened and
pleasing murmurs   It was, in short, one of those spots the mind loves

when excited by joy or sorrow   at once, and by a strange contradiction, a trusting place for lovers and a grave for suicides

The twilight was now far advanced—the soft summer twilight—and a young moon shewed a gentle light through the clear blue sky

Evine came to a halt about the centre of the bridge   She had left the lodging house in haste, without waiting to make any alteration in her attire   Her hair therefore in its luxuriance unconfined by any head dress played in light golden ringlets over her forehead and down her neck The beautiful symmetry of her slight figure was undisguised by mantle or shawl and clad in a garment of light hue stood out in bold yet fairy like relief   more shadow than substance from the foliage behind   Nature had bestowed on her personal attractions that required no artificial concur rence either of dress or circumstance to impress the spectator with their matchless beauty   yet where is the perfection that cannot be heightened by such advantages ?   In the glare and splendour of a ball room she would have borne away the palm as the fairest of mortals   in that se cluded and dark spot, by the light of a young moon, attired with careless grace, if she lost anything it was the colouring and identity peculiar to mortality her form seemed spiritualized into a phantom of ideal excellence

Edward was struck with her appearance   but the emotion it pro duced amounted to a feeling more dignified than admiration for an attrac tive form   To him the mendicant s daughter seemed at that moment, as a creature of near affinity to heaven,   yet exposed to all that earth pre sents most degrading and perilous in trial   His heart was rung with anguish composed of noble elements admiration for loveliness compassion for distress,   such a sentiment as (if a comparison between mortals and beings of a higher order can be admitted) a guardian angel may be sup posed to entertain for the object of his care

She soon broke the silence

" We are going from the town   she said

" Immediately ? asked Edward

" My father is preparing to leave   I have seized the moment to speak to you   I have something I wished to say,   answered Evine

" I am glad to hear you have decided on leaving P—— immediately Had I seen you before, it is the step I should have recommended, observed Edward

" You would have recommended it !   repeated the maiden, with apparent surprise   Wherefore ? Are you then of my father's opinion that we are watched dodged by those who wish us harm ? Yet, how should you   you a stranger

" Has your father such suspicions ? enquired the youth, interrupting her

' Yes ' continued she ' but for them he might have done some good for himself by passing a night in the town   From what has past he thinks it more prudent to go forward to night

' Tell me   said Edward, who now began to think he might be spared the painful task of repeating what he had learned from Grasp provided he found they were sufficiently on the alert to secure themselves from

No 8

the threatening danger "tell me what induced you to change your intention what gave rise to your suspicions ?

'Many things said Evine "strange faces hovered about us followed us up and down enquiries had been made after us of the woman of the house besides father slept an hour or two this afternoon and had such terrible dreams and I dreamt too, last night, such a dream ''

This was no time to speculate on the validity of dreams and there seemed stronger reasons to confirm the suspicions of the mendicant Edward had however yet to learn whether Welbourne was acquainted with the real nature and cause of the persecution, which, by his preparing to avoid he evidently dreaded

'What is the danger he fears ? enquired Edward

Alas, that is a mystery to me ' said Evine "If I enquire, he tells me that I am too young too childish to be entrusted with it

"But have you no suspicions ? asked her companion

'Oh yes ! replied she ' and in times of alarm such as this, it wears my mind out to think of them At times I have thought him fearful on my account but that cannot be who would care for a helpless creature such as I am ? Then darker suspicions cross my mind I am afraid to listen to them even in thought I cannot tell them to you he is my father and I dare not

Edward felt embarrassed as the mendicant, however appeared alarmed and had decided on leaving the town, he considered it would be the wisest plan to keep his conjectures a secret, and not perplex the father and daughter by discovering to them a new cause of fear One thing however, occurred to him

'Your father is not in a very fit state to travel ' remarked he, though in referring to that circumstance he betrayed himself

No ! he is in his most dangerous temper and I wonder he sees the necessity of leaving the town but she added in a tone of surprise who told you of my father s state ? '

' I remarked it myself ' said Edward and he would have added in what manner had not Evine interrupted him

"Ah ! you thought of us then ? Twas kind of you few care for the poor beggar

"I have thought of you ever since we parted and shall not cease to do so when we are still further from each other What direction do you take ? asked he

We go to S—— far from the London road But I must loiter here no longer my father waits for me, and would be vexed, did he know we were together

' Why so ? enquired Edward ' have I offended him ?

"Alas ! misfortune and persecution have made him suspicious of all men and though your conversation gave him pleasure this morning he now fears that you were not so friendly without intention Oh ! forgive him for such a suspicion my poor father has had much to embitter his mind indeed he has ' said the poor girl

' Your request would obtain forgiveness for a more serious injury, said Edward, in a tone of deeper friendliness than he was perhaps conscious of

It will then, perhaps, obtain for me a favour that I scarcely dare to ask added Evine, with a blush that the moonlight but scarcely concealed

'It will obtain from me anything within my power replied the young man warmly

'Oh! you can do it, if you will yet I am afraid to offend you by asking it—indeed I am,' said she

"I give you my unqualified promise that no request you can make will offend me' replied Edward

'Are you very, very sure?

"I think I have sufficient self command not to receive offence from any request you can make, was Edward's reply

'You are going to London?' asked Evine

"Such is my purpose was the response

'To better yourself?

"I fondly hope so'

Tis a large place—a great, crowded place I was there once

Then you know something of its splendour?

Much of its misery there the poor die unnoticed the rejoicing of he great drowns their very moans tis a hard place for the poor

'You do not encourage me much by your description, in the furtherance of my plans he observed

'No continued Evine, 'I must discourage you to gain my request

'I am puzzled to conceive its nature, said the young traveller

"In London all is dear friends are rarely to be found there to get on in your way of life, you will have to mix with great people you must wear good clothes, and look respectable

'Alas! I have foreseen these difficulties more easily than I could prepare to meet them but why these cautions, my good monitress? asked Edward

You will *then* want money added Evine, with an increasing and an agitated hesitation, as she placed her hand in her bosom much money

'Alas, yes! exclaimed Edward, as his small means occurred to him "but God will aid me, he added with hopefulness I am sure of it I have a mother's prayers'

"He *does*! retorted Evine, drawing her hand from her bosom and holding the purse given her by Lady Minhurst the preceding night at arm's length "Here is gold *take it*!"

Evine stood near the centre of the little bridge, and Edward remained on the bank of the small stream the arm of the latter stretched out towards him was accordingly over the surface of the water The young man started back a pace or two it was a request that of all others he was the least prepared for

Never! said he with firmness

'You fear to take it you doubt my honesty I am a beggar's child how should I have gold?

" By heaven no ' exclaimed Edward, betrayed into an oath   " I am as persuaded of your honesty as of my own, though our acquaintance does not date from four and twenty hours

" Then why not take what you so much need ?

" In offering it to me you overlook your own necessities   Your provision and raiment are scanty and coarse   if it is useless to you, your father could employ it well   But why should I say this to you   you cannot have forgotten *him* ?

" He has not been overlooked when I made you this offer   gold to him is the most dangerous of gifts   He despises it as the chief tie that unites man to man, and exchanges it for dangerous liquors, whose effects he deplores in his sober moments   Gold for my father !   tis his aversion and his bane '

' Put up the purse   it is worse than madness to give to others, when your own wants are extreme

" Believe me I have no wants   yes one   to hear of your success-- no other   I never was better clothed, better fed   or better housed, and I have fared worse   where then are my wants ? But you   did you not tell us but to day   that for you the present was all want, that you existed but in hope?   How will these hopes be realised without the aid of money ?   Take, take the purse '   almost imploringly urged the maiden

' Never ' never '" said he

" You refuse me then this favour ?—the first I have asked—the last I shall be able to ask '

' I cannot comply   it would burthen my conscience

Will no consideration induce you to take a gift it costs me no sacrifice to part with ?   asked Evine

" None ' ' firmly responded Vivyan

Then let it sink to the bottom of these waters ' ' cried she, raising her hand, as she spoke, to drop the purse into the stream beneath her

' Rash girl '   exclaimed Edward, as he saw it glitter in the moonlight   " would you throw away the means of existence?

" Tis valueless to me, if it does not benefit you '   she returned

' This is madness '   Gold '   gold '   we live by gold '

" If you think so, take it ' '

And she hurled the purse from her with such violence, that it fell heavily upon the grass at Edward s feet

He was too startled by this sudden action to perceive that Evine had taken flight by a path leading from the bridge on the side of the stream opposite to that on which he stood   In two or three moments however, he pursued her, bearing in his hand the treasure so wantonly thrown away   Those few moments, however, favoured her escape   on reaching the other bank he was bewildered by a variety of paths   He looked around, but no living thing was within sight   he listened—no footfall met his ear

When satisfied that she was really gone, he returned to the public house, determined at all hazards to visit the mendicant at his quarters and restore the money   This attempt was also fruitless   he learnt from the woman who kept the place that the mendicant had left the town half an hour before

Such was the case Evine anticipating Edward s refusal, and deter mined to confer on him a gift that she felt would be of essential service, had contrived a pretext which left her at liberty to join her father about a mile on the road to S—— That point was easily gained by a path leading from the bridge, and turning to advantage her knowledge of the country, she thus forced her gift on Edward Vivyan

But he was not easily disconcerted a plan immediately suggested itself—he would trace them to S——, endeavour to learn her name, deposit the money at a bank, and then apprise her by letter that it re mained there for her use

Breathless with a long run, during which she had not dared to cast a single look behind, Evine came up with her father When she slack ened her motion, and had recovered from the effects of her rapid pace she found herself a prey to agitation of another kind—which she had been far from suspecting It was a wild, trembling 'emotion—by turns the pleasing consciousness of having done a good deed, the triumphant exultation that accompanies success against obstacles, and that strange uncertainty as to the propriety of our actions—only known when we have hazarded some bold attempt, and most known to those who are in love

"Have you brought it ? asked her father, enquiring for the object she had contrived to leave behind, in order to obtain a private interview with Edward

Here it is, she replied holding up a tattered article of dress—yet far too important a portion of their wardrobe to be thrown away

' Where was your head, child, that you did not think of it,' continued the old man

' I scarcely knew what I did, father you seemed afraid—and when you fear, I may well grow bewildered, was the daughter s excuse

"Well ! well ! no matter ! Did I seem afeared ? Who knows ? who knows ? There may be no danger, but I have lived long enough to learn to be wary It is not every face I trust Evine—no, no !—but that youth, this morning—I should not have suspected him !

"He can wish us no harm, father I am sure he does not

The old man looked searchingly in his daughter s face

"Poor child ! poor child ! she cannot couple a handsome face and a black heart Well ! well ! Who knows ? But why should he be better than others child ? why should he ?

' He looked so, father, was her simple reply

"Nonsense ! looked so ! how do you mean ?

"He did not look like one who plots and schemes

"He was very grave nevertheless—a very grave young man—I don t like your solemn youths Hang me ! I was blind not to see through it

' Yes, father but he looked grave like one who is sad at heart, but not cross like a wicked man

This was nice discrimination for Evine s years and it drew another searching glance from her father

" So, so pretty one ' said he   you see the difference between the
gloom that comes over us to pass away again, and the gloom that is
settled within—to abide there for ever ?   Tis early, though—tis early !
Poor child ' poor child '

I am very sure, father, he had much to make him unhappy without
having a black heart and forming wicked plots   Think, he had left a
mother and was going to London all alone without money, and without
friends

" May be ' may be ' But a poor man is a weak man   Who knows ?
who knows ?—a piece of gold might induce him to betray a strange
beggar whom he would never perhaps meet again

' That he would not, father '   cried the maiden, with an earnestness
that sounded like vexation

" Who knows ? who knows ? Why should he not ' said the father

" He has an honest face and could not

' So has many a rogue continued the mendicant somewhat more
sternly

" He has a noble heart ' rejoined the earnest girl, " and dared not '

Well, well ' Why the puss pleads like a big wig ' But never tell me
—I ll have nothing to say to any more travellers though they be ever
so good looking ' D ye hear, Evine ^ I won t   But come on, child
or we shall never reach our quarters

Do we stop at the next town ? asked Evine

We shall not reach it by daylight, if we travel all night, replied
the mendicant   ' No ' no ' we must pitch our tent as we did last night,
in some lonely place   Let me see ' some six miles on there is a place
will suit us we ll make for it child we ll make for it

He fell silent and as Evine followed him she observed with some
regret the bold curves he described on the grass as he walked totteringly
along   He had drank freely but this was by no means an extraordinary
circumstance, and but for his unusual alarm it would have given her
little uneasiness   As it was, however she could have wished he had
been in a state of greater wariness and vigour   He plodded on with
considerable briskness notwithstanding the stupor produced by the
liquor   On such occasions he was rarely talkative and Evine was
accordingly left to her own thoughts   These were novel if they were not
pleasing, and we are not prepared to say they were without the latter
quality   Our fair friends will solve the question with ease if they give
themselves the trouble to recal their feelings after the first interview
with the man whom they regard above all men   Let it not be supposed
however that we ask for a confession we respect such emotions too
highly to disturb their privacy they form the Schekinah of that sanc
tuary the heart, and none but the initiated in love are permitted to be
hold their glory

It would have been fortunate for Evine had her happiness depended
only on the excellence of the youth thus thrown in her way but alas ' it
was qualified by the reflection that she had seen him for the first and
last time   Still the mind takes a pleasure in contemplating the beautiful
though it may be remote from all connection with ourselves and by the

same law the poor wandering maid thought with gentle, not unpleasing melancholy of her young friend If it grieved her that their acquaintance could not be continued she felt that not to have known him would have been a greater loss as the morning's adventure had furnished her with a delightful object for contemplation There is a strange faculty in the heart of dilating that which it loves of prolonging its pleasure by dwelling on a thousand petty details existing and imagined and this power was in vigorous exercise as Evine took her nocturnal midsummer way to her leafy domicile Under how many phases did Edward's countenance occur to her mind ! a thousand signals she remembered as flashing from love's telegraph the eye then the few sentences he had uttered were pondered on till every one claimed a hundred meanings each meaning recalling higher beauties of mind and feeling and all these thoughts too came over a mind that had received no training a nature unformed by education so vigorous and tuneful are the heart's chords, when fanned by the first warm breathings of love

Thus glided away two short hours save a few moments that at different times were spent in listening to sounds that resembled a distant footfall For a second or two, her heart would perhaps give place to a passing fear but the transient agitation was speedily quelled by the absorbing thought Her father was the first to break silence

To the right said he ' This is our resting place we shall not meet a better to night

They turned off from the narrow path which they followed for it did not deserve the name of road and after making their way through some feet of underwood reached a little nook of verdure not unlike their place of halt on the previous night The arrangements for converting the spot into a sleeping place were soon made From the centre rose a venerable oak, the large dimensions of whose decayed trunk offered one of the travellers at least an effectual shelter from the heavy dew Each party was reluctant to enjoy this natural luxury to the privation of the other and Evine only consented when her father effectually pointed out to her the necessity he was under not only to watch through the night but also of being on the alert and unshackled in case of a surprise

A surprise ! cried the alarmed girl "Do you indeed, fear a surprise ?

Who knows ? who knows ? There are many who would not be sorry to take me if I come in their way but it is scarce worth their while to pursue a poor man like me

How you frightened me dear father

' Silly child ! silly child ! a beggar's daughter should not fear even if they were *there* But in you must go Poor thing ! no bed last night nor to night poor thing !

And he proceeded to spread a rough outer garment on some dried grass in the hollowed trunk of the tree In this couch he insisted on Evine's reposing and having kissed her cheek as she laid upon the rude pillow covered her head with a clean kerchief that formed the envelope of their little bundle He then lighted a fire and took his station in a sitting posture before the opening of the trunk By this time the effects of the liquor had passed away, and Welbourne found little difficulty in executing his intention of keeping watch through the night

All this was decided upon and executed in less than a quarter of an hour, and the mendicant warmed by the genial heat of the bright flame and sheltered from the breeze by the tree at his back, soon fell into the deep rumination peculiar to his solitary habits and turn of mind In a few minutes, the hard breathing of his daughter, satisfied him that she had yielded to sleep whose demands at that time of life are as refreshing as its influence He was himself nearly overcome by the same power when a slight rustle of the leaves aroused him With all the wakeful ness of an alarmed man, he felt inclined to spring to his feet and stand on the defensive, but his presence of mind instantaneously suggested the propriety of reconnoitering as far as he could from his position, without manifesting any appearance of alarm Though a second sound, so slight as to pass unnoticed by any but an accustomed listener reached his ear not a muscle of his body moved his chin remained pointed towards his chest in the posture of a sleeping man while at the same time his keen eyes from beneath the slouch oil skin hat glanced round the circle of foliage before him They were not long in meeting an object on which

to repose Between the branches of a low bush he met the gaze of a pair of eyes that beamed with an expression of savage exultation, too horrible to be taken for human but for the harsh printed features of the rest of the face, on which the flame flashed vividly

The heart of Welbourne beat quick at this sight his whole treasure slumbered unconsciously behind him and though unaware of the precise character of his pursuers, his past life gave him sufficient reason to apprehend a rencontre with the emissaries of the law especially in a neighbourhood that had been the scene of its most faulty incidents Still he felt that his safety depended on dexterously eluding rather than confronting the parties and awaited without flinching, to see how they would proceed A greater trial however awaited his courage

" Here they are ' here they are ' reached his ears in a low whisper but sufficiently distinct to announce the joy of the speaker

" The girl ' I do not see the girl ' exclaimed the same voice, in a tone of desparation

" She cannot be far, rejoined another voice that proceeded from a different quarter

" We must have the girl continued the first speaker " Fifty guineas for him who secures the girl '

Welbourne s blood ran cold they were then numerous—they wanted his child He cursed the great in his heart for by such he now supposed his pursuers were employed who would deprive a poor man of his only wealth

" She must be near, resumed the person by the bush secure the father—the old man sleeps

" D——n it ! shoot the beggar shoot him !

For the first time the mendicant perceived a pistol levelled at him with a steady aim by the man he had first seen and which escaped his notice in the dark shadows that bounded the reflection of the fire light

The wretched father shuddered through every limb—in a moment he might be a corpse, and his Evine unprotected still he moved not, for he heard the first fellow reply —

" Aye, if he move he sleeps soundly like a drunken man secure him from behind—on him on him '—but the girl look well to the girl —a hundred pounds to him who secures her '

Scarcely were these words uttered than Welbourne heard the slow movement of four men through the grass the direction they took to execute the commands of him who appeared to have the lead, threatened at once to separate him from his sleeping daughter No time was now to be lost in preparing for defence, and grasping firmly the staff that lay at his side, he sprung to his feet as the men came within a few paces of the tree, intending to fell to the ground the first who approached The action was perceived by Grasp (for it was the little lawyer himself), and firing his pistol, he wounded the mendicant in the arm and effectually disabled him Mad with rage and terror, Welbourne listened to the shriek of his daughter as aroused with the pistol shot she sprung from her hiding place to find her father in the power of four armed men He dashed towards her in a state of desperate phrenzy but encountering a heavy blow on the skull from one of the wretches he fell senseless to the earth

A very long interval had not elapsed, before he was brought to himself by the application of cold water to his temples   The look of solicitude that returned his first glance on opening his eyes, satisfied Welbourne that he had not fallen into the hands of a stranger   In a few moments he was sufficiently relieved to recognise Edward Vivyan

' Evine ! Evine ' he faultered   Taking Edward for one of the gang ' If you are human, do not deprive me of my child ! '

' Where ? where is your daughter ?' cried the young man, with an energy that satisfied the father he had no part in the plot   " if she be in danger let me know it, that I may fly to her rescue

At that moment a loud shriek rang through the wood the mendicant pointed in the direction, with a look of entreaty that could not be mis understood and Vivyan darted off to save the unfortunate Evine The old man rose to follow, but having dragged himself a few paces, he again sank apparently lifeless on the grass

---

CHAPTER VIII

GRASP and his companions concluding that the mendicant was inca pable of pursuing them, bore off their prize with less speed than they would otherwise have done   For a short distance they met with no obstacle from Evine   when she saw her father felled to the ground, and herself captured by four ruffians who had taken the precaution of dis guising their features with black crape, she sank into a long swoon, pro duced by terror and grief   This circumstance, though it rendered her powerless, was that which most immediately favoured her rescue Grasp, satisfied with the effect of his fire, and exulting at the capture of Evine, considered it would be prudent for his own reputation to withdraw his presence from an expedition so successfully conducted   He had no fear of trusting its completion to the other men   They were old and well tried hands at awkward jobs, and years had increased the thirst for gain which first brought them within the lawyer s power   His first care was, however, to see the senseless captive so bound and manacled, as to pre vent her profiting by any remissness of vigilance on the part of her guards   He then described the route most screened from observation that led to the hovel where he intended Evine should pass the night and enforcing his exhortation to speed with a large fee, rode off, purposing to enter P—— in an opposite direction to the scene of the night s adven ture

Compassion is not easily driven from the human heart, however vile and degraded it may become this divine principle, as it is its chief or nament, so it is the last to leave its sullied place of sojourn   The men employed by Grasp were always ready to execute any deed that promised to procure them gain and had all undergone the penalty of the law nevertheless, if anything made them halt in the execution of the project it was the appearance of the captive Evine so beautiful, so pale so inanimate, excited in her unconscious state, then compassion She continued senseless so long a time, that pity at length gave way to fear   Alarmed for her life, a halt for the purpose of using restoratives was deemed adviseable, and met the approbation of the four   They were near a narrow brook and placing their charge gently on the bank they removed the cords with which she was bound loosened her dress, and, applying water freely to her brows were soon repaid for their care by signs of returning animation   Her opening eyes however, resting on the same black countenances, she uttered a second shriek and again became sense less   Evine was unaware that her despair had given an effectual signal to a zealous deliverer

When she next recovered, it was to meet the anxious gaze of Edward Vivyan

"Where am I? slowly exclaimed the exhausted child as she gazed round a small room indifferently furnished, and perceived Edward and a decent looking woman standing at her side

" In the hands of friends " replied the former   " Do not be alarmed you have nothing to fear now

" My father ! where is my father ?

" Bless the poor young thing it goes to my heart to see her, said the woman, turning away her head to conceal an involuntary tear

" Has anything happened to him ? repeated Evine, whose fears were increased by this ill timed display of sympathy   ' Stay I remember those dreadful men—they struck him down Is he — her terrified countenance supplied the word she was unable to utter

"No! no ! not dead ! said Vivyan   "when I left him to snatch you from the power of those wretches, he was recovering from the effects of their violence '

" Thank God !   Was it you then, who delivered me ? asked Evine

" What a blessed providence it was to be sure interposed the land lady, for it was a solitary publichouse that afforded them shelter ' Poor young thing !   What would the villains have done with her ? tis dread ful to think of !   Gracious me ! that men should be such rascals !

' But how came you near us, continued Evine ' you were going to London a different road ?

' It is no time to enter on an explanation, said Vivyan unwilling to state the motive which had induced him to take the same route as the mendicant   ' try and compose yourself, while I return to the spot where I left your father, and apprise him of your safety "

" Why did he not follow you ?   Ah, he was wounded and unable

' Slightly wounded he certainly was, but I hope there is no danger, returned Edward   " Endeavour to get over your alarm, that he may have the pleasure of seeing you composed when I return with him

" I am composed quite, quite composed   said Evine rising, when she saw Edward prepare to depart   "and will go with you

" Goodness gracious !   What run into the very lion s mouth again when I have such a nice bed ready for the poor young thing to rest in !' exclaimed the woman of the house in surprise, and with a cordiality in spired by the sight of a half guinea which Edward had thrown down to gain an entrance into her dwelling "Better stay with me, my good girl, and let the young man go alone

"I cannot, I will not' exclaimed Evine with energy "I shall die if I may not go to him

Her looks betrayed intense anxiety and Edward satisfied that he had effectually dispersed the ruffians, and having no doubt of Welbourne s safety, thought it prudent to comply

'We are three,' said ne to the landlady as he left the inn, which was a wretched cottage that promised but scanty and mean accommodation 'and will return to sleep if you can let us have beds

"Don t be afraid sir I make up three every blessed night things are very dull in these parts and we have had no travellers drop in to day Gracious goodness! times are so bad' Depend upon it, sir I ll keep the beds and the little bustling dame watched Evine and her companion till they were out of sight

As they drew near the spot where Edward had left the wounded mendicant Evine s anxiety became very great Her father was the world to her so essential was his well being to her happiness, so fully and completely did her being depend on his, that she conceived no idea of existence unconnected with him Though their precarious mode of life subjected them to many and strange vicissitudes, none in the whole course of her recollection had so signally threatened to destroy their happiness, by separating them from each other She made it is true great efforts to rally against her fears, and to repose in the assurance Edward had given of her parent s safety but the effects of the shock were not so easily got over and the worse kind of alarm, a dread of something indefinite and vague weighed heavily upon her spirits Vivyan for his part, had little doubt but Welbourne would wait for him in the spot where they last met prudence, as well as his wounded disabled state, would lead him to adopt that course It was impossible for him however, not to see the distressing anxiety of his young companion Her arm trembled as it hung on his as she clung to him, he could feel the pulsations of her heart, while her small quivering feet scarcely touched the grass over which they rapidly passed

The thicket was at last gained, and Edward was on the point of has tening first to the spot for the purpose of preparing the father for the good tidings of his daughter s recovery, when Evine releasing her hold prevented his design and rushed into the circle The abruptness of her action took Edward by surprise he followed however, immediately, and in another moment had gained the spot No mendicant was there Pale as death Evine reclined for support against the decayed tree, which had been intended for her resting place during the night, and her eyes were fixed with the wild stare that announces the vacancy of horror on a dark stain that saturated the grass near the embers of the expiring fire

From this abstraction she was aroused by Edward, who, fearing the worst and apprehensive of the consequences to her mind drew near gently and took her by the hand

'Evine!' said he in a soothing tone

She started as if she had heard an unexpected sound and looked full in the face of the speaker. It was the first time he had called her by name, and she was accustomed to hear it from no one but her father. Heart rending was the disappointment depicted on her countenance and only surpassed by the forlorn look which succeeded it, when returning the pressure of his hand, with a grasp of agony, and pointing to the black horrid spot.

"Blood!" she faultered "*his* blood!"

The next moment Edward clasped a senseless body to his bosom

He had so fully depended on meeting Welbourne that he was scarcely prepared for this unexpected result. Nor could he account for it con jecture succeeded to conjecture but none with stronger grounds than those which preceded it. At first he hoped the mendicant might have been induced by anxiety to follow him to the rescue of Evine. To con firm this opinion he examined the grass in that direction but there were no marks to allow him to suppose that any wounded bleeding man had crawled that way and Welbourne's disabled state led him to abandon this most satisfactory way of accounting for his absence. He then feared that the men from whose power he had rescued the daughter had in their flight fallen in with the father and profiting by his weakness secured his person, or taken his life   He was, however too little acquainted with the history of the parties to form anything like a probable conjecture   his first care, therefore, was to conduct the unfortunate girl thus strangely left to his protection, back to the inn, and having seen to her comfort, to ponder at leisure on the next steps to be taken to obtain tidings of her father

On arriving at the inn he confided Evine to the care of the landlady entreating her to spare no pains to restore and comfort his young charge Widow Bustle went to her task with considerable alacrity, and while she was placing the poor girl in a bed in her own room, Edward, satisfied that no immediate danger was to be apprehended from the long fits of fainting, into which Evine successively fell, strolled through the adjoining meadow, where he could consider the different particulars of his situation more calmly than in doors   He remained out for a long hour and spent the interval in deep thought   To account for the events of the evening was utterly out of his power, and the only way of obtaining information on the subject, seemed to be an immediate application to the officious stranger, who in the tap room of the Cat and Gridiron had manifested in so singular a manner an interest in the fortunes of the unfortunate travellers   This person the reader must be aware was none other than lawyer Grasp, who, though he had superintended in person the attempt to carry off Evine, had yet through an affectionate regard for the welfare of his own person so contrived to keep out of the way that in the hurry of the moment he had escaped the notice of Edward His confederates had taken precaution to disguise their features   Thus he could obtain no clue to the circumstance from any one but Grasp and even in that quarter the attempt would be attended with some difficulty   Though the lawyer had great notoriety in his county Edward devoted to study and confined to his school labours, was unacquainted with Grasp s person, and only hoped to find him out by an application to the hostess of the ' Cat and Gridiron   In the event of his successfully tracing the person who had sought his services that afternoon, Edward had too good reasons to suppose he was himself implicated in the attempt made upon Welbourne and his daughter, to decide upon applying to him directly   Envolved in difficulty however, as the matter appeared he determined for the sake of Evine to have recourse to some active measures without further delay and in pursuance of that resolution determined to return to P—— early in the following morning

But the events of the night were not yet terminated, and before morning changed the intention of our adventurer

CHAPTER IX

EDWARD was aroused from his reverie by Mrs Bustle

' Young man ! young man ! cried the widowed hostess, panting for breath after a hasty waddle across two or three meadows " Come haste to the house I have prime news for you

' Is her father within ? anxiously asked Edward, having Evine s situation still uppermost in his mind

" Better nor that, may be, ' replied she

' In heaven s name let me know what it is I am in a state of mind ill calculated, my good soul, to endure suspense

' Speak low, there s a good young man or you may be the death of me Consider, continued Mrs Bustle, "I m a lone widow, and if them there ruffians was to take a spite against a body—mercy on us, there s no knowing what they would do !

" Have you heard of the villains, then ?' enquired he

" Hush ! hush ! you will be my ruin, as sure as a gun, if you can t be calmer Walls have ears, they say, and so have hedges, said the old woman, looking round with terror at the underwood bathed in moon light

" Tell me what has happened since I left the house in God's name, do not mortify me !'

" Well ! you must know, after a sight of pains, I brought the poor young thing to her senses like but, mercy on us ! as different from what she ought to be as cream from butter milk Well, as I was look ing quite sadly on her pale features bless em ! they looked as handsome as any angel in heaven need be, for all they had no more colour than the sheets and thinking what a sorrowful heart the poor thing must have had to make her stare about so wildly, up runs my niece—I never had a chick of my own, though my poor man, who has been in heaven this many a long year, was as kind a husband as may be—to tell me there were two strange looking fellers just drop t in as wanted beds So I told the child to look after the lass, and down I steps to see what sort of articles they were for you must know, ever since I've been in the public line, I have made it a rule not to take in every one

" Another time you can tell me your rules—they are all very proper, no doubt—but what of these men ? said Edward impatiently

" As I am a living woman, when I cast my eyes upon them, if I wasn t struck dumb ! Such figures I never set eyes on afore in all my born days Not a foot should they have set in [my house, if so be I hadn t a sort of misgiving that they were the very men as had done all the mischief to that poor young thing

' Did you admit them ? did they stay ? are they in the house now ? cried Edward, in a breath involuntarily quickening his pace, without waiting for the old woman s answer

' Goodness gracious ! at what a rate you do gallop I can t walk at that pace and talk too, I promise you, my master '

Edward walked slower to gain more information

'As luck would have it, Tim Wilkins and Jesse Grim, the parish clerk, had just stept in to take their evening glass Mr Grim is as nice a man for a bachelor as ever lived—always calls for a drop of the best—so I thought I should nt want a protector, if they chanced to turn out bad customers '

So, you allowed them to come in ? said Vivyan, his impatience increasing

'Lord bless you' and a precious deal more When a good action is to be done, you may ask the whole parish, and every man will tell you that widow Bustle was never backward In I let s em come, and to keep em till your return, I promised to sleep em, and drew all the liquor they chose to call for though I haven t seen the colour of their money, and the Lord in heaven only knows if I ever shall !—and it is for a lone widow, like me, who toils hard for a crust to expose herself to get swindled, and robbed, and murdered in her bed, for anything I know ''

Edward assured Mrs Bustle she should not be a loser by her efforts to assist either himself or Evine, and tried to confine her conversation to the subject by asking some direct questions respecting the appearance of the men

'Downright knavish looking fellows, I promise you, replied the landlady

"But in what way?' asked Edward, for whose sagacity this reply was far too general what do they look like ?

'Lord a mercy' like two thorough bred rogues ragged, dirty, lousy rascals with such lean faces that you wouldn t suppose they had a penny in their pouches, or a bite in their bellies '

"Did they make any enquiries ?"

"Not they, trust me The villains are old files—a precious sight too deep for that But if they didn t use their tongues, they seemed no ways inclined to be idle with their ears You see my niece had been telling all about it to Mr Jesse and so when I'd set the new comers, the brutal ravishers I mean I can t find a name that s bad enough to call 'em the wretches' down to a mug of ale, what does Mister Jesse do but, says he to me, is she pretty Mrs Bustle? meaning the poor young thing You wicked old man,' says I, just to turn the conversation like, 'to be thinking about the wenches at your time of life Then I turns me round to the shabby vagabonds Gentlemen, says I in the public line we learn how to palaver folks wouldn t you like to walk into another room as is warmer and more privater than this ? At first they didn t seem much inclined to stir but I wheedles em and wheedles em, till in they went, and there they be now box d up safe enough

"A thousand thanks, my good cautious landlady' Your ready care demands ready recompense, said he, drawing out the purse given to him by Evine, into which he had placed his own scanty supply of money, and presenting the poor woman with a crown piece I must see these men, and you may reckon upon a much larger reward if they turn out to be any of the party who attacked us and I succeed in bringing them to justice Let us make haste I long to confront them

The old woman safely deposited the coin in her huge pocket and inwardly congratulated herself on having to do with a guest who could display so well garnished a purse

As for meeting them face to face she continued as they approached from behind the premises of which she was the worthy mistress ' I know a trick that s worth ten of that if so be you will just follow the advice of a lone widow like me

" I will do anything that will enable me to discover the fate of that unfortunate young female s father, and to bring the perpetrators of the outrage to the punishment they so richly deserve

' I don t think somehow twould be of any use letting them two chaps know as you be under the same roof with em gracious goodness ' they are so cute them sort of folks, they would take to their heels in no time and never so much as think of the reckoning

' It would be their most prudent plan if they be the persons we take them for

' Then you follow me, young man I ve got a plan as will just catch em or my name is not widow Bubble

So saying the landlady moved on with an alacrity truly wonderful for her age and size, while cautioning Edward to proceed as stealthily as possible led the way through a low shed, large enough for a pigstye but dignified with the name of stable A door led from the building into the house

" Go in there, said she hear all, and say nothing I ll go round to the front door, and see if they want more drink— twill make em speak out '

' Do so, rejoined Edward, softly raising the latch, ' and be under no apprehensions about the reckoning If the gentlemen are short of money, or find themselves in too great a hurry at their departure to think of settlement, remember they drink at my expense

With these words the young man entered his place of concealment and Mrs Bustle resumed her functions as landlady, to the great satisfaction of Jesse Grim and the other guests who graced the settle of her humble kitchen

Edward found himself in one of those domestic receptacles destined to receive the lumber and filth of an establishment, and when on the humblest scale devoted to cleansing operations of every description It was with some difficulty he found his way through tubs pans brooms brushes, and other broken ware, to a chink in the wall, from whence issued a stream of light and the sound of voices betraying to our adventurer his post of observation Having succeeded in reaching it without noise he was able to observe at leisure the adjoining room and its occupants

It was rather a closet than a room and separated by a thin partition from the common apartment of the ale house a contrivance lately made at the suggestion of Jesse Grim whose experience of the world led him to assure the landlady that nothing was more likely to attract parties to

No 10

a place of public resort than its possessing the attractions of private accommodation

The present occupants seemed however but ill satisfied about the privacy of the place their conversation was carried on in low whispers Fortunately for Edward s purpose they had stationed themselves on the side nearest the place he occupied, and if a word was occasionally lost, he was well able to make out the sense of their conversation His first care was to examine carefully the appearance of the two men before him The persons from whose hands he had rescued Evine, were masked, and he accordingly gained nothing from his careful examination of the features of the new comers There was nothing either in their height and figure to lead him to form any conclusion, and it was out of all question to attempt to form an opinion from their dress, as they had evidently been making considerable alteration in their attire Edward was satisfied of this from their appearance being more respectable than the account of his landlady had led him to expect and further from a dark heap of apparel, the different objects of which it was impossible to distinguish by the dim light of a farthing candle, which strewed the floor of the room After this unsatisfactory inspection, Vivyan found that his only course was to observe and listen In pursuing this plan he did not indeed entertain much hope that the men before him were those he had encountered in the wood On consideration he did not think it probable that persons concerned in an unsuccessful depredation of the kind would take up their night s quarters so near the scene of action The appearance however of the strangers even in their more decent apparel was sufficient to excite his curiosity and influenced partly by a desire of satisfying himself that they were not the men he desired to see, and partly by the spirit of observation peculiar to his age, he determined to witness for sometime at least their tete a tete

The garb of both was of that fashion worn by respectable persons of the middle classes, but shabby and out of repair The elder of the two had assumed by the help of a wig, a sleek, saintly appearance while the younger, who appeared scarcely to have attained the age of twenty one, was endeavouring to give by the assistance of a japan tea tray that served for a mirror a dandy like turn to his hair

Your coat wants a stitch under the arm, said the eldest

Yes yes ' vid a leetle mending,' replied the other whose accent betrayed his country to be la belle France, "it vill do veery vell '

Wants a button or two '

' Ah Mistare Tomkins, you are a veery vicked man you do determine as you do say in English, to make von hole in my coat

" No difficult matter that, I take it, Monsieur Le Beau

In about half an hour, their conversation which had proved them to be most abandoned characters was suspended by Mrs Bustle, who entered to know if they wanted anything It was amusing to see the surprise depicted on her countenance on observing the metamorphosis the guests had undergone To this charge Edward would have attributed the alacrity with which she replenished the drinking vessel had he not known she was influenced just then by purer motives than are generally assigned to landlords and landladies   When she had left the room—

"Do you try S——? enquired Tomkins

"Ah, mon Dieu! de wretched town—I have tried it—no compassion for my distress   I left de town vidout a good coat I vas obliged to sell, because nobody give assistance

"And where are you bound?

'I shall exploiter—try I think you say de town of P—— but before I do go dere I must see a French lady—dey say lives vid one Lady Min—Min—ah vat is de name?

"Minhurst?

"Yes yes dat is it de French lady is a demoiselle de compagnie to de great miladi Minhurst   Dey come from London yesterday I vas told   so I shall go dere to morrow

"Yesterday? You are lucky to get your information so soon

"It vas a great fortune for me   I hear it from von leetle man vid a veery sharp nose and shin I did meet in de vood he tell me a veery terrible story   Ah! de Englise are great coquins   He asked me if I had seen a young man and young voman   I had seen noting at all de whole evening   Den he tell me an old man and his daughter valk along veery quietly—

Edwards attention was now deeply excited, as he felt aware that the mendicant and his daughter were about to become the subjects of the conversation

Vell, continued Le Beau   a young man come along he look at de young voman fall in love vid her, and knock down and kill de old man and carry off his daughter

"Villain! muttered Edward, restraining with effort his indignation, when he thus learnt in what way the events of the night were likely to be reported through the ingenuity of their contriver

A romantic story upon my word Monsieur Le Beau—just suited to your French taste

'A veery nice story for your Englise taste too rejoined the Frenchman "The old gentelman vid de sharp nose did give me a crown to pay my expenses till I should see my countrywoman he did tell me about   He said f I would open my eyes and find de young man and de young voman or de young voman alone, I should have fifty gold guineas for my peine'

'Indeed!

'Yes, dat he did   He seem veery much to vant de young voman

In that case my good fellow the best thing we can do will be to make it our business to seek them to morrow and in case of success, share the reward   What say you? Two are better than one, and twenty five guineas are not earned every day

Ah! dat vill be fameux said the Frenchman

'Let us to bed then, for in that case we should be moving early to morrow

And draining their glasses, they called on the landlady to conduct them to bed

Mrs Bustle before she complied with their request went in search of Edward, to ascertain whether he had obtained any information respecting her guests. She met him emerging from his retreat. He was at a loss how to answer her enquiries. he had not time to relate the purport of the conversation he had overheard and he was unwilling needlessly to alarm the widow by acquainting her with the true character of the strangers.

'They are not the men you supposed them to be he said briefly when you have shown them to their beds he added, 'I must see Evine we ought to start before day break to morrow and I wish to satisfy myself that she is in a fit state to undertake the journey

'Goodness gracious' before day break? exclaimed the astonished landlady

'Yes' I have my reasons for leaving so early. But your guests are waiting

In a few minutes Mrs Bustle ushered Tomkins and the Frenchman into the only dormitory of her establishment. It comprised the whole of the only story the little tenement could boast. Above were the rafters supporting the roof undisguised even by white wash and through the sundry interstices occasioned perhaps by havock done to the tiles during the nocturnal excursions of the grimalkin tribe, the light of the moon streamed comfortlessly into the wretched apartment. Between the crevices of the floor the light in the room below might also be discerned in spite of the sand liberally scattered either to conceal or prevent the accumulation of dirt. There were three truckle bedsteads, of very aged and mean fashion with their corresponding bedding stationed in this room while a cord drawn across the lower end separated one of them from the others—an accommodation dictated by decency for female travellers when chance brought them to this forlorn asylum. No other furniture was to be seen and a rude ladder and trap door was the only way of access to the room

A candle end stuck on an oyster shell by way of candlestick was flaring on the floor. Le Beau had already thrown his coat on the bed to supply the deficiency of clothing and the foot of the landlady was on the first bar of the ladder on her way back to the lower part of the premises, when she was thus accosted by Tomkins —

"Who sleeps in that bed? pointing to the one he alluded to

'A young man as is just come in—a very respectable young man, I can assure you gentlemen replied the widow whose respect for them had increased greatly since the alteration in their appearance 'You need not fear all my lodgers is decent people—I don't take in the first as comes

'Are you quite satisfied of his respectability? continued Tomkins who, bearing in mind the account Le Beau had given him of the affair in the wood wished indirectly to sound the landlady

"Gracious goodness' to be sure I be. I haven't been all my life in the public line without discerning what's what. not me indeed—trust widow Bustle for a good pair of eyes

"Dey are veery bright indeed, yawned the Frenchman, not exactly understanding what she meant but concluding that the mention of eyes called for a compliment

It is not so pleasant, resumed Tomkins, 'to sleep in the same room with strangers unless one is satisfied about their character

'Lord love you' replied the widow this here young man is as innocent as a lamb, and pays like a lord—he has too full a purse to be a dangerous chum

"Has he been here long? said Tomkins deciding to catechise the widow till he ascertained whether the rich guest of the ale house was in any way a likely person to lead to his gaining the reward offered for the recovery of Evine

It is probable he would have obtained from Mrs Bustle information on the subject of a more satisfactory nature than he could have possibly hoped for, but the good fortune of Edward having brought him at that moment to the foot of the ladder he overheard the questions addressed to the landlady and effectually stopped the reply by summoning her to descend When she reached the kitchen and had brewed him a glass as requested, and of which she was invited to partake, he cautioned her to observe the strictest secrecy respecting himself and Evine and desired to see his young charge before he went to bed, in order to make arrangements for their early departure early the next morning

In the mean time the other travellers sought their beds

"Let him be who he may observed Tomkins to his companion after commenting at length on what he had learnt respecting the person who was to occupy the other bed "he has the ready rhino, and we must take it out of him

'I wish to mon Dieu you may were the pious evening orisons of the Frenchman

'I will try for it these are no times to be idle So saying Tomkins wrapped himself snugly in the scanty clothing and awaited the coming to rest of our adventurer

In another hour all was quiet in the humble hostelry With the wariness of a young traveller Edward had deposited his money safely under an apology for a pillow on which his head reposed and with the wariness of an old rogue Tomkins had not failed not only to observe this precaution, but also to examine as carefully as the feeble light would permit the personal appearance of the young man

The day had been one of great exercise to a person of Edward s sedentary habits and he soon yielded to the combined influence of sleep and fatigue His slumbers however were neither deep nor refreshing he acted over in dreams the events of the night—again he saw the bleeding mendicant—again he contended with the wretches who had carried off his daughter at times the countenance of Welbourne would occur to his mind bearing all the signs of death at others he heard the voice of the maiden claiming his protection as an orphan and destitute One of these visions came over him with more force than the rest he fancied himself stretched on the same miserable pallet whereon he actually reposed—but bound fast bound with cords of iron strength By the bed side, stood the two men he had overheard conversing during the evening

Iheir countenances glowed with malicious tiiumph, and they weie en
gaged in completing then precautions to fasten him to the bed with a
violent plunge he stiuggled to get free it was in vain and the next
moment the cords were drawn round him with a tightness that threat
ened suffocation at the same time the men withdrew he saw them dis
tinctly as they gradually disappeared through the trap in the floor half
a minute passed and then a long and loud shriek the shriek of Evine
such as he had heard it in the wood again rung in his eais His agi
tation awoke him and he started with a bound from his bed Before he
had time to satisfy himself that his companions were still in their beds
a loud cry reached him fiom below he knew the voice well and his
worst feais awakened by the dream seemed to him on the point of being
confirmed He darted down the ladder and pushed open with violence
the door of the room from whence the sound proceeded Here he found
Mrs Bustle in a night dress busily engaged in striking a light which
she speedily brought near to the bed that Evine occupied The poor

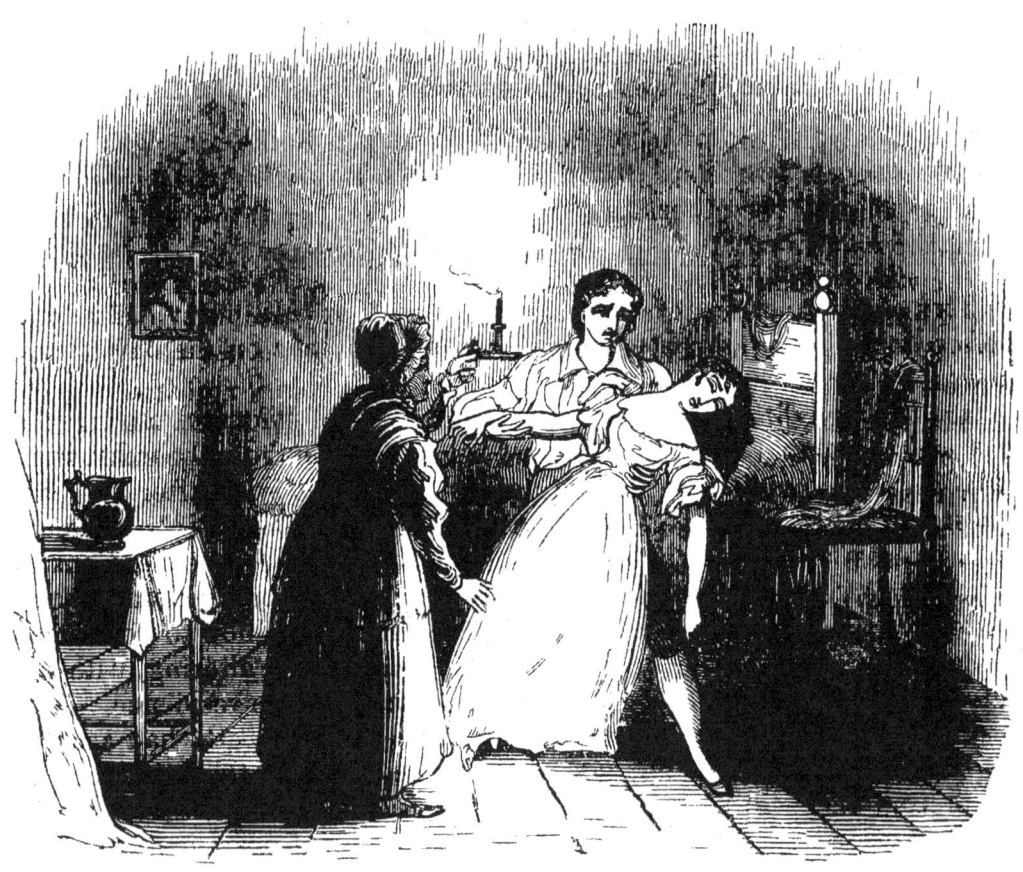

girl s teriors pursued her even in sleep she had started from her slum
bers and her bed with a terrific scream and her alarm had been followed
by a return of the fainting fit They found her stretched inanimate on
the floor

Edward was much relieved when he found out the cause of his alarm, and lent the widow all the assistance in his power to bring Evine to herself The swoon was long and deep, and more than once both he and Mrs Bustle were alarmed for the life of the sufferer As Evine came to her senses the sight of Edward contributed a great deal to console her, and he remained by the bed side clasping her then feverish hand until she again fell asleep

"Do now go and try to get a nap said the considerate widow, when she saw their young charge had fallen into a calm, gentle slumber ' here take this candle

' 'Tis unnecessary rejoined Edward   daylight is streaming through the shutters It will not be possible to set out as I intended, so I may as well sleep an hour or so, as you advise

So saying he drew near the ladder and, on reaching the top was much surprised at the fresh breeze which fanned his forehead A glance satisfied him that it came from a low casement which had before escaped his notice He advanced towards it it had been forced open, and the blanket which swung from it aroused his suspicions The beds were empty, and rushing to his own he looked behind the pillow for the purse it was gone The two men had taken advantage of the confusion, and left him to welcome the opening day, a pennyless man, and laden with the fortunes of a young destitute, and unhappy female

CHAPTER X

THE sobriety of country life was observed at Minhurst and long before midnight the party assembled there to dine on the day of the dowager's arrival had broken up

Though delighted with the little intercourse he had had during the day with his father and sister Ronald began to suffer from the exhaustion of a protracted vigil and retired to his apartment soon after the last guest had taken his leave It was natural for the young heir to examine with interest the family mansion but apart from all considerations of that nature, the rooms assigned to his use possessed strong claims on his curiosity Viscount Minhurst had a mania not uncommon to gentlemen of large fortune and secluded habits —for constantly altering, with the intention of improving be it understood, his favourite residence The original building, which dated from the time of Elizabeth, had accordingly undergone greater changes since it had been in the possession of its present occupant, than at any other period of its existence, for no preceding lord had spent so much of his life free from the turmoil of public business These changes, though generally contrived with taste and judgment gave imperceptibly perhaps to the owner an air of whimsicality to the ensemble of the edifice In no part of it was this more apparent than in the little wing or pavilion appropriated to Ronald's private use The apartment on the ground floor retained all its pristine and cumbrous ornaments, the elaborate carving of cornice and panel, and the ever excellent, though somewhat faded painting of a celebrated artist of the sixteenth century   Adapted for summer use, its numerous windows opened on a colonnade surrounding it on three sides, from whence the park was easily gained by gradual flights of massive steps protected by a balustrade and at that season profusely garnished with exotic plants To this apartment an upper story had been recently added communicating by a long dark passage with the house, and gained from the lower room by a light spiral staircase of great elegance and exquisite proportions   This staircase, having rendered the passage unnecessary, it had fallen into disuse, and the door which led to it was concealed by the handsome tapestry of Gobelin fabric that covered the walls, yet so contrived as to keep the door still practicable in case of an emergency

Ronald was ushered into his apartment by the lower room, and having admired its situation and arrangement, proceeded up the staircase, he himself leading the way, in order to reach that most desirable of all places to the wayworn traveller, his bed-chamber   He found the upper story divided into three rooms of moderate dimensions   The first he entered, the one nearest to the main building, was fitted up with a few study luxuries   The selection of the library plainly told that the person superintending it, had in view its present destination   it containing such literary stores as a father of refined taste and thorough learning might be supposed to procure for a beloved and hopeful son   The inspection of these parts of the fittings up had an effect upon Ronald s warm and susceptible nature, that prevented him from observing a portrait or two, with some specimens of sculpture that ornamented the room   The adjoining apartment formed a commodious dressing room, and beyond that, overlooking from three sides the extensive park and surrounding country, was a spacious bed chamber   A fire had been kindled in the study, for the purpose of airing rooms that were now to be occupied for the first time and Ronald sank into a capacious arm chair beside it, while Robert made the necessary preparations

"Why do you stand there, Robert ?" said his master, observing the valet hesitate to leave the room   "I am impatient to get to bed have you anything to say ?

"I had, sir,   replied the old and faithful servant   "but the hour is unseasonable I—'

"If it be important, never mind the hour

' It would save an old man s legs a short journey,

"Let me hear what it is   I can but tell you to desist if the matter wearies me

' There has been an old man below waiting to see you, sir, ever since dinner time

"To see me ? an old man did you say ?   You should have asked his errand, and informed me of it

"He begged us not to disturb you sir   He must see you alone, he said, when you could hear what he had to say and implored permission to wait till you were at leisure

"Poor man ! some one, probably, who stands in need of the little I have to share, and has had too sad experience of the world to let his story reach my ears through any one but himself   Pon my word, it is too great a tax on my charity to require an interview to night   give him money, Robert—something liberal and let him return to morrow "

"I have tried that plan sir but the old man protests that to ask alms is not his object   he has something important to communicate something for your private hearing

"Will not to morrow do ?" asked Ronald

"I told him you would be more at leisure then   my refusal made him dejected, and more earnest in his request to see you to night   In short sir to tell you the truth he looks so old and feeble and seemed so distressed when I denied him that I promised, almost without thinking what I did to let you know he was waiting   I hope you will forgive me sir but I could not refuse an old man who looked so near his grave "

"Willingly Robert   your description interests me   A young man can at all events bear fatigue better than an old one, and if his business is not decidedly frivolous, I shall feel the happier for having saved him a little trouble.   Let him come in if he still waits '

Before Ronald had time to conjecture what could be the nature of the old man s communication   Robert returned with the aged petitioner

Nothing could be more favourable than the stranger s appearance It presented a living portraiture of venerable and decrepid worth   amidst the decay of age you could read a life of industry and virtue   Ronald was pleased and moved at his aspect   all sense of fatigue and all alarm at being detained by impertinent garrulity, was instantly forgotten, and the youthful son of a peer drawing forward a chair, motioned to the aged peasant   for his garments did not bespeak a higher condition

" Excuse me sir   said the old man, sinking into the proffered seat with every appearance of extreme exhaustion, and in a tone of natural politeness that increased the favourable impression Ronald had already received   I beg a thousand pardons for taking this liberty, but I am old, sir—very

" Do not mention it   it is for me to apologise   How I regret, con tinued Ronald glancing towards Robert to withdraw, ' I was not ap prised of your wish before

' It is not new for me to wait a long while when I wish to see my betters, said the old man   I don t complain about it   twas always the order of things, and always will be

A pause ensued   Ronald wished to leave it to the old man to state the object of his visit   With his last words, however the eyes of the aged visitor had rested on a portrait suspended above the mantel piece, and were rivetted there with an abstraction that at length excited the curiosity of his companion as much as it tried his patience   The picture bore the marks of age, and its sombre frame stood from the wall with so little relief that it had hitherto escaped Ronald s notice   He now examined it with the help of his glass   It represented a young female of great beauty in a fanciful costume   with some surprise Ronald felt that the features were familiar to him though he was at the time unable to recal where he had seen them   The age of the portrait prevented him from supposing that he had ever met the original

No 11

' Do you know that portrait ? said he to the aged man

The person he addressed started, and looked vacantly at the speaker like waking up from the vivid illusions of a dream, and unable for a moment to recollect his actual situation

' Excuse me, Sir I am a weak old man trifles set me wandering.

' You appeared to consider that portrait with peculiar interest

I am glad to see it here it assures me that I shall be a welcome visitor—that the messenger will be welcomed for the sake of the message

' Do not deceive yourself I am as strange to this apartment as you are and notwithstanding some faint resemblance of features similar to those delineated on that canvass occurs to me I do not know whom it is intended to represent

Unknown in her own house ' sighed the old man   ' No wonder he continued in a fit of abstraction the children of the stranger sit at her hearth '

' You knew the original I presume ? inquired Ronald, at a loss to account for these strange expressions unless by ascribing them to the imbecility of age

' Well ' very well ' an angel a blessed angel ' You remind me, Sir hat I come here to discharge a duty that may be left undone if I do ₊not make haste

As he spoke the old man evidently made an effort to concentrate his remaining energy   The apparent struggle between a great weakness and a desire to rally terrified Ronald and he placed his hand on the bell to ring for assistance

Do not ring I am well now interrupted the other " my task will soon be done There is no fear I shall die in my own bed—I am sure I shall

There was an earnestness and sincerity in the speaker s tone and manner that awed the young man into silence   During the short pause that followed, he looked on the old man before him as a messenger from the tomb commissioned to reveal secrets of the past he waited for him to proceed with the solemn silence of one in expectation of an oracular response

It is the portrait continued the mysterious stranger ' of the first Viscountess Minhurst—I mean the first wife of the present Viscount s father

" The predecessor of the present Viscountess, you would say ' rejoined Ronald

' Of your father s mother said the man with an emphasis that gave an arousing signification to the words, but were lost on the hearer from his ignorance of events that a few more hours were destined to reveal to him

" I knew her well I was her lord s valet You have, perhaps, heard of Caleb Walton ?

" The name does not occur to me answered Ronald

No doubt ' no doubt ' When the old lord followed his lady to the grave, I was no great favourite with the survivors they tried to forget me—I knew too much

The old man s tone assumed a bitterness of spirit which his appearance belied

" Remember, Sir, you are speaking to his grandson, ' said the young man haughtily

' You do well to remind me of it, ' continued Walton Children suffer for their fathers sins but do not inherit them or it would little answer my departed lord s purpose for me to obey, as I now am endeavouring to do, his dying bequest

" I trust good man, these imputations will not end in an impertinence if so they are unbecoming your years Remember, you hold life by an uncertain tenure '

' Another wholesome hint, my worthy young gentleman forgive me —an old man will prate

Come to the purpose '

' When the late Lord Minhurst died none were near him none, I mean to whom he could speak in confidence but myself

' Where was the Viscountess my grandmother ?

' If my answer give you pain recollect you sought it—he could not trust her '

Not trust her ! exclaimed Ronald in astonishment

I have almost accomplished my errand resumed Walton, taking no heed of his companion s surprise my dying master was a deceived and injured man—how, or in what way, I never sought to know, though I had suspicions

' Speak out, old man speak out ' cried Ronald by this time violently excited

' The duty of a servant is silence when he only suspects I have never forgotten my duty

' What may you mean then by these hints—these imputations—for such they are

" I am old and foolish, and do business clumsily but heaven knows, I meant them to preface my dead master and lord s own words which I am about to relate

' How ? impatiently enquired Ronald

Wilton drew a packet from his bosom

From this you will learn all The reasons that kept my lord silent at his death made him wish to render the disclosure of his secret as remote as possible for his son s sake the present Viscount My poor master ' though a lord he had none to trust with his soul s thoughts but his humble Wilton In his last hour he gave me this packet Keep it, Wilton said he 'keep it till you feel the hand of death upon you then make it your last care to deliver it into the hands of the next heir of Minhurst I promised, and am come this night to fulfil my engagement

The old man spoke as one labouring under powerful emotion but his manner had an impressive dignity as he placed the packet into the hands of Ronald, that carried a conviction of his sincerity to the mind of the young heir The singularity of the circumstance deprived the youth of his presence of mind, and he looked with astonishment at the document he held

'And now added Walton "my task is over Pardon me if the warmth of my feelings has drawn from me any disrespectful words and grant me permission to return home to die

The old man rose as he spoke but overcome by his exertions fell back into the chair Ronald rang for assistance and Robert was soon at his side When Walton was sufficiently recovered to understand what was passing

"You had better remain here for the night, said Ronald "you can be easily accommodated

No' no' cried the aged man with great energy 'I would die at home—let me die in my own home ! Besides he whispered his eyes at the same time turning faintly round in the direction of the packet, 'you may have reason to wish my visit here kept a secret

His request was complied with though it was with difficulty Ronald could be induced to allow him to depart on foot and alone The old man, however adhered too pertinaciously to his request to be withstood, and he accomplished the journey on foot but followed by two men who were directed to keep out of his sight, so as to render him assistance in case of need

The next morning the passing bell was heard in the village, and the gossips amused themselves with the oral biography of Caleb Walton

A strange mysterious foreboding, the cause of which is not easily traced often rests upon the mind when trial awaits us though at the time we are wholly unconscious of the evil to which we are exposed When, however the first faint glimmerings of impending danger burst upon us this feeling increases with an overwhelming rapidity proportioned to the magnitude of the danger with which we are threatened Then the vigour of each mental faculty as if reserved for moments of emergency bursts forth with an intenseness that astonishes its unconscious possessor memory ransacks the past with painful fidelity, and brings from its unexplored recesses every incident that can accuse the conscience or awaken fear Imagination, at all times a powerful auxiliary of terror or hopefulness because ever ready to answer the summons of either then lavishes profusely her luxury of fancies, creating fresh and horrible conceits from slightest circumstances, and bring them forward with such promptness and ingenuity that the sufferer alarmed by the terrible and fantastic throng acknowledges present fears to be

Less than horrible imaginings

To this species of mental torture Lady Minhurst found herself a prey on retiring to her apartment The insipid character of the society in which she had passed the after part of the day had scarcely sufficed to afford her a transient respite from the painful thoughts awakened by the incidents of the preceding night and morning The dullest society has, however, a claim on our attention and the effort it required to satisfy this demand, postponed to a moment of solitude the deep harrowing of heart and conscience from which she was destined to suffer. The mind knows not a greater pain than that she endured yet by a strange but deeply seated principle of our nature t is a torture often sought as though the sufferer found comfort in his torment by regarding it as an expiation for his guilt or as part of that repentance which forms the condition of his forgiveness in the sight of God

This was the case with the Viscountess. Her reflections of the morning had been of the most painful nature yet so far was she from dreading a return of them when she retired for the night that she dismissed her attendant abruptly, and thus seemed to seek the anguish of mind she knew solitude would not fail to produce

"Mon Dieu! mon Dieu!" exclaimed Eugenie when she learnt that her mistress would not require her assistance to undress that evening 'vat is de mattare I vondare miladi no vant me?—go to bed alone! Ah, it must be de leetle monsieur of de morning vid de pointed schin cause all dis change! Oh, vat a ding is love!'

This soliloquy was uttered by the lady's maid in the antechamber, as she withdrew for the night

Lady Minhurst sat alone in her bed room—that awful room connected with so many dreadful recollections. The tapers stationed on a side table were not sufficient to dissipate the gloom that overhung the vast dimensions of the apartment. The hangings of the windows and the bed were indistinctly seen in the obscurity, and the dark shadows of their massive fold assumed the appearance of dire and giant shapes The old clock clicked heavily beneath its gorgeous frame work and, as its measured sounds reached the ear of the lone lady, they increased the impressiveness of the unearthly silence of midnight. Could a stranger have entered the apartment a few minutes after Ma amselle Eugenie had retired, the appearance of the Viscountess herself would have inspired him with awe. She sat for some time motionless in a remote corner of the room, beyond the influence of the feeble and pale light emitted by the tapers. Heat and fatigue had removed the artificial colour from her cheeks and the palor of remorse and terror which replaced it, was heightened by the dark hue of her dress. Yet her figure was tall and stately her features bold and handsome so that the majestic outline, with the impressive and contrasted colouring formed an object well calculated to inspire dread. All expression, however, falls immeasurably below the feelings of the heart in moments of extraordinary conflict. Words cannot express all that lonely and silent lady endured. Dire scenes were reenacted in her memory bitter words and horrid sounds seemed again to assail her ears her heart felt as if once more hurried on by the violent passions which impelled its action two score years before But worse than all, the room appeared peopled with reproaching crowds forms delineated by the painter's skill started into life from their frames, like miraculous incarnations not a hanging in the apartment but drew back to discover its hidden phantom not a chair but had its ghostly occupant. The mission of each seemed to be reproachful and prophetic the reproaches were of a nature to wither every hope, and the prophetics told of impending ruin. Then the multitude of shapes would pass away

to be succeeded by others, each presenting the same form and each ex-
hibiting the same countenance—a young female face of great beauty and
great sadness   That calm smile of patient and saint like resignation
spoke louder of doom than a thousand prophecies to the beholder   In
vain she tried to avoid the stedfast glance beneath which she writhed
on all sides above, below, around it seemed to gaze on her   the walls,
floor, cieling appeared alive with swarms of the same pale lineaments—
they were present to her mind   Minutes wore away, and the horrid
multiplied vision seemed to concentrate   the multitude of figures sub
sided into one, whose terrible resemblance to reality was increased by its
solitariness   It stood, or appeared to stand like a lifeless thing, by the
tapestry that concealed the door of the passage we have already had oc
casion to notice   Thus it presented itself before the mind of the conscience stricken woman till her heart beat with alarming violence, and
she felt ready to sink with terror at the imagined presence of an inmate
of the tombs   Still, however, reason had power to reject what remorse
and superstition conspired to conceive and yielding to the former in
fluence, Lady Minhurst started from her seat and darted towards the
entrance to the passage, as if to prove whether the shape existed only in
her brain   So great was her excitement that she conceived it had glided
into the passage and throwing open the door she followed down the
dark corridor the retreating creation of her distracted mind   The rapid
ity with which the Viscountess moved and the presence of other objects
than those on which her eyes had rested for the last half hour, most
effectually dispelled the phantom, and she was smiling bitterly at her
alarm, when a light, streaming through a crevice at what appeared the
opposite end of the passage diverted her thoughts for the time   A light
issuing from such a quarter very justly gave her ladyship surprise   She
was not acquainted with the alterations recently made to the mansion,
and perfectly well remembered from events connected with her own
history that the passage had formerly conducted to a staircase and
private outlet from the building   A strong and unaccountable curiosity
induced her to approach the aperture from whence the light proceeded
she found a door which easily yielded to her endeavours, and opening
outwards discovered heavy hangings that thanks to an unskilful uphol
sterer, were so arranged as to make it no difficult matter to know what
was passing on the other side   Her ladyship observed a small room
furnished with books, &c , and nearly opposite the aperture through
which she looked her young grandson was seated before a fire, with his
back towards her and deeply occupied in reading   Another look satis
fied her that she really beheld her grandson, Ronald   The passage
which had formerly ended in a staircase and outlet was now terminated
by the new story we have before described   The Viscountess had no
longer any reason to fear intruding on the nocturnal student, and it
seemed a favourable opportunity to dissipate thoughts too painful to be
endured   Nevertheless she raised the tapestry with hesitation   so ter
rible a foreboding of calamity rested on her mind that she dreaded the
consequences of the most trifling and common actions   and it imparted
so great caution to her then movements that she stood near the chair of

the reader before he was aware of her presence From her position she
saw that her grandson was engaged in perusing a manuscript another
step and she recognised the hand writing—the autograph of her deceased
lord the late Viscount Minhurst

A heavy pang shot across her breast at this discovery she did not
suspect the existence of any document in his lordship's own characters
but those in her own possession and to which, as his sole executor she
had a legal claim The purport of the paper in Ronald's hands and
how he obtained it were questions therefore at once started for her
curiosity to employ itself in solving Lady Minhurst was no longer the
person she had once been the imperturbable self possession the faculty
of facing an awkward or discreditable circumstance intrepidly was gone
her spirit was unnerved by a vague but oppressive fear Much as she
desired to make herself mistress of the nature of the document at once
and unperceived by her grandson her agitation prevented an attempt
that called for great coolness and dexterity Indeed so great a mastery
had her fears obtained that her hard drawn breathing at length revealed
to Ronald the presence of a second person in the room He turned and
beheld the Viscountess at his elbow

'Dearest mother' (so he was accustomed to call her) Here at this
hour ! Has any thing happened ?

"Nothing I slept during the day, and feeling wakeful I have been exploring and you see to what unexpected regions I have penetrated You were reading I think? Any thing interesting ?'

"Not extraordinary replied the grandson with an affected indiffe rence and awkwardly striving to push the manuscript more out of sight than he had at first succeeded in doing

Neither his action or his manner escaped her ladyship

"It is manuscript, I think coolly observed the lady

"Yes—not exactly—that is—yes it is a manuscript

'There is always something amusing to be found in an original ma nuscript, however dull its contents Is it original ?

"It professes to be so

"May I ask the author's name ?

"Really I fear I may not I am at a loss how to satisfy your lady ship, replied the confused grandson

'Oh, do not give yourself any trouble I think I know the hand writing

"Ah ! you saw the handwriting ? asked Ronald unguardedly, at the same time directing an enquiring glance towards the Viscountess for the purpose of ascertaining from her countenance how she had been affected on recognising the hand, if she had really done so

"You were so deeply interested in the document before you and I stole on you so unexpectedly that I could not avoid seeing the writing Ronald, I have been too familiar with those characters to have forgotten them

'Your ladyship knows then—

"The handwriting of her own husband Is that so extraordinary that you should look on me thus strangely ?

No ! it is not singular but I am taken by surprise

'Ronald continued her ladyship, seeing his confusion and finding it was now time to use plain dealing you will not either think it ex traordinary that his wife and widow should be anxious to know the pur port of papers of whose existence she was ignorant up to this hour

Would to God my refusal to satisfy that curiosity could not be deemed more strange!

"Am I to understand Sir that you refuse to let me know its con tents ? said Lady Minhurst with assumed haughtiness while she visibly changed colour

'I am not at liberty to communicate them

Are their import then so mysterious ? she asked with the agitation of one who fears to hear his condemnation in the reply

'In God's name, do not question me ! I cannot answer you I must not !

A terrible struggle took place in the bosom of the Viscountess during the few minutes which elapsed before she resumed From Ronald's reluctance to impart to her the contents of the papers she feared they contained the worst of revelations for her character and that after all her long and careful watching of her husband during his last moments he had contrived to elude her vigilance and transmit to posterity the story of her shame   Her lips were livid with terror, as she arose and drew near her grandson

Ronald   she began   "the existence of those documents is a proof to me of their importance   They affect us Ronald—I know they do—yourself, your father sister, me, the whole family   Have we then not a right to know their purport ?   From a child you have had my care no mother could spend more vigils in scheming for her child s welfare, than I have done for your s Ronald   Will you, then, leave me a prey to anxiety, agonising fear perhaps merely because you find it an easier task to suppress than to declare the truth   or because an old man in the caprices of life s last stage has enjoined your silence ?   Let me conjure you speak !   I have been very very unhappy, of late   Some misfortune seems to threaten our house—to blast our hopes   Oh ! my son, be kind, be compassionate   put an end to my suspense   tell me the worst !

Lady Minhurst s terror imparted a wild energy to her language that Ronald could not resist   On ceasing to speak, she had sunk on her knees at his feet   and to see a person of her peculiar character voluntarily assuming the position of a suppliant, was alone sufficient to shake his firmest purposes   Raising the Viscountess with one hand   and seizing a taper with the other   he held it up before the portrait suspended over the fire place

'Do you know those features ?   said he

They were briefly glanced at by the unhappy lady   her worst fears seemed all to be confirmed

'Mercy ! mercy !   she shrieked   cowering in agony from the look of her grandchild, and the inanimate gaze of the portrait   'Hide me   hide me from her—there—there   everywhere   Is there no escaping from those dreadful eyes ? '

It was Ronald s turn to be alarmed   the papers had made no revelations tending to compromise the Viscoun ess, and her grandson was far from suspecting her remorse, or the cause which gave rise to it   Though greatly astonished   and unable to account for her emotion, he clasped her gently in his arms

'My dearest mother   said he ' why this terror ?

' Your mother !   do you still call me so ?   Do you not indeed spurn me ?

Spurn you !   spurn the worth and excellence I have ever been taught to revere ?   Mother   what wild   unmeaning words are these ?   Why should I spurn you ?

"Those papers !   she replied fearfully

"Threaten to deprive me of my right to the peerage,   rejoined the youth   no more

"They do not then   Ronald ! Ronald ! I am weak and foolish   I have had to night dreadful fears   But is that indeed all they do reveal ?

"So limited is the information to this particular that I hesitate to believe, because I hardly comprehend what is asserted

"Heaven be praised !   exclaimed her ladyship in a suppressed tone, and then adding   somewhat more energetically, as she tried to read

No 12

Ronald s thoughts in his countenance " Why then did you ask me it I knew that portrait

'Because one of these documents refers to the person it represents

Ah ' what is said of her ?

It is implied that she has been wronged that herself, or child may be living to claim the title and estates of Minhurst

" She living ? Impossible ' She is interred with your ancestors in the family vaults, at the village church

Tis an inexplicable mystery, said the young man, handing the papers to the Viscountess " read'

Lady Minhurst did read It was drawn up in the hand writing of the late Viscount and simply stated that the writer at the time of his death was wrung with remorse for injuries done to his first wife, but through regard for his son by the second he was induced to postpone to some future period the disclosure of the probable existence of another heir and with design purposed placing these writings in the hands of a confidential servant, with a strict charge to deliver them into the hands of the next heir of Minhurst whenever he (the servant) should be led to apprehend his own demise The document then proceeded to entreat the next heir whoever he might prove to restore the inheritance to the parties having a prior claim and even begged him, as he might value the enjoyment of a quiet conscience in this life and future felicity hereafter to take active measures to find out the lawful heir and restore him or her to their rights

No attempt was made to account for the existence of tne first Viscountess Minhurst whose solemn interment was yet in the memories of many in the neighbourhood neither was there anything that seemed to accuse any one besides the deceased lord himself as a party to the fraud

The perusal restored Lady Minhurst to her wonted confidence When she found it contained nothing to implicate her character her ambitious hopes revived and with a lofty head and steady tone

And how does the next heir to Minhurst intend to act she enquired

To obey the injunctions of the departed said Ronald solemnly

To submit to be juggled out of both name and fortune, you should say

Not so I hold that request from one on the brink of the grave and I shall obey its contents to the letter

'A silly prejudice' This old parchment exists for none but yourself let it perish even for you she said pointing to the fire

Its contents are already copied on my heart

You provoke me, Ronald If you were sure of the authenticity of these manuscripts it would be a different thing

Mother ' said the youth fixing his fine eye upon her for the first time with an expression of mistrust did you not recognise the hand writing ?

That is easily imitated besides this supposed heir may not exist or your attempts to find him may be useless pains

They will satisfy my conscience replied the young man,

' And in the meantime all the high expectations you are entitled to cherish as heir to a coronet are to be abandoned ? '

' I hope I have courage to make the sacrifice

Lady Minhurst felt risings of indignation against her grandson and pupil at this first display of what she considered worldly inaptitude about a quarter of an hour before however, she had been reminded of the precipice on which she stood and prudence dictated the suppression of anything like wrath for the moment

" One favour I must request of you, Ronald she said, taking the arm he offered to conduct her in obedience to a sign she had given to her apartment In return for the years of anxiety and care I have spent on your account, you must promise me however you may act in this matter, to keep the contents of this packet a secret to every one until they can be disclosed to purpose

Ronald considered for a moment and then made the promise thus requested

---

CHAPTER XI

' And who may be the original of this pretty sketch ? asked Ronald when, on the following morning he surprised Mira busily engaged with the pencil in her favourite retreat

The young lady made a slight attempt to withdraw her performance but a second thought changed her intention, and with a slight blush she exposed it to her brother s inspection

' A very handsome face, said he

' A silly whim—an idea that beset me as I waited in idleness for your appearance, my dear brother

" Very handsome indeed ! continued the youth I have no acquaintance who can claim resemblance to this drawing you must introduce me to the original Mira

' Nonsense, Ronald ! exclaimed the half blushing girl

In sober sense, this is no beau ideal

' Perhaps not In my humble attempts I follow the custom of other artists and gleam my materials where I can

' I understand you can find a mouth at the dinner table, pick up a nose in the street and take an eye or two from your admirers now and then is it not so ? A kind of depredation on our personal attractions artists are allowed to perpetrate with impunity for the sake of their high vocation I am not quite satisfied however that these beautiful and well harmonising features were thus gathered from all quarters No Mira I have caught you in the flagrant theft of some unfortunate Adonis face

" Will you wink at my offence ?

' It might be more serious had the transcript been made elsewhere than on this paper and I may be induced to do so, when I know the name of the original '

' That I must tell you because he is a person I wish you to take an
interest in

Very pretty' very ingenious indeed'   You wish to excite in me
an interest for a very handsome person in whom you already take I
suspect a very considerable interest yourself   For this purpose you
show me an irresistible portrait, with all the indifference and simplicity
imaginable and having first attempted to make me believe it is com
pounded of the features of a dozen anybodies, at last acknowledge that
I must give somebody my countenance

' How you talk'   This somebody is nothing to me   there—I will
tear up the sketch to convince you—

Stay   said the brother taking the paper from her hand, " I would
rather it should be kept to compare with the original   The artist s fidelity
will help me to a conclusion   besides tearing it up would be no proof
of indifference   you could afford to amuse yourself at destroying a thou
sand copies, while you retain a proof impression somewhere else

Mira blushed she knew not why and protested for want of something
better to do   at length she added —

' You shall see the original this morning, if you like, Ronald   He is
a village schoolmaster and though his features are handsome enough to
be transferred to paper I hope you give me credit for sufficient prudence
to keep them out of my heart   He is moreover a poet very poor and
very clever and your patronage would be useful to him

' His name ? enquired Ronald

I almost forget—indeed I am not sure that I ever heard it—his sur
name I mean   His Christian name is Edward

The proposition was acceded to and the happy pair were soon on
their way across the park to the village church in the chancel of which
the scholars of Edward Vivyan daily assembled   They met the Vis
countess Minhurst and her son as they drew near the private gate which
opened into the churchyard   Mira in her zeal for her protege, was the
first to mention their destination, and the elder parties having nothing
better to do agreed to bear the others company

They passed through the gate and were at once within a hundred
yards of the church a time worn building simple and venerable screen
ing its decayed ornaments with a thick mantle of luxuriant ivy   The
churchyard through which they advanced differed but little from other
churchyards   the grass was as brightly green the grave stones, in all
positions between the horizontal to the perpendicular, chequered the
sward with their usual appearance and some stately trees, in the redun
dance of summer pride waving like giant hearse plumes, threw over it
wide and sombre shadows   They advanced, Mira leading the way,
towards a low arched door, half way hid by a huge butment and appro
priated to the use of ecclesiastical functionaries from the portly rector to
the gossiping sexton   A hum of youthful voices burst from this aperture,
as its heavy oaken door was pushed open—sounds so exuberant with
mirth and the energy of young life, that they might seem to deride to the
passer by the grey and crumbling orifice that gave them issue

He is not here, said Mira, in a tone of disappointment, when she perceived that an aged man of spare figure and harsh features occupied the seat usually filled by the comely person of Edward

' Is the young man ill who used to teach you ? she enquired of a curly headed urchin who stood near

The other master be gone replied the boy

Gone ! responded the fair enquirer

' Yees, my lady, and this be Andrew Wornout, the great scholard from the Workhus as be come to teach us

' Where is your old master gone then ? asked Ronald

" Whoy they says as how he be gone up to Lunnon to meak his fortin '

Ronald was silent he thought of the contrast of hopeful, aspiring youth leaving scenes of early and humble tranquillity to justle with the crowd and disappointed weary age forced from the hard repose of a pauper s asylum to drudge out the last hours allotted to his earthly course Mira also grew pensive and amidst a great deal of mental confusion, her thoughts reverted to the verses she had received on the preceding night for the first time she perceived that they must allude to his da parture, and that they breathed of farewell

" We will call on his mother said the young lady ' she is a worthy woman and will want consolation in this bereavement '

' I have an acceptable present for her, rejoined Ronald, who had preserved his sister s hasty pencil sketch

" Ronald, you surely will not, began Mira, with a confusion that would appear like the reluctance most lady amateurs manifest to allow their productions to get into the hands of some friendly connoisseur, but which might have had its source in a deeper feeling

' Why not ? If it should prove a likeness, the poor mother will wel come it as a treasure replied the young man

" Mira ! Mira ! what an oversight is this ! observed Lord Minhurst, who had not overheard this short parleying between the brother and sister had I known of this young man's departure, I might have been of ser vice to him "

" Edward has always puzzled me, papa he would receive with mani fest pleasure my approbation of his poems, but he has invariably thwarted my indirect efforts to be useful to him, when he could do so politely

By this time they were arrived at the threshold of the little cottage occupied by Edward s mother They had no leisure to remark its neat ness, for at the door stood Mrs Vivyan in earnest conversation with lawyer Grasp

' Grasp here with this poor woman ! thought Lady Minhurst "before he brings me tidings of the important errand on which I dispatched him last night ! What can this mean ? It is not the manner of his cloth to neglect a rich for a poor client

' I tell you, my good woman, said the lawyer, who appeared remon strating in a very high key, " it is he—it must be he—it can t possibly be any one else ''

" It cannot be, Edward ! indeed it cannot Sir he is incapable of such an act, replied the poor woman, who had a very decent appearance, and seemed violently affected

"Lawyer Grasp your servant,   said the Viscount coming forward you are not too hard on this poor widow I hope ?

"Hope your lordship is in health—your ladyship well—ah Miss Mira Mr Ronald I presume   heard of your arrival   quite well, I hope

While the little lawyer was uttering these words wi h great rapidity and bowing at each pause a pantomimic mode of punctuating he practised on ceremonious occasions, the poor woman curtseyed as often and as well as her distress and the unexpected appearance of such visitors would allow her

' Was only communicating to this good woman here a strange circum stance   happened last night   her son, a principal party, indubitably evident   to this effect

' Indeed it could not be my Edward, your lordship ' sobbed the poor afflicted mother

'Like very much to know who else it could be ?   interrupted Grasp ' Judge of the facts yourself, my lord

And here the artful attorney detailed at length how a poor traveller a very aged man, and his young and beautiful daughter had been attacked the preceding evening on the road from P—— to S—— by a young man who after wounding the father to a degree that threatened to prove fatal, had contrived to carry off his child   When this story had been told with all due professional embellishment he proceeded to show in what manner he had discovered the delinquent to be none other than Edward Vivyan   and further to mention the corroberation his suspicions received from the absence of the young man from his post as school master

All the party listened to the tale with great interest   Mira fairly reddened with indignation when she heard Edward accused

"Mr Grasp it is impossible that Edward could have been concerned in this transaction !" she exclaimed

" I do not think your suspicions very well grounded, Grasp, ' said his lordship   " It appears you saw the person who is supposed to have com mitted the deed in the course of the day   but, by your own admission, you are not personally acquainted with this good woman s son

" I have good descriptions   young man not at home at the time ' observed Grasp

" I think I can settle this at once,' said Ronald, holding Mira s sketch of Edward so that both the widow and the lawyer could see it   ' Do you know for whom this is intended ? '

'Tis my son, my own boy !' cried Mrs Vivyan with delight, hoping the avowal would avert every suspicion from her son

' Tis he   the very wretch who did it   I should know him from a thousand ' exclaimed the merciless man of law, retreating at the same time to the door   Good morning, ladies and gentlemen   my business is done here my suspicions are fully confirmed   depend upon it he shall not escape with impunity a very good morning   He then withdrew

Mira and Ronald, with the Viscount hastened to assist the poor wo man who had an intuitive fear of all lawyers, and had fallen into a faint ing fit when she heard Grasp thus denounce her only child

Lady Minhurst availed herself of the confusion to follow Grasp. The story he had told revived all her fears, and she hastened to obtain further information.

The lawyer turned to look behind him on leaving the cottage, as if he expected what would happen. On seeing the Viscountess, probably with a view to avoid observation, he entered the church. It was noon, the rustic scholars were disbursed, and in a minute or two Grasp and the Viscountess walked up the main aisle of the venerable building.

'What is this strange story?' asked the lady with breathless anxiety.

'True in the results, though something varied in the facts,' said the lawyer.

The Viscountess urged an explanation.

Grasp told her ladyship the whole of the night's adventures as they really had happened, and during his narrative the worthy pair unconsciously left the principal aisle, and at its conclusion found themselves in the company of certain knights in armour and ladies in ruffs and huge

petticoats, kneeling and recumbent, most elaborately sculptured from solid stone. They stood among the monuments of the Minhurst family.

'The girl is gone then?' said she.

Grasp nodded.

'And the father?'

'I will take care of him   he is in my power

' Confine him until we know more, said the Viscountess

" His wounds will do that   rejoined her agent

At this moment Ronald having left his father and sister to console the agitated and unhappy widow, entered the church   The family monu ments were to him novel as well as interesting   Examining the first that came in his way unconscious of the presence of others, though within hearing of their voices when after a pause, they resumed the conversation

" And this girl this beggar girl who stands in the way of my scheme,' said a voice which Ronald recognised as his grandmother's ' we must find her and get her out of the way at any pains let no cost be spared

' At any cost my lady   repeated the lawyer, pointing at tne same time to the inscription of the stone on which they were then standing

This gesture was observed by Ronald who, unwilling to overheai a conversation intended to be private was at that moment unwittingly advancing towards the parties

' Grasp I am a desperate woman   I must have this girl in my powei, though she make a second victim aye such another as the woman whose name I tread on

We are observed,' whispered the cunning lawyer and gliding behind a pillar, they disappeared

' As Ronald reached the spot they had left his eyes rested on the inscription

It was simply

'EVINE VISCOUNTESS MINHURST,
OBIIT MDCCXXX

Ronald thought long and darkly on the words he had overheard

CHAPTER XII

It will be necessary to detain the reader sometime longer at Minhurst in order to make him acquainted with a few circumstances that occurred in the course of the day thus auspiciously began

The parties so strangely brought into collision at Minhurst church in the morning, returned to the mansion suffering (we may justly use the term) from the influence of their visit   Viscount Minhurst enjoyed the greatest ease the deepest emotion of which he was conscious amounting only to a deep sympathy with the lonely widow, and regret for the sus picions thrown out against her son though his charitable nature would not allow him for an instant to give them credence   On nearly similar grounds Mira attempted to account for the depression of spirits she experienced on her way home and though we are disposed to think she deceived herself on this point yet as nothing to that effect ever fell from the lips of the young lady we conceive it would be indecorous on our part to dwell at length on the subject Happy indeed would it have been for Lady Minhurst and Ronald, had their melancholy been pro duced by similar causes Every hour seemed to darken the prospect of the former every step she took served to complicate rather than unravel the meshes of the net she had been so long and unconsciously weaving for her own destruction Three nights before, she had slept in security yet that short interval had sufficed to place her fortune reputation and peace of mind in hopeless jeopardy On the preceding night she had learnt that the offspring of her victim still existed—existed perhaps to inflict upon the author of her mother s ruin a terrible and just vengeance For the last four and twenty hours she had been scheming laboriously and anxiously scheming, how to conceal the injury done to one victim without making another how to conceal guilt without adding to its enormity Her mind thus worn by anxiety, and harrassed by remorse had undergone a severe trial, stood exposed to a danger that threw every other species of peril into insignificance when an accident placed in the hands of her adored grandson—the child of her care and hope a clue to the guilt of her early career The combination of feeling thus excited was powerfully oppressive, and could have not been concealed by one less practised in dissimulation than Lady Minhurst. This mental agony was the recompence of crime the germ of delayed and dreadful retri bution Ronald s condition was most pitiable a sudden blight seemed to have fallen on his young heart his faith in the excellence of human kind had received a potent shock His nature so trusting social and sanguine, had met with disappointment there where his admiration was most excited, and his confidence most fully gained circumstances wear ing the force of proofs had aroused suspicions, too horrible to be indulged, against the guard an of his youth, the mother of his own father and the only mother he had ever known How his heart recoiled from mankind from himself, though unconscious of any crime, at this discovery of mortal frailty his bright visions of excellence were bedimmed and all the energy of emulation vanished in his soul It was a relief to the whole party to find they had reached the mansion in time to prevent the depar ture of unexpected visitors

"My dear Lady Minhurst'' exclaimed a voice of no very harmonious tone, as they entered the drawing room "This *is* a pleasure'

"Not unexpected as far as I am concerned, retorted the Viscountess with her best grace ' foremost among the gratifications I expected to derive from my visit to the country stood the pleasure of meeting my very old friend the Earl of Wagmouth

The noble earl thus graciously accosted, was a great man of little sta ture, notorious for long speeches and shallow thinking with very urbane manners He was accompanied by two young gentlemen and two young ladies the former of whom Lord Silliton and the Hon Francis Fluent leigh, have already been introduced to the reader at the dinner party of the preceding day and the latter we have now the pleasure of introducing as the ladies Mary and Augusta, daughters of the most noble the Earl of Wagmouth

This done, in justice to the persons whose biography must be glanced

No 13

at in the course of this history we must keep in our mind that excellent maxim 'brevity is the soul of wit by passing over all the good things then and there conceived and delivered and merely present the reader with a summing up of a short dialogue between the two male cousins who ac companied the carriage on horseback, on their return to Brenton Hall the seat of the noble earl

"What is the matter now my susceptible coz? asked Frazer effect ually alarmed by the lack a daisical face exhibited by Lord Silliton

That beautifully, adorably lovely Mira! sighed the man of ad verbs

"For once I must do you the justice to say that you have fallen in love without making a sacrifice to taste

"How demnably maliciously severe you are coz I tell you I am really and truly, and wholly in love That girl shall be Lady Silliton I'll go over to morrow on purpose to propose

The Minhurst family sat alone in the drawing room for some time after the departure of their visitors

' The earl of Wagmouth has a fine family' said the Viscountess, with the tone of one who wishes to direct the conversation to a particular topic at the same time glancing at the young folk as if expecting to hear their opinions Her eyes however rested on objects that most effectually checked the excitement and satisfaction the visit of an old friend had produced Ronald wrapped in thoughts too plainly of the most sombre cast reclined against the draperies of a window, looking vacantly on the extensive landscape it overlooked He had been surprised by one of those absorbing reveries that for a time subjugate the mind, and make it unconscious of outward objects and yielding to its influence he disclosed by his countenance a dejected and wretched state of mind

The law of sympathy operates quickly in youthful minds they soon feel if they do not always understand each other and Mira from a distant sofa was as deeply engaged in trying to read what was passing in her brother s mind from the expression of his countenance, as he himself was occupied by a crowd of dark and oppressive thoughts

It was with some pain that Lady Minhurst saw her grandchildren thus absent the one reflecting if she did not share the depression of the other In the looks of Ronald she fancied she discerned more wretchedness of heart than the discovery of the preceding evening could warrant The occasion was not however a fitting one to make an en quiry, and turning to the Viscount with an ill suppressed sigh she resumed the conversation about the Earl of Wagmouth and his family

Mira observed her brother s melancholy with much sorrow She knew very well that it was impossible to form a proper opinion of his character from their short intercourse but she was much surprised at the singular contrast between the light hearted open manner of Ronald on the preceding day, and the gloomy, heart stricken demeanour he then assumed One more versed in the ways of the world would have con cluded that he was infected with the romantic spirit so fashionable with young men of the day but Mira with the straightforwardness of inex perience, attributed it to a mind ill at ease she had too much natural affection to rest satisfied with this conclusion What might have caused this dejection, and what might alleviate it, were immediately brought forward for mental discussion The first appeared inexplicable, and nature whispered that a sister's sympathy would not be altogether useless with regard to the second The thought had scarcely crossed her mind before her light form bounded across the apartment towards the recess in which Ronald was standing

'How deep in thought you are' said she

"Excuse me, dear Mira I forgot you were present, or I would not have indulged my thoughtful mood at your expense

It was a painful indulgence, or I am mistaken, returned Mira raising a fine pair of blackest eyes, and fixing them on her brother's countenance with a look of tender enquiry

'Did I seem so melancholy? I know not why then I have no cause to be unhappy

"I am very glad to hear you say so your looks gave me pain I suppose I must ascribe your abstraction to the powerful glances of Lady Mary or Lady Augusta ' continued Mira playfully

'Oh, do not mention them' replied Ronald whose voice was harsh and morose, for as he spoke a painful reflection occurred to him

'Is it so very bad? persisted his sister, either mistaking his meaning, or wishing to joke him into gaiety 'that you cannot bear to hear them named? It cannot be both which is the one? Come, Ronald, you must tell *me* '

"Dearest sister, said the young man in a wild and distressed tone, clasping her round the waist and hurrying with her into the grounds on which the window they stood near opened 'how will you bear to re nounce the society your tastes and habits have made congenial? How will you endure the coldness and neglect of early friends? My poor sister!

'You frighten me dreadfully Ronald What can have happened?

'What, indeed, Mira! Unheard of things! We are the sport of fortune *She* has raised us to a splendid eminence my sister, nurtured us amidst life's refinements and, great God! the transition would be bearable, if it involved no dishonour

"Ronald! Ronald! you speak in riddles your words distract me! Does anything horrible threaten us?

The singular and sudden emotion of the young man had by this time excited great alarm in the mind of his companion the colour had left her cheeks, and she shook violently as she threw herself in the arms of her brother and implored him to explain This simple gesture seemed to Ronald like an appeal for protection and it affected him powerfully His eyes had scarcely caught sight of the expression of terror depicted on her countenance than they were blinded by the torrent of tears that came to the relief of his swelling bosom Bitterly did he chide himself for suffering emotion to get the better of discretion, which thus had be trayed him into the disclosure of fears that for the present no matter at what mental torture, ought to have remained deeply buried in his bosom The secrets however, he had become possessed of within the last two days were of a nature so extraordinary and terrible, followed each other with such sudden rapidity, and effected so entire a change not only in his own condition, but also in that of those who were dearest to him—that he felt unable to ascribe to weakness of mind the unfortunate expressions he had uttered in a paroxysm of anguish Still he could not forgive himself for the effect they had produced on Mira, and he longed to counteract it

Speak, brother ! pray speak ! ' she exclaimed, still quivering in his embrace

' It was weak and foolish of me to alarm you my dear sister   believe me, love, we have nothing to fear now   I mean *immediately*

' But your words   your agitation   surely some danger must threaten us !

" Where is the family free from the vicissitudes of life Mira ?   What wealth and rank to day can reckon on wealth and rank to morrow ? In unison with my present feelings allow me, my dear sister, to quote a few lines from the celebrated author of the ' Essay on man '

TO DAY AND TO MORROW

To day man s dressed in gold and silver bright
Wrapped in a shroud before to-morrow night
To day he s feeding on delicious food
To morrow dead unable to do good
To day he s nice and scorns to feed on crumbs
To morrow he s himself a dish for worms
To day he s honoured and in vast esteem
To morrow not a beggar values him
To day he rises from the velvet bed
To morrow lies in one that is made of lead
To day his house though large he thinks but small
To morrow no command no house at all
To day has forty servants at his gate
To morrow scorned—not one of them will wait
To day perfumed as sweet as any rose
To morrow stinks in every body s nose
To day he s grand majestic all delight
Ghastful and pale before to-morrow night
True as the Scripture says   Man s life s a span
The present moment is the life of man

Yes, continued the brother, " and our very reputation can hardly be said to be in our own keeping, Mira, when the deeds of those connected with us can so blotch and sully our name, as to make us the scoff and reprobation of a generation   Believe me it is so   I cannot say that anything will happen yet thoughts of this description so constantly press and prey upon me, that I am at times most gloomy and unhappy '

' I am scarcely happier from your assurance that no danger awaits us, said the sister with somewhat less emotion, since from the very impressive manner in which you repeated those exquisite lines, I can too plainly discover the melancholy turn of your mind   Yesterday I thought I fancied you to be so light hearted how you deceived me !

A sigh escaped from the young man as he thought of the change he had undergone since the preceding day, and the unexpected cause that produced it

'You have seen me gay you see me sad, he replied "and there is nothing within your knowledge to account for the alteration So is it, Mira with the vicissitudes of life they are as evident, and too often as causeless What a preservative, my sister, against the misery they inflict, should we be armed with, were we accustomed to live in expect ation of the worst transitions, and not to trust so blindly and fondly in an imagined security

" These are wise words, Ronald but they are too like forebodings for me to give them a cheerful welcome

" Believe me, love, there is nothing in my speech more than it implies I am, as you will say, when you know me better, of a sad soliloquising mood '

The brother and sister were now more composed, and they walked hand in hand silently through the most retired part of the grounds

Of the various kinds of mental distress, few or none, unless it be ab solute despair, could have remained insensible to the influence of the scene and hour It was the close of a gorgeous summer afternoon the most beautiful flowers lavished their fragrance on the tepid air shrubs of the greatest variety and luxuriance waved in the breeze, and threw fairy like shadows on the paths Even Ronald rallied from his despond ency as he gazed on the life around him He had not one fear the less he felt conscious of an internal energy ready to meet the worst

Age is more matter of fact than youth the former shudders at the prospect of danger, the latter prepares to encounter it While Ronald was paralysed at the new and unexpected prospect opened before him, Lady Minhurst was revolving and even disclosing, however premature such steps may seem, schemes for placing the fortunes of her family on a surer footing Taking advantage of the sudden disappearance of her grandchildren, she at once broached the subject to the Viscount As family councils seldom possess much general interest, we will spare the reader the details, and pass at once to the result of their long tete a tete

" Believe me, Wilfred, it gives me much pleasure to find that we are for once agreed respecting the children, said the Viscountess

' You understand I make one reservation, rejoined the worthy father " I force no plan of mine upon my children Those we have been considering, are the most important steps they can possibly take in life and will cause them much misery, unless they enter freely and heart ily into our views I can have no objection to the union, if Mira has not

' Mira is no woman if she refuse the heir to an earldom

' I shall be disappointed in my own daughter, if an earldom have much attraction for her, when a man like Sillton must go with the title

' I can make all allowance for the sentiments of seventeen but the young man has good hair, good teeth, a fine figure, genteel manners and to crown all fifty thousand a year

The father sighed ' In every thing but mind

" Wilfred, you put me out of patience What has an earl with fifty thousand a year to do with mind ?

The conversation was here interrupted by a servant who announced to her ladyship that Gregory Grasp Esq was waiting to receive her commands before he quitted Minhurst

' You seem to have many affairs to settle with your agent, observed Lord Minhurst, as his mother rose to give the lawyer an audience in her apartment

A cloud passed over her brow as she replied

' My long absence from the neighbourhood has thrown the small matters I entrust to Mr Grasp s management into some confusion."

For the plans concocted by the Viscountess and the lawyer, we must refer the reader to their execution and results as they will be found recorded with due detail in the course of our story It may be necessary to direct his notice to one trifling circumstance connected with the lawyer s departure from the mansion

It was the dining hour when Ronald next found himself alone, that is alone with his faithful servant Robert The effort he was obliged to make in order to counteract the impression his emotion had excited in the mind of Mira, had in some measure lessoned the gloom that hung over his mind while he continued in her company But the moment he exchanged the important duty of consoling a sister, for the trifling affairs of the dressing-table, it returned with renewed weight His mind sickened with disgust as he went through an operation he generally performed with the greatest attention to nicety He had discovered guilt and unsoundness in the dearest object of his reverence and love, in the brightest ornament of his social circle , and with that resolution of feeling peculiar to inexperience, his affections were chilled towards his kind What to him was society now, that he should be studious of its ceremonies, or solicitous for its favours ? He turned from it with disgust so sudden is the transition, when heavy woe assails us, from the warmest sociability to the gloom and isolation of the misanthrope Almost unconsciously he went through the daily process of decoration, and at its close, with the eagerness of one released from " durance vile, he rushed to a window, and threw it open with violence Here his eyes met another object than the charms of nature which prove an inexhaustible source of comfort to the unhappy, and from that object he recoiled as from some monstrous deformity It was the little lawyer who, his conference ended, mounted with no great grace a well worked and ill fed hack The dreary church aisle, the mysterious and dreadful words of Lady Minhurst, the confidential tone of Grasp, and the cold stone slab with its simple inscription, ' Evine, Viscountess Minhurst, came with rapidity to his mind, and reaching from the window, he called out to the horseman, intending to stop and interrogate him at once He was however, too late The hoofs of the lawyer s horse already clanked down the long avenue of the park, far beyond the reach of his voice

" I cannot question her, said he, his heart bleeding as he spoke ' but that man the accomplice yes, yes, I must wring this horrible secret from him Learn who it is continued he aloud, turning abruptly

towards Robert 'who has just left the park   his name, residence, call
ing every particular   do you hear ?'
The valet was about to obey   Ronald called him back

' Enquire with discretion, Robert   as if curiosity alone induced you
you understand ?
The man retired, and the heir of Minhurst was again alone
" I will see him this night' cried he   wrest the mystery from his
heart of hearts   God' will it never be dark ? he added as he glanced
at the sun still far from the horizon, and thought of the tedious cere
monies of dinner and dessert—from which he could not absent himself
without singularity if not suspicion

CHAPTER XIII

IT had been a bright warm day   but towards evening the gathering
clouds and still and sultry atmosphere portended a storm   By none
were these indications viewed with more regret than the widow Vivyan

The various difficulties of her son s arduous journey on foot to the me
tropolis even under the most auspicious circumstances, had occurred
to her mind with the vividness a mother s forethought only can impart
and as she watched from the quiet garden of her cottage the appearance
of the sky, it grieved her to the heart to think of the additional incon
venience he would be exposed to by inclement weather   There was no
sign however, that promised the storm would pass over or be of little
consequence   Cloud succeeded cloud, each heavier than the former
until the whole of the heavens were covered , while on earth every object
took deeper hues than the twilight generally gave them   Not a breeze
stirred the roses that decked with prodigal profusion the widow's humble
porch   the flowers shrunken by a long drought, drooped from their
stems, directing their gorgeous chalices towards the earth, as if dreading
the violence of the approaching torrent   The elms of the churchyard
so richly verdant in the sunshine stood out like black and spectral
figures in harsh relief from a leaden sky   and above towered the belfry
of the church with its crest of ivy, an image of chilly age seeking warmth
in a funeral pall   A thin, grey horse the property of a poor curate
who had the duty to perform of a distant parish stumbled over the graves
as it glided at a phantom pace to a huge yew for shelter and the monu
ments and tombstones looked whiter and wilder than ever in the impend
ing darkness   It was a gloomy scene for a light heart and brought
more heaviness to a sad one   Large drops of rain forced Mrs Vivyan
to desist from the evening labour in the garden, which, now Edward was
gone (it had been his task when at home), closed her hard working day,
and took shelter in the cottage   As she fastened the shutter of her only
window, previous to sitting down to pass an hour at needle work, the
first faint lightnings glimmered in the horizon

With a sigh that was all for Edward, she drew the bolt, and turned
away to take her seat at a low table on which rested the materials for
her proposed task   On raising the half finished shirt (one of half a
dozen on which she intended to bestow all her skill, and to forward her
son as a surprise, when he got settled in London) she uncovered the
sketch by Mira, which had remained there concealed since the morning
The presence of her noble visitors was alone sufficient to confuse a
person of her quiet habits and the accusation Grasp had brought against
her Edward so completely bewildered her, that she had lost sight of the
portrait, and hid as it was beneath her needlework she concluded some of
the party had taken it away with them   She gave it welcome as a lost
treasure unexpectedly recovered

A thousand treasures are connected with the possession of a portrait
of those we love   We scarcely require a symbol to remind us of one
whose image is impressed upon our hearts and yet how many precious
moments will such an object revive even in the most faithful memories
We gaze upon well known lineaments the skill of the artist has imparted
to them their habitual expression the tracery seems to have life it is
the face we loved to look upon   We are conscious that the pencilling
is permanent those lines cannot deviate into another object than that
they first designed, yet, as if by miracle, the lip is curled into a smile

the eye varies in expression more frequently than the multiform devices of a kaleidescope fancy imparts to it animation memory, influenced by love, gives it a thousand beautiful phases that we loved to note and still delight to recal it teems with life, and is nevertheless but a shadowy semblance contrived by an ingenious hand—a lifeless portrait

The mother looked on the very accurate likeness of her child with those feelings which are only known to a mother she had reason to be proud of her son's beauty, but with far greater reason she rejoiced in the certainty that his heart answered to that handsome intelligent countenance

As she sat contemplating the hasty but to her invaluable drawing a host of recollections crowded to her mind she was again a young and happy wife, and watched, as she had so often done in the same cottage her husband, as he gambolled with the little Edward then she acted over the sad scene that left her a widow and the boy fatherless His features recurred to her as she had seen them, when he kissed away the first bitter tears of widowhood that fell in torrents down her cheeks the day after the funeral these features were not very unlike the face depicted on the paper before her—they were perhaps something rounder and might have a shade more colour, yet in the man she could trace the child She pursued this mental biography sketched by a mother s memory through the gay hours of childhood the more weighty school days, and only stopped at a period of her son s history which dated a few months prior to the present stage of our history It was then she had first traced the impress of care upon his brow then for the first his faded cheek betrayed an aching heart Her solicitude on that occasion was great, for Edward was all to her yet she asked no questions but watched solicitously in his behaviour some clue to his heart s anguish She soon perceived rendered acute perhaps by personal experience, that her boy loved without hope, that the beauty of a peer s daughter had found a way to a peasant s heart Mrs Vivyan had much faith in the strength of those affections which untried spirits hastily explode as romantic she knew their reality and bitterness At first the discovery gave her great pain and she watched with torturing anxiety the growing distaste for his usual pursuits and pleasures but too manifest in her son s conduct and the symptoms of declining health too evident in his appearance Yet she soon perceived a remedy—the only and desperate remedy for strong and hopeless passion Edward had high and dangerous gifts and a mind capable of great ambition She had long been conscious that her son possessed the mysterious treasures of the mind, and had looked forward with trembling to their development now however it was her care to foster what she had hitherto repressed—in the enthusiasm of poetry in the aspirings of ambition she hoped to find a cure for love Alas ! they are made too often the stepping stone to forbidden heights

All these and many more remembrances were dwelt on with pensive pleasure peculiar to memory until the mind of the widow was brought to ponder on the circumstances of the day How speedy alas ! did the thousand pleasant thoughts of bye gone days vanish before the few but painful topics of the present Her son was not there at her fireside, as he was wont to be, no sweet strains of simple youthful poetry, the

No 14

produce of the morning's rumination met her ear and what they were ever sure to do her approbation   He was gone, and a stranger had been there to slander him—him her gentle Edward—for slander it must be that could impute a deed so savage and barbarous to her own son.   She would then remember that slanders take their rise in truth and her heart sunk within at the thought of some vague accident that might have befallen him   Yet, she reasoned " it may be nothing after all—some mistake perhaps by this time he may be near London safe and well Mercy on us ! that thunder clap—surely I heard footsteps

The lonely woman listened but no sound could be distinguished save the heavy pattering of the rain through the trees and shrubs without.

She resumed her ruminations they looked forward to the future. How would her husband's brother a rich man report and receive his poor nephew? would he try to forward his views and with what success ? were among the questions she propounded for consideration when a foot-fall amidst all the hurry and rage of the elements again caught her ear

'There is surely some one at my door ! ' said the worthy woman   and she rose to meet *her son !*

Edward !   she exclaimed

' Mother ! cried the youth, clasping her to his arms, and only check-ing her hasty kisses to glance rapidly round the room

You are alarmed my son !

'I must take every precaution said he " against surprise , and as he spoke he advanced towards the door of the cottage, and drew the rude wooden bolt into its socket

Gracious God ! It is all true then ! ' cried the mother, sinking pow-erless with terror into her chair

' Have they been here then ?   Mother, what have you heard ?' asked the youth sustaining her in his arms

Oh, Edward ! how could you have done so ! but tell me all   let me hear it from your own lips—it cannot be so bad as they say

What have they said, dear mother ?   Has any one dared to slander me ?

No, no ! it cannot be true you never looked like a villain, and you do not now, repeated Mrs Vivyan looking attentively at her son , " but tell me all that has happened—what brings you here—what makes you fear to be surprised ?

Edward was so eager to hear who had accused him, and the nature of the accusation and his mother felt so anxious to know what had tran-spired since his departure that it was some time before either of them could sufficiently conquer impatience as to allow the other liberty to speak   At length both parties explained at full   Edward learnt that a report of his adventures of the preceding night similar to that which he had overheard in the conversation between Tompkins and the French man had been made to his mother

" The wretch !   he vehemently exclaimed, as soon as she had done speaking

'Tis a lie then— tell me it is a lie, Edward, and I shall be happy ! '

It is true that I bore away the poor girl but then—I rescued her from the villains who I conclude, wounded probably murdered her unfortunate father

"My son' my own son' exclaimed the mother thrilling with terror at the danger she imagined he must have undergone and overpowered at his deliverance again pressed him fondly to her arms

" And are you unhurt Edward ?

' I received a bruise or two that I feel no longer

And where is the poor girl ?

" I have left her in as private a lodging as I could procure she is I suspect pursued for some bad purpose and it would have been impru dent to have brought her in this neighbourhood

Edward then proceeded to relate the particulars of the whole trans action carefully recounting his first interview with the mendicant and his daughter what had taken place at the Cat and Gridiron and how he had come up to the wounded Welbourne in time to run to the rescue of Evine He also mentioned the adventure in the road side ale house forbearing however to allude to the loss of the purse lest it should lead his mother to insist on his accepting assistance from her scanty resources

' This poor girl is thus thrown upon my protection he concluded " I cannot forsake her or quit the neighbourhood until I learn tidings of her father and restore her to him if he is still alive It will, I fear take some time to evolve this mysterious affair and from the reports which are in circulation I cannot be too thankful that I determined in the first place to apprise you of what had taken place I have thus spared you some anxiety But what villain brought this lying tale to your ears mother ?

' A strange man to me

Short and thin with sharp features ?

" He was that kind of person

Have you any clue by which I could find him—his name calling residence ?

Have a care Edward how you fall in his way remember he accuses you, and as he is better off in the world than we are, he may do you great injury

" For your sake mother I will do no imprudence but, I beseech you if you know any thing of him, do tell it me

' While he was here said the widow thinking for a minute or two before she resumed ' some people happened to come in—they told me his name

' Let me hear it ' gasped Edward

" Mr Gregory Grasp replied the widow who gathered her inform ation from the style in which she had heard Lord Minhurst accost the lawyer

The rascally lawyer of P—— retorted Edward he is notorious throughout the county—I will see him to morrow

For heaven s sake be careful Edward he is powerful

' Fear not mother our interview shall take place in the presence of a magistrate

This explanation over, it was time to refresh the young traveller after his long and stormy journey across the country—for he had judged it unsafe to take the high road

You are wet to the skin   Edward   give me your coat—there—I will step up stairs and bring down your old suit   My poor boy ' I little thought you would want it again so soon   I ll not be long. When you have changed we will set about supper   you must surely be faint with hunger

For a few minutes Edward was left alone   Seated on a chair, his arm reposing on the table, he looked thoughtfully at the fire which his mother had kindled during their recent dialogue with the rapidity of enchant ment   As he changed his position the rustling of paper drew his atten tion to the sketch

A sheet of white paper among his mother s sewing was a novel object and his curiosity was increased when he perceived as well as the twilight would allow him that there was a drawing on the paper   He poked the fire and holding it near the flame beheld a well executed likeness of himself   His surprise knew no bounds   such a drawing was an article of luxury far beyond his mother s means to procure   and the village or the neighbourhood furnished no artist competent to the task   He ran with vivacity to the foot of the old staircase

' Mother ' mother !   cried he, his heart beating violently as he spoke   tell me I conjure you, how you came by this likeness "

' What is the matter ?   enquired Mrs Vivyan the question having been uttered too vehemently to be very distinct slowly descending the stairs as she spoke

Her foot was scarcely off the last stair before Edward held the picture directly opposite the light she carried and gazed on it with great intent ness—his eyes almost starting from their sockets, his countenance beam ing with an expression of outrageous joy, while his whole frame shook with excitement   Mrs Vivyan looked alternately at the picture, and then at her son, with the air of one amused at his surprise

' Who drew this? said he hurriedly

The mother now began to regret that her agitation had prevented her from concealing an object which she feared would give rise to painful and useless emotions   Mrs Vivyan was not so short sighted but she guessed the draftsman

'Tis she—it must be she ' muttered Edward, after a few more se conds rapturous contemplation of the drawing

" Who my son ? enquired the widow scarcely knowing what to say

' Yes ' yes ! her own hands drew it see ' see ' he cried, hastily snatching the light and holding it nearer the picture   ' there in that corner mother—see you not ?

In a corner of the drawing, with the aid of her spectacles, Mrs Vivyan, though not without some difficulty made out, mysteriously entwined with other pencil marks the letter M

' Dearest mother   said he with eager rapidity ' did she send this to comfort you ? did she come herself ? she is an angel mother her heart is full of heavenly dispositions   What condescension ' what feeling this act betrays for the sufferings of others '

" It was certainly kind of Miss Mira, said the widow ' but do not my dear son think too much of this small trifle—done perhaps merely to divert an idle hour, and brought hither by accident

' Mother I am not that fool ' exclaimed Edward in accents that were made moderate by great effort " I do not argue from this sketch more than it warrants She could not have made this paper breathing with myself without thinking of me could she mother ? Well then, a thought an occasional thought—tis a trifle perhaps—yet it is the height of my ambition—all I desire and expect—and she gives it me, mother she gives it me!"

Here the dialogue was suspended by the surprise a loud knock of the door occasioned

" Who can it be ? whispered Edward, looking at his mother with alarm

" I expect no one, she faltered

The knocking was now repeated with redoubled violence.

' Step out of the way—up stairs—in this cupboard—while I see who it is

' I will not hide myself, exclaimed Edward indignantly I am un conscious of guilt and do not fear

For my sake ' implored the mother ' Remember the reports abroad recollect the poor girl whom it is now your duty to protect

A third and louder rap at the door, distinctly audible, though at the same time a peal of thunder loud as the voice of ruin rattled through the heavens, enforced the widows entreaty—Edward stepped out of sight

" Who is there ? asked Mrs Vivyan, advancing to the door in great consternation

Another peel of thunder, longer and louder than the one which pre ceded it shaking the very roof of her humble dwelling drowned the poor widows enquiry

An awful silence prevailed and the widows heart breathless with anxiety quailed within her at the thoughts of impending danger

' A stranger at such an hour ' and on such a night ' thought she ' who can it be ?

Another loud knock roused her from this reverie.

' Who is there ? repeated the widow

' Open the door ' said a voice more assimilated to the tone of a screech owl than that of a human being ' open the door I say ' '

Who is it that thus demands admittance at this late unseasonable hour ? exclaimed the widow with nervous energy

It were well for you not to keep me any longer in this drenching rain my good woman open the door, I say—my patience is well nigh gone

The words of the speaker were uncourteous enough to warrant a longer resistance on the part of the mistress of the dwelling but the voice grated on her ears in tones so harshly stern and so well known, that with forebodings almost amounting to terror, the poor woman withdrew the bolt and opening the door in the lightning flash that quivered for a

moment through the air she beheld the spare form and disagreeabl
features of the lawyer Grasp

An involuntary shudder seemed to seize her whole frame and she
stood motionless before him

'Are we alone? said he striding into the apartment

We are, replied the widow retreating before him and contriving
dextrously to cover with the cloth the preparations for supper which but
too plainly announced that a third person was in the cottage

This action fortunately passed unperceived and a pause followed
during which the lawyer glanced cautiously round the room, as if he felt
it important to assure himself that no one was at hand to witness what
might transpire during their interview

"I thought I heard voices said Grasp "while I waited at the door

"I am a lone woman and talk to my cat sometimes it makes the
minutes pass away faster

'You kept me waiting a long time

It was a wonder I heard you at all, while the thunder was pealing
loud enough to make one deaf with fear

'Well! well! Dare say it is all right Quite alone, no doubt If
any one were present it would make no matter—my business is fair and
honourable—maxim with me never to do anything to be ashamed of

' You may be a very honest man no doubt, Sir but, as I am used
to rise early and it is long past my bed time already I should take it
kindly of you to tell me your pleasure at once

Grasp looked at the widow like a man who fears to come directly to
the point and yet must either do so or give up the only chance of re
ceiving important information   On his way home from Minhurst it had
occurred to the lawyer that Edward would no doubt correspond with his
mother and that by her means he (Grasp) might perhaps with proper
management obtain a sure clue to Evine s retreat.   On this bright idea
he immediately acted his impatience to find out the mendicant s daughter
being wonderfully increased by the liberal addition the Viscountess had
made to the reward she had promised him if he succeeded in placing
Evine in her power at their last interview   He accordingly turned his
horse s head in the direction of Minhurst church and alighted at Mrs
Vivyan s door at an advanced hour of the evening, as we have already
seen   Now that he sat tete-a-tete with the mother of the young man
whom he had that morning so imprudently and unsparingly slandered
his first object was to sound her, and judge from the result how far she
might be safely and usefully employed in his main scheme—the recovery
of Evine   Even the abstruse calculations of lawyers have often been
foiled by the ready wit of woman but we may observe by the way it
does not follow, that the sex do well to rush into such struggles.   Their
skill depends on the affections, and when these are roused, cunning and
zealous must be the man who can compete with a female advocate   Mrs
Vivyan was considered a clever woman in the ordinary duties of female
life and now that she had to contend with one of the most crafty minds
ever enrolled among the ranks of Themis   a mother s love supplied her
deficiency for the contest   With an intuitive wariness she kept the
lawyer in the dark respecting the information she possessed and drove
him to make enquiries by which he unintentionally betrayed a thousand
things to his disadvantage

I came to converse with you about your son Mrs Vivyan, began
Grasp

" My poor boy ' sighed the widow

" Rode over on purpose

" Very kind on such a night, rejoined his companion with ill dis
guised sarcasm that did not escape the lawyer s notice

' See how it is—not forgiven me for what I said this morning You
are a sensible woman Mrs Vivyan and should know better than to bear
me ill will for being the bearer of bad news

' I cannot believe it—I never can—my Edward could not have done
so

' It certainly was very bad but young men will be young men, you
know '

True   but to act in that brutal, lawless way '

' Not so unaccountable either   Consider Mrs Vivyan, young men s
passions are strong very   your son loved this young girl we will say
became rather familiar perhaps very probable in a young man you
know   well, the father grows restive they quarrel blows follow   old

bones easily broken—the man is stunned, and off trips the daughter with her lover   a very good opportunity don t you think ? '

This edifying way of accounting for and even justifying the **trans** action, did not escape Edward s quick ear who burning with indignation found it necessary to exert all his patience in order to remain quiet in his place of concealment   He longed to give the lawyer then and there the chastisement his lies deserved, and only refrained in the hope of obtaining an insight into Grasp s motive for persecuting an unoffending girl

" If you think it so slight a matter, resumed Mrs Vivyan, " why did you talk about it so bitterly when you came to my cottage this morn ing   then you talked as if the crime you are now pleased to term a folly deserved the utmost rigour of the law

" Justice must be done, Mrs Vivyan in my capacity I must steel my heart against all tender sympathies   Difficult task ! very often im possible as in this instance   How can I pursue your son with severity, when I know that the punishment due to his offence would leave a tender hearted   worthy mother, childless and alone in the world ?   I could not do it, Mrs Vivyan I could not do it it is out of my power quite

" It is very good of you to have so much consideration   and must be very troublesome to you, Sir, in your way of life

" Very, Ma am, I assure you   never more so than in this instance '

' Then why do you interfere in it at all ?   asked the mother

This was an unexpected question   poor people seldom presume to ask the motives of a wealthy minister of justice, even when they suffer from his abuse of the responsibility he is invested with

" Hem ! hem !' coughed the lawyer as he considered what reply he should give, while Edward scarcely dared to draw breath in his impa tience to hear it

Why should you interfere, and endanger my poor boy, when it goes against your heart ? repeated the widow, who was aware of the advantage she had gained

" To tell you the truth, began Mr Grasp slowly, as if afraid to trust his words beyond his mouth, " I am placed in this matter in a most awk ward predicament   between a father and a mother as it were '

" How so ? enquired Mrs Vivyan filling up a pause, during which the lawyer caught a stronger hold of his idea

" Thus, ' he resumed " the father comes to me, to restore and avenge his child   and the mother of the guilty author of the offence begs me with tears to spare her son

" Tis a lie ! thundered Edward darting from the closet, while Grasp staggered to the further end of the room half dead with terror   ' the mother of an innocent child never sought the indulgence of a false, base knave   the father of a lost daughter never employed the hoary villain to recover her who contrived the project for carrying her off   My mother ! he concluded pressing Mrs Vivyan to his bosom, who trem bled as she saw the violence of her son and the guilty terror of his ac cuser

Not a word fell from the lips of the lawyer pale with rage and fright he slunk towards the door   Edward perceived the action, and rushed between him and the entrance of the cottage

"'You shall not stir from hence,   said he, resolved not to lose sight of his accuser

" By what right do you detain me ?   faltered Grasp, becoming somewhat uneasy at the very determined manner which the young man had assumed

" As the friend of a helpless girl whom you have deprived of her lawful protector '

'This is fine language from the poor man s murderer, rejoined the other recovering some composure it will not do with me unhappy young man let me pass, I command you'

" Miserable wretch ' you are in my power !' shouted Edward, with that firmness which a good cause never fails to produce on an upright heart unjustly maligned

" You will not kill me ' cried Grasp really alarmed at Edward s infuriated look, although he was unable to suppress the rising craft of his heart, which led him to add " as you did the other

" You are my accuser,   rejoined Vivyan, " and I insist that you substantiate this charge, nor shall you leave me until we have been before a magistrate '

These words had a terrible effect upon the lawyer   At once he saw the necessity of securing his safety, and of avoiding an immediate examination, which might seriously compromise him   The emergency made him desperate, and with more courage than he could have given himself credit for,

' Say you so ? he exclaimed drawing at the same time a brace of pistols from his pocket, which he always wore when on the road after dark, and presenting one at Edward, and the other at his mother   'let me pass—a word from either, and I fire ! added he, his appearance assuming that of great desperation

The suppressed scream that came from Mrs Vivyan at the sight of the fire arms, had more effect upon Edward than the threat   Silently and sullenly he removed from the doorway, while Grasp with the same caution moved towards it, but still levelling the instruments of destruction at the two inmates   He was within a foot or two of the doorway, when his movement so changed the relative position of the parties, that the body of the son masked the mother   This was an opportunity not to be neglected   like lightning the young man darted on his retiring foe, and struck the pistol from one hand, while he seized him by the wrist of the other   Struggling desperately, they both tottered out of the cottage and the poor mother awaited in the greatest agony of mind the issue of this struggle

She heard their hurried unequal footsteps along the path of the little garden—the wicket gate swung to behind them

" Edward is the strongest, she thought, " and will force him to go to the nearest magistrate my boy is innocent, and his assertions will be believed

Scarcely had the thought passed her mind, when she was startled by

No 15

the report of a pistol   Frantic with terror she rushed out, nor stopped
till she reached the yew tree in the churchyard   Against it pale and
aghast leant Edward   near him, bathed in blood, was stretched the
lawyer

They had proceeded thus far Edward yet firmly holding Grasp by
the wrist of the hand in which the latter still clenched his pistol   In
their struggle that death dealing weapon had exploded, and its muzzle
was at the time directed towards the unhappy man

CHAPTER XIV

In a small room, about fourteen feet by twelve, divided into two com
partments by a wooden partition nearly the height of a middle sized man
and terminating in a rail, sat a personage, for whose fortunes, peculiarities,
sentiments, and performances, we respectfully solicit the attention of the
reader

Mr Dobie Snitch—such was the honourable appellation chance and his progenitors had bestowed on the four feet eleven of skin and bones we had nearly written flesh, a slip of the pen which would have led the reader into a most lamentable error respecting the personal appearance of our worthy—which constituted all that was visible and physical of the head clerk (fifty weeks out of the year, the only one) and factotum of Gregory Grasp, Esq , solicitor, and master extraordinary in Chancery

It was between the hours of eleven and twelve, P M , on the evening of the day in which the memorable events described in our last chapters took place, that this individual began to experience all the ordinary symp toms of a protracted sitting on his usual post of eminence—a high round wooden stool, which answered the purpose of raising the little man to his inky and notched desk, and also to a proper elevation for recon noitring through the aforesaid rail all those attending at the office of his employer

It must be understood that this apartment was situated at the further extremity of a large house, whose frontage towards the street was adorned with three tiers of ten windows each whereof that of the little office formed the first   The entrance was under a gateway, on the right hand side, and was ornamented with the usual quantity of brass plates and bells   At the end of the room was another door leading to an upper room—the sanctum sanctorum of the man of law—and communicating with the house

In this locality sat Dobie Snitch   His cheeks were lank with hunger his face pallid with a hard life of desk-plodding, the effects of which were but indifferently counteracted by sundry red tinges of a blueish cast that rested on the more predominant features, and betrayed an attachment to spirituous tippling

Every appearance of work had long been laid aside, and the weary clerk amused himself by cutting into pens the stumps of several quills an economical practice he had learnt from an attentive observation of the habits of his master

' I am a fool to do it, said Snitch, admiring the graceful nib he had manufactured from the worthless remnant of a goose quill   "a precious fool and so I am told every blessed day of my life   I wonder now what the governor does save by me in the run of a year   I ll just make the calculation, if it s only to pass the time away   In the first place, if he had not me, he must have a managing clerk, and a copying clerk, and a junior clerk, and a messenger or two   oh Lord ' oh Lord ' that is five individuals   what a precious sum it would cost, to be sure ' and I do it all for seven half crowns a week '   What a blessed fool I am ' To be sure it is regular money   paid down on Saturday night as sure as clock work   Only to think of the wages of all these people ! there s a pretty sum I put in his pocket every year, not to mention other savings ! Who but a precious fool, like myself, would take care of his twine, his sealing wax, candles, candlesticks hard bottomed stools, quills, and such stationary, I should very much like to know ?   Then he is always re minding me of the gratitude I owe him, for taking me out of the work house   as though I shouldn t have found the way out of it myself in time I don t know what I have got by the change, not I   A precious nice house this is for work, and no fib at all Well! I suppose my turn must come some day Where can the governor be at this blessed hour of night?

Such were the cogitations of Dobie Snitch, when sounds from the upper room, just as he was in the act of laying down his thirtieth pen, broke upon his reverie

" There he is, said he, seizing the light—a candle snuff glimmering from the socket of a tin office candlestick " just in time ; a minute later and not a precious spark of light would he have found in the place wish he had— tis his own fault—why don t he leave out more candles thinks I eat them, I suppose ' And with sounds that might have been signs of merriment, but which very much resembled a growl he advanced to the narrow staircase leading to the lawyer's private cabinet At the head of this staircase was a door that gave access to the other parts of the building, a vast pile by the way, which furnished the maiden ladies of the place matter for wonder, as to what mysterious purposes it could be devoted by bachelo Grasp

Now it so happened that at the moment Mr Dobie Snitch protruded his head through the door at the foot of the staircase, holding high in the air, as most people do when they take a candle into the dark, another head protruded through the door at the top of the said staircase, while the individual to whom they belonged held a similar expiring candle-snuff and its receptacle in the same elegant attitude

Fortunately the expiring snuffs still emitted sufficient light to disclose to either party the face of the other who, it was no wonder, were friends, for in both countenances age, ugliness, craft, and theft were strongly depicted

' Mrs Deborah Swill, by this blessed light !"

" Is it you, Dobie Snitch?

" I thought you was the governor, said Dobie

" No but here is a gentleman wants to see him '

" At this blessed time o night'' exclaimed Dobie, shuddering at the prospect of a more protracted vigil " Better say the governor s out, Mrs Swill

' So I have, Mr Snitch The gentleman says he must see master to night I came to tell you, Mr Snitch may be tis particular

' A young gentleman, Mrs Swill?

" Very young, Mr Snitch

' I ll come directly—this precious moment '

And with movements very similar to those of the insect yclept by children ' daddy long legs, Mr Dobie Snitch transported his little person up the stairs to the side of the female factotum in the domestic depart ment of Gregory Grasp s establishment

A loud ring at the front door bell—an issue of the building seldom used, and not from time immemorial at that hour of the night—sum moned them to attend to their respective duties Dobie Snitch to wait on the client, Deborah Swill to attend to the door

On reaching the passage leading to the front entrance, Snitch per ceived a tall young man, whose appearance bore such signs of affluence as invariably drew from the clerk the most polite attention

"Your obedient, Sir ' he began while Mrs Swill, thrown into a tremor by louder raps at the door, and most alarming attempts on the bell wire which fortunately failed to produce a ring, fumbled in vain to extricate the door key from her pocket, which with the precaution of a prudent housekeeper, she had placed in that very miscellaneous receptacle, in order to prevent the premature departure of the stranger during her absence to summon the clerk

"Drat the key ' cried she, giving another tug that relieved her pouch of various articles, among which a screw of paper containing half an ounce of tea a piece of soap, the end of a wax candle, balls of thread of all sizes and hues, with a huge thimble were most conspicuous   I won der who the plague it is comes at this unseasonable hour ' There goes the wire ! snapped in two I ll be bound '

"Mr Grasp, probably, intimated Ronald (for he it was whom Snitch had addressed), and coming to this conclusion from the very authoritative attempts made by the new comer to gain admittance

"Stuff and nonsense ! replied the matron, tugging more heartily than ever with one hand, and gathering up her exposed treasures with the other ' master comes round the back way, and lets himself in always Pooh ' pooh ' it can't be master '

"What may be your pleasure, Sir ? reiterated Mr Snitch

"I wish to know when Mr Grasp is expected home, replied Ronald

"That is rather more than I can say, Sir the governor is precious irregular in his movements 'tis a blessed long while, though, since he went out—never knew him absent so long before. Can I do anything for you, Sir ?

No ' I must see your master to night I come some distance, and will wait for him

"This way then, Sir, if you please '

As Snitch was on the point of conducting Ronald to the office, Mrs. Swill applied the key to the key hole

'One moment, Sir, said the clerk, halting to see the new comers

The key creaked harshly in the lock the door turned heavily upon its hinges, and several voices from without were heard to complain of the tediousness of the operation

'Mercy on me, what a posse ' exclaimed Deborah giving a last pull, which drew the door wide open

A pretty time o night to keep folks at the door ! cried one

"The man will be dead before you get him into the house ' shouted another

'Lord have mercy on us ' Dead ! What do you mean ? ' enquired the housekeeper, stretching her neck out into the street to distinguish, if possible, some one among the many who were thus assailing her mas ter s mansion

"What can it all mean ? I should very much like to know ' inter posed Dobie peering into the darkness over Mrs Swill s shoulder

Damn it, woman ' stand aside, and let us come in, will ye we are ready to drop under our load as it is , ' and the brawny arm of the speaker putting the aged lady aside with little ceremony, made a passage for the rest of his party to enter

The storm had long since ceased but the light from within streamed out on a score of rough peasant faces   Two or three of the foremost figures carried an object of some weight and bulk   anxiety and alarm were strongly depicted on the countenances in the back ground   The men entered the house with their load

"A corpse! cried Mrs Deborah

"Not quite, Mrs Swill,   articulated a faint voice proceeding from the burthen carried by the men

'Heavens above, my poor master!   sobbed the housekeeper

"Good Lord, if it isn t the governor!' cried Dobie with a significant wink at Ronald

"Don t stand wringing your hands , let us get the old gentleman to bed—he can t last long

A moan from the patient seemed to enforce this request, and the housekeeper led the way to the lawyer s bed room

The features of the wounded man were ghastly pale, and begrimed with gore   The eyes opened from time to time, and gazed wildly round, but closed again with a speed that revealed the effort it cost the sufferer. Once they rested on Ronald and he thought he observed the expression of the countenance change as they did so   He however stood aside, and as they proceeded up the stairs interrogated the persons at the door

'How did this happen?' he asked

"Lord in heaven knows!' said a man at his elbow   "it serves the old codger right   many a poor man s heart has he caused to ache—tis just his turn should come at last!

'How was it done? was it an accident? was he attacked?'

"Devil a bit!   cried another   "the old rogue could nt abide the cries of his guilty conscience, and shot hisself to silence 'em

'A d—d sight of conscience!   interposed a third   "take my word for t, one o the hundreds as he s ruined has giv the villain tit for tat'

Ronald shuddered at remarks which, however merited, under the circumstances of the case appeared cruel and unfeeling   Perceiving near him a person of better aspect than the rest, he again made an attempt to ascertain the particulars of the disaster

"I was at the doctor's when they brought him in, said the man "and I believe I heard all that is certain about the business'

"Was he attacked, then?'

"No one can tell   He was brought to this place by two men who say they were passing the road that runs by Minhurst church   some time before they came up to it they heard the report of a pistol, but the night being stormy they disregarded it   On reaching the churchyard, however, about ten minutes after they heard low moans, and, guided by the sounds, found lawyer Grasp weltering in his blood   Not a soul was to be seen , so they applied for a light and assistance at a cottage hard by '

"I know,' observed Ronald   "a neat, pretty cottage, inhabited by a widow, I think

"The same, Sir   The poor woman seemed agitated when they entered, she had heard the report, she said, but being alone feared to leave her cottage

" Natural enough Did you gather any further particulars ?

" A pistol was found near the tree

" Do they think it will lead to the detection of the murderer ?

" The doctor recognises it to be one of a brace he sold to the unfor tunate man a few months before

" It would seem then to be—

" Suicide," said the man finishing the phrase Ronald had began

On receiving this intelligence, our young friend became thoughtful an attempt to commit suicide, he argued, would imply remorse and he hurried towards the staircase in order to profit by the few moments of life that might be spared to the wretched man, whom he hoped to find in a state of mind favourable to the disclosure he wished to extort from him

Already the house manifested the signs of a heavy domestic visitation The remaining part of the household, a shock head stable boy, now ap peared to add to the shew of bustle, and followed in the wake of Mr Dobie Snitch and Mrs Deborah Swill, as they ran to and fro displaying a zeal and sorrow highly becoming in such faithful servants

To Dobie did Ronald address himself, as that personage hopped down the staircase to expel and silence the crowd which had gathered around the door

" Has your master received a serious injury ? asked Ronald, endea vouring, notwithstanding his anxiety to obtain information, to repress his impatience and give a form of decency to his enquiries

' A precious business this ' ' replied the man , ' it s all up with the governor, and no fib '

" Is there immediate danger ?'

" The men who brought him home say it is the doctor s opinion he cannot last through the night

' Has he his senses ? continued Ronald, almost gasping with his anxiety for a reply

' I should say the governor had poor soul, he wanted so to come home '

" I had important business to settle with him—business of the greatest consequence I am unwilling to disturb the repose of a dying man, but my visit will probably add to the comfort of his dying moments '

' Is that it ' exclaimed Snitch with a look of cunning intelligence " comfort the governor s dying moments, eh ?

" I am mistaken if he would not ask to see me, did he know that I was within call

" What does the young gentleman say ?' asked Mrs Deborah Swill, who now emerged all bustle and distress from the scene of approaching death

" Wants to see the governor, Mrs Swill , but I have an idea it cannot be just now—

" Oh Lord, no ' 'Tis all over with my poor dear master !

" Good God ' Is he dead ? ' exclaimed Ronald

" Not exactly, Sir but very near it—too near to see any one but the parson

" Precious near it added Dobie " I shall book no more six-and eight penny attendances, I take it

' He gets worse and worse, Mr Snitch I really do think I heard the rattles in his throat Poor soul ! Wouldn t you do well to go and learn his last wishes He made me a sign all the world as if he meant to express his desire to see you, Dobie

' His danger makes it imperative that *I* should see him,' said Ronald assuming a sterner tone

" Impossible ! replied the female

" Quite impossible ! ' echoed Snitch

I will see him ' ' rejoined Ronald here is gold conduct me at once to his chamber "

" Five guineas, Snitch ! said Mrs Deborah, looking at her fellow factotum

" There could be no harm if the gentleman wouldn't forget the con dition the governor is in, said that functionary, returning her glance with one that forced compliance

' You will be still as a mouse, Sir, ' continued the woman, leading the way to the door

" Nor forget the poor governor is dying, added the other faithful guardian of the peace of the departing soul

" I shall not want your attendance, exclaimed Ronald with impatience as he stood on the threshold of Grasp s chamber " if your master grows worse, I will ring—you may depend on me

As the door closed upon the young man, Dobie and Deborah exchanged glances that imported considerable astonishment, as well as great awe at the commanding and mysterious manner of the stranger

' ' Do you think it is all right ? asked Deborah

' I don t like the young man s way, ' replied Snitch " but what are we to do ? he added, pointing significantly to the five sovereigns in the palm of his hand

" Better let us go halves, and leave the young man to say what he has to say in peace

" I think we can t be very well uncivil to him besides I have some thing to attend to

" In the office, I suppose, added the venerable spinster " some valuable bits of paper there— eh, Mr Dobie Snitch ?"

" Paper isn t like plate and linen,' replied the clerk with a significant wink " I presume you have a little business in your way, Mrs Deborah Swill "

" I was thinking about seeing all right in the store room Mr Snitch

" Just what I intend doing in the office, Mrs Swill Extraordinary emergency this !

" Clever woman that,' said the male factotum, as he entered the office

" Shrewd little man, observed the female factotum, as she prepared to ransack the store room of the dying lawyer

As soon as Dobie Snitch had shut the door leading from the office into the house, he drew a key from his pocket, and holding it up in the light appeared to contemplate it with an exultation little short of rapture

"My turn now! my turn now!" said he giving the little instrument sundry triumphant shakes as he held it aloft "Let me see, let me see," he continued applying it to the key hole of Grasp s private room "now to explore the 'secrets of the prison house,' as governor used to say when he chose to be funny and pleasant Poor soul! he will never be funny and pleasant again"

The key creaked in concert with this dolorous note, and in another moment the door opened to lay bare to a prying, dishonest menial, passages in his master s life known only to the conscience of him who figured in them and the searcher of hearts

It was a room of small dimensions, but compactly arranged, and crowded to the utmost with boxes, cases, and shelves

There, in time worn and dusty envelopes, were papers drawn up by aching hands and perused with weeping eyes the marriage settlement of the fair and youthful bride rested on the last testament of the man of wealth—wrung from him perhaps by hungry heirs in moments of infatuated dotage here the same covering contained the parchment by which affection sought to procure a provision for its dearest object, and the deed by which that object bartered such memorial of love for the means of obtaining prodigal and shameful gratification papers drawn up for the innocent reposed, unconscious of the contaminating neighbourhood, beside the elaborate depositions of false witnesses, cunningly arranged, and expensively obtained, to save from merited punishment the debased perpetrator of some hideous crime right and left were piled silent but emphatic testimonials of human depravity, and human trial on all sides materials might be collected for tales that would have sounded strange and horrible in a hall of justice, and disgraced the secrecy of the confessional

Dobie loitered on the threshold of the room He stood in great awe of his employer, and had always been accustomed to enter the presence chamber with the feelings of a slave approaching an eastern despot a disposition Grasp delighted to perceive, and never failed to cultivate, either by the rigour of his commands or by the acerbity of his sarcasms. But where now was the harsh and haughty master? No longer on his tyrant s throne, the office chair before a bureau groaning beneath a load of papers and parchments the instruments of his power—but impotent as a child he was hastening to his long home Nevertheless, so strong is the force of habit, that on throwing open the door, the clerk stood in the trembling, hesitating attitude in which he had so often awaited the reprimands of a man then scarcely able to articulate a faint request Snitch saw before him the little office invested with its simple and mighty paraphernalia—for which, by frequent and dreadful proofs of their effects he possessed feelings that rested little short of reverence There was the vacant chair of authority before it a pair of slippers apparently waiting their owner s pleasure and thrown loosely over the back of it a morning gown, that a few hours before covered limbs now waiting for a shrowd

On the table was a waste sheet of paper scrawled over with memoranda yet fresh and black, of the preceding day, and near it lay a pen still moist, with which they had been written

A slight glance brought to his mind the details we have been some time describing, and they left there an impression similar to that the actual presence of his employer would have produced For a moment he trembled, but the next he recollected that the least delay would take from him for ever the golden opportunity that now presented itself

" The dead will be stripped one way or the other, argued he, yielding to that strange propensity of wickedness to solace itself with sophism " and I may as well have the pickings they are my due—I have worked hard enough for them "

Fully persuaded, and greatly encouraged by this very sound reasoning, he strode into the room, and having carefully closed the door, proceeded to search for that object which seemed most deserving his attention on so unusual on occasion   A strong fire proof chest was viewed with an eye most decidedly covetous but two potent reasons placed all depre dations on its contents out of the question   Their value was sure to have entitled them to a place in a certain will, the existence of which was no secret to Dobie Snitch though all his conjectures as to its pur port were far enough from the truth and the chest, moreover, was one of those then very modern contrivances that so cleverly and effectually baffle the designs of individuals possessing the organs of theft and in quisitiveness   With a suppressed sigh he accordingly passed on to a deep closet, from whose recesses he drew a small coffer rendered by its construction exceedingly eligible for examination and plunder   It was some years back that an accident made Snitch acquainted with its exist ence and it had since been honoured with a considerable share of his observation and notice   More than once he had surprised his master poring over its contents, and by paying very minute attention to its po sition he had discovered that no day passed without its being taken down and replaced, in which exercise he presumed it was not indulged merely with a view to its improvement or comfort, but more probably for the convenience of its owner   Impressed with this conviction, and to put his sagacity to the proof, he exposed the coffer to certain operations of lifting and shaking, from which processes he further learnt that it experienced almost daily changes in its weight, and from certain clinking sounds, exceedingly musical and not at all ambiguous, he came to a pretty certain opinion respecting the nature of the weighty part of its contents   In these suppositions he was very much borne out by other observations he remarked, for instance that increase of weight in the coffer was invariably followed by an entry on the credit side of the cash book, and whenever a payment of specie was made into the bank the mysterious chest as invariably grew light   These facts satisfied Mr Dobie Snitch, as indeed they might have done any person less gifted with discernment, that one of the uses of the said coffer was to hold any monies from the time of their payment until they found their way to the banker and the almost daily change in their contents assured him that they could not possibly be recorded in any of those inconvenient docu

ments which state so very correctly and minutely what people are pos
sessed of at the time they think proper to retire from the world and leave
to others the enjoyment of their good things   It soon occurred to our
sagacious friend that it was most desirable to keep such a valuable ap
pendage constantly in view, and accordingly he conceived for it so extra
ordinary a friendship, that he allowed no day to go by without bestowing
on it sundry affectionate hugs and shakes which were generally responded
to by the musical clinking from within   These friendly duties had not
been omitted on the morning of the day whose eventful close we are de
scribing and Snitch had perceived symptoms of unusual wealth in the
coffer it will not therefore appear a matter of wonder, if on this occasion
he felt desirous of becoming more intimately acquainted with his favour
ite   In the absence of a key he felt no scruple at performing a violent
operation on the lid he wrenched it open, and his eyes glanced with
delight as they gazed on the glittering spectacle beneath

Bright gold and brighter diamonds sparkled in the rays of the small
candle he held, sending back in return ten thousand others a thousand
times more brilliant

"There must be a thousand, said he, as he took up a handful of
guineas "these jewels must be worth three times as much   stay, these
papers will perhaps tell all about it   he concluded, taking a bundle of
papers from the coffer, and a loose document that bore the appearance
of a recent date

The latter first gained his attention, and most satisfactorily accounted
for the presence of the gold and jewels, giving also an estimate, a usurer s
estimate be it remembered, of the value of the latter   It was the rough
draft of a debtor and creditor account—a kind of hastily struck balance
sheet   The business like habits of his employer satisfied Snitch that it
was only a private note to assist some calculation, and not the copy of
a document duly signed and delivered

"So! so! cried the clerk as he read ' Debtor the Dowager Viscountess Minhurst to Gregory Grasp Creditor   "Oh! oh! that s the
way the wind blows is it   he added casting his eyes over the items

" ' By cash advanced on jewels, three thousand pounds '   Better and
better these gew gaws here must be worth six thousand, if Gregory
Grasp advanced three   Well, this is a lucky find and no fib!   Let me
see—' To bill bearing date from —num ' very pretty sum total indeed !
Nice client, a precious nice client that old dowager ! ' To monies paid
for expenses incurred in the pursuit of the girl E—— five hundred a
blessed item that ! Who is the girl E——? I should like very much
to know ' Balance One thousand— Hem! hem ! ' Balance paid
June, 17—   What have we here ? continued the clerk, looking at the
bundle of papers which formed the remaining contents

It was a large collection the date of each paper was announced by
its hue, some of them being worn with age while others were as fresh
as if added to the heap but yesterday   They were tied together with
red tape and bore a hastily written endorsement

" ' Minhurst Family letters, documents registers &c , ' resumed
Dobie, reading the label, ' Now I shall know all about them, ' he

added, drawing out the uppermost of the pile with great eagerness "was always sure there was some mystery to be brought to light in that quarter —what is this?

The paper Snitch held in his hand was the copy of a letter bearing date, 12 P M, on the preceding night, addressed to Dr William Wilder, Lunatic Asylum Pentonville, London, and ran thus —

> SIR,
>   The bearer Mr Townsend, will deliver into your keeping, till further orders, James Cobb an unfortunate lunatic related to one of my clients His case is very desperate he persists in calling himself one Wilfred Wilbourne and raves about a lost daughter Your vigilance is requested, and will (you understand) be handsomely rewarded You need be under no apprehensions about detaining him I have seen to everything and will take all the respon sibility I refer you to Townsend, whom you may treat with confidence, for further particulars
>
>   Yours truly,
>   G G

Dobie gathered very little from this epistle, further than the fact that his employer had been busily engaged on the preceding night while he had been snugly sleeping off the effects of his evening potations It puzzled him a little to trace the connection between the lunatic and the Minhursts The next paper proved to be the copy of another letter It was addressed to the lawyer s London agent, and requested him to send a person to watch the arrival of the coaches from that (Grasp s) part of the country for some days to come in order to intercept a young man and woman who had left P—— under peculiar circumstances It need not be added that the description of the fugitives answered to the persons of Edward and Evine It appeared that this letter had been forwarded with the other

"What can be at the bottom of all this, I should very much like to know, thought the factotum, as he turned up the ends of each of the papers and looked at the endorsement it bore "So, so! they go back for twenty, twenty five, thirty—ay, forty years! A blessed story they will tell, I warrant, when I have time to put them together These are mine, fast enough, said he, putting the papers up together, and transferring them to a capacious pocket "who can tell they may one day stand me in as good as a stock in trade The diamonds I won t touch it may be, when the lady finds the old man is gone off the hooks she ll make a noise about them The gold is another matter Who is to know anything about that?' and with great dexterity he contrived to stow it away by handfulls in various private receptacles about his person, that appeared made for the purpose, so well they retained the golden treasure

"Now then to put the key back in its place said he, having restored the coffer to the recess and removed all marks of violence from its surface 'That young man is gone, I suppose, that——Stay I will creep in by the dressing room and see I thought my turn would come one day, and no fib at all, he observed complacently tapping his well filled pockets, as he drew to the door and locked it after him

There was another door in the office opposite to the one by which
Snitch had entered it was furnished with strong bolts on either side,
and led to a dressing room communicating with the lawyer s sleeping
apartment the three rooms forming a small suite, and constituted the
only part of the mansion used by him on ordinary occasions Availing
himself of this mode of access, Dobie drew back the bolts with caution,
and crossing the intervening apartment on tip toe, stood before the
entrance of the chamber of death Here he paused to listen no
sounds reached him from within, and concluding Ronald was gone he
stole in The hangings of the bed were partially drawn, and screened
him from observation, preventing him at the same time from observing
what was passing in the room Prudence suggested to him the pro
priety of ascertaining who might be there, before he ventured round to
that side of the apartment where the lawyer's coat from the pocket of
which he had adroitly managed to withdraw the key of the office—had
been carelessly thrown For this purpose he drew near the heavy cur
tain, and through a small hole that had escaped the notice of Mrs
Deborah, he was enabled to observe all that passed

Immediately before him, and scarcely a foot and a half below his eyes
for Dobie as we have seen, was short of stature—lay the wounded
man The sudden occurrence of the accident, and perhaps also the cu
pidity of his attendants, had led to the neglect of those cleanly precautions which so much increase the comfort of the sick His face was
still bespattered with mud and gore the hair, clotted in masses, fell in
two or three large, thick, blood stained flakes on his forehead , and the
part of his skin exempted from this hideous and unnatural colouring
displayed the livid hues of approaching death There were few signs of
animation in the body, but the wide open eyes fixed with a horrid stare
of recognition on Ronald, whose pale, anxious countenance, stood out in
bold relief against the dark curtains The old man s deathy eye fixed
on the youth with so much stedfastness and was met by a look so full
of anxiety and terror, that Dobie forgot his own excitement to watch
with interest what was going forward

A minute or two of dead silence ensued, and operated powerfully on
all present Grasp at length heaved a deep groan, and closed his eyes
in a way that too plainly disclosed how much he shrunk from encountering the person before him It was impossible for a bye-stander to
suppose this note of anguish had been extorted by bodily suffering --it
bore all the impressive symptoms of a tortured mind So powerfully did
it appeal to Ronald s heart, that notwithstanding the interests he had at
stake, he upbraided himself for embittering the last moments of the
dying

"It is the last spark of life thought he, retreating from the bed
side "a treasure of inestimable value and I perhaps am helping to
extinguish it

'Stay ! said a low voice, sepulchral as a sound from the tomb, though
it was uttered by the living

Ronald turned and looked towards the bed The patient was strug
gling to rise, and with much difficulty succeeded in raising himself a little

in the bed, supporting his body by one arm   With straining eye balls
he surveyed the young man his bosom heaving violently with his
attempts to breathe, and every muscle thrilling with agitation

"You should be Ronald—son of Wilfred Minhurst' faltered the
lawyer
   The young man bowed
   "Why do you come to trouble the last moments of the dying ?
   "To bring to day a terrible secret   believe me I would not willingly
trouble your repose—nay, I hope to give you ease, by putting it in your
power to perform an act of restitution to the wronged '
   A sarcastic smile played over the features of the old man beaming in
hideous alliance with the glare of his eyes, over which the film of death
was rapidly creeping
   "He ! he ' he '' chuckled he   repose ' restitution ' a hundred lives
spent in ceaseless labour would do but little towards it '—Restitution '—
impossible '
   "You may have aided to injure one who is no longer living to benefit
by any amends you can make   If I mistake not her children live, and
for your own peace of mind, I implore you as a dying man—
   "Who calls me a dying man ? interrupted the lawyer with asto

nishing impetuosity for his weak condition ' Driveller ! fool ' ass ' begone ' Leave dying to old women ! Who thinks of dying ?—who talks of dying ?—I don t, not I—are you a doctor ?

Ronald shook his head

' Then talk not of dying ! Are you a priest—a parson ?

No ! ' was the reply

" Then talk not of peace ! Leave peace to those who seek it—prize it—want it—to the fearful, weak, and canting—to those who have neither virtue to merit it, nor courage to do without it—leave peace to them— to them, I say—I want no peace—never did—never shall ! "

This incoherent raving was uttered with all the wildness of insanity Ronald conceived the best plan would be to humour it, and accordingly observed with mildness,

" You must be solicitous about your reputation, Mr. Grasp ; can you leave unimpaired any injury you may have done to others ?"

" I tell you, young man, the labour of a hundred lives would not do it Repair injury ! Pooh ! pooh ! It was my delight to do it , shall I undo my favourite work !

" Good God ! Is this possible ?' exclaimed Ronald , " and in the face of death !

' Aye, aye ! Though the flames of h- l flashed in my face, I'd say it shout it—glory in it ! I lived to injure, young man -lived to injure, mark you ! "

Exhausted with the effort, he fell back on his pillow, and gasped fright fully for breath, the cold sweat-drops streaming on his brow In a few moments he continued, in a low voice, so feeble that his companion caught the words with difficulty,

' None of your grovelling money seeking wretches—no ! no ' Gregory Grasp was never one of them I loved money as the means of power the mighty engine that set my rack a going never for itself I ve paid the world the debt I owed it returned its past kindness I drew breath in a workhouse sucked hate not against one, or a score, but against all men at my mother s breast Look you, my lot was drudgery my food the bread of bitterness was tortured throughout my early days, days that enjoyment and hope should have brightened, until my passion, my fondest object was to torture again To obtain the power to torture, I studied, laboured strove Well ! my day came, and I vomited on all around the accumulated gall and venom of years -aye, vomited, and will vomit my task is not done !

The sick man paused again and seemed to be collecting his remaining energies Raising his body once more on his hand,

" D ye think me a wretched old man ? he resumed " Death at hand, racked with pain tortured in mind, dying in solitude must be a very wretched old man eh ? I ve a luxury you know not of more evil to achieve injuries to inflict, not to repair ! '

The vehemence of manner, rapidity of utterance, and spectral appear ance of the dying man, were alone sufficient to appal the beholder but accompanying, as they did sentiments the most detestable, they drew from Ronald an involuntary shudder Pity, horror, anxiety transfixed the young man to the bed side, and he stood motionless and silent a reluctant and powerless hearer of blasphemies from lips already bearing the impress of death

'Injuries to inflict on you   on you   do you hear me, Ronald Minhurst? shouted Grasp with all the energy of a man in full vigour " on you Ronald Minhurst!

" In God s name spare yourself this dreadful excitement!" said the young man   " You can do me no injury that can be felt more deeply than that you have already contributed to inflict

The wretched man eyed the speaker for more than a minute, and then said in a whisper, which had in it more malice than precaution,

" Has *she* then told you?

'Who ?' gasped Ronald overjoyed to find the lawyer giving to their conversation the turn he most desired and at the same time afraid to receive the terrible intelligence he foreboded he should hear

" She—the upstarted Viscountess—the usurping Viscountess—the false Viscountess—your grandmother, young man—your *own* father s *own* mother!

" How is she false usurping?   in the name of all you prize and hold sacred tell me how she is so?

Ronald s countenance was deathly pale his lips quivered all the expression of a heart harrowed to its lowest depths was thrown into his last question   It drew a frightful and exulting grin from the lawyer

" Did I not tell you so, Ronald Minhurst? I can yet give pain   Do not attempt to deny my power   tis manifest   Your heart bleeds, young man, for your cheek is bloodless

'By the pleasure you take in my misery, I entreat you to proceed or you will drive me to deprive you of the pleasure the sight of my anguish affords,   exclaimed the half frantic youth

I will, I will   Damnation! I can t   I can t   I choke - choke   I choke

A convulsion, apparent'y that of death had come over him   [His inanimate frame sunk heavily down on the bed the arm giving way which supported it   every sign of immediate dissolution was to be seen his countenance wore the livid hue of death, and his hands grasped the bed clothes with the agony of one who feels every thing giving way beneath him

Ronald, overpowered and aghast, made no attempt to call for succour his powers were absorbed by horror for the man he considered as dead, and the secret lost with him   Dobie Snitch from his place of conceal ment witnessed what he likewise considered the last agonies of his master, but saw no necessity for betraying himself to procure assistance   He had no longer any need of Gregory Grasp, and wished in his heart that the governor would oblige all parties by getting through the last scene with as much expedition as possible

All, however was not over   After a few convulsive throes, the dying man again opened his eyes, and again they settled with the same cool fixed, blighting gaze on the youth at his bed side   Gradually conscious ness and vigour returned

Have pity on me ' exclaimed Ronald observing with joy the signs of intelligence that again played over the lawyer's countenance, and resolving to make a last appeal to his compassion by yielding to his deep, unfeigned emotion have pity on a most unfortunate young man who has a long life—a life of infamy probably—before him and let me know the worst Speak' oh speak for the sake of that dread Being before whom you were but this moment on the point of appearance '

Ronald's knees gave way from beneath him as he spoke he knelt at the side of the couch and tears, the hot tears of agony streamed over his cheeks.

' Tears! exclaimed Grasp rising on his seat with more energy than before and looking stedfastly in the young man's face as though each drop gave him infinitely more pleasure than as many pearls beyond price could have done to the most avaricious miser why let them fall Ronald Minhurst for you are titled and wealthy yet have you no name no rank, no wealth' Illegitimate and a beggar is your father illegitimate, and a beggar is the son' Ha! ha' ha' the proud Lord Minhurst' He' he' he' the brave heir his son' Ho' ho' ho' for his fair sister!—she shall marry an earldom

Ronald buried his face in the bed and for a few moments sobbed convulsively as he thought of those so near to him and so dearly loved whose bright expectations were so unsurely founded and so fated to wither by the blight of fortune

' No' no' he almost thundered starting suddenly to his seat ' this infamy—this degradation—must not light on them '

' It will ' responded the dying lawyer in a tone as loud or louder than that of the vigorous and healthful youth ' She who wronged her who had a better claim to Minhurst and raised herself to an unsure eminence, shall fall therefrom and drag all with her—you your father, sister —

' It cannot be' we are not reserved for the shame of this disclosure

"It shall! it shall' roared Grasp I have taken measures I I - Ha' ha' ha'

His laugh was loud and discordant, and rang shrilly in the ears of Ronald, till a rush of blood rising to his throat changed the note of triumph into the silence of death

The short space of five minutes brought the mortal course of Gregory Grasp to its close His harsh features, distorted by suffocation, lay hideous and lifeless on a pillow saturated with the gore that oozed from his mouth Ronald turned from the disgusting spectacle to summon assistance and the artful Dobie seized the opportunity to replace the key in the pocket of his deceased employer

These papers said he hugging to his bosom the bundle he had taken from the coffer ' are worth their weight in gold Dobie Snitch if they don't make your fortune, you must be a precious fool, and no fib at all' '

Satisfied that the wretched man had ceased to breathe, Ronald rushed from the house much agitated by the scene he had witnessed, and but little forwarded in his search after information on the topic which was

No 17

nearest his heart　He walked rapidly towards the inn where he had left
his horse, and hastily mounting it　gallopped　homeward with all speed
It was not till he had advanced some distance　and found himself　in the
silence and darkness of an unfrequented bye road in the depth of a moon
less night, that he fully perceived how much additional light he had
gained by the recent interview　In the short space of two days his suspicions had been excited, increased　and were now terribly confirmed　-
confirmed not by that slight and ambiguous evidence barely presumptive
that leaves the sanguine mind still grounds for hope but by the testimony
of a competent witness and accomplice, delivered almost uncalled for,
and with the greatest freedom amidst the hurry, the anguish, the solem
nity of dying moments

His worse fears were now confirmed　they rested on facts　the nature
however of those facts had not been ascertained　he only knew that
they had existed in the past, but whether chronicled, or where and how
remained doubtful and obscure

As he passed rapidly along, the foremost and oppressing thoughts
present to his mind were anguish and disgust, excited by the discovery
of guilt in one he had been accustomed to view with reverence and much
affection

"There is no doubt of it　he exclaimed　'she　my own father s
mother !

And he rode on faster and faster till his horse chaffed and foamed
beneath　as if he sought by rapid motion to expel the agonising thought
from his mind

He came to a steep ascent, and was brought to notice surrounding
objects by the gasping of the panting animal　As he walked the horse
up the hill　he felt for the first time since leaving the lawyer s house
the night breeze cool and refreshing　to his fevered brow and suffered
his eye to rest on the composed and softened objects around him　The
heavens were now cloudless　the storm had cleared them of every vapour,
and from their surface of deep blue thousands of stars shed a soothing
and melancholy light　On reaching the summit, he brought his horse
to a halt　the animal turned towards the hedge to browse, and at length
placed his head over a style or gate　the one at which Evine and her
father had seen Edward Vivvan on the day that made them acquainted
with each other

The eyes of Ronald rested on the mansion of Minhurst　a dark out
line rising above the massive foliage of the valley in which it stood　The
sight awoke new thoughts, and though the new ones promised to afford
little comfort, they were yet a relief to the dark and horrible reflections
that up to that period had engrossed his mind　He thought of his father
and sister　they were reposing peacefully　happily in the midst of afflu
ence and rank, unconscious that they owed all, even the lowest necessary,
to ambitious crime

"Why am I entrusted with this dreadful secret ?　thought he　" 'tis
a cold philosophy which teaches us to regard the ills of life as wisely
designed　why am I exposed to this dreadful discipline ? why am I
doomed to this reverse of feeling which drives me to hate where I loved,

to view with abhorrence her I most esteem? why am I entrusted with the secret of her guilt, and made, oh bitterness! the messenger of guilt, beggary, and infamy to the unoffending the worthy? My home! my happy home! God, that my heart should sicken at the sight of it! no longer will it be to me the quiet resting place where worth and virtue contribute to enjoyment! It is another's a stranger's!'

He turned in despair from the tranquil landscape and rode away. In the midst of his anguish but one redeeming hope dawned upon his mind, but one rallying point appeared around which he could summon fortitude and resolution the accidents that made him a minister of ill tidings to his kindred made him a minister of justice to the wronged. He felt himself summoned to the arduous struggle between duty and inclination between broad inflexible right and the longings, the affections of human nature. But, alas! at what sacrifices was it to be sustained how would his heart bleed and sicken in the arduous contest!

As he rode up the broad avenue of the park, he lingered, reluctant to approach the home that a short time before he had sought with all the eagerness of pure affection. From one reposing beneath that roof he felt severed for ever the tie between them, that long years of intercourse had riven a day a night had violently and effectually sundered and but for others to whom his heart yet clung, he would have galloped from the spot to visit it no more.

For the sake of these he summoned up his energies, and sought, as the morning broke, a couch for the first time destined to be sleepless.

CHAPTER XV

Evine expected Edward with much impatience. Heavily went by the hours of the dreary day and drearier night that intervened between his departure and return. In obedience to his counsel they were spent in strict solitude. The reasons for this precaution were obvious it was the surest way to guard her from the attempts of her pursuers during the absence of her protector, and also the most effectual means of preventing those endless surmises the arrival of a young female in the company of a young man would most inevitably have given rise to in the small country town. The uncertainty he was in respecting the issue of his enquiries made him especially desire to avoid becoming a subject of slander in the neighbourhood. He knew that, if he failed to restore the father and child to each other, the latter would be dependant on him for existence, until some way of life suited to her sex and condition might present itself. At first he thought of procuring for her an immediate asylum beneath his mother's roof, but this idea, pleasant and proper as it appeared, a little reflection obliged him to abandon. The neighbourhood would, he feared, expose her to the inexplicable persecution already so dreadful in its effects and at the same time such a project would impose on his parent a burthen she was unable as he was satisfied she would be willing to bear   To make the poor forlorn girl the partner of his journey to London seemed the only course to be pursued did his enquiries prove fruitless but even this course became impracticable when the adventure of the ale house deprived him of his little means   On discovering that he was robbed of all his money he despaired for a moment of executing his generous project of standing by the mendicant s daughter in her trouble   Hope in a youthful breast is made, however of stubborn materials and it soon suggested new expedients   His small valise was examined, and the few articles of value his portable wardrobe could boast   articles procured by the only pardonable avarice, the avarice with which a parent amasses treasure to lavish it on his child   were instantly placed at the disposal of his unfortunate fellow traveller   From the hostess of the road side ale house he succeeded in obtaining in exchange for his watch decent garments for Evine with a change of linen and a trifle of money sufficient at least to procure them food and lodging during the few days he intended devoting to a diligent search after her father   Clad in her new attire which, though plain and coarse fitted neatly and aided the charms her discarded rags served to conceal Evine accompanied Edward to the nearest town   As her costume was not at all inferior in respectability to the worn suit in which the young man travelled for economy, it was agreed between them to pass for brother and sister and under that title he hired a room for his charge in a clean humble cottage where she might await his return in, at least outward tranquillity

Having completed these little arrangements Edward set out and as we have seen directed his first steps towards the cottage of his mother His chief object in so doing was to save her anxiety by forestalling any report that might reach her ears, and also by informing her of the true cause that delayed his journey to London

The result of this project the interview which took place, and its fatal consequences, have already been related

When Edward beheld the lawyer stretched at his feet apparently a corpse he reeled horror struck backward, and was only kept from falling to the earth by the trunk of the yew tree behind him   The shriek of his mother who, on hearing the report, had hastened to the spot recalled him to his senses   He clasped her fondly to his arms

' Mother I am guiltless ' ' said he

" Thank God ' exclaimed the widow, giving the readiest assent to a truth her heart wished to hear

In a few words she was told the whole particulars and learnt how strangely the pistol had exploded in the hands of the wounded man Mrs Vivyan had a vigorous mind in a moment the circumstance that preceded and accompanied the accident were present to her thought and she saw at once the equivocal and even dangerous position in which it placed her son   She also foresaw the part his affection for her would induce him to take in such an emergency, and in an instant, with admi rable presence of mind and resolution, she decided on the plan she would pursue

Edward!' she exclaimed in a composed tone, and looking steadily and affectionately in his pale horror stricken countenance " here is warm blood spilt on the graves of the dead   This is a solemn scene, my son

Mother, dear mother" sobbed the young man

' I see your heart, Edward   it is paralysed   it leaves you no power to act   I did not see him fall   I did not clasp his hand at the time as you did   I can therefore consider this horrid accident with more calmness than you are able to do   Not far from this spot are the remains of your father, Edward   as you revere the memory of the dead   as you reverence the request of one who though she is now alive to make it, must soon join him in his last cold bed   you must promise to do my bidding

' In this dreadful moment can I refuse you anything ?   I will do it to the letter, dearest mother

" My boy, my own boy' sobbed the distressed parent overcome by the grief she had so long struggled against   " you must away from hence immediately

" Mother, fly like a culprit ?

' Ay, like a culprit Edward, or break a mothers heart by suffering like one   Appearances are against you '

" Merciful God! exclaimed the young man in a tone of despair

" Fly, my son' fly''

A groan, a long drawn groan from the wounded man seemed to enforce the injunction, yet both stood rivetted to the spot   Footsteps and voices in the adjoining road were plainly heard

They come this way   fly' implored the widow in a whisper of agony

" Mother' sobbed he embracing her

" Tis not for ever   God will undertake for us, Edward   Begone'

The youth darted out of sight   When the men who discovered Grasp beneath the tree came to the widows cottage for assistance, they found her agitated   they had surprised her on her knees

It is time to leave this digression, and resume the thread of our story by returning to Evine

To a restless feverish night succeeded a long and anxious day   While the daylight continued however her countenance would from time to time brighten up as smiling through torrents of tears she pictured the pleasure of their meeting if Edward should indeed return in company with her poor father   Such reveries were not long entertained she justly feared they were too bright to be realised   She remembered that she had seen her parent struck to the earth   that Vivyan had reported him as seriously wounded when he left him in the wood to run to her rescue   and she felt it was indeed vain to hope that she would soon welcome him to her neat lodging which, poor and humble as it was, surpassed her highest conceptions of comfort and magnificence   Yet she thought if Edward returned with tidings of her father, the nature of his wounds, the place where he might be found how very gladly she would receive him, and how eagerly she would fly to comfort and succour the parent wounded in her defence

In alternate fear and hope the day glided away but the latter grew more and more faint as the shades of night fell round her   Ten o clock came and with it no Edward   The habits of the people of whom the lodging was rented required them to retire early and with an aching heart she complied with the regulation   The night, though spent in a bed softer and cleaner than she had hitherto known proved, however, a long and dreary vigil   Anxiously did she count the strokes of the neighbouring clock as they announced the flight of the hours and in vain did she spend the long intervals in intense listening to catch some sound or footfall that might betoken his approach   The new day dawned as the preceding one had closed solitary, and much more unhappy, she perceived the first sun beams struggling through the woodbine on the outside, and the small white curtains on the inside of her window   She heard the people of the house rise and commence their daily toil, and she too rose to be ready to give Edward welcome   Her first steps were directed to the little garden overlooking the road it was small and rustic, but gorgeous with blossoms dew drops, and sun shine   A mile of road could be seen from its gate, but no one traversed it   Disappointed and oppressed, she seated herself in the shade of a rude arbour here her attention was soon attracted by the rustling of boughs at her side she looked out a young man had just bounded over the hedge it was Edward   She flew to him, and her countenance better than words expressed the pleasure it gave her to see him   In silence he returned the grateful pressure she gave his hand, and leading her back to the arbour, sunk exhausted on the rude seat

"My father ? faintly articulated Evine

"My poor friend I bring you no tidings of him, ' said Edward

"Have you met with no means of tracing him ?

"None ! retnru ed the young man

Evine sunk on the seat opposite to the speaker, and the chill of despair seemed settled on her heart, till it found relief in a torrent of tears She would have indulged longer in this solace of the unfortunate, but she was drawn from her own grief by the sobs of her companion   She never remembered having seen a man weep and she looked at Edward, as stretched on the bench he fairly watered it with his tears, with the surprise a naturalist might be supposed to feel on discovering some new peculiarity in the animal he studied   Her own sorrows were in a moment forgotten for his advancing gently towards him, and placing her hand on his shoulder,

"Why do you weep thus ? ' she asked

There was so much gentleness in this show of sympathy, that it was unnoticed by Edward, in his torrent of passion overpowered and uncon scious of every thing around him, he writhed and sobbed convulsively

"My mother ! my poor mother' were the only words that Evine could distinguish   A conviction that some misfortune had befallen him, and that while exerting himself in her behalf, flashed across her mind.

'Pray speak to me!' she sobbed "let me know the worst, if I can not help you

This time she succeeded in attracting his attention   He looked up on her mild countenance deeply suffused with compassion, and imme diately rose, ashamed of the unmanliness into which the violence of his feelings and the weakness of his frame exhausted by the arduous efforts of the two last nights, had betrayed him   Her own suffering lost sight of she perceived for the first time his jaded and wretched appearance The handsome, neatly apparelled stranger she had met but two days before was not to be recognised in the pale, haggard countenance and dirty dress of the young man before her

"Whatever has happened was unavoidable   occurred while discharging my duty   I chiefly regret it as for some time at least it will deter me from seeking your father

Has anything so terrible happened

It is a long story   let us go into the house, and you shall hear the particulars dry your eyes, my good girl   your father is, I trust, alive, and let us hope will soon embrace his daughter again

If I could think so I would endeavour to be happy   But you are tired and hungry   I will prepare you some breakfast, and then listen to your story

They went into the house and notwithstanding his great exhaustion Edward could not forbear noticing the unaffected skill Evine displayed in arranging their humble meal   A female of the lowest class accustomed to an irregular life would have found fault with the cooking and service, yet were both performed with cleanliness and dexterity   But the charm of the repast consisted in the kindliness and grace of the young housewife   It was not sufficient to present the food to her deliverer with a beaming countenance but with earnest supplication she implored him to eat and looked on with solicitude as she perceived him reject the food long fasting had rendered necessary, but which excitement and anxiety made difficult to take   Often was the neglected mouthful allowed to cool on the fork while Edward attempted to begin the story of his adventures since they parted and as often did Evine refuse to listen until he had satisfied the demands of nature, and done due credit to her preparations for his repast   In these little disputes she proved victorious and when the meat had disappeared and the tea smoked in his cup, the young man was allowed to proceed with his narration   It excited the greatest interest in the listener   Her feelings were fresh and warm no long acquaintance or familiarity with the stirring events of life, either in reality or fiction had blunted their vigour, and they were very natu rally powerfully wrought on as she learnt to what extent of danger her preserver had been exposed in her cause   He dwelt as slightly as possible on the trying manner in which he had been forced to separate himself from his mother   nor was a long detail necessary to fix the attention of his youthful auditor   Her own situation was too similar to allow her to listen with unawakened sympathies to this part of his story   Indeed when we consider the obligations she was already under to Edward, his many qualities which alone rendered him an object of great attraction it will not be a matter of surprise that circumstances thus appealing to their filial sympathies became a firm bond of union with each and moved in its lowest depths the heart of one of the two whose sex and age ren deied her the weakest

A torrent of pure and youthful tears   early tears whose bitterness is so softened that in after life they become entitled to rank with our past pleasures   fell from the eyes of each as the speaker ceased, and the peculiarities of their mutual situation were presented in the most painful light to their minds   My father' 'My mother' they sobbed in concert with the childishness of spirit deep distress will ever impart And thus it was that they came to disregard that reserve of manner which some knowledge of the world had bestowed on Edward and the natural modesty of the sex lent to Evine   for when both felt most keenly the solitariness of their position, Evine found herself locked in the arms of Edward   and that by a movement so sudden and simultaneous that it would have been impossible to say which action took place first the extending of the arms or the rush towards them   But there they stood the streaming upturned eyes of the young girl meeting the down cast and melancholy glances of the young man both youthful, both un happy and each thrown as it were upon the other, the elder for comfort, the weaker for protection

You will not forsake me implored Evine with indistinct accents

' Never ' exclaimed Edward with vehemence, impressing a kiss upon her smooth forehead in confirmation of his word, an action into which he was betrayed by the impetuousness of his emotion

As fair a cheek as ever met the day buried itself in his bosom, to conceal that curious compound of modesty and feeling the first blush of maiden love

It is strange how our best moments are interrupted by the most trifling incidents of chance "There is a special providence in the fall of a sparrow, says Hamlet and judging from the circumstance that occurred to our young friends, the fall of a crushed sheet of paper may also have its special providence for when their embrace was fondest, and they were most drawn from outward objects to each other, a crumpled page fell to the ground from the bosom of Edward, and served to warn him of the dangerous nature of the emotion in which he was indulging The reader may probably wonder what could possibly endow a soiled paper with so high a mission it is fortunately in our power to enlighten him on the subject. It will be remembered that Grasp interrupted the interview between Edward and his mother at a most interesting moment to the young man—while the portrait of himself, sketched by the hands of Mira, formed the subject of discussion When the loud knocking of the lawyer drove Edward to his hiding-place, he took care to conceal the drawing, and a feeling of covetousness perhaps, as well as precaution, induced him to find a place of concealment for it in his own bosom There its shrunken proportions had reposed in entire security during the hurry and excitement of the events that followed, and now, for the first time, it made an unaccountable capricious attempt for liberty We will not waste our time in conjecturing the motives that induced the sketch to fall to the floor at that particular moment, but rather give our attention to the consequences of so unexpected a movement Edward stooped to pick it up, and conveyed it back to the place it occupied with something like precipitation As he did this, he sighed deeply, and gently disengaged himself from Evine s embrace Till that moment he had not questioned the propriety of the little display of feeling they had just enacted, but it now appeared to him in a light so improper and unbecoming, that he decided on bringing the scene to a close Such wonders may be effected by a piece of crumpled paper

" This will not do, said Edward, gently loosening the hold of Evine as the image of Mira came vividly to his mind, adorned with all the advantages of rank and education, and we need not say how unfavourably for the mendicant's daughter ' we must not suffer sorrow to weigh us down—to make us hopeless Take courage our prospects will brighten '

Evine raised her head as he spoke the blush still suffused her countenance a faint smile, symbol of hope and confidence, played round her lips and sparkled in her eyes, still moist with a lingering tear

She looked beautiful—exquisitely beautiful light locks of golden hair a transparent complexion tinged with the faintest pink eyes of the deep blue only to be seen in a tropical sky, and shaded by lashes that, at the will of their mistress, could convert their brilliance into the most voluptuous languor, and a slight form of perfect symmetry, formed a creature of rare loveliness   To these outward attractions, great in themselves, simplicity of mind and warmth of feeling lent an indescrib able fascination   and well occupied indeed must that heart have been that could long have resisted its magic influence   To be proof against such a combination of charms was no part of Edward s nature, and it might have been presumed that, thus entrusted to his protection, they would have weakened the passion he had already conceived for one im measurably beyond his reach   The romantic and unjustifiable affection he felt for Mira was, however, no love of *fancy*—no cold predilection to be effaced by the first object of superior beauty that came in his way The impression was heart-deep—graven on his mind with those indelible lines an ardent imagination is alone able to imprint or sustain   The rare beauty that stood before him was therefore powerless   he saw—he almost felt, but he dare not own the charms of Evine   His deeply rooted, though almost hopeless love of Mira, made her the only idol whom he would permit his soul to worship   Not so with Evine, whose affections had never been attuned to love   Such had been her chequered life, that hitherto she had seen few young persons of either sex, and had never conversed so long and intimately with any as she had done with Edward   and those occasionally thrown in her way, while she travelled with her father, had excited far more disgust than pleasure   Vivyan s worth was therefore as novel to her as it proved attractive, and had already sunk so deeply in her heart that, had a sudden separation parted them for ever, long years would not have sufficed to obliterate the im pression two days of intercourse had produced   Though, therefore, there was nothing harsh in Edward s manner when he saw fit to give another turn to their interview, yet without knowing why, Evine felt dissatisfied with the action which disengaged her arms, and the words that accompanied it

It was an undefined regret, unsupported by, but, nevertheless followed by a pang—a chilling dread of some future misfortune   This feeling was rendered with faithfulness by the countenance   but the heart s in terpreter is not always read with skill   and Edward was far from sus pecting what was passing in the mind of his companion   Had he done so, it is more than probable that he would have felt an additional motive for placing a restraint upon his feelings   Necessity, as well as prudence, put an end to their interview   It was impossible to prosecute his journey to London without means, and Edward s first object was, therefore, to endeavour to obtain some employment in the town or neighbourhood This delay was rather agreeable than otherwise   it kept both himself and companion on the spot, should any favourable turn occur in the for tunes of either   The first and most pressing difficulty to be met, was therefore to find the means of subsisting   After attempting to render himself as respectable as his scanty wardrobe permitted, he sallied forth into the town with this object

The town was not large, and all it possessed of wealth and bustle was exposed on either side of the long straggling street, through which ran

the high road between two of the most important cities of the kingdom
The only building approaching to a mansion scowled from the market
place in solitary grandeur, and one or two other edifices that seemed
greatly encumbered by additions, which the bettered circumstances of
their owners had enabled them to construct

This was discouraging for our young friend as it held forth little pro
spect of employment for a stranger   but on his way down the street he
passed several doors on which the word " Solicitor' seemed to invite his
entrance , he had gained the further end of it however before he could
conquer the repugnance he felt for his very necessary errand   He stopped
blamed himself, and again determined to make the effort   and though
these censures and resolutions within himself were not accompanied with
outward gesture, yet his thoughtful appearance attracted the attention of
one out of the few who passed him

This person was short and pertly   in excellent keeping, though not
clad in the most respectable attire   Indeed his apparel seemed to have
been selected from wardrobes of various dates, persons, and climes   his
hat and wig were of modern make, and the former would have better
suited the sconce of a younger man

'I beg your pardon,' said this odd looking personage   'you are from
London, I presume ?'

" I never was there,   replied Edward

" I hope no offence,   said the stranger   " I expected a young gentle
man—our leading man—he is two days later than he promised—a very
awkward circumstance—very awkward indeed "

Thereupon they separated, and Edward betook himself to accomplish
the object he had in view, smiling at being taken for a leading man,
without exactly knowing the import of the term

Resolved now to lose no more time, he boldly entered the door of the
first of these ' solicitor s offices that came in his way   On entering, he
contrived to get through a body guard of clerks and messengers, and
stood in the awful presence of the most experienced lawyer of the place
This gentleman had had considerable practice but his coffers were filled
and he now began to allow himself the enjoyment of well earned indul
gences   His practice had decreased   yet he still kept up the parade of
business, and Edward therefore found him more at leisure than the tur
moil of the outer offices led him to suppose   In a few words our adven
turer stated his business, and in return had to stand the probing of
twenty questions, in succession, uttered with great rapidity   This process
was undergone with heroism and as his replies were most satisfactory,
our hero became very hopeful as to the result of so much catechising
When, however, the enquirer seemed to have taxed his invention to its
uttermost, and perceived he had to deal with too acute a person to be able
to inflict on him a repetition of his question, he pushed his feet a little
farther into his Morocco slippers adjusted his morning gown, hemmed
twice or thrice, and in short as far as circumstances would permit went
through the various movements that are regarded by the profession as
preliminaries to a summing up

' Very sorry, Mr ——, I beg your pardon—your name is ? Exactly
sorry Mr Vivyan, to omit this opportunity of securing the services of
so clever a man of business but unrecommended as you are Sir and
inexperienced in the profession I could not in justice to my numerous
and increasing clients possibly come to an arrangement with you Good
morning, Mr Vivyan

The lined inner door and the heavy outer door closed upon the
young man, as with feelings gradually becoming less and less hopeful,
he took his way to the next legal practitioner s abode   Here he met
with no better success, and learnt that he owed the courteous audience
he had received at the preceding lawyer s to the leisure that gentleman
enjoyed owing to his rapidly declining practice, and that the young men
he had perceived idling about the place were employed more for display
than use

Determined to try them all, he proceeded with the like success to the
remaining offices, and at length stood with a trembling hand at the door
of the last   It was the last, yet Edward prepared to enter it with more
hope than he had approached either of the others   It was based how
ever on the slightest grounds—the recommendation of a neighbouring
practitioner

" Take my advice, said that gentleman go to Mr Chentless—he will be sure to employ you He has newly begun to practise and has leisure to train a clerk—to put a young man in the way, as it were I have no doubt, Mr Vivyan, you will be an acquisition to him

Away went Edward with this very pleasant information knocked at the door, was desired to enter, and made his bow before Mr Chentless

That gentleman was the son of a wealthy tradesman, for many years an alderman of the borough his wealth authorised him to bring his son up to a profession and that young man, after trying for many years to acquire a practice with but little success, had at length been unanimously elected mayor by the corporation He was now engaged in discharging his magisterial functions, and before him stood the remarkable personage who had accosted Edward in the street.

' And when do you open, Mr. Share ? said his worship

' As soon as my leading man arrives, said Mr Share, with a dignity very becoming his character and office as the manager of (to use his own words) a very respectable company of itinerant comedians

Depend on my patronage, Mr Share I am a friend to art in whatever vehicle it may be conveyed, and as a magistrate and a professional man shall always patronise the drama You may depend on one bespeak from me at least, Mr Share, said Mr Chentless, who having no business, conceived bespeaking an occasional play would add to his popularity

Mr Share bowed and prepared to withdraw

And now sir, I am at your service, said Chentless, turning to Edward, in a tone so very bland and obsequious, that it went against the young man s conscience to destroy the hope of a client by revealing the object of his visit Necessity, however is no bad orator and he spoke out The lawyer s countenance lost something of its radiance as he replied—

' It grieves me sir to say, that my limited practice precludes my making any immediate increase to my establishment '

I can work hard, and will work for little, said Edward using what his short experience satisfied him were the most powerful pleas that can be used on similar occasions

" I make no doubt of it, sir but I have no occasion for your services —none, I assure you Tom, the door Good morning, gentlemen.

Tom—a little imp lost in the obscurity of the apartment—opened the door and forth issued Edward with Mr Share at his elbow Overwhelmed with disappointment, and unable to decide on the quarter in which he could next make an application, Vivyan turned in the direction of his lodging A sigh occasionally escaped him as he strode rapidly on and when he thought himself unperceived he drew from his pocket their supply of cash—scarcely amounting, silver and copper to the value of half a crown—and contemplated the coin with the dull heavy despair of one exposed to deep and inevitable poverty He had scarcely given vent to his feelings in a brief ejaculation of despair before the little manager who had followed him at a short distance stood by his side Comparing what he had overheard in the office of Mr Chentless with the dejected appearance of the young man Mr Share had no difficulty in obtaining a tolerable insight into his circumstances

'Hard times these, observed Manager Share, unab   to resist any longer his desire to make Edward's acquaintance   "it is not an easy matter for a young man to make his way in the world now a days '

Edward sighed because he could not help doing so, and remained silent because he felt no disposition to encourage what he deemed an intrusion

'Mr Clientless might have given you something to do," continued the other   but I suppose he has not more business than he can manage A country town affords no opening to a young man. You should try London

"It was my intention to have done so, ' rejoined Edward, won over to good humour by the really considerate tone of his companion "cir cumstances, however, will not allow me to continue my journey '

"I fear you will not meet with much encouragement in this place, continued Mr Share.

'I have already met with much to discourage me   returned Vivyan

'Have you made many applications similar to that I witnessed ? en quired the manager

"I have visited every one in the town I thought likely to give me employment

Poor fellow ' I am very sorry for you '

Edward felt indignant at this communication   but a poor man is an object of pity and must learn to endure it

"Have you any encumbrance?   continued the other, after they had walked on a few paces without speaking, as if some project had suddenly occurred to his mind

"What do you mean ?   asked Edward

"In plain terms are you alone?

"It is my misfortune to have another dependant on my exertions

"Poor fellow ' When a young man s purse is low, he must not be very nice as to the means he employs to recruit it

No measure of distress can justify a dishonest action '

"Right young man ! you are very right   That has always been my maxim, through thick and thin and I have had my share of both, I assure you   When I said a young man should not be over nice, I did not mean to assert that he should do anything to compromise his prin ciples No ! no ! I am not the man to say that   But there are certain prejudices, very respectable no doubt, when we can afford them, which must be held lightly if they stand in the way of our bread and cheese— do you understand me, young man ?

'I think I do and wish I could see as clearly how your remark bears on my case   I would sacrifice my oldest and dearest prejudices, if, by so doing I could make my way honestly

"I thought you would say so   I knew you to be a sensible fellow, when I took you for my leading man, at the end of the town an hour or two ago   Now, if you only act up to what you profess, I think that I can do something towards assisting you

"If you can procure me employment, I shall be obliged to you for ever.

Manager Share retired a pace or two from Edward, and both came to a halt. The latter underwent a complete scrutiny from head to foot and that over, the comedian throwing himself into a dignified attitude, continued,

"You will do—admirably well—I am sure of it Good figure—expressive countenance—tuneful voice—the best qualifications! Oh, you will be sure to do!'

"For what, pray ?' enquired Edward

' Would you like to try the stage young man ?

"I have no such ambition,' rejoined Edward with a smile at the idea of turning actor

' No doubt! no doubt! I know what people think of my profession and to be candid with you, from what I know of it myself, I cannot censure them   But if your circumstances are bad as they appear to be, the little remuneration I could give would perhaps be an object

Edward thought of his disappointment that morning he remembered his low purse and Evine occurring at the same time to his mind, he was induced to enquire,

"And if I consent, what will be my duties ? for, to say the truth, I am such a novice in the world s ways, that I never witnessed the performance of a play '

' No !' exclaimed Share with astonishment, for being the descendant and heir of a manager, he had scarcely an idea of existence without plays and play acting "never seen a play! that is against you, to be sure you will have all the stage business to learn—but never mind—we ll see what you can do

"Your proposition is a kind one it requires, however, a little consideration before I can accept it

"Certainly it does   This is my lodging walk in no ceremony, I beg '

Edward entered the manager s home, and left it a most reluctant recruit under the banners of Thespis

---

CHAPTER XVI

NEARLY a week had elapsed since the interview described in our last chapter, during which period the arrangements for opening a theatrical campaign in the town of S—— had advanced rapidly   This event was attended with all the difficulties and disasters peculiar to undertakings of such paramount importance   Innumerable were the vexations and disappointments Mr Share had to contend with in his attempt to metamorphose a large, dreary dilapidated barn into what the bills termed a commodious, elegant, well aired, and splendidly illuminated theatre   In due time, however, the perseverance and enterprise of that gentleman accomplished the wonderful change Rows of seats rose one above another to a perilous height in the portion of the barn, ycleped house for the time being devoted to the audience Saw dust and red cloth denoted the boxes saw dust and old cloth distinguished the pit, while the gallery was only denoted and distinguished by the extreme roughness of the unplaned boards prepared for the reception of the gods

While the theatre was gradually approaching a state of completion, the company arrived one by one in the town They were certainly shabby enough in their apparel but by no means deficient in the dignity required for the due enacting of regal and other grand parts But, amidst the accomplished band, as the manager having examined their respective merits termed them to be, no leading man was to be found How to get on without a leading man was a question that baffled a managerial saga city that had never learnt in the metropolis how to gull an audience Ldward, destined at first for a subordinate part, having acquitted himself so much to the satisfaction of his employer at an early rehearsal, was looked upon as the person best calculated to extricate them from this dilemma

The next difficulty was to fix on an opening piece that might suit the powers of the new actor

" You will find it hard work to study a long part by Monday,' observed Mr Share 'you are so little acquainted with plays, that I presume you cannot be more familiar with one than another ?

" A volume of Shakespere once fell in my way," replied Edward " I read, and read it, until I had every line in my memory With this ex ception I know nothing of the drama."

" Shakespere ! Not so bad We might open with one of old Billy s stirling pieces What plays did the volume contain ?'

" Antony and Cleopatra -

" Antony and Cleopatra ! Stuff and nonsense ! Shakespere never wrote anything about Antony and Cleopatra You mistake, young man, it could not have been a volume of Shakespere

Edward smiled at the manager s lore in dramatic literature, and would have attempted to make him wiser, had not Mr Share spared him the difficult task by enquiring what other plays were in the volume aforesaid

' King Lear, Hamlet   was the reply

" King Lear won't do we havs no ladies good enough to play the women Hamlet let me see Polonius myself Richardson the king Miss Drawley the queen yes, Hamlet s the play Do you think you are studied in the part ?

" There is not a scene in the play but I know

" What every scene the whole play ? '

" The whole play '

" Well ! you are a clever fellow, that s all Learn a play by heart ! why I never read one through from beginning to end in my life You will soon be on the London boards at that rate It is decided then that Hamlet shall be the play I ll make out the cast and the town shall be billed to morrow Here Richardson ' ' continued the manager calling to a very thin man that was scraping away on a violin at one of the wings "this is Mr —what shall we call you Sir—your theatrical name, you know ?

' Somers, said Edward, mentioning the first that came to his mind

"Very good Mr Somers will play Hamlet on Monday, when we open and you will have your old parts in the piece The gentleman is a novice so you must oblige me by going through the business with him

The actor put down his instrument to signify his consent, and manager Share wishing both a good morning withdrew to attend to other duties

"If you are walking my way," said Richardson to Edward, " we will go over the scenes at my lodging it is rather more comfortable than this barn "

To this proposition Edward readily assented, and during their walk he had an opportunity of observing more attentively his companion Mr Richardson engaged to do the low comedy in the company of manager Share, was one of the most singular as well as one of the poorest follow ers of Thespis He had served twice an apprenticeship to his profession, on every kind of stage from a barn to a theatre royal In every situation he met with a considerable share of success, for he had talent to win the admiration of his audience, and good fellowship to gain the esteem and even affection of his comrades yet now that the prime of his professional course was attained, he could command no engagement more profitable than a share in a company of strollers A fellow of infinite mirth, his excentricity was his bane Strangely allied to a rich store of comic hu mour, he had an irresistible penchant for the horrible As a clown, or a demon, he was admirable on the stage, and to crack a joke over the bottle, or assist at an execution, formed his favourite amusements in real life This strange combination of fancies imparted a singular and almost wild diversity to his appearance When silent and thoughtful, his irre gular features, sallo complexion, and lanthorn jaws, made a most pitiable object to look upon yet in livelier moments his physiognomy was as laughter inspiring and irresistible as ever was Grimaldi s in his blithest days This peculiarity of character had a powerful influence on his conduct it presented opposites as wide and as sudden , the friends he acquired to day he lost to morrow, and that through some caprice of humour which had nothing to do with his heart that ever beat truly to those for whom he professed attachment It was, in a word, the unhappy lot of Maurice Richardson to pass his days in lightening the moments of thousands, while ne dragged miserably through life in poverty and distress

He lodged at a small publichouse, an asylum preferred by men of his peculiar calling and temperament as tending to increase the kind of popularity which ensures a bumper on a benefit night No sooner were our histrions—for even Edward must for a time come under this deno mination seated themselves in the sanded room constituting Richardson s domicile, than a soiled newspaper, a day or two old, attracted the notice of Vivyan

"Excuse me,' said he, taking it up with eagerness "here should be news to interest me

No 19

Oh play don t mind me ! said Richardson who to amuse himself
the while, drew his violin from a bag that had once been of a very res
pectable green baize but now of a very yellow hue, and began to rosin
the bow, and tune the instrument

With an agitation that brought the blood to his cheeks, Edward
glanced rapidly down the columns of the paper   Not one was omitted
but all the eloquence and wisdom of the provincial press lavished on any
event however important, would not have detained him in his desire to
find some paragraph relating to the event which had so materially changed
his fortunes

Excited indeed was he when he at length read the words, 'Inquest
on the body of Gregory Grasp Esquire Solicitor   &c

His eyes ran hastily over the depositions   they were numerous, and
seemed to justify the verdict

Thomas Dobbs constable of Minhurst parish, was first sworn   he
deposed that, on the night of the great storm he was called up by James
Wright and Edward Willis who informed him they had just discovered
a man severely wounded in the churchyard   On going to the spot he
recognised the lawyer of the neighbouring town whom he had frequently
met at justice meetings   he was not dead   they bore him to the nearest

cottage, where he recovered his senses and earnestly begged them to convey him home they then procured a cart, and his wounds having been dressed by the surgeon of the place, he was taken to his own house in P——, where he left him in the hands of his family

James Wright and Edward Willis were next sworn their evidence corroborated that of the constable Deceased appeared sensible of what was taking place around him and made efforts to speak he was however unable to utter anything more than a request to be taken home this he urged earnestly they heard nothing from him that could throw any light on the fatal deed there were no footsteps to be traced near the tree under which he was found the rain fell in torrents witnesses produced a pistol found very near the body of the lawyer he was living when they took him to his house

The landlord of a small house of entertainment at Minhurst stated on oath that lawyer Grasp had put up at his house on the same evening he partook of some refreshment, and left his horse, stating he had some business in the village which might detain him an hour or two before half that time had expired witness was called upon to procure a cart to convey the wounded man to town

The evidence of the surgeon proved that death had been caused by the wounds such wounds might have been inflicted by the deceased himself witness knew the pistol produced by Wright and Willis to be deceased's property he had sold it to Mr Grasp some time before

Mr Dobie Snitch and Mrs Deborah Swill, managing clerk, and housekeeper of the late Gregory Grasp, deposed to the wounded condition in which deceased was brought home on the night of his death they had caused no medical attendant to be summoned his wounds were dressed and his case considered hopeless deceased was sensible before he died said nothing respecting the events of the night was busily engaged in conversing with a strange gentleman the interview was private deceased expired during the interview witness had observed nothing unusual in their master's behaviour knew of no occurrence likely to have driven him to the commission of a rash act when he left home he was in good spirits believed he had been absent from home a long time on the preceding night could not say where he had been, or for what object did not know the gentleman who was with their master when he died had never seen him before supposed him to be a client

he left the house abruptly during the confusion caused by the deceased's death deceased never rode out at night without arms

James Hodge, a labourer, swore that he had seen the deceased in company with some strange looking men on the night before his death met them in a bye road it was then past midnight the men seemed to be in liquor and were at high words with deceased heard them say they had done their best to carry off the girl threatened they would do for him (Grasp) if he did not keep to his word deceased promised to see them the next night witness swore positively to the last fact

Several other witnesses were called, who swore that on the evening of his death deceased was in a sound state of mind, and betrayed no dejection that would lead them to suppose he contemplated self destruction

The jury, after some hesitation, returned a verdict of Murder committed by some person or persons unknown

The perusal of this report by no means promoted Edward s tranquillity There was something dreadful in thus reading over the circumstances of an event already graven on his memory with the deep impress of horror It was painful to bear in his mind the frightful detail of that catastrophe but it became deadly so when he found that those details, as collected and examined by the appointed authorities brought them to form an opinion injurious to his own fair name and safety   Such, however, was the result of the inquest a verdict of murder had been given   It was an additional matter of grief to Edward to find that public opinion attached suspicion to parties who were in no degree concerned in the event.   It was very evident that the verdict of the jury was based principally on the deposition of Hodge   and the companions of Grasp on the night before his death would be sought after as the supposed perpetrators of the crime   Overwhelmed by these considerations, which flashed almost instantaneously across his mind as he finished his reading he let the paper drop, and seemed plunged in the painful abstraction of bewildering thought

Richardson soon noticed this singular deportment, and, in his turn letting both hands fall to his side one holding the bow and the other the violin with an extravagant stage grimace rendered natural by long habit consisting of a lowered jaw and raised eyebrows intended to indicate surprise, he gazed in silence on his new friend   Finding Edward s fit of abstraction likely to put his patience and curiosity to a severe test,

" A friend dead ʼ he ventured to enquire

" No ʼ   replied Vivyan aroused only to relapse into deeper reverie

" A friend married perhaps? asked the comedian, betraying by the question no very elevated notion of the matrimonial state

' Neither ʼ worse my good friend much worse ʼ

Richardson shrugged his shoulders, and then raised his violin to the proper position for playing   He thought it useless to interfere further, as any calamity more grievous than death or matrimony was utterly beyond his conception

Do I disturb you ? said he, as he drew his bow across the strings, at the time directing towards Edward a very grotesque look, that never theless was inspired by very sincere compassion

" Not at all my good friend   I fear you will find me a dull scholar just now—I have seen news that ruffles me   If you please, we will post pone the duties that brought me here another hour or two "

" When you like Sir   If I can assist you in any other way, I shall be glad   said Richardson once more desisting from his musical exercise " if you can make any use of me do now I beseech you

There was so much sincerity and cordiality in the tone of the actor, that Edward returned his offer with a heavy pressure of the hand an action that is very often useful in carrying off the overflowings of the heart

Not now my good friend, said he

Well then, don t make it late before you come again that s all I have to say   I expect a glorious night of it in the little parlour of the King s Head   snug party of us   two lawyers clerks, and an auctioneer   nothing but choice spirits there   so don t make it late it   Sir

Edward gave his word   and hastening from the apartment, sought to soothe and relieve his mind in the solitude of the fresh green meadows surrounding the town

He strolled about till dusk—now revolving the particulars of his situ ation   and now finding it impossible to fix on any immediate and decisive point of action   striving to banish the incidents of the past few days by giving up his mind to the study of the part he was to enact   Even the verse of Shakspere, and the absorbing interest of Hamlet, were insuffi cient to draw off his attention from realities   and by turns, his mother, lonely and anxious—the innocent men who were no doubt suspected by the jury as the murderers of Grasp, and his own circumstances so equi vocal so distressing and so unmerited, pressed painfully upon his mind At times he was on the point of going off at once to his mother to ease her anxiety by his presence   but he dreaded to approach the spot, lest he should awaken suspicion   and he was further deterred by the recollection that, to absent himself at that time, would be throwing away the only opportunity he had of succouring the unhappy Evine   Another time he thought of hastening to a magistrate, and stating the whole transaction and the share he had borne in it   But the terrors of justice impartial and inflexible, judging from facts, requiring blood for blood   would then occur to overturn his resolution   and he abandoned as rash a project that at first appeared just

" I would see no man suffer, he reasoned " and remain silent   No ! the moment suspicion attaches itself to any one and drags him to the bar, I will speak, to save him from unjust punishment   But why should I an innocent man, unluckily accused by appearances, run madly to my own ruin   when it can benefit no one ?

Notwithstanding this conclusion, night came on before he could release his mind from the weight that oppressed it   Innocence, however, will rally in spite of all oppression, and go forward in the dawnless pride of her inexhaustible resources

The hurry attendant on the opening of the theatre and his first appear ance   with his anxiety to succeed for the sake of the paltry emolument a'tached to success, confined his attention to duties connected with his new vocation   during the few days that ensued   At length the eventful night arrived   the penny candles flared in their tin chandeliers   the bassoon from the church, and the clarionet from the chapel, grumbled and squeaked in harmony with Mr Richardson s fiddle   smock frocks filled the gallery, and smart gentry the boxes   actors and actresses were capering gaily behind the curtain, the ominous bell rang, the music and talking subsided, and in all the stateliness of tragedy in a barn the piece began

The whole entertainment went off to the great satisfaction of the audience, who declared to a man   that they had never laughed so much in all their lives   The success of the evening procured for Edward an eng igement in the company   and the promise of a free benefit—terms that p omised to supply the immediate necessities of himself and Evine

CHAPTER XVII

In a small domain shut in on all sides by a circle of diminutive hills, well wooded, and watered by a silvery stream was situated Tranquil Dale, the residence of Sir Matthew Melter   In the little parlour opening on the lawn sat Miss Merriville, the worthy Sir Matthew, and his somewhat antiquated sister Miss Clothilda Melter

'Dear me, brother ' I hear a carriage driving up the avenue,   ex claimed the latter lady

Mira Minhurst, I declare, and alone too ' ' ejaculated Marian, rushing on the lawn to meet her friend, without waiting for the formality of an announcement

If you please we will not go into the house immediately,   said Mira, as the two friends embraced each other   my visit is to you and as the weather is so fine, we can talk in the grounds   and to tell you the truth, I am gratified at your thus having given me this opportunity, for I am in such low spirits that I do not wish to meet your aunt and uncle

'What has happened, my dear Mira ?   Is your brother worse since we last met ?

'Poor Ronald ' he grows worse and worse every day   But that is not it   In fact Marian, I scarcely know where to begin—we are all in sad confusion at home

' A few weeks ago, when your grandmother and Mr Ronald arrived, you seemed all so happy '

' Alas ' how little we know what is for our advantage   Their arrival, to which my father and I looked forward with so much pleasure, has been followed by a succession of nothing but unpleasantness '

"I am surprised to hear you say so   your brother has been successful in his opposition to Mr Fluentleigh   surely you must feel proud to have a brother so young returned to the senate of his country

I would rather see him in good spirits than a prince of the blood, Marian   You saw Ronald when he came to Minhurst   what did you think of him—I mean with respect to his disposition ?

" He seemed to me the merriest and freest person I ever met

' And so he was, Marian a gay, joyous creature, and as free from care as his noble nature deserved to be   The change in his demeanour is unaccountable

" What is the cause of his melancholy ? '

I canot divine   All the family remark it, but none have been able to obtain his confidence   When questioned, he complains of slight indisposition and turns away   indeed something seems to deprive him of all energy, and, alas his rallying seems hopeless '

' Have you no suspicions, dear Mira ? '

" Marian, you are my only friend—I come to you to unburthen a sor rowful heart—I know you will not shun my confidence

The two friends kissed each other   and, entering a bower, Miss Mer

riville requested Mira to keep her no longer in such needless and ago
nizing suspense

"It is very painful to feel coldly towards those we ought to love yet,
Marian, I cannot, dare not love Lady Minhurst!

I am hardly surprised to hear you say so, Mira—she was a long
while at variance with your father

"Would they were still at variance! Avowed enmity is better than
the intimacy now subsisting between them '

' She does you no harm, I hope ?

'Me? No! yes! At any rate I intend to defend myself But you
shall hear that part of my story presently I felt love, much love, for
my grandmother, when on the morning of her arrival she treated us with
kindness and affection Alas! a few days made a great alteration in my
sentiments My brother grew pensive, gloomy, and on more than one
occasion displayed a vehemence of manner that was alarming Unable
to obtain his confidence, I resolved to watch his conduct when I soon
observed that he shunned always, and evidently with intention, the so
ciety of her ladyship I saw she noticed this, and that it gave her pain
—more than pain perhaps—for, Marian, I have seen her lips and cheeks
blanched and ashy white I have seen her tremble when she has chanced
to meet the stern, searching glance of Ronald Is it not dreadful ?

It does not strike me as singular that the Viscountess should view
with solicitude on your brother s altered manner

' But to quail before him, as I have seen her do, Marian? Oh, I
have terrible suspicions! There is something rankles in the heart of
Ronald that he dares not bring to light and it must concern my grand
mother, or his open nature would not retain it to oppress and harrass
him

"Do not torment yourself by suspicions wait for facts before you
judge harshly of the Viscountess

"Have I not facts, Marian? do I not see my own brother pining
under dreadful depression, and can I not trace the cause of it to my
grandmother? I was taught to believe he loved her, and I find them
shun each other! I am very unhappy

Here Mira hid her face in the bosom of her friend, and indulged in a
hearty flood of tears

' Cease, dearest Mira pray cease this weeping " said Miss Merri
ville, with the thousand affectionate caresses women love to interchange
' consider you may be putting a wrong construction on appearances
you are unable to account for Perhaps your brother s melancholy may
be produced after all by some romantic love affair I do not see that
you have cause to consider yourself so very unhappy "

' Alas! I have not told you all Were my suspicions as far from the
truth as your friendship would wish me to suppose, this proud, imperious
woman—

" Mira! Is it from you that I hear this language—and applied to so
near a kinswoman ?

' Do not think it so strange '' continued the peer s daughter with
bitterness " when our dearest privileges are inroaded, we easily forget

the courtesy due to those who have done us the wrong   Lady Minhurst would control my heart dictate to my affections, Mirian—aye, would betray me into a marriage with a man I loathe '

You Mira, with so kind a father to protect you ?   Impossible !"

Lord Silvester Sil'iton has become my avowed suitor !

' I heard such a report but rejected it as absurd

" You did wrong   he will soon be my accepted suitor, and, God knows how soon, my husband !

" Nonsense, Mira ' If you go on in this strain, I shall think you are mad indeed   Lord Minhurst would never impose such a trial on his daughter !"

' Alas, he must not know the pang it costs me ! I must wed this man with a cheerful face, Marian   at least so declares my grandmother '

" You will make me even hate her, if you tell me so   What reason does she give in support of this strange request ?

" Heavy pecuniary embarrassments ' I do not understand it but I am told that my father s present retired mode of life is consequent upon breeches made upon his fortune by early prodigality in short I am given to understand that my father is a ruined man if I do not con sent to this hopeful alliance !

' Incredible '

' So I have thought so I fondly still think but who is to satisfy me on that point ? '

" Your father himself !

" You do not know how good he is, or you would not say so   He would suffer the shipwreck of his fortunes a thousand times before he would make my happiness the price of their preservation yet it is a price I would make with pleasure, Marian, could I be persuaded that all is right.

" Consent to nothing, my dear friend, till you see clearly the circumstances of the case

" Lord Silliton s father presses the match   They talk to me inces santly of an earldom, jewels, and mansions, as if they could inspire affection, till I sicken with disgust Who can I consult for information ?

" If you cannot apply to his lordship, I should say your brother is the most eligible person you could fix on for an adviser in this emergency

" I have longed to do so but when I find him weighed down by his own sorrows, my heart will not allow me to burthen him with mine

" On the contrary your confidence would perhaps divert his mind from the subject he dwells on so intensely

" Do yo think so ?'

" I am sure of it   Come, Mira, I must insist on your taking this step nay, if you wish it I will return to Minhurst with you, to see that you follow my advice I can return with my aunt and uncle, who are invited there to dinner What do you say to my proposition ? '

In a few moments the young friends were in the carriage

" I have a call to make, said Mira, " I know you will bear me com pany '

It was a golden morning   The sun threw on every object its most brilliant light. The grassy graves, richly enamelled with summer flowers, seemed enviable resting places: and a thousand insects so light in form and so gorgeous in colouring, as to appear like the denizens of a brighter purer world, buzzed over them in gay and sprightly dances. The door of the church was open to give admittance to the children of the school, the majority of whom were making the sojourn of the dead resound with their youthful voices. As the young ladies advanced towards the widow's cottage, they perceived Ronald entering the church by the door appropriated to the use of the school.

"It is my brother!" observed Mira.

'You cannot have a better opportunity of making your sentiments known to him. Take courage Mira, go to him at once and ask his advice.'

In a few moments the light step of Mira was heard in the aisle of the church, as she sought her brother. They met at the further end, behind the altar, in a deep recess that in Catholic times had been a chapel dedicated to the Virgin, and which contained the monuments of the Mnlhurst

family. Mira reached the chapel by one of the side aisles and, being struck by the pensive appearance of her brother, whom she found leaning on the monument of the late Viscount, paused before she entered

No 20

Monuments of every description crowded the walls on either side a fantastic collection of cold white devices here and there relieved by larger sculpturings proudly reared their giant and spectral imitations of the human frame   Among these, so still and thoughtful, that but for the dark hues of his garments he might have been taken for one of them, stood Ronald his head inclining downwards, and his eye fixed intently on a large slab in the centre of the pavement   A solitary sun-beam, that by some strange circumstance forced its way through the thick foliage gilded as with molten gold that part of the flooring, and gave great prominence to the solitary word—for the rest of the inscription was lost in the shade—EVINE

Mira gazed alternately on her brother and on the word that so powerfully engrossed his attention but unable to trace any connexion between the living and the dead, she ventured, after some minutes of exemplary patience, to enter the chapel and disturb the dreamer

Ronald started as she placed her hand on his shoulder the eyes of both brother and sister met a pale and anxious countenance, that brought to each an instantaneous conviction of their being united in the brotherhood of misfortune   A fond embrace followed and tears exchanged by the persons who shed them glistened on the cheek of either

"Why are you so melancholy ? asked Mira the object of her visit being for the moment far from her thoughts

"Is it singular, my dear sister to be so when we commune with the dead ?' replied the brother

"You are as melancholy when you mix with the living ! ' dear Ronald

' I have greater reason perhaps,   fell faintly from the lips of the young man, and both were silent   There was a pause of some minutes during the interval Ronald s eyes wandered towards the slab, and rested on the inscription as intently as before

"Why do you look so fixedly on that tomb, Ronald ?

' There is a story connected with it, ' he observed starting at the question, and turning his eyes with an expression of deep melancholy on the enquirer

"What is it ?   asked the sister

' It is too dark a tale for your ears, dearest   God keep you from the knowledge of such deeds, Mira ! '

The tone of the speaker went to the young lady's heart.   She looked at him fondly and searchingly—then added, with slow emphasis,

"Is it the cause of your distress of mind Ronald ? '

" The dead affect me but little,   he replied evasively

'What is it then ?   Why are you so sad and unhappy ?

"Am I sad ?   Then bad spirits seem to have fallen on us all   you are not so light hearted as you were when I first saw you, Mira   It is not a month since and the change is very great !

Mira looked down, and a blush covered her pale cheek   her brother continued,

' You are blushing, Mira   and I owe to certain rumours and conversations my suspicion from what cause that blush arises   I hope however Lord Silliton is not the object of your unhappiness

The ice was fairly broken, yet Mira had not composure or presence of mind to enter into a formal statement of her case

"Dear Ronald, tell me truly, what *you* think of such an alliance?' she exclaimed

There was a simplicity and earnestness in this appeal which brought a deeper shade over the young man s brow

"Will you give a sincere answer to a plain question?' he enquired after a pause

"There s no question my brother could ask that would be answered otherwise

"You are saying a great deal, Mira   The human heart will have its secrets the heart of woman especially claims the privilege of silence on a subject that touches it most nearly   To that my question refers, and unless it meets the most candid reply I must withold all advice on this important step

"Speak, Ronald   In all things you may rely upon my candour '

'I will then venture to ask you, Mira, a question, which I could not put to another of your sex for fear of tempting them to falsehood   Is your heart free have you never yet seen the man to whom your affect ions cling with unconquerable energy?

"Never ! replied Mira, in the clear, firm accents of decision

"Then I would advise you to accept the proposals of Lord Silliton Do not interrupt me, Mira   I can interpret your heart that shudder as I pronounced his name, tells me what I before felt sure of that you do not love him   Nay, do not weep or you will drive me to suppress the severe things I ought to say   If your heart was engaged, my dear Mira, I would deprecate this step, because I believe passion is invincible, and am persuaded a union with another, while love exists is incompatible with happiness   But *your* affections are disengaged the duties of a wife will keep them so in time perhaps fix them on your husband   Again you tremble   You can never love him, you would say   Perhaps not. Do you then see no attraction in an earldom and wealth that baffles calculation? '

"They have no value to me, Ronald, unless they can confer happiness on those I love you know they have not   You think you have read my heart because my girlish weakness betrayed me into a tear, a shudder Mind, Ronald   I have not opened my lips to say I approve or disap prove this marriage and you have no right to suspect what I do not choose to reveal   But enough of this   In your turn, answer me as candidly as *I* have answered you does anything affect the fortunes of our family threaten my father s honour or comfort?

' All before us is uncertain, Mira, ' replied the brother, relapsing, as though the speaker had struck some harsh chord in his bosom, into his most dejected manner

"This is evasion, Ronald, not reply   I have dealt sincerely with you will you not do the same with me?   Do you treat me as one whose girlish fears cannot sustain the shock of what you have to reveal ? or do you think so lightly of me as to suppose that I am not ready to make any sacrifice that

Sacrifice!' interrupted Ronald clasping his sister to his bosom and bathing her in a torrent of scalding tears my poor Mira we are all called to a dreadful sacrifice! Heaven help you to endure your part!

Pray be calm my dear brother you frighten me

'Calm! impossible! the dead the dead are opposed to our tranquillity!' and insensibly his eyes again rested with the fixed and frightened glare of an astounded man on the inscription

"There is a dreadful mystery in all this said Mira "Ronald! dear Ronald! my brother! He does not hear me that stare that insensibility! this is madness! Oh who can help him!

With these words she hastened from the chapel in search of assistance for the unfortunate young man whose state of mind fell little short of her fears

At the door of the church Mira met Lady Minhurst The death of lawyer Grasp soon reached the ears of the Viscountess, and it was not without reason she regretted the death of so valuable an agent She deplored this accident the more as it seemed to overturn the plans she had formed for her own security These plans rested wholly on the power she could obtain over the person of Evine In Grasp she had lost the only person she could entrust with an enterprise she had no means of conducting alone While in extreme perplexity and indecision she recalled the scene that had taken place at the widow's cottage on the last morning of Grasp's life She remembered his accusing the widow's son of carrying off Evine, and concluding that he would be likely to communicate with his mother she determined to see the widow at the earliest opportunity and was just leaving Mrs Vivyan's cottage after a very unsuccessful visit as Mira came out of the church

Lady Minhurst was the last person Mira wished to meet for she well knew the presence of that lady would aggravate rather than allay her brother's distemper So greatly however had her fears been excited by their recent interview—so lively were the apprehensions she entertained for his sanity, that she had neither the prudence nor patience to delay her application for assistance till she met with a person better qualified to give it

Pray go to Ronald my lady said she advancing rapidly towards the Viscountess "his state is dangerous—I am sure it is Pray go to him!

Ronald in danger! How? where is he? asked the astonished lady

' In the church among the old monuments Oh! I have seen him weep torrents of hot tears! now, he seems to have lost all consciousness —does not heed me when I speak to him, but raves wildly of the dead

Of the dead? repeated her ladyship in a tone that sounded to Mira more like terror than astonishment I will go to him Your friend Miss Merriville waits for you at the widow's cottage you will do well to join her Trust me I will see to Ronald and with hasty steps she sought her distracted grandson

Notwithstanding this injunction Mira would have followed but she

was deterred by an authoritative wave of the hand peculiar to her lady
ship which never failed to secure obedience The young lady loitered
a few minutes in the churchyard to gain composure before she joined her
companion A few tears relieved her mind and having executed her
errand at Mrs Vivyan s, she hastened with Miss Merriville to the
carriage

What does your brother advise dear Mira? enquired the latter
when they had rode about a mile in silence

When Lord Silliton does me the honour of proposing, he will be
accepted was the reply

CHAPTER XVIII

RONALD continued for a long time in the position in which Mira had
left him his mind brooding as intensely on one torturing thought as his
eyes gazed with vacant stare on one chosen object Not a word fell
from his lips, but a long weary argument—weary because it led to no
conclusion—was carried on in his mind It would not bear utterance
the thoughts occurred too rapidly were at times too confused, and at
others too dreadful yet as far as words can be symbols of mysterious
thought the following may possibly give the reader an idea of that inward
conflict

It requires no further proof, said he to himself "the crime is
evident I know not the details I desire them not the certainty of the
deed is sufficient My heart sickens at my wretched lot ! God knows,
I care little for the proud honours to which I fancied myself born I
have little ambition and could have passed my days blessedly content in
an obscure and honest condition But to be raised thus high—to sink
in the social grade—sink how low? Oh God ! so low as to have no
claim not even the smallest on the world s respect so low as to become
the object of its scorn illegitimate, base born a usurper of titles not
my own Had a strange hand brought this misfortune on me and did
it light only on myself I could have bowed to it with submission But
my father s mother ! the bosom on which I have nestled to harbour
thoughts thus villanous ! My father, too left nameless, destitute in his
old age my poor and guiltless sister, deserving the happiest lot on
earth, driven to seek a provision for her necessities at the price of her
heart s liberty her bosom s peace ! All this sum of misery can only be
avoided by giving the preference to guilt—by burying this secret in my
breast and retaining wealth and honours not my own retaining them
while those who can assert a truer claim wallow in poverty and crime !
No ! no ! I cannot stoop to that Yet what motives urge me to it ?—
a father s peace, his mother s reputation my own sister s welfare !
Merciful powers ! how have a few days embittered my whole course of
life !

Thoughts like these, and many more, had passed through the mind of

Ronald before he was discovered by Lady Minhurst   His appearance made her hesitate to intrude on his solitude   It indicated a wretchedness of mind that awakened in her bosom the worst fears   She had noticed his melancholy from its commencement   a gloom so deep in one so young she felt convinced could proceed from no slight cause   and if at times it occurred to her that it might be caused by some untimely discovery of her own early crimes, she wanted courage to linger on the thought, and to consider how far it might be true   She had, however, a strong maternal regard for Ronald   nor had guilt so weakened its force as to induce her to view his dejection with unconcern   She had hitherto been withheld from making enquiries by a vague apprehension of the truth   but the decisive moment had now arrived   accident so confronted them that it was impossible for either to recede   while her grandson brooded over his fears, Lady Minhurst at once dreaded and sought the confirmation of her own

Her spirit impatient of delay, at length induced her to approach him   With the soft soothing tones a man only hears from a mother or a wife, she enquired the cause of his depression   The pale countenance that turned towards her, as she finished speaking, betrayed an agony of mind that would have wrung a harder heart than Lady Minhurst's   He made no reply, and she repeated the question

' My sorrows are my own, my lady,   he answered in a voice of affected coolness

They may be lightened by confidence   come—I must share them

' Oh, there is no occasion for confidence' he rejoined, while a smile of scorn lightened his features that went like a dagger to her heart "You are but too well acquainted with my secret,   he added in an impressive manner, and passing the Viscountess with a low bow, he retreated from the chapel

What unuttered and unutterable things a look may convey' how often it interprets the heart when the lips want courage to perform their task Ronald's severe expression of countenance removed all doubt from the mind of Lady Minhurst   she felt satisfied that his affections had undergone a terrible revolution before he could have thus looked on her

' He knows all,   she exclaimed, as a prey to the most agonising feelings she leant for support against the nearest monument   Two objects were present to the wretched woman   her mental vision retained the pale, reproachful countenance of her grandson , and her eyes rested on the time worn word EVINE

There was much festivity that evening at Minhurst   but the family who gave it derived but little enjoyment from the entertainment,

Ronald, who had stood with success for the borough of P——, had set apart that day for a farewell dinner to be given to his intimate friends previous to his departure to London to enter on his political career   A few months before he would have ranked such a day with the happiest of his existence   but now the highest enjoyments of life were become flat and wearisome   A stigma, secret indeed, but never to be effaced, rested on his family   Name he had none, though bearing that of an illustrious race   and of all the privileges of elevated caste, he only pos sessed the expensive tastes acquired during years of false expectation Why then should he court the distinction that personal merit actively employed in the service of his country would justly procure since every distinction would aggravate the disgrace which he felt must inevitably fall on himself and those connected with him Nevertheless, from the hope of giving pleasure to his father, and of securing in an established political career the means of retaining that position in society which he now held by a surreptitious title, he submitted as a necessity to what is sought by other men as an honour and found the congratulations that followed success a most intolerable tax on his patience and good nature His melancholy begot in him feelings of misanthropy very foreign to his nature and he looked with coolness, occasionally with abhorrence on the well known faces that in other circumstances he would have welcomed with the sincerest friendship and on this occasion he saw them withdraw with a feeling of thankfulness and he found no real relief till, in his own apartment, he began to prepare for his return on the next day to Town

Having taken an affectionate leave of his father, he next hastened to Mira For his sister he had much tenderness, and fully sympathised with the cruel alternative her situation presented

" May we be happier when next we see each other ' said he, wiping away with a kiss the tear that trickled down her cheek

" It will be at my marriage, thought the unhappy girl, but no words escaped her lips—she felt that the merit of her suffering consisted in its secrecy

Ronald made no attempt to see his grandmother, nor did she throw herself in his way

---

CHAPTER XIX

IT was an October morning, bright and beautiful the trees and hedges, still wearing the luxuriant foliage of summer, were tinged with a thousand rich and varying hues and no part of " merrye Englande " looked more glorious in her sumptuous autumnal garb than the environs of a small town in a western county where Edward and Evine were then staying

On the outskirts of that old fashioned borough was a lane of singular rural loveliness It led off from the turnpike road a short quarter of a mile below the town, and formed for some distance a boundary to the grounds of the wealthy incumbent of the parish It had long ceased to be a thoroughfare of importance, and, except in harvest time, it was rarely disturbed by the presence of cart or waggon, though at that season it received from the ponderous chariots of Ceres marks the whole year failed to efface The heavy cart ruts however, bordered a carpet of the fairest green, and by no means scared away the sentiment loving lads and lasses from their favourite retreat It terminated in a road, and nearly opposite an old barn—the last building of a long straggling street at the back of the town

In this lane—about the hour of ten the sunny quiet hour when the lounger may be sure of a lonely saunter, the busy being at their avocations, and the idle but preparing for another day of listlessness—we beg leave again to bring Edward and Evine before the notice of the reader

The chimes of the town clock were tinkling their " fairy like music far away amongst the dense foliage on his left as Edward, thoughtful and alone turned from the high road by the vicar s mansion

Edward s new mode of life had not improved his appearance He was thin and pale and his clothes (as clothes will persist in becoming, to the great annoyance of seedy gentlemen) were something shabbier than when he engaged in the company of Mr Share A shallow purse accounted for the shabbiness of apparel the neatness of the wearer could not disguise, while anxiety of mind and an employment revolting to his taste and sentiments had gradually imparted a worn and haggard expression to his countenance

During the few months that had elapsed since he embraced, in a moment when necessity left him no alternative the arduous and precarious calling of strolling player Edward had drawn consolation from two sources that appeared exhaustless and enabled him to endure with courage the privations of his new mode of life—the study of Shakspere and the gratitude of Evine In the former he found an apology for the frippery of the stage it was a task that gave an indirect dignity to his new pursuits the latter was at once his motive to exertion and his exceeding great reward

Eleven was the hour appointed for rehearsal, and according to custom he chose the lane as the most agreeable though a very circuitous route to the rustic playhouse Having a full hour before him he sauntered along at a slow pace, occasionally conning his part and as frequently indulging in the desultory musing which the words he studied or the scene around him gave rise to

Since his sojourn in that town this lane had been his chosen haunt There are spots in the natural world which have an affinity with our natures not unsimilar to that which heart must have with heart to form the alliance called friendship spots towards which our feet involuntarily turn where the mind ever experiences congenial and soothing influence These haunts seldom boast attraction for the stranger their beauty is only discerned on intimacy and then we discover in them as in the face of a friend a daily and a varying loveliness, when no striking excellence of feature would have led us to imagine its existence

Such was this spot to Edward he was sufficiently familiar with it to have exhausted its power of conveying enjoyment the outline of its foliage was graven on his mind he was familiar with the short lived story of its loveliest flower he had seen it beautiful with every variety of light and shade—gilded by the sun silvered by the moon, smiling in reply to the laughing heavens above and drooping like a weeping outcast

in the " pelting storm   yet was it still prolific of pleasure—the pleasure
only known to the student of nature, who, deep read in the wide volume,
is ever wrought on by its eloquence

On that morning he was in a happy mood   his mind basking in a
moral sunshine as warm and brilliant as the sun beams around him   and
his enjoyment was not a little increased by the pamphlet he held in his
hand   It was the play for the evening, and by a strange coincidence, so
suitable to the present situation of Edward, the sylvan play " As You
like It

But melancholy men are not destined to find their paradise on earth,
(if solitude be paradise to them) any more than the sociable part of the
species   even a dull and out of the way lane will have its intruders   If
we may judge however from his manner as he advanced to meet them
it was not in this light Edward regarded the ladies who now made their
appearance   The elder of the two was stout and comely in person of
bustling manners and beneath the smart open bonnet beamed a merry
chubby countenance that reconciled you to the wearers eccentricity
Never was a better heart than Mrs Bondells, or Mother Bondell, as
she was invariably called by the many who had made proof of her goodness of nature and simplicity of mind   The friendly shake hands with
which she returned Edwards salutation will satisfy the reader that she
belonged to the *profession*   With her fifty years complete, her buxom
figure, merry face excellent heart and dowdy finery, with all these ad
vantages and disadvantages, Mrs Bondell was nothing more and nothing
less than a country actress   She was, be it observed to her credit, no
stage struck lady regretting amid old age and poverty the illusions that
in youth tempted her to embrace a precarious and wandering life   no
predilection had raised her to the boards   she was born in a theatre, bred
up by the glare of the foot lights   and gay and light hearted as she was
for the greater part of half a century, had known no better lot than the
obscure and despised condition of a female performer   The scanty
earnings of her juvenile talent from her earliest recollection, had contributed to her parents income   and when, at their death she was left
' mistress of her choice," she possessed neither the connection nor the
training necessary to embrace a more respectable career had she wished
to have done so   Fortunately for her peace of mind her first love at the
age of sixteen terminating in marriage she was preserved in the domestic
circle from temptations peculiar to her calling   Mr Bondell was a
player like herself and they lived together happily for many years   At
his death some ten years before the date of this narrative, he left her to
support three grandchildren the offspring of an only daughter long since
dead whose prodigal husband having first brought his wife to the grave,
deserted his own children   For the support of these orphans she had
heroically continued to contribute to the amusement of the public while
her heart was racked by the pangs of bereavement   and now that a
relation of her worthless son had come forward to share some part of her
burden she still devoted all she earned above her immediate necessities
to the education of her young charge   Such was Mrs Bondell, an
exemplary woman, though throughout life an outcast from what is called

society, and often viewed with prejudiced scorn by persons of her own sex

Warmly as Vivyan greeted the elder lady, the younger one had evidently more claim on his attention and regard A straw bonnet projected from the sun features of great beauty but by no means concealed the soft brilliance of large blue eyes, nor confined long tresses of golden hair She was a beautiful object to look upon, and after the first salutation was over, Edward continued some time gazing with admiration on the lovely creature

He felt more than the enjoyment the sight of beauty produces even when it attains the enthusiasm of love the satisfaction only known to pure benevolence, mingled with his admiration The beautiful female before him was in some degree his work he had raised her from vagrancy to rank one day as he hoped among the reputable and useful of her sex

It was no slight improvement Evine had undergone during the last few months At an age when the mind is susceptible to every impression and yet pliant enough to receive any direction that may be given to it—brought, with all this promptness to conceive and readiness to execute suddenly into connection with persons whose habits of life though obscure and simple, were luxurious and refined compared with the coarseness and penury of the vagrant tribe she had been accustomed to, Evine felt the advantage of the change and applied herself zealously to the acquirement of those manners her new position in life required

Soon after he had joined the players Edward discerned the worth of Mrs Bondell and for the sake of Evine s reputation as well as for her general improvement he tried to dispose the actress in favour of his charge This was a very easy task, when supported by the interesting countenance and amiable disposition of the mendicant s daughter After a brief acquaintance censured by all the women of the company, and by many of the men as imprudently short it was agreed that Evine should share Mrs Bondell s lodging while Edward should hire a room in the same house This matter once settled the process of training was commenced with great zeal, and the willing, able pupil made a corresponding progress

Her infancy passed in beggary and her first education undertaken by a strolling actress it may be supposed that Evine s character would be marked by eccentricity and waywardness, if it escaped worse defects nor shall we be ready to abandon the supposition when we remember that a poet and self instructed scholar as her daily companion and most intimate friend had also some share in its formation But if a Providence can be traced in all the events of life in none is it more visible than in the training by which men are fitted for the capacities they are destined to fill in the world Evine s mission in society remains to be seen but it is certain that her childhood prepared her for suffering and vicissitude, and brought her with a quick, observing mind to the study f duties belonging to more civilised life

On Mrs Bondell devolved the task of instructing our heroine in all feminine pursuits, from the dropping of a curtsey to the darning of a stocking while Edward undertook to teach her to read and write As however, he held a leading situation in the company the study of new and difficult characters left him but little leisure to bestow on his pupil, but, to turn all he could spare to the best advantage, it was his custom as soon as she had mastered the first rudiments of reading, to blend his lesson with her s and make selections from the play in which he had to perform at night the subject of the morning s tuition

Thus it might be said that Evine s first book was Shakspere if we overlook the great volume of Nature which she had often conned in childhood with all that alacrity of observation peculiar to persons whose minds have not been fettered in infancy with that restraint mistermed education But we must resume our story

" You are the very person I wanted to see began Mrs Bondell "I thought we should meet you here—you are walking towards the theatre I perceive shall we accompany you? To come to my point at once I must beg of you to chide this obstinate sister of yours the little thing will work herself to death in spite of all my scolding I can t get her to leave off for a moment I was obliged to use main force to get her to take a walk this morning The fact is she has such a passion for shirt making that I never saw anything to equal it never

I know Edward must be in want of them faltered Evine

But it does not follow that you should lay yourself up with work I wouldn t do it for any man alive—and I wont let you!

' How is this Evine ! you must not let your zeal injure your strength

Well! interposed Mrs Bondell as she has learnt to stitch the collars and wristbands so well and so quickly, we must not say anything to her this once But another time— and the good humoured soul held up her hand in a menacing attitude one of those comic gestures, on which she relied when on the stage for producing applause from her audience But here comes Richardson to summon you to rehearsal, how time flies when people stand chattering, to be sure '

By this time the little party were in sight of the barn at the end of the lane It was the playhouse and it seemed to view with gloomy distance the merry group of shabby men and tawdry women that loitered about its dilapidated door

Good bye Somers ' said Mrs Bondell turning back I shall not trouble you this morning I have enough of thebarn when I am wanted "

" You will come back as soon as you can Edward, whispered Evine

' Let me see some good writing when I do he replied as they separated,

* * * * * * *

It was approaching rapidly towards midnight, and the single candle that lighted the apartment of Mrs Bondell was expiring in the socket

Ten minutes to twelve ! exclaimed that lady rubbing her eyes and poking the fire what can detain them so long at the theatre to night? Put up your writing my child Mr Somers will be ravenous when he comes in

A loud knock at the door and the noise of many voices without now excited their attention Before Mrs Bondell had scarcely time to renew the light, Evine opened the door and drew back with surprise and at or as she beheld the pale, thin countenance of Mr Richardson wearing an expression of great concern

'Do not be alarmed ladies,' he began in a tone by no means calcu lated to check any terror his appearance might have inspired ' only an accident, a trifling accident the doctor assures me it will be attended with no serious consequences'

'Who who is hurt?' cried Evine pushing him aside and closing her eyes with a shudder, as she perceived Edward pale bleeding, and appa rently unconscious borne into the room on a shutter

'Hush my dear girl! restrain yourself' said Mrs Bondell, coming forward ' Poor Somers! how did this happen?'

'In a moment you shall know all but first let us put the poor fellow to bed His wound is dressed and the surgeon will be here to see him again as soon as we have made the poor young man comfortable'

Very active exertions were made to effect this no useless display of grief was indulged every one lent prompt assistance—Evine acting with more presence of mind than even the men, although her blanched cheek bore witness to the most painful anxiety and alarm

The surgeon soon arrived, and renewed the dressing of the wounds, which before had been merely slightly performed to enable the patient to be removed to his home He learnt from Richardson that the accident had been occasioned by the fall of some scenery and on examination discovered that the injury amounted to some severe bruises and a broken arm Having bestowed the necessary care on the young man he took his leave, assuring Mrs Bondell and Evine that a long confinement was the worst evil they had to apprehend

This however soon proved terrible enough The first few days, it is true, were passed by Evine in watching by the sufferers bed side, who seemed to endure great pain and the fever increasing to an alarming height, for a long time his recovery seemed almost doubtful While he continued in this state she had no thought but of him and, indeed nearly the whole care of nursing devolved on her From Mrs Bondell she received some invaluable directions but that lady was too much engaged with the duties of her calling to support the long vigils and wearisome attendance that a sick chamber required The loss of Ed ward s services forced the manager to bring forward the other description of talent found in his company and consequently a greater demand was made on the time of Edward s kind and useful friend

Evine s affectionate gratitude sufficed however to procure her patient every comfort and consolation and it was not till the burning fever had left him, and he seemed again endowed with the power of enjoying life though in a feeble degree that she grew alarmed and anxious respecting the means to be resorted to to his and her own maintenance until he was again able to resume his duties Edward had been unable to save anything from his scanty earnings and Evine saw with much pain that Mrs Bondell had already deprived herself of many humble comforts to contribute to their convenience A circumstance one day occurred which determined her to take immediate steps to ward off the evil of destitution she had been plying her needle in silence for several hours and imagined Edward was asleep one or two heavy sighs announced a disturbed slumber and unconsciously desisting from her work she remained for a few moments perfectly still Edward was awake and revolving with all the torturing anxiety of a disabled man his distressed circumstances She was soon aware of this and listened with deeper attention

'Merciful God! What will become of us' he exclaimed

The words seemed to come from a broken heart and she rose hastily to soothe him His face was half buried in the pillow and he was evidently betrayed into that excess of weeping which is peculiar to cases of great debility Large round tears trickled down the bed clothes and unable to endure the sight Evine turned away to summon Mrs Bondell, who fortunately was at liberty to relieve her

Before another hour had elapsed Evine waited on manager Share Whether it was her object to make an experiment on his generosity and whether she succeeded in so doing it is not in our power to say but we can assert on Mrs Bondell's authority, that when next she took her seat at the invalid's bed side, her countenance was more hopeful her step more light than that lady had ever seen it

A few nights after when Edward was better able to observe what was going on around him, he perceived an unusual bustle in the room, hitherto kept so scrupulously quiet At times he perceived Mrs Bondell and Evine exchange an anxious glance, and the latter, for the first time, was too busy to read to him once or twice too, when he turned his head in the direction in which she was sitting, he noticed a quick movement of the hands by which she contrived to put her work out of sight, in a word, there were many visible symptoms of domestic mystery, and they drew him into a chain of conjectures each more extraordinary than the preceding, till they plunged him into a dose that lasted for some time

When he awoke the evening was far advanced the rush light burnt dimly on the hearth and he wondered at being left alone He had however an attendant Richardson sat quietly behind the curtains ready to help the invalid if he required it but otherwise unwilling to be seen by him

It soon became necessary for him to leave his hiding place to answer Edward's repeated call

You here Richardson' he exclaimed with surprise

Richardson nodded like the clown in a pantomime

Where is Evine? asked the young man with alarm

Hush! don't be frightened she is safe enough It is Mrs Bondell's benefit—money takers can't always be trusted'

True! said the invalid with a sigh of exhaustion "Evine is gone to help her—that is very right and he added falling again in o a dose ' it is very kind of you to come and sit with me Richardson

The next Saturday Evine was able to quiet Vivyan's uneasiness by placing in his hand the usual amount of his week's share

This is generous of the manager observed Edward I long to be about again to requite him you must have had good houses this week, Mrs Bondell'

Both the females smiled but made no reply
Evine had that week made a successful appearance on the stage '

CHAPTER XX

In a large cold looking room, on a miserable straw mat rass, and wrapped in a tattered blanket was stretched Wilfred Welbourne It was winter, and the frost was severe   The rays of the moon streamed through the grated window and fell cheerlessly on the wretched man   His limbs

were benumbed with cold and galled by heavy fetters and his mind was a prey to the most agonizing feelings
For weary months he had been a captive   Setting aside the torment in being unjustly confined the treatment he received in his odious prison tended much more to increase rather than mitigate its severity   If he complained of his confinement if he sought to know why he was detained or ventured to express the anxiety he entertained for his unprotected child, he had the mortification of finding his words were regarded

as the language of insanity and often met with brutal treatment in reply
In an asylum professing to be a retreat for unhappy people deprived of
reason, he had met with such accommodation as a felon might have justly
exclaimed against as merciless and compared to which even the privations
of his usual mode of life were comfortable and luxurious   To the loss
of liberty, the want of food and clothing to the brutality of his keepers,
Welbourne would have submitted with cheerfulness, could he have known
that his daughter was provided for and protected : but distracting anxiety
about Evine drove him alternately into paroxysms of violent passion, or
the terrible prostration of despair   Into such violent excesses had his
agony betrayed him that there were moments when the sordid keeper
of this den of torture felt inclined to part with so unruly a guest but
the stipend remitted him by Grasp through the instrumentality of Lady
Minhurst having liquidated all demands that might accrue for six months
to come, his avarice got the better of his fears and he contented himself
with inventing new methods of cruelty for restraining his captive   It
would be tedious to enumerate the modes of torture devised, and carried
into practice   Food was withheld until the sufferer wanted strength for
the violence to which rage and hunger prompted   at other times he was
supplied with nauseous masses the pangs of starvation alone induced him
to devour   To increase the weight of his fetters till they brought the
wretched wearer to the ground or so retarded the circulation that the
black and swollen veins seemed on the point of bursting and deep and
festering scars were produced on the galled flesh—was the favourite tor
ture to which he was daily exposed   Often was he left to shiver through
the night, in a condition little removed from nakedness on the cold flags
of an underground cell, and he had long grown habituated to the incon
venience of filth and vermin   Yet all this would have been supportable,
could he have been satisfied respecting the welfare of Evine.

He had that morning gone into such excess of passion as had disturbed
the whole community   In his desperate struggles he had snapped his
fetters, and, driving every one from the yard appropriated to exercise
kept for a whole hour the keepers at bay   In his phrenzy, however he
overshot himself, and was betrayed into the lonely apartment he then
occupied   A massive iron door was immediately closed upon him and
it was determined to keep him there until reduced to submission by
hunger unless he preferred to release them from further trouble by sui
cide   Wilfred was bound too firmly to life by the thoughts of his child
to adopt such an alternative

Ten hours of solitude fasting and anguish had gone round when he
awoke with a loud yell from a short dose He had had a frightful dream
his child was confined like himself enduring treatment such as he had
undergone and still under the influence of his vision, he started up in
his bed shouting for assistance

' Hush ! ' exclaimed a low voice near him, while he felt a hand placed
gently on his bare shoulder

He looked at the speaker with alarm, but it was speedily exchanged
for astonishment

' Is it you, Mary ?   said he

' Aye, poor daft Mary! They would beat you this morning to keep you quiet I could have told them better I knew what was the matter —it was about the heart, all about the heart! Poor daft Mary knows what that is ,

' How came you here ?

" I stole the key from under Dodds pillow They take no heed of daft Mary but daft Mary can serve a poor man a good turn.

" Was it you who brought me fresh water when I was locked up in the strong hold for eight and forty hours ?

" Aye! aye! I could get nothing better

' And two days ago exchanged my mouldy crust for good bread and cheese ?

May be I did! rejoined the poor woman, relapsing from a sudden appearance of intelligence into her habitual silliness of manner.

' I can t help you much now, poor man,' she continued but you shall have half daft Mary s supper

' I cannot eat! said the man, turning sullenly from the food ' let me die!

His visitor looked at him compassionately

' Let us talk! said she after a pause

' I have no care to talk ' he replied

" Come, come! talk to me as you used to do when you first came— about the pretty maid it did you so much good to talk of, as I dressed your wounds

' What is become of her now ? sighed Welbourne

" God feeds his lambs! whispered daft Mary

' Bless you! bless you! Who knows—who knows ? said the broken hearted father, as yielding to his companion s wish he allowed her to lead him to the window

' We will sit here—in the moonshine—and talk a bit continued the female, seating herself at the window seat ' we can t often talk—Dodds would suspect us I took a liking to you, œhen you first came I always liked you because I knew you were not mad like the rest I am not mad either—that is not always—but sometimes I feel strange

The unfortunate pair sat silent some time a sigh from Welbourne again drew the attention of his companion

" Don t think about her! said she ' God will take care of her, pretty maid Come tell me how you came to get in here ? '

" Rogues! rascals! vociferated Welbourne

" Hush! hush! rejoined Mary, looking round with alarm "you were entrapped into this place—I know it—but we won t talk about that —I see it vexes you—and it might drive you mad, you know What shall we talk about ? '

"Will you tell me your story ? asked Welbourne, scarcely knowing what he requested

Poor daft Mary looked thoughtful, and drawing her hand across her brow —

It is not all here now she said "but it will come as I talk I have not always lived here No! no! daft Mary was rich once!

" Poor creature ' sighed the mendicant

" 'Tis a tedious while since then—more years than you have seen My name is not daft Mary," she added in a low voice as if afraid of being overheard

" No ?

They would have taken my name from me, as they did every thing else It was such a change when they brought me here ! It seems as though I had passed into another world all cold and gloomy You won't call me daft Mary when Dodds isn t near, will you ?

" What shall I call you ?

" Call me by my own name '

" But you have never told it me

" Oh, I forgot ' I thought you knew it Once every body knew my name but now they all think me dead—Evine is my name

" Evine ' Strange— tis my child's name, and was my mother s "

" Did you ever have a mother ? enquired the woman, again deprived of the gleam of intellect which but a moment before had assisted her

" I never knew her " rejoined Welbourne , " she was torn from me while I was yet an infant the persons into whose hands I fell found in my bundle of clothes a document that made them acquainted with my mother s name they had me called after the person to whom that writing was addressed '

Did they tear her from you ?' exclaimed his companion " poor, poor mother ' So did they with me—tore me from my child Hold off, villains ' It s your death to touch me—you shall pay for this Help ! Mercy ' Help '

And the frantic creature enacting again a terrible passage of her early life, ran wildly round the room like one escaping from pursuers

Either alarmed for the safety of the phrenzied woman, or fearful that her noise would reach the ears of the keepers, Welbourne followed her, endeavouring to convince her of the error under which her disordered imagination laboured His attempts only aggravated the evil running round the room with more rapidity, and shouting in a louder key, she made the place resound with dreadful shrieks By suddenly darting across the apartment, the mendicant contrived to seize her in his arms, and as she struggled to get free,

" Silence, for God s sake !' he exclaimed tis I—your friend Wilfred Welbourne, and no pursuer '

" You lie ' she shouted, bursting from his arms you want my Wilfred —my boy ! You shall not have him no, no, you shall not '"

Overcome with emotion she sank lifeless to the ground by the window near which she stood Welbourne raised her, and as he gazed on the countenance worn with the sorrows of sixty years revealed by the moon light to his view, he felt conscious that he pressed to his bosom his long lost mother

CHAPTER XXI

EARLY on the morning that followed the event related in the preceding chapter, Dobie Snitch awoke from the first slumber he had taken in a metropolitan bed

Having made a substantial breakfast off the various luxuries which an inn in the neighbourhood of Fleet Market could provide he was prepared to encounter all the opening day might bring forth   From a very ominous blue bag he drew one by one a collection of papers, which he placed in a pile on the table

" You are a lucky fellow, Dobie Snitch   he soliloquised, " and no fib at all '   These papers will do my business for me   and if I don't make them bring me in a hundred times their weight in gold I am no better than a fool   Let me see   first certificates of the marriage of Evine, Viscountess Minhurst   then we have the settlement made to the said Evine   So so ' that s all right   This is the register of the interment of that very   same Viscountess   a mighty pretty farce that interment, I take it—a sham burial—these letters prove thatt   The whole correspondence between the present Viscountess and my old governor Whew ! how she would wince if she knew I possessed in her own hand writing all the plans and contrivances she invented to get her predecessor and rival out of the way   A very nice woman this dowager Viscountess ! Dobie Snitch, Dobie Snitch, you ll come in for a taste of her ladyship's generosity, I take it   Pity there is no scrap of writing to give me a clue to find tne true Lady Minhurst, if she is still alive   But no mattei   her son, this Wilfred Welbourne, will do as well   So, my proud viscount, I Dobie Snitch the lawyer s clerk, can strip you of title and fortune   and restore their lawful owner to his rights   So, this is the letter to the keeper of the madhouse in which he is detained and see what he will give me for the job   After all the best bidder shall be master of Minhurst, or I am not Dobie Snitch '

Here he was interrupted by the entrance of the waiter

Morning newspaper ' said the man, presenting him one of the epitomes of a day that emerge every morning from the printing presses of the metropolis   and a letter, Sir   Eight pence to pay if you please

As soon as the waiter was dispatched with the postman s fee, Dobie broke the seal, and made two or three attempts to decypher the hieroglyphics of Mrs Deborah Swill

' Poor dear soul '   he exclaimed as he came to the conclusion of his very puzzling task   " how she does doat upon me to be sure '   Well, never mind, Deborah ' a little more patience and, trust me, if between us we don t prove that we didn t serve poor old Gregory Grasp for nothing   Thereupon he took up the paper and with the method of a long practised reader of the daily prints sought the column containing the leader   As he ran over the summary of the preceding night s debate, he met with the following paragraph

"We have great pleasure in directing the attention of our readers to the eloquent and important speech delivered by the youthful member for P——   We are ever ready to welcome the entrance of youthful talent into the political arena, but especially do we feel gratified to recognise sentiments so liberal, talent so distinguished, and experience so matured in a young man destined by his rank one day to grace the benches of the upper house   It will be remembered that a petition was brought before a committee of the House against this gentleman's return He is the only son of Viscount Minhurst, a nobleman whose private worth amply atones for his inactivity in political life

"Ha! ha! ha!   A mighty great man, no doubt!   chuckled Dobie, as he read   I warrant these editorial gentlemen would tell a different story if they knew all that I do   But no matter   Only let the old dowager come down with a round sum, and the young member for P—— may talk the Commons deaf, and sit with the Lords till his bones ache again, for anything I care   but if she is stingy, I'll bring a man from a madhouse to spout to the 'lords and gentlemen, and no fib at all'   No great change for him after all, poor man, from Bedlam to Parliament I will read on   a newspaper's no bad help"

Finding nothing more attractive than the above paragraph in the leader, Dobie's next attention was devoted to the miscellaneous columns

In this catalogue of numberless calamities and innumerable felicities peculiar to humanity, he noticed two facts with evident pleasure   They were as follows

"The Earl and Countess of Wagmouth give an entertainment this evening at their incomparably elegant mansion in —— Square   This is the first given by that nobleman since his coming to the title.   It will be one of the finest fetes during the season

"Ha! ha! ha!   laughed or rather roared Dobie, as he read   "there they go again —The Countess of Wagmouth, forsooth! the daughter of a nobody who enjoys through a fraud the title of Viscount   What would the old Earl say were he alive to know that his son and heir had married a nobody's daughter

After this comment he continued his perusal in silence, until some new information called for another fit of laughter, which now seemed more than ever like exultation

'We understand   he read "that the late contest for the borough of P——, and the petition brought before the House against the return of the present member, have cost his opponent, the Hon Francis Fraser Fluentleigh, not less than twenty thousand pounds'

"A ruined man that a ruined man!   shouted Dobie in exstacy, and, as though a sudden thought had come to his mind, he strode towards a bell rope suspended from the middle of the room, and gave it a furious jerk

"Call me a coach!   said Mr Snitch to the waiter in a most decided tone   "a coach instantly!

A coach was called accordingly, and into it Dobie sprang, with an alacrity he had not manifested since the death of Gregory Grasp Esq nor did he utter a word   or gaze on a single object   so intensely was he occupied with his new plans, till the vehicle drew up before the door of the asylum which had now formed for some time the residence of poor Wilfred Welbourne

I am very glad to see you, Sir, was the reply of the principal officer at once the proprietor and governor of the establishment as soon as Snitch had announced himself and stated his errand ' I was at a loss to know, continued the man, " what to do with the last person Mr Grasp confided to my care the time stipulated for his stay and for which I have been paid, expires to-morrow; and as I knew Mr Grasp was no longer alive, I had made up my mind that the best course I could adopt would be to let the man go about his business Now you are come to see about him, Sir, the affair presents a different face—and I should recommend a few months more discipline

" Bless me !' interrupted Dobie ' do you think he is quite mad then ? '

" That depends on how you define madness," returned the man ' it may be so defined as to exempt none from the failing, or you may form such an idea of it, as to conclude that the most raving Bedlamite has the enjoyment of his senses

' But this man is he very mad ? enquired Dobie, concluding that the keeper himself was not exactly in the perfect enjoyment of a sound mind

" Sometimes very , and sometimes not very Would you like to see him, Sir ?'

' Do you think he would hurt me ?" asked Snitch, alarmed at the idea of confronting the inmate of a madhouse

Being assured that no danger was to be apprehended from an inter view Snitch submitted to be ushered into the presence of the mendicant

He was shown into the room in which the meeting of the mother and son had taken place the night before Though it was winter the sun gleamed brightly through the grated windows, and bathed in a flood of golden light the mendicant who was seated on the floor, and his mother who, stretched on the ground, reclined her head on his lap

On recovering from her swoon that unfortunate woman enjoyed a lucid interval and understood, or seemed to understand all that Wilfred said of their relationship It is true she was soon plunged again into mental darkness nevertheless, the kind and soothing tone of her son had a powerful effect upon her spirits, and they talked on, sometimes with a shew of sense and sometimes with strange incoherence, till slumber overtook them with the dawn

They were both asleep when the visitor entered, and Dodds, who accompanied him, took care to manifest his astonishment and dis pleasure

" Did you ever see a better than that—those old wretches asleep in each other s arms ? I ll teach them to go courting at their time of life '

' Poor creatures ' Let them sleep on ' said Snitch, evidently affected by their wretched appearance and the deep slumbers of fatigue into which they were plunged

"Let them alone!" shouted their keeper; "a very pretty joke indeed! I dare say I will let them alone too   What do you suppose now would become of the morality of this establishment, if we were to sffuer de pravity of this kind to pass unnoticed?"

'Get up, you hoary headed sinners! Arn t ye ashamed of yourselves? he roared applying to each with a heavy stroke a thick bludgeon he held in his hand

Both sleepers started at once to their feet, and throwing around them a wild look of terror ran into each other s arms

"Do not leave me! *he* will kill me   cried the female appealingly

'Never mother never! responded the man.

"Aye mother! that s right old boy, call her mother—she might be your mother twice over   Away with you, you infernal disgusting hag! Come tramp!

As he spoke he began to take measures to tear them asunder

"Never! burst forth Welbourne with vehemence, hurling the man from him and clasping the female closer to his bosom   man shall never part us!

There was a determination in the tone and manner of the mendicant but too well understood by Dodds and Dobie Both of them hurried through the door

" I must seek some help, said Dodds, fastening the door behind him there is no doing anything with that fellow I must let him go, he will murder half of us, and drive the rest out of their senses '

" He seemed gentle enough to that poor woman '

   Crazed folk always are so where they take '

' Is she indeed his mother ? enquired Dobie

" His mother ' Lord bless you, no !

" How came she here ?

' 'Tis now five years ago since she was transferred here from another asylum long since broken up A very large sum was paid for her maintenance but none can tell who she is

' What is her name ?'

' The people of the house call her *daft Mary*—a name a Scotchman gave her who was here when she arrived

' But does she answer to no other ? do you never hear her call herself by any other name ?

" Sometimes she calls herself Evine

Dobie started at the last word uttered by Dodds

" She *is* his mother ' muttered he to himself

" Did you speak, Sir ? asked Dodds

" No ' resumed Dobie I was thinking aloud perhaps ' I wish you to take special care of these two unfortunate people I will pay your trouble to any amount—take this as an earnest

' As he spoke, he placed a guinea in the keeper's hands

" You will hear from me again to morrow," said he, walking towards the door I shall remove these persons shortly

In about half an hour after the foregoing conversation, Dobie Snitch knocked at the chambers of the Honourable Francis Fraser Fluentleigh During the contest for the borough of P——, and while preparations were making for the petition, Dobie had been of great service to that gentleman it was even surmised among the gossips of the place that the services of the ci devant clerk were of a nature to give him great claims on the rejected candidate He however met with reception very different to what most men experience when claiming their due, for his name was no sooner announced than he was ushered into the presence of Fluentleigh

" Ah, my friend Mr Snitch ' I am exceedingly glad to see you—extremely gratified, I protest

" You expressed a wish to see me, if ever business called me to town, and I take the earliest opportunity to wait upon you '

" You have done very right, my dear Sir your services during that unfortunate contest when I say unfortunate I do not mean in a personal sense—by no means—I call it an unfortunate contest, inasmuch as it added to the number of young conceited noodles for after all, Sir, what is this young Minhurst, but a noodle—who already crowd the benches of the House but I was observing that your services were invaluable during the contest, and I should have been grieved had you not given me the earliest opportunity of shewing my gratitude

" The whole busmesss must have cost you a pretty sum Sir " observed Dobie

" A fortune, Mr Snitch, a fortune '

" The Viscount s son paid a pretty round price for his seat ' ' rejoined Dobie

' In that particular I was most lamentably deceived, Mr Snitch I never imagined the Minhurst family had the means of opposing me

' It should be a rich family insinuated the lawyer s clerk

" It was, but the present Viscount spent a very extravagant youth and what he contrived to spare, his mother, the dowager Viscountess, took care to expend

' The ruin of such a family would, no doubt afford you pleasure, Mr Fluentleigh after the losses they may be said to have caused you ?"

The disappointed candidate stared at his companion as though he were astonished at his impertinence for presuming to intimate a supposition of the kind but, reading design in Snitch s countenance he lolled back in his chair, hummed an air for two or three seconds, and then replied

No ' not particularly they are rather a fair family the Minhursts rather haughty but that arises from their rank and long standing in the peerage

' If that could be shaken ? observed Dobie slily

" What ? enquired the other struck with Snitch s manner, but very much at a loss to conceive his meaning

" The Viscount s claim to the peerage, retorted the clerk

" I do not exactly see how that can be

" It is well you do not These things should not be too evident Twenty years service in the office of the dowager Viscountess Minhurst s confidential agent, you will allow, gave me an opportunity of obtaining some insight into their affairs

" It should do so yet how they can have no claim to the peerage, I am at a loss to conceive Pray explain !

" First, Mr Fluentleigh, I must beg you to be candid with me Tell me how you are affected towards this family The communication I have to make can serve you no turn unless you bear them sufficient hatred to rejoice in their disgrace and ruin

' I would stake all I possess to ruin them ' exclaimed Fluentleigh with eagerness

" I will do the job for half that sum said Dobie, drawing his chair closer to Fluentleigh and accosting him with the familiarity low men invariably assume towards their superiors when circumstances bring them to the same level

We will spare the reader a prolix account of what followed Snitch artfully managed to obtain a written promise of an ample reward to be paid him as soon as he should have accomplished the ruin of the present Viscount Minhurst and family, without giving Fluentleigh the slightest insight into the means by which this purpose was to be effected

" Do what you propose and your fortune is made, Mr Snitch, said Mr Fluentleigh as the former took his departure

To return to the madhouse was Dobie s first care On his way he began to think how he should dispose of himself in the after part of the day

"I'll go to the play said he, advancing at the same time towards a shop window to read the bills of the performance Having ascertained that a young lady was to make her first appearance in the character of Juliet at Drury Lane, he decided upon going to that house, and was turning away to pursue his walk, when his attention was attracted by a man at his elbow, with whose features he seemed familiar

Before he could recall the name of the person at his side, the man had passed on, and Dobie quickening his pace hastened towards the asylum At last he gained the gloomy building, and as he was entering the door, he again caught a glimpse of the individual whom he had so fruitlessly endeavoured to recognise

It was Townsend, the active servant of the dowager Viscountess Minhurst

CHAPTER XXII

ALL the Minhurst family were now in Town the dowager occupied her usual residence in Upper Grosvenor Street Mira, now the Countess of Wagmouth, lived at the mansion of the Earl Ronald had chambers and Lord Minhurst divided his time between his mother and daughter

It was an important day with Mira the death of the late Earl of Wagmouth having taken place immediately after the return of his eldest son and his lovely bride from their wedding journey, the young couple had been condemned to the privacy of mourning and now for the first time were enabled to resume the festivities for which the mansion of the earls of Wagmouth had ever been remarkable during the fashionable season

This first fete in her own mansion the young Countess regarded as an arduous ordeal and for the purpose of obtaining advice on the infinite details of such a ceremony, she determined to pay an early visit to the Viscountess her grandmother, on the day appointed for the entertainment

' My dear child, how very ill you are looking ! were the first words, after the usual salutations the Dowager addressed to her granddaughter

" My present mode of life is so different to the quiet habits I observed at Minhurst, replied the young Countess

" Do not mention your early habits I cannot hear them mentioned with patience they are so opposed to the advancement of young people besides, it will never do to complain at the commencement of the season How pale you are, Mira ! your eyes are quite red I hope nothing makes you unhappy '

" Oh, no ! I am not unhappy

" I should say nothing could make you unhappy A countess, with a princely income ought not to be unhappy

'No indeed, rejoined Mira, a sigh escaping from her lips as she spoke.

With the handsomest man in London for your husband continued Lady Minhurst conceiving it necessary to indulge in a little humour, to which she very rarely stooped, in order to remove the evident low spirits of her granddaughter

'"Possibly,' thought Mira and she restrained herself with difficulty from uttering the word.

A gentleman whose manners are perfectly suited to the position in society his rank and fortune accord him, continued her ladyship not perceiving, or affecting not to perceive the beseeching looks with which the young wife implored her to desist from her unwelcome panegyric

"Your ladyship will excuse me, faltered Mira, rising from her seat "I am in no mood to hear raillery

'"My poor child have I offended you ? I thought I knew too well the courtesy most agreeable to a young wife I see I have made a sad error Will a little abuse atone for it ?

'Neither your abuse nor your encomiums, Lady Minhurst can alter my opinion of the Earl I came here she added making a powerful effort to rally "to converse on a subject to me of infinitely more importance—to learn how I should comport myself as his wife What *he is* I know *my* new duties *I* have yet to learn

Mira spoke in a determined tone, which she contrived to soften by assuming a playful manner The words and the manner of the young Countess, however, gave the Viscountess a greater insight than she had yet been able to obtain into the domestic relations of the new Earl and his bride Drawing herself up with much dignity—

'I shall be most happy she replied, in a haughty, measured tone "to give the Countess of Wagmouth any advice she may require respecting her new station

'Dearest grandmamma exclaimed Mira running towards her, and bursting into tears, 'not this coldness I cannot bear that; indeed I cannot!'

"You are a child quite a child' said the Dowager, raising the head that would have nestled on her shoulder and pushing it gently away: "these emotions are very unbecoming exceedingly detrimental to your personal appearance And she smoothed down the rich lace of her dishabille with most exemplary composure

'Forgive me my lady I am not very happy I look forward to the evening with alarm and my mind is easily jarred

"If you came to consult me about the evening's entertainment, nothing can be more proper nor could I on any other subject more willingly impart to you the result of my experience Entertain no fears I will be constantly at your side

'How kind of you'

At this moment Ronald was announced

Both the ladies advanced to meet him with cordiality The ardour of Mira's welcome was a little checked by the presence of the Viscountess, and for once Lady Minhurst herself overstepped the glacial limits he

No 23

refined notions of decorum induced her to impose at all times on her emotions

He returned his sister's greeting with an eloquent and cheering smile to the elderly lady he made a cold and distant bow

'This is a favour' cried the grandmother   it is an age since I last saw you Ronald to what circumstance may I attribute this visit?

"I perceived my sister's carriage at the door and hastened up to pay my respects to her replied the young man, with a mortifying coldness, that deeply wounded her ladyship, and served greatly to embarrass Mira

You accepted the Earl's invitation, so I suppose we shall see you to night Ronald inquired his sister

"I am looking forward to that pleasure'

'I wish you would call for me! once more ventured Lady Minhurst I am averse to going out alone

I must beg your ladyship to excuse me I have an engagement for the early part of the evening A friend has engaged to dine with me at the Club and we go to Drury Lane afterwards

Lady Minhurst reddened sensibly at this second slight

I have been much amused by your last night's speech she observed, wishing to conceal her annoyance   I am sure the Ministers must be very much obliged to you they ought to repay your labours with some handsome appointment

Your ladyship is considerate *I may need an appointment very soon*

These words were uttered in a tone of such deep dejection and pointed sarcasm that they violently affected both ladies though in a widely different manner

Ronald—my brother! exclaimed Mira in a soothing but surprised tone

We will wish Lady Minhurst good morning if you please Mira I will beg a seat in your carriage'

To this proposition his sister consented forgetting in her desire to hear from Ronald an explanation of his conduct, the impropriety of re tiring at such a juncture   As the Countess of Wagmouth's handsome grey horses dashed along the streets, she tried to induce Ronald to ac count for the unseemly deportment he had assumed towards her grand mother

I am not so patient a sufferer as you are Mira said Ronald "when my heart is oppressed my indiscreet temper betrays me   In you my sweet sister the canker is not so soon perceived—it cannot provoke you to a harsh word but it chases the bloom from your cheek You are unhappy'

You shift the ground ingeniously but do not hope so to escape *my* curiosity   What did you mean by *needing* an appointment?

The vicissitudes from the evil effects of which I hope your marriage will ever secure you may render an appointment under Government a timely provision for me

'For you Ronald I cannot understand you

"I would to God, Mira I found the same difficulty in interpreting your pale looks nnd reddened eyes ! Does Wagmouth treat you un kindly ?

No ! Ronald he does not it is I that am silly He has made me a countess, and it is exorbitant to require him to give me his love as well ! '

" *His* love ! Wagmouth is not capable of love Excuse me, Mira but your settlements are handsome happier days are in store for you - till then bear it, my poor sister if you can

The carriage had by this time reached the place of Ronald s destination, and the brother and sister separated

They had left the Viscountess alone in her boudoir but her solitude was soon interrupted by the appearance of Townsend

' What news ? she enquired as soon as he stood before her

Vat a morning I has had of it ! began the man " out o one coach into another I m blest if I aint been all over I onnun pretty nigh

Lady Minhurst understood the hint

" Pay yourself, Sir, she said presenting him with money and now let me hear your tidings "

" Grasp s man is in Town !

' So I feared, thought the Lady do you know his errand ?

' Vy I did take the liberty of seeing vat he vas agoing about but your ladyship must make head or tale out on it for I can't

Where did you see him ?

" I stopped to see vat vas agoing on at a playhouse, and there vas he a reading the wery same bills

' Well ! did he know you ?

" Vy, your ladyship he did look precious hard but the deuce a vord had he to say to me then I took the liberty of valking behind him, and on ve valked a precious vay till he turned into a gloomy house t'other side of the town

" And then ?

" I steps into a shop to ax em vat that ere large house vas ' A mad house, says they

" A madhouse do you say ! I hen I fear his errand But would he dare ? No ! I cannot believe it Yet why did he not come to me ? Will you be able to find this madhouse again Townsend ?

" No doubt of it, my lady

" And this man is it likely you will meet him again ?

" I vas too vide avake to leave that to chance my lady so I followed him back to his quarters

' You have acquitted yourself nobly Townsend here is more money you see I reward zeal liberally That will do be in readiness I may want you at a moment s notice

When Townsend had left the room her ladyship threw off the restra nt she thought proper to observe in his presence and paced the apartment rapidly

' I am on the precipice I fear it, and I shudder Ronald my grand-child, views me with a contempt that seems an omen of approaching nfamy Ungrateful boy ! How am I to avoid the fears that harras me? A bold determined stroke in what way? Shall I see this man this tool of Grasps or watch him narrowly? That madhouse, no doubt contains the heir was I going to say? —no, no ' not that, not the heir! To work, to work, my poor brain ' desert me not in this ex tremity '

CHAPTER XXIII

THE evening set in wet and gloomy, and carriages were already cir culating with rapidity in the neighbourhood of the theatres, as Evine' attended by Mrs Bondell stepped into a hackney coach at the door of their lodging in the New Road, and drove off in the direction of Drury Lane

' Don t be nervous, my dear, said the latter lady, adjusting herself in the vehicle to the great risk of a huge bandbox they had biought with them into the coach you will succeed there is no doubt of it

' If I could be sure of that and once have it in my power to make you and Edward a return for the kindness you have shewn me how happy I should be ' indeed the obligations I am under to you my humble services never can discharge '

" Why will you vex me by talking in this manner you know very well it has cost me no trouble, but given me a great deal of amusement Then as for Mr Somers I am very suie he considers himself amply repaid by the care you took of him during his illness

But we must here leave them in order to give the reeder a brief account of what had happened to the mendicant s daughter since her last appearance

Evine met with great success on her first dramatic attempt Indeed her rare beauty giaceful deportment, and harmonious delivery excited a sensation in the little town almost unprecedented in theatrical annals ' The young strolling actress soon became a common topic throughout the county and was a prevailing toast in the town long before the news of her debut reached Edward s sick chamber, where notwithstanding the hours she was obliged to spend fiom home, at night Evine would insist on taking her post by the bed side of her wounded friend but where the regularity of hei absence and the many little additional comforts provided for him soon however awoke Edward s suspicions, and at last he learnt the truth from Mrs Bondell

" If she is not on the London boards before she is two years older, I am very moch misteken said that lady on concluding her account of Evine s success

" But the *life* Mrs Bondell—I know I may say as much to you without giving offence—the life is so injurious to a female s character !

" Poor dear creature What you say is alas but too true ' yet she has succeeded, and promises to make her way in the profession—so we can hardly do otherwise than encourage her to persevere But we must take care of her Mr Somers

" She shall never want a protector while I have strength, ' said the young man

" Nor shall she want advice while I am at hand to give it, retorted the worthy Mrs Bondell

Edward gradually recovered and was soon able to add his earnings to those of Evine, whose great success had already procured her flattering overtures from several country managers   Fortune however had better things in store for her   A gentleman of great reputation in the legal and literary world having accidentally witnessed her representation of one of the heroines of our immortal bard struck with the talent she displayed felt so much interest in her success that the removal of our two young friends to London was at once determined on where that kind gentleman s influence proved to be so great that Evine s engagement at Drury Lane was almost the immediate consequence   Edward too soon felt the beneficial effects of this introduction   it was his fate to make one of those lucky hits which raise a few to affluence and renown which thousands perish in aiming at—in a word through the fostering protection of their new friend Mr Wharing in a few short months the verses of the young poet were in every mouth and the remuneration for his literary labours greatly increased his powers of improving Evine for her forthcoming effort

Vivyan s circumstances thus altered he wrote to Mrs Bondell to cancel her engagement with manager Share and begged her to join them in London   He felt the necessity of providing Evine with a suitable companion of her own sex   and though he might for a moment have wished to have supplied her with a companion from a less equivocal station in life, the peculiar relation in which he stood to Evine together with the profession which he began to think she was justified in adopting, induced him to abandon his desire

For the comfort of his friends, he rented a small neat cottage in the neighbourhood of what is now called the New Road in which they were installed on Mrs Bondell s arrival   He took up his own residence in the same neighbourhood and to note Evine s progress in her various pursuits formed his pleasing relaxation from the severer studies in which he was now so deeply engaged

Her improvement now became so rapid, that the beggar s daughter and the actress of the barn were no longer to be recognised in the elegant and accomplished girl, who was now attending in Drury Lane the requisite rehearsals   It was an anxious interval for Evine   but she gave her whole energy to her new duties and went cheerfully through the drilling

At length,

Heavily in clouds came on the day

on which the young lady so long announced was to make her appearance Mr Wharing knew Evine s history as far as it was known to Edward tempted by its singularity that gentleman had communicated it, with some restrictions, to a few intimates, who, in their turn, beset by the same temptation had detailed to others the history of the new actress,

suppressing and adding as their fancies guided them until a most ro
mantic story was in general circulation the hero and heroine of which
tale of sentiment bore the names of Vivyan and Somers

This circumstance in connexion with the kind exertion of friends,
drew an unusual crowd to the theatre   The men rushed to catch the
first glimpse of the extraordinary beauty as the debutante was already
styled in the elegant phraseology of the public press   while the women
submitted to the martyrdom of a London mob to see that phenomenon
of their sex—a person whose fair name report had kept unsullied while
it exaggerated her adventures with unlimited invention   Of all this
Evine was, however happily unconscious   and it would have amazed the
multitude could they have known the childlike simplicity and purity of
heart possessed by the great object of attraction on that most momentous
evening

As usual a crowd of dirty men and boys were loitering at the entrance
as the hackney coach drew up to the stage door   The lamp in the door
way gave a faint light just serving to make visible half a dozen grimmed
and sickly faces   but among them peering between two shoulders was
discerned a pair of eyes, with whose broad brutal stare to Evine seemed
familiar

" Tis *she*   uttered a voice in a low tone but so distinct that it reached
Evine s ears   It was to her a well known sound   and she shuddered as
she turned her head in the direction from whence it proceeded   Again
she met the gaze of the eyes she had before noticed   this time she knew
them *well*

This circumstance which has taken some time to relate was the work
of a minute   Within that space the coach had drawn up deposited its
load and drawn off again   As Evine, unnerved by what she had seen
and heard sought her dressing room leaning tremulously on the arm of
Mrs Bondell Townsend—for he it was—moved away from the stage
door and mingled with the crowd, bustling over the dark and shiny pave
ment of Russell Street

" I think I know a tale will bring my lady from Grosvenor Street to
Drury Lane before St Paul s clock strikes seven   said he as he hurried
off in the direction of the Dowager Viscountess s residence

" I am sure I saw *him*   said Evine, scarcely aware that she was
speaking aloud, just as Mrs Bondell to the great discomfiture of another
female in attendance had succeeded in adjusting the white silk robe of
the representative of Juliet, the character in which she was about to make
her debut

" Saw who child ?   enquired Mrs Bondell, who had long since in
dulged in very maternal epithets, when accosting her young charge —
" saw who ?

" A man I saw once before in very frightful circumstances the night
I lost my poor father   replied Evine as a tear started to her eye

' Bless you ' rejoined her companion kissing away the living pearl
that trickled down her cheek and throwing back from her forehead a
beautiful ringlet   " how lovely it looks '   What would your father say
if he could see it now ?

He would feel no pleasure, sighed Evine "it ever irritated him to see me looked at

"Not a word more, or I shall scold How dare you encourage these gloomy thoughts now! Your success depends upon your spirits The way to recover your father is to succeed and make a fortune

My kind, kind friend cried Evine throwing her arms round Mrs Bondell's neck, and assuming a cheerful manner, ' you shall not have to complain again

At length the summons to the green room was heard and, preceded by the manager the ladies took their way thither through the litter and trumpery of the stage

To a *debutante*, the green room presents a more formidable audience than the house The envious and critical glances of the sisterhood, the low deportment of many of the brethren and chiefly the intrusive impertinence of titled and wealthy loungers require an exertion to encounter The company assembled on that occasion had however sufficient sympathy to dispense with the usual ceremony and impudence All eyes were turned towards Evine as she entered and returned the salutations of those nearest her A very welcome and flattering murmur from all sides of the apartment followed

Evine looked anxiously round her in the hope of perceiving Vivyan When he called that morning he had told her not to expect him till after the play 'These people said he observe among themselves a degree of decorum that will render my protection unnecessary My presence this evening might give rise to unpleasant reports From an obscure corner of the house I will therefore watch your triumph, and come round to congratulate you when it is complete

'She fully justifies all that has been said of her, thought Ronald, who had just entered the room after an attentive but unperceived survey of Evine "but I am not a stranger to those features How pure and modest an expression! Where can I have seen that countenance? It reminds me of the portrait in my study at Minhurst No it cannot be that' Yet that smile—I am sure I have seen it before Stay! was it not round the lips of the wandering girl I met on Wedgemoor Heath that I have seen it play?

A frown gathered round his brow as he came to this conclusion but before he had time to cherish the feelings that occasioned it, his attention was diverted by the conversation of a party at his side

'She does look very young and innocent, observed a lady, who had very evidently long since abandoned all pretensions to those qualities

'What very great hypocrites you women are! rejoined a gentleman, whose voice Ronald recognised to be that of his opponents, the Right Honorable Francis Fraser Fluentleigh

You don't mean to say that she is one?

"I do

And Ronald looked round with indignation on the man who could injure the reputation of a lovely creature placed in circumstances of peculiar trial the subject of a scandalous gossip After a hasty glance at Evine, he turned hastily towards the last speaker

Do you know, Sir you have uttered contemptible slander? said he

Sir! to listen to a conversation not intended for your hearing, is not the act of a gentleman stammered Fluentleigh who was taken by surprise

To slander an unprotected and innocent girl, Sir, is the act of a coward!

Sir, this insult—

"Oh Sir I am ready to give you satisfaction

And before the loud voices of the disputants had drawn a crowd around them a challenge had been formally given and accepted

At this moment the first bars of the overture were heard, and a general bustle ensued and not long after Evine was summoned to take her place from which she was to make her entry where wrapped in a shawl, with Mrs Bondell at her side she watched attentively the business of the stage The lamp lights flared around her till her eyes ached and the vapour of a thousand breaths already came oppressively upon her

At length the cue was given, and starting from her hiding place, with the light bound with which the custom of centuries requires Juliet to answer the call of her Nurse, the Beggar s daughter stood in the presence of her audience

A slight murmur hailed her appearance increasing as she acknow ledged it, and the spectators became impressed with the beauty of the figure that had thus sprung into their presence, until it became a deafen ing din of hearty rapturous applause For some time the play was sus pended, and Evine with downcast eyes and a beating heart curtsied her thanks to the gratified assembly Gradually, after four or five successive outbreaks each more enthusiastic than the last the applause subsided and every one became mute and breathless to catch her first accents She now ventured to look on those who had given her so kind a reception, but the dead silence of those beings whose heads formed a succession of rows from the footlights to the roof was more appalling than their ap plause A feeling of giddiness and stupor seemed to seize her, and she felt unable to articulate a word Fortunately her part required her to speak almost immediately on her entrance and her first words floated like silver notes in the silence of the vast and thronged area As the business of the scene went on she gained confidence, and when, in answer to Lady Capulet s question—

Tell me daughter Juliet
How stands your disposition to get married ?

she had to reply

It is an honour that I dream not of !

she gave the line with such exquisite and elegant simplicity in a tone so audible and full of music yet so unstrained and natural, that a second peal of applause proved that she had already gained the enthusiastic ad miration of the house

It would be tedious to follow her through the play It will suffice to say that the interest increased with every act and in the more impas sioned scenes she exerted over her audience that influence which invests the scene with so close a resemblance to reality as to awaken the deepest emotion and suspend applause In her hands the character of Juliet resembled a strain of sweet music commencing with a mild and playful prelude gradually mellowing into tones of melancholy and sorrow, fol lowed by a wild and irregular movement of despair, and then subsiding in a gentle cadence

A gratified audience gave her the most flattering proofs of their satis faction at the close of the piece but far more dear to her than the shouts of the multitude was the smile of Edward Vivyan which greeted her as she came from the stage

Ronald was among the first to leave his seat at the fall of the curtain he had watched the performance with the greatest interest and long before its termination dismissed the supposition that had flashed across his mind when he saw Evine in the green room.

It cannot be the same person said he elegance and taste like that could not in so short a space of time have been imparted to the child of a vagrant No! no! it is but a striking resemblance, thank God Were this actress the person I imagined her to be, heavens! in what perplexity should I be placed

No 24

Thus he reasoned as he passed through the thronged lobbies. While waiting under the portico however his opinion was considerably shaken by the appearance of a lady, who, closely hid in a large cloak, was hastening to her carriage.

A glance satisfied him that it was the dowager Lady Minhurst.

CHAPTER XXIV

ABOUT eleven o'clock on the same evening, Mira Countess of Wagmouth was doing the honours of her first route amidst the splendour of a gorgeous and thronged suite of apartments in —— Square.

Envied by every mother and daughter present receiving from every one the most flattering homage the young Countess was far from experiencing that buoyancy of spirit a youthful and untried bosom might be expected to prove in the midst of the choicest enjoyments of refined life. It was not that she had the morbid temperament of the sentimental girl who obstinately persists in closing her eyes on the sun shine of life nor had she writhed under those passions the penalty as well as the glory of our natures which leave upon the heart a settled melancholy repugnant to every pleasure. To neither of these causes could her indifference to the gaiety of the scene be attributed yet imperceptibly a deafening influence was creeping over her spirit. Her new state, though splendid as the most ambitious heart could desire brought with it a cumbersome ness that destroyed the elasticity of youth and in depriving the heart of its freedom robbed it for ever of enjoyment.

Her husband comported himself towards her as well as a fashionable husband might be expected to do who in marrying a beauty for the gratification of his vanity could neither discern nor appreciate the worth of mind she united to her personal charms.

When he had no occasion to make a parade of his handsome Countess she was left to herself while he hurried from home to gratify the propensities of low and depraved tastes. Many wives would have been perfectly satisfied and even very happy with the liberty Mira thus possessed of disposing of a large portion of her time. For her however prevented by pride and virtue from supplying the vacancy occasioned by her husband's absence, the hours passed by with chilling listlessness and every succeeding day brought no emotion no hope nor fear no joy nor sorrow, to remove the irksome inanity of a vacant heart.

Her only resource was in the few pleasant recollections with which a short life had stored her memory. The materials were few but the solitary spirit can wonderfully dilate the subject matter of its broodings and Mira beguiled her solitude by recalling old faces old scenes and old emotions till the sole enjoyment of her dull existence became the dreamy and protracted vision of the past.

This habit grew so strongly upon her that a fit of absence would sometimes surprise her in society and into this social sin was she be trayed on the night of her first rout when an interval in the tedious ceremony of reception left her for a few minutes unoccupied A very lovely girl had been presented to her a moment before whose pretty joyous countenance betrayed an ecstasy of spirits that made a great im pression on Mira   As the young lady turned away the lines

> May heaven guard thy gentle heart
> From every maiden sorrow

occurred forcibly to the mind of the Countess it was the wish of her own heart expressed in the language of another

The lines of the poet led her very naturally to think of their author, and she was soon plunged into a very profound study of the well known and often admired lineaments of Edward Vivyan   She was very far from suspecting the pleasurable emotion with which she dwelt upon his memory traced image she deemed it natural to give *that* welcome as well as any other object connected with more happy hours   But it never struck her that a welcome similar in kind might differ in degree

She was lost in one of these meditations, when some one approached her she looked up and was betrayed into something more than a blush on perceiving at her side the person her mind had been dwelling on so intently

"My dear Countess said the Earl who in the presence of strangers assumed a silly show of affection towards his lady, "allow me to present to you Mr Vivyan Mr Vivyan the Countess of Wagmouth You have heard of Mr Vivyan, dearest ?

"We have met before said Mira extending her hand with great cordiality to Edward Mr Vivyan it has long given me pleasure to hear that your talents were appreciated by the public, and I am happy to have this opportunity of making you acquainted with my sympathy in your success

' As you are already acquainted Mr Vivyan will have no trouble in making himself at home said the Earl who knew nothing respecting Edward s history, and cared as little about the *breed* of the *lions of the day*, provided he could secure the attendance of a great many of that formidable tribe at his sumptuous but rather miscellaneous entertain ments

There was something embarrassing in the situation of the young people Mira the young timid shrinking bride stood blushing in the presence of the successful literary Colossus, (for such was he become in point of celebrity,) who two years before, at their last and almost only interview, had received from the clever and then light hearted girl, the encouragement so agreeable, and so necessary to a youthful worshipper of the Nine   Edward on the other hand found himself the honoured guest of a lady whose slightest notice he had been taught to consider as a work of condescension, and whose smile he still regarded as beyond all price

We shall see you often I hope, Mr Vivyan, said Mira, after an awkward pause of some moments, actuated partly by a desire to enliven

the dull society with which she was surrounded by the frequent presence
of a man of acknowledged genius and partly perhaps by a sincere wish
to furnish Edward with an opportunity of extending his acquaintance
with the rich and powerful of the higher circles

'I am sensible of the honour you do me replied Edward, bowing
profoundly, while a blush mantled over his cheek

Another lady now joined them, and prevented Mira from commenting
on his reply Had she done so however, the evasion of the young poet
would have probably escaped her notice Yet *evasion* it was for, while
he thanked the lovely lady of one of the most fashionable and wealthy
establishments in Town for the honour she conferred upon him he inwardly
determined to shun the dangerous snare she was unconsciously preparing
for his peace Could he have done so without unpoliteness, he would
have immediately withdrawn from her presence, since his heart loudly
admonished him that to linger in it was to court temptation If his
unhappy passion had not been subdued by the distance between them he
felt that he could not with impunity indulge in friendly intercourse with
its object

So far from giving him comfort, his presentation to Mira in her own
house and the courteous reception she had given him effectually disturbed the calm that constant literary labour, and an unvarying tide of
success, had produced in his heart To the emotion occasioned by their
meeting succeeded the poignant agony of hopeless love, aggravated by a
combination of circumstances till it imbittered all that seemed joyous in
his then condition, and cast deep shadows over the bright prospects he
had recently cherished with the fondness of hope He had seen her in
the pride of her beauty himself adorned with the guerdon of merited
fame, she had welcomed him with the smile of friendship her eye had
beamed with pleasure as she spoke of his success but what to him were
her congratulations ? what to him her gracious smiles ? Alas, an ignis
fatuus to betray him into the darkest depths and desolation of unrequited
passion !

The peerless beauties, flashing with the brilliancy of eyes and jewels
glided by him in harmony to the magic music but he saw them not
to him the gorgeous fete no longer yielded enjoyment, and retiring to a
recess, formed by the projection of a bow window he gazed vacantly on
the soothing star lit heavens

Edward Vivyan was not the only sad and weary spirit in the thronged
halls of the Earl of Wagmouth

The dowager Viscountess Minhurst as she had agreed to do in the
morning dressed at an early hour for the purpose of assisting her grand
daughter in the formalities of a first reception night The arrival of
Townsend, however and his account of what he had witnessed on his
way to the two shilling gallery of Drury Lane theatre materially changed
the plans of his mistress It was with great reluctance she gave credit
to his story—that Evine should in so short a time have been raised from
the degradation of mendicity to fill a situation in the first theatre of the
metropolis appeared to her ladyship an impossibility When, however
he reminded Lady Minhurst that he with others under the direction of

Grasp had torn the mendicant s daughter from the arms of her father, and borne her in their arms long enough to become familiar with her features she began to consider his story as deserving consideration and desiring him to wait her return, drove directly to the theatre A private box happening to be disengaged she witnessed the debut of Evine and recognised in her the poor girl who had been the unconscious cause of the anguish and anxiety she had proved since they last met

If Lady Minhurst had been astonished to hear Townsend s story her surprise was still greater when she found the object of her persecution not employed in any mean capacity but as a leading tragic actress On ascertaining however that it was a first appearance her hopes revived and leaning back in her box she watched the progress of the performance As the clear musical tones of Evine came to her ear imparting even to the verse of Shakspere the charm of vocal melody her spirit again sunk within her and she trembled at the thought of having to contend with a person enjoying the distinctions of talent and public favour Scene suc ceeded scene the increasing applause rang discordantly in the ears of Lady Minhurst yet when the curtain fell, and the young actress came forward to receive the ovations of the multitude, the dowager like one spell bound still lingered in the box

Frightful visions had crossed her mind during the performance of those five acts—visions so terrible and absorbing that the interval scarcely seemed as many minutes Evine the actress the gossip of the crowd the heart s queen perhaps of some wealthy titled fool, could not be driven from her mind Happy would it have been for her ladyship had Evine s image only haunted her in this light but she was pursued by Evine conscious of and clamouring for her rights supported by the terrible and resistless influence of popularity The events of the night came over her like a sudden astounding shock, and produced such deep felt dismay that it was not till the night breeze fanned her heated brow, as she rode towards home that she had sufficient freedom of thought to perceive and shudder at the violent measures to which she might be prompted by despair

Townsend awaited her return and by the time she confronted him, her active mind had found a new errand for her faithful and well paid emissary

'Townsend, she exclaimed, as soon as they were closeted "you will return at once to the asylum whither you followed Grasp s man this morning and present to the governor of the house this letter it contains a request that he will immediately deliver to you one of his patients Have a coach ready and take with you sufficient force to manage a strong hale man should he prove restive The person delivered to you you will bring here

"But if the give nor doesn t treat your ladyship s letter like a gentle man, and doesn t do as you bids him l'

Her ladyship smiled at the suggestion

"There is no fear of that, my good Townsend

Lady Minhurst was right The keeper of a suburban madhouse—an establishment so private as not to come under the notice of the magis tracy—was not a person likely to reject the golden bait held forth to tempt him to her purposes

' Does your ladyship think the feller will be very obstrepolous ?

' You may use what precautions you like   This note   she added, displaying at the same time a Bank note of the value of fifty pounds   is not too great a reward for your trouble when the man is once within my doors   Be discreet and expeditious   Let me not return from the Countess of Wagmouth s before you get back

Lady Minhurst had not been more than an hour in the drawing room of her grand daughter before she was accosted by Ronald   As she per ceived him approaching she trembled violently   His countenance lat terly on all occasions pale and melancholy looked haggard in the extreme and the disorder of his costume contrasted with the careful toilette of the gay throng of beaus among which he mingled   The fitful light of violent agitation and indecision beaming from his eye convinced her ladyship that something had gone wrong   and, like the conductor to the lightning she attempted to guide the blow she could not ward off

' Are you ill Ronald   she enquired, meeting him and extending her hand   ' you look wretchedly

Without replying he took the proffered hand   and led her ladyship into a small boudoir that terminated in one direction the suite of recep tion rooms, and was at that moment deserted

" Your ladyship was at the theatre this evening,   said Ronald, accom panying his words with a glance, that made his companion quail at heart   no trace of emotion, however, was apparent on her countenance

' I was at Drury Lane

" To witness the first appearance of a young actress ?

" Just so '

' This interest in the drama is novel to your ladyship

' Our tastes seem to have taken a similar turn   From your informa tion, I judge you were there also   but I see an old friend I wish to speak to   give me your arm into the next room   And she made a movement to withdraw

' Lady Minhurst, I wished to speak to you touching that young actress   Oblige me by taking this seat

The young man s tone was solemn and painfully decisive   and was uttered with a look that prevented refusal   Her ladyship sank into a seat he had wheeled forward   Ronald seated himself beside her

" Is she not handsome ?   said he, while his eyes seemed to read the soul of the person he addressed

" Beautiful   I confess   but this trifling subject we can discuss at any time,   she replied   making an effort to rise

It cannot be discussed too soon for my own peace '

' What do you mean, Ronald ?

" Lady Minhurst   you remember the beggar girl we met on our way to Minhurst   did she not resemble this actress ?

It is so long since I cannot judge,   faltered her ladyship, trembling violently

Lady Minhurst, you have not forgotten the portrait in my study at

Minhurst I should say this actress was the original should you not?

' Ronald these are wild fancies you look distracted Hold me not or I give the alarm '

I have but a few words to say Madam and you *shall* hear them In the church of Minhurst there is a tomb it bears for inscription a short name— Evine —but it surprises you to hear this actress answered to the same

These were terrible words coming from whom they did to the wretched woman who heard them but the look with which they were accompanied—a look of abhorrence from one she doated on went to her heart s core

Mercy ' she exclaimed scarcely able to keep her seat with emotion

' Is it so, then ' said Ronald with frightful coldness, leaving abruptly his seat and walking away

To rise and seize him by the hand were the work of a moment

' Ronald hear me in God s name ' No word of this go not hence compose yourself I will tell you all I am guilty but wretched very wretched

He disengaged himself from her grasp and made another movement to retire

'Distracted boy ! what will you do ? whispered the agonized woman, throwing her arms round his neck, to detain him "will you bring ruin on us all ? Look ! see you not your father among the crowd ? Would you *kill him* Ronald ?

Again releasing himself from her hold

I can be discreet said he and hurried from her presence

It was impossible to pass through the crowded rooms unobserved to escape notice he approached the nearest recess it was the one at which Edward Vivyan had taken refuge

As soon as Lady Minhurst recovered from the shock she had received she ordered her carriage and hastened home During the ride her reso lution which had been entirely overthrown in the brief but momentous interview with her grandson returned and she began to consider the exact position in which she stood and to prepare to meet the worst

He knows all ! she reasoned " An hour ago I would have sacri ficed every thing to keep him ignorant of my early crimes now it is no longer possible I cannot hope to command his silence longer than his father lives—Ronald is too just to enjoy the heritage of another What can be done ? The father the real heir must be already in my power this girl this actress, how can I remove her ? The public character of her profession defies concealment the emolument it yields places her above the temptation of my gold Lost and ruined woman that I am !

When the carriage drew up, Lady Minhurst found Townsend waiting in the hall

Come to my private room said she

The man followed her in silence to the great discomfiture of Ma'am selle Eugenie who yawned frightfully at the prospect of another hour before her services would be required

'Well Townsend said the lady, you are ready to receive your reward I presume ?

'If your ladyship particularly wishes to pay it in advance, replied the man

"How ?

'I haven't got him !

Does the fellow refuse my request—my noble offer ?

Not he my lady he's a trifle too cunning to do that I fancy

'How is it then you return alone

It's prudence as dictates my lady They says the man is terrible hobstropolous and couldn't well be moved without a row so the giv nor adwised us to leave the business until to morrow

'Have you no brains man ? By day light the attempt will be doubly hazardous

'The feller's breakfast's to be drugged my lady

'How Townsend ? asked the wily woman

"No harm in the world my lady It will only compose him into a nap vile we brings him away

Enough see to it that the man comes by no harm and let it be managed early in the morning In the mean time you will step to the theatre, and ascertain the dd ess of the actress who has just made her first appearance   Put no restraint on your liberality   spare no pains to find this out '

" You shall have her address at breakfast to morrow, my lady, said Townsend

They then separated, and Lady Minhurst spent the night that ensued, not in tears of penitence, but in laborious scheming how to conceal her crime, and avoid its chastisement

---

CHAPTER XXV

It was long past midnight scores of carriages were drawn up in —— Square, and innumerable lights flashed from the windows of its proudest mansion   Occasionally a vehicle was called from the line to take up a guest but this happened at rare intervals, and the entertainment seemed yet to be in the very height of its splendour as two gentlemen well wrapped in cloaks passed through the crowd of lackeys in the hall As they descended the steps of the door a servant approached one of them, but his services were refused, and the two friends turned in silence from the square into an adjoining street. As they threaded the then dimly lit avenues of the town they by degrees fell into conversation, and at length though not until they had walked a considerable distance, indulged in free and hearty intercourse   They might have passed for intimate friends so familiarly did they converse with that enjoyment known only to the intercourse of familiar friends did they exchange argument and repartee, until their words and laughter echoed through the deserted streets

In their merriment however there was no true joy   the heart of either had been betrayed in its fondest hope, and the gaiety they indulged in was that wild mirth that more betokens the existence of grief than joy   Yet on they kept walking with a quicker step, and in more boisterous laughter, till their exultation might have passed for phrenzy or intoxication

Their progress was at last arrested by the blazing lights of a tavern, as its doors were thrown open to allow the egress of a party of revellers The friends entered, and soon found themselves in the midst of a crowd of modern Bacchanals   Here, then as now, the peer squandered the heritage of a noble ancestry, and the apprentice scattered prodigally the scanty sum obtained by a long system of fraud on the property of his employer   Wine and women were the deities of the place, to whom golden offerings were joyously made, and their giddy worshippers were favoured in return with high priced wines of the worst description, and the hollow smiles of that race of fallen angels to whom destiny has assigned the pave of the town for a lighting place

In all the excesses of the scene the friends plunged wildly, even madly men who to obtain the love of one virtuous woman, were capable of a life of sacrifice and achievement, placed by circumstances beyond the pale of hope suffered the degrading embrace of the harlot, and sought to efface sorrow in the debasing exultation of the drunkard

Their riotous revels were carried into the night or rather morning of the new day and when they sallied from the scene of their debauch, the lamps burnt dimly in the grey of dawn, and many an artizan might be seen hurrying to his daily toil

'Six o'clock by heavens ' said one of them, raising the dial of his watch towards a lamp "I have an appointment at seven Will you do me a service, Vivyan ?

"I am yours to command, to the utmost of my ability, replied that gentleman

"I had a quarrel last night, and Seven is the hour appointed for adjusting the difference

'A duel ? '

'Exactly so Will you be my second ?

'You have my promise to serve you as far as I am able but is there no way of reconciling the matter by means less serious ?

"None, I assure you '

"Your quarrel then must have been important ? '

"Infinitely important—about an actress '

"And you will throw your life away on a worthless woman, perhaps '

"As far as worth is concerned, she ranks, I suppose, with the rest of her sex in beauty she is a paragon But you know her—I saw you at the theatre last night

"You do not speak of the new actress—*the Juliet ?*

"I speak of *the* Juliet By heavens ' you do well to call her *the* Juliet the poet himself would have been charmed with her "

"Has any one dared to insult her ?

"Oh ' oh ' Sir—are you interested in her ? I beg a thousand pardons but I cannot possibly transfer to you the task of chastising a scoundrel, though by your looks I see you would fain pass for her knight errant

"I am more deeply interested in that young lady than you imagine, observed Edward "if through protecting her you are involved in this quarrel, I heartily espouse it '

"Then let us lose no time ' rejoined Ronald "give me your address, and I will call with my coach and take you to the place of meeting, some other time you must tell me how you are connected with this charming creature '

'There is nothing between us to prevent Miss Somers from receiving your respectful homage She has a mind above listening to other proposals

"I am happy to hear you say so although I felt sure of that when I undertook my post of champion '

After a few more words the friends separated, to encounter in another hour the Honourable Francis Fraser Fluentleigh and *his friend*

On the same evening when the fete at the Earl of Wagmouth's was at its height, Wilfred Welbourne, stretched on the straw pallet of his cell, suffered in silence from the agony of mind which had so long racked him Since we last had occasion to refer to the wretched father, he had undergone torture of the most aggravated kind, inflicted with relentless perseverance by his heartless keeper   Long since would the wretched man have been released by death from his miserable and hopeless condition, had not the flame of life been constantly renewed by the mysterious influence the mind exercises over the body   One desire, one strong life giving desire enabled him to endure the hardship of his lot—the desire however hopeless, of again embracing his lost child

Indeed the only actual enjoyment of his condition was connected with Evine   the remembrance of her smiles, her caresses, some incident of her childhood, or her lineaments as they appeared to him when he last beheld them, constituted his only recreation and comfort unless the faint prospect that glimmered like sunshine on his wretchedness, of a happy meeting in store

His mother had likewise a share in his thoughts but these were of no pleasurable nature   Long years of suffering had reduced her to a sad state of imbecility, and the few lucid moments which she experienced, could hardly be hailed as a blessing, since they were invariably followed by protracted seasons of mental darkness   He had not seen her since the day that Dodds had surprised them when overcome by fatigue and emotion they slumbered in each other s arms   This led him to conclude and such indeed was the case, that she was no longer considered the harmless creature the keepers had been accustomed to conceive her and that she was accordingly watched with greater vigilance   At times he was distracted by the thought of the cruelty by which her endeavours on his behalf might have exposed her although he hoped that long experience had taught her poor idiot as she was, how to conciliate her persecutors

Such was the hourly terror of the poor mendicant s internal life   externally it was equally monotonous and painful—the same damp cell, the same filthy garments, and unwholesome fare awaited him

The morning was drawing on rapidly when the hand of daft Mary once more rested on the ill clad shoulders of the mendicant   He started and looked round

' Hush ' she whispered, raising her hand to prevent his half uttered exclamation of surprise ' throw the rug over you, and follow me

He complied promptly   guessing immediately that the poor creature had some scheme in view for his benefit—probably their escape   It was not however till they had threaded numerous passages, and descended various flights of steps, that she ventured to address him

' You will promise to take me with you,' she said, suddenly turning round and raising the lantern in her hand, so that the feeble light it yielded fell on the features of Welbourne   " tell me, you will not leave me here ?

" Do you then hope to escape ?

" Hush ' she again exclaimed, cautiously surveying the place, and then added in a whisper ' promise to take me with you

' If you can indeed enable me to escape, I should be worse than a fiend, mother, to leave you behind

Mother ' Did you call me mother?   Then I am sure you will not

leave me   But you should not call me mother   it is not true   I never
had but one babe and you are not like him

And the poor woman seemed to have forgotten her design   for she
stood gazing vacantly in the face of the mendicant as if comparing the
worn features of the man with the fair image of the babe memory had
traced on her heart

Welbourne looked around him with impatience   They were in what
appeared to be an under ground room of the asylum   it was half filled
with straw, shavings, and other rubbish, and presented no outlet to his
view save the door by which they had entered   Notw thstanding its
underground situation, it was not very far removed from a sleeping-room,
for the loud snoring of sleepers at frequent intervals disturbed the dead
silence

' This will not do ' said he, at length   " If escape is possible, let us
in God s name make the attempt

His words fortunately took effect the unhappy woman came to herself,
and with a promptitude and clearness that astonished her companion,
proceeded to acquaint him with the steps she proposed taking

We must close this door said she pointing to the one by which
they had entered   that we may not be overheard

By what way then are we to get from this cellar ?   inquired Welbourne in a tone of surprise and dejection

Fear not, my brave man,   replied daft Mary—for we prefer still
calling her by her old cognomen—assuming an air of exultation , ' only
keep Dodds out and the worst is done

And acting in accordance with this opinion, she placed the lantern
on the ground and having closed the door with such fastenings as it
presented began, for it opened inwards, to form a barricade against it
with the straw and rubbish   The mendicant at a loss to conceive her
plan looked on with astonishment, and perhaps a little mistrust   With
a vigour really wonderful for her age, she raised the pile higher and
higher till the upper part of the door alone remained visible

" Ha! ha ! ha ! she shouted, surveying the result of her labour with
satisfaction; " I defy them now to approach—aye, aye I defy them 'Tis
a weary work yet," she continued, looking round on the heaps of rubbish
that nearly filled the other half of the place   will you not help me ?
Ah ! you have no child to seek or you would not stand looking on with
folded arms, when you might once more breathe the free air

She now resumed her occupation, and Welbourne concluded from her
impatience to remove the rubbish, that there was some outlet beyond
it   The moment he saw the object of her toil he fell to work with an
effort only to be exceeded by her own   Though she had accomplished
much in securing themselves from surprise by fastening the door, much,
however remained to be done   The rubbish had been collecting for
years, and though chiefly of the lightest materials, grew more and more
dense as they approached the conclusion of their labours   Scarcely
uttering a word they had toiled for nearly an hour, when they both
paused to gather fresh strength as Welbourne looked round he perceived the candle was burnt nearly to the socket of the lantern   and

still, a vast and discouraging pile arose between them and the wall. The prospect of being left in darkness stimulated him to renew his efforts · he tore down the masses that obstructed his way with the energy of desperation, till the clouds of dust that accompanied every fall impeded his vision, and threatened both himself and companion with suffocation. Having undermined a heap for a considerable distance, a powerful effort brought down the upper part with the violence of an avelanche, and he violently escaped being buried beneath the load   As, however, the dust gradually dispersed, a cry of joy broke at once from the lips of mother and son—a faint glimmer a little above their heads betrayed an aperture.

'Tis there ' tis there ! cried the female, almost in a paroxysm of joy , ' beyond that grating is the road ; we may gain it easily

"A grating ! repeated her son despondingly

"Aye, the bars are stout   but I have that will make them yield,   returned the mother, and she drew from her bosom a stock of rusty blades, bars of iron, large nails, &c , a collection she had been many years in forming

'Let us work then,' cried Welbourne, selecting the implement he conceived most likely to serve him, and springing on a heap of rubbish from which posture he could pursue his work on the bars with ease an effect

'Bring here the light, he exclaimed, after he had been a few moments in this posture ' stay, not yet—some one passes   Hide it, in God s name   tis the watch '

The woman hastily concealed the light   Wilfred crouched low down against the wall   and the breathing of both was checked as they heard the heay footfall of the night guard on the pavement without   While thus silent, they could still hear, though more subdued the snoring they had heard before, and when the tread of the watch died away in the distance Welbourne rose to renew his work

"Shall I light you now ? asked the woman

"I fear I cannot do without ' rejoined he

And with a swift foot daft Mary advanced towards him   As she endeavoured to raise herself to the same level as her son, the pile on which she trod giving way from beneath, she was precipitated to the ground

Before Welbourne was well aware of the accident, for she had presence of mind to check the cry of terror she was on the point of uttering, a bright flame illuminated the place, and in an instant the whole cellar was in a blaze   The cause of the misfortune was evident   the candle falling from the hands of the aged female on a heap of straw, the unfortunate fugitives were threatened with the horrors of a frightful death.

'For your life ' gasped Wilfred, as well as the smoke would allow him   "Rise ' for your life aid me to throw what we can upon the flames   it is our only chance

As he spoke, he dashed as huge a mass as his brawny arms could lift upon the burning heap   For a moment the place was plunged in darkness   but the fire had taken a strong hold, and in the next it blazed forth with terrific vigour

The mendicant looked round in despair   his eyes rested on his com panion She stood gazing on the flames with distended eye balls and her features illuminated by the horrid glare seemed to recall to Wel bourne s mind some horrid vision of the past

The door she cried—"the door! we cannot gain the door—we have sealed our own tomb!'

Frantic at the thought of the death that seemed to await him and more so at the idea of witnessing the burning—the slow, cruel burning— of his helpless insane mother, Welbourne dashed towards the aperture and again laboured to snap the massive bars or to wrest them from their stone-resting places Motionless in his grasp they baffled his efforts, though the sweat drops ran in torrents down his cheek and the blood spurted from his fingers, as he desisted for a moment, exhausted by his furious attempt

"Back, back mother for God s sake' the flame will catch your clothes if you do not move, said he but perceiving that terror had deprived the poor creature of all power to act he pulled her towards him, and once more renewed his efforts to save her

A bright star light night had succeeded to a wet evening and as it bore away, a sharp drying wind had risen   Fortunately for Welbourne and his mother it blew directly through the grating   and though it in

creased the violence of the flames, it nevertheless carried them in the direction of the door, and so postponed—at least for a few minutes—the danger which threatened them

Long, however, their destruction could not be delayed · dense smoke floated through the cellar, and the flames, finding no egress, played round the walls till the rubbish taking fire on all sides, threatened to enclose them in a circle of flame

"My God, my God! shouted Welbourne, in agony, as he saw his mother sink to his feet, overcome with heat and terror

At that moment a gust of wind came through the aperture and while it drove away the rapidly approaching flames, as it blew over the mendicant's brow, it seemed to inspire him with fresh and mighty vigour Once more he seized the opposing bar the violence of his jerk would have dislocated the strong arms that gave it, had they not succeeded in moving it Welbourne thrilled with joy as he felt it yield to his grasp another effort, and the bar was wrenched from its position and hurled to the ground

Notwithstanding the roar of the flames the cellar echoed with his loud cry of joy His mother was raised hastily in his arms,—a kiss imprinted on her senseless lips in another moment, mother and son were free

As he fled swiftly along the road, Welbourne cast an anxious glance around No one was in sight Already a few feet behind him rose black and dreary the house of cruelty, in which he had so long been confined Above its gaunt outline was a cloudless, star-lit sky, faintly reflecting the flames that now began to flash from the building. The sight of the fair heavens, the invigorating breeze that fanned the precious burthen he bore, his own desire of freedom,- -all urged him onward He sought a quarter of the town he knew and when the alarm of fire was given, Welbourne and his mother were beyond pursuit.

In less than three hours the whole building was reduced to ashes, leaving no traces how the fire originated, nor any clew to the flight of the fugitives, who were supposed to have perished in the flames. Nearly all the inmates escaped; and of the four who perished, three were said to have sought their fate. One of these was a poor woman, whose mental derangement was caused by the burning of her own house, when her only child perished She was seen to throw herself into the midst of the ruins, shrieking out to those within hearing to aid her in the rescue of her boy Another, though loudly urged to leave the burning ward in which he was discovered to have taken refuge, raved of martyrdom, and crowns of glory All efforts to save him were ineffectual and from time to time his voice was audible, chaunting a hymn of triumph, till the fire reached him A third whose unhappy malady led him to conceive he was transformed into stone, defended himself with great vigour from those who tried to take him from the building and persisted in believing himself fire proof, till the falling in of the floor ended the delusion with his life The other sufferer was Dodds a just retribution for knavery and cruelty like his

The usual number of fire men, fire engines, curious idlers, and thieves,

were drawn to the spot, and lounged about it nearly all the ensuing day
About eight o clock, two persons greatly interested in the events of the
night added their important though by no means bulky persons to the
crowd   Dobie Snitch came on foot for the purpose of obtaining an' in
terview with Welbourne   and Townsend drove up in a carriage, in the
hope of successfully executing his fifty guinea job

Both these gentlemen met, as the reader will suppose, with great dis
appointment and were the only persons who knew him that deplored
Dodds wretched fate   As it was, they each retired to console themselves with a good breakfast, and then repaired with the tidings to their
respective patrons, Lady Minhurst and the Right Honourable Francis
Fraser Fluentleigh

CHAPTER XXVI

It was within half an hour of the appointed time of meeting when
Ronald reached his chambers   Persons less opposed, and more accustomed to rencontres of the kind than he was, would in most cases have
spent the preceding night in preparations suitable to an event that leaves
but the alternative of flight or death   To him, however, the latter result
appeared almost desirable   for though he had too much courage to entertain the thought of self destruction   yet sad experience had disgusted
him with the character of his race   his hopes were for ever blighted
dishonour certain, if distant, threatened his family   and now that a
fortunate marriage   had provided for his sister, the only helpless
member, he felt regardless of life, and preferred losing it to incurring
the remorse attendant on slaying, though in a duel, a fellow-creature

Under these circumstances he had no preparation to make, save a
hasty adieu to his father and Mira   and having committed these to
paper, he prepared for the encounter in the same reckless spirit which
had led him into a night s debauch, as unusual to his habits as was incon
sistent with his tastes

A brief halt for the purpose of taking up Edward, was the only inter
ruption he met with on his way to the place appointed, and the two
friends were the first on the ground

It wanted five minutes to the time agreed on, and they paced in silence
the dreary suburban field, till a neighbouring clock struck the hour

"No one here ?   observed Ronald   "this is very strange !

" A man is coming towards us,' returned Vivyan, and the eyes of
both were directed towards the person who now made his appearance

It was a ragged ill looking man, such as may be seen at an early
hour wandering about the town   seeking any employment that may pro
cure food for the day, and shelter for the night

When he came up with Ronald and his companion, he held up a letter,
and mentioned the name of the former

"From whom ?" inquired Ronald of the messenger, looking at the same time with surprise towards Edward

"That you must guess, your honour, if the letter don't tell you. Faith' and a cunning feller I should be to tell your honour who it came from, seeing I never saw the cratur afore who gave it me in all me born days

"Was it a gentleman ? ' asked Edward.

"May be he was that is a gentleman s gentleman, your honour, for, sure he had gold lace about enough to make me a gentleman for ever and ever'

"Enough ! said Ronald, throwing a shilling to the man, and preparing to open the epistle

"God bless your honour' You re a jontleman every bit of you May be your honour would be wishing to send back a moisel of answer now ?

"I shall bear the answer myself, replied Ronald, crumpling the paper, in a paroxysm of rage You can go !'

As soon as the man was out of hearing, Edward enquired with anxiety, the cause of Ronald s emotion, for the letter evidently gave him great distress

"What does he say ? asked Vivyan, "if our short acquaintance entitles me to make such an inquiry

"You are a party in this business, and have every right to be made acquainted with the rank and character of the person whom you have consented to serve in the capacity of second, retorted Ronald, with a bitter sneer, putting the letter into the hands of Vivyan

To his great astonishment, the latter read as follows —

"The Right Honorable Francis Fraser Fluentleigh regards his appointment with the person styling himself Ronald Minhurst as annulled. He cannot condescend to meet a man who holds no other rank in society than that he has hitherto maintained with (to do him justice) the skill of a consummate impostor "

Surprise and indignation mantled on the cheek of Edward when he became acquainted with the contents of the note,

"Cowardly slanderer ' ' he exclaimed

"Defer your decision, ' interrupted Ronald, in a tone of deep dejection, as he took back the note, " there is too much truth in the assertion '

"How so ?"

"The tale is too long to enter into now , very shortly, or I mistake, it will be told by a thousand tongues For the present, my kind friend, allow me to see you to your home, and accept my best thanks—the only return it is in my power to make—for your services on this occasion.

"And where will you go ?

"My first step will be to call on the writer of this note

'Then, by your leave, I will accompany you. Nay, do not refuse me Am I not the second you fixed on in this affair ? Believe me, I cannot forego my office so easily, until I am persuaded the differences between you are settled

"Be it as you will , but you may repent your zeal I fear I cannot give the lie to the author of this charge

No 26

" There is some mystery about this business I cannot penetrate , whatever the issue nothing can shake the esteem I bear you "

Ronald returned this sincere protestation of friendship by a hearty pressure of the speaker s hand   and the two friends, springing into the cabriolet, determined, *nolens volens* to disturb the morning slumbers of the Right Honourable Francis Fraser Fluentleigh

On their way it was agreed, after some little discussion, that Vivyan should remain in the carriage, while Ronald sought an interview with his antagonist   This determination suited the purposes of each   Ro nald, unacquainted with the extent of Fluentleigh s information respect ing himself, and the source from whence he derived it, felt that it would be imprudent to admit Edward to their interview, while Vivyan s motive in wishing to accompany him was to guard his friend from any rash measure into which he might be hurried by provocation or insult   Ne vertheless, he felt both curious and impatient, as he walked the cabriolet up the street, while waiting for Ronald s re appearance

Ronald found some difficulty in penetrating into the presence of the Right Honourable   A few minutes later indeed, he would have been unable to see him as that gentleman desirous of guarding against any unpleasantness arising from his laconic epistle, had immediately, on despatching it, begun to make very active arrangements for a trip into the country

Being known in the hotel, and having had occasion to pay Mr Fluentleigh a visit or two, Ronald contrived to find his apartments   In an ante chamber, he met that gentleman s valet who showing very evi dent signs of opposing his entry, our young friend took the liberty of putting him aside, and in another minute he stood in the presence of his man

Fluentleigh was very clearly taken by surprise   Concealing it as much as he cou d, he desisted from his task of packing and, surveying the intruder with the greatest indifference he could affect—

" What is the reason of this intrusion * he enquired

Ronald drew the note from his pocket

" Are you, said he, holding it in the view of the Right Honourable, " the writer of this note ?'

Notwithstanding his satisfaction, the disappointed candidate for par liamentary honours found it difficult to command sufficient firmness to conceal the uneasiness excited by the appearance of his early guest, and nearly a minute s pause ensued before he ventured to articulate—

" I am ' '

" Then I must request you to oblige me with an explanation of its contents

" I can hold no communication with an impostor   Nor would he disgust me with his presence, unless he sought a public exposure

Ronald startled and turned pale at the word *exposure*   The dreadful dilemma in which he was placed immediately occurred to his mind   to retire, was to plead guilty to an odious charge   to maintain his post, might draw infamy on himself and family   Consciousness of innocence

emboldened him, however, to make an attempt to soften his recent oppo
nent and now implacable foe

" Impostor I am none ' said he   " By Heaven, you wrong me '

" Possibly I am mistaken   the son only perpetuates the crime of the
father '

The Right Honourable could not have employed a more successful
word to intimidate his visitor   The word *father*, like a powerful conju
ration, brought before the mind of the unhappy young man all the worth
of his parent, and all the misery to which he stood exposed   A cold
shudder came over him , he tried in vain to speak   and his companion
taking advantage of the pause, rang the bell violently

" You will show this person the door, said he, to the man who an
swered the summons

Ronald reddened with indignation   In a paroxysm of rage, he ad
vanced towards Fluentleigh

' Have a care how you misconduct yourself,' exclaimed that gentle
man   " remember, you are in my power '

' Entertain no fear Sir   rejoined Ronald, approaching the door
' we shall meet again

" I trust not detestable canaille ' muttered Fluentleigh, as the door
closed on his discomfited visitor   and he again breathed freely

With rapid steps, and excited almost to madness, Ronald reached the
street   While he waited at the door of the hotel the drawing up of his
carriage   he was accosted by a mean looking man

' Beg pardon Sir   I won t be sure—but I think I have the pleasure
of knowing you '

The young man glanced rapidly at the speaker   and, by the rapid
process of association it immediately occurred to him to what source
Mr Fluentleigh was indebted for the information which led to his extra
ordinary letter   Affecting an air of the greatest composure, Ronald
stretched out his hand towards the stranger, whose low bow, in return,
plainly bespoke him deeply impressed by the honour conferred

" What, my old friend from P——, said he " positively you did me
a service, the night your old master died, that I have vainly 'onged to
requite   Come, you will do me the favour to discuss a breakfast with
me ?

" I have breakfasted, I thank you, Sir, replied Dobie Snitch, (for it
was he) who having had other interviews with Mr Fluentleigh since the
one we reported, was on his way to visit that gentleman, to find how the
links wanting in his chain of evidence through the fire at the madhouse,
might be supplied by other means

" Be it a luncheon, then, returned Ronald " come, you must oblige
me

" Excuse me   continued Dobie, evidently hesitating between his
desire of gain and his love of good cheer " but I am going to call on—

' Mr Fluentleigh I understand   You will find that gentleman by
no means disposed to receive a visitor so early   I have just found it so
You had better postpone your visit to that gentleman till you have shared
my luncheon

" I think I might as well, said Dobie, affecting a little more simplicity that long legal practice had left in his nature

After giving a few directions to his servant (for the coach had now drawr up) and making an appointment with Edward for the after part of the day, Ronald entered with Dobie into a neighbouring tavern encouraging a faint hope that his affairs might yet take a favourable turn

While Dobie was devouring with great enjoyment a luxurious luncheon, Ronald resolved in his mind the best method of drawing from the ci devant lawyer s clerk the information he so much required, in order to ward off the momentous blow that threatened his family   He was too ignorant of his companion to light at once on the master-key of his heart, and, accordingly, as soon as the cloth was removed, Ronald determined to catechise him at random, until he should succeed in making him communicative.

" And the good old woman, Mr Snitch, your companion at ——, is she still living ? '

' She isn't so very old   replied Dobie, with a sly wink of the eye, and smacking his lips in a most ungenteel way after a sip of his wine

" Is she not ? '

" No, bless you ' 'Tis care, poor thing, that makes her look so   but she ll be happier now, I take it.   We are going to set up in a small way of business in London——Deborah and I   she is not a bad hand in the public line, and it suits me uncommonly '

" I am exceedingly glad to hear you are so well off in the world, Mr Snitch   Allow me the pleasure of drinking Mrs Deborah s good health, Sir '

" With all my heart   Here s to Mrs Snitch that is to be ' ' ejaculated Dobie

As they replaced their glasses on the table after this toast, Ronald tried another subject

" Settling in London is an expensive affair, I should think '

" Cost a few hundreds, responded Dobie thrusting his thumbs into the arm hole of his waistcoat as he grew more and more elevated

' You must have lived frugally Mr Snitch the stipend of one in your situation of life hardly leaves a prospect of saving a few hundreds '

" We have our perquisites, said Dobie first glancing suspiciously at the speaker and then drawing himself up with great importance

" I understand a douceur [now and then from rich clients for expediting business   from such a man as your friend Fluentleigh, for in stance

" Can t say much for him, replied Dobie who had not become quite so fuddled as to forget he was speaking to Fluentleigh s opponent, and consequently, conceived he was bound to disparage that gentleman out of courtesy to his entertainer ' he is not what you call a liberal man towards those who transact business for him

" It would very much surprise me to hear the contrary, rejoined Ronald with affected indifference   " he must be, besides, a ruined man not worth a thousand pounds

"You don't say so," cried Dobie with some alarm, setting down the glass he was in the act of raising to his lips "Mr Fluentleigh not worth a thousand pounds''

"I have very good grounds for what I say interposed the other, finding that he had succeeded in gaining the profound attention of his auditor 'Fluentleigh never possessed more than twenty thousand pounds Half his fortune was squandered in the first year after he left college He turned politician in despair, and, as you very well know expended another fifteen thousand for the pleasure of opposing me So you perceive so far from possessing a farthing, he is to my certain knowledge indebted to the amount of a round five thousand

"Oh Lord! oh Lord!'' roared Dobie, what a precious fool I am to be sure! Oh Lord! oh Lord!

"You alarm me, my good friend I hope you are not a creditor of this gentleman

"Yes I am,' replied the man with great solemnity, admirably qualified by his libations to look lack a daisical

"Are you indeed? Poor Mr Snitch! I most sincerely sympathise with your case I have no doubt but Mr Fluentleigh will start as soon as possible on his continental tour '

" And I shall get nothing at all   nothing but promises   Oh Lord '
oh Lord '   I dare say you would have given me more

' For what, Mr Snitch ? gasped Ronald, trusting he had brought
the little man to the point

" Oh nothing ' nothing ' that is   you won t be angry   some other
time   I ll tell you some other time   Oh dear ' oh dear '   Not a farthing
shall I get   and it would have set us up in business so nicely   Poor
Deborah Swill ' how it will break your precious heart to know what a
fool I have been ' '

" If you would let me know the particulars Mr Snitch, I might pos
sibly assist you   Come take a glass of wine to compose yourself

" Oh ' to think he should have got such a secret out of me for paltry
promises and a rubbishing ten pound note to pay for preliminaries   But
he hasn t got the papers—no ' no '

" There are papers, then, enquired Ronald with an eagerness that
betrayed his motive and drew from his companion a look of suspicion

' Did I say anything about papers ?   said Dobie, looking suddenly
exceedingly simple

' Aye ' aye '   What papers were they ?

" Bless you,   my master   left cart loads of papers behind him ' re
turned Dobie, now awake to his imprudence and giving a hiccup or two
to protect himself against further questioning

" This will not do, Mr Snitch, said Ronald seeing through him
" You hold papers that concern me   and you would have parted with
them (if you have not already done so), to this Fluentleigh, to the great
prejudice of my family

' Lord bless you ' not I   again muttered Dobie still persisting in his
attempting to evade the discovery his imprudence had brought about

" I have Fluentleigh s own hand writing to confirm what I say   ex
claimed Ronald drawing the note from his pocket   The charge here
brought against me is founded on your information, communicated by
you '

l inding it impossible to deny that he had held communication with
Fluentleigh on these subjects, Dobie clung to the chance of making a
better bargain in another quarter   " I certainly have papers," simpered
he

" They are still in your possession ?

" Safe enough   they were to have brought me in a handsome sum
from Fluentleigh   As he is not a very sure man, I don t mind letting
you have them for the same cash, on delivery, you know '

Ronald paused a moment

" You were confidential clerk to Gregory Grasp, I think,' he then
added

" Almost as many years as you can reckon

" The Dowager Lady Minhurst was for many years one of your
late master s clients ?'

" One of the best,   said Dobie, rubbing his hands with delight, as
the remembrance of sundry liberal donations from her ladyship crossed
his mind

" At the death of your employer,' continued Ronald, sternly, " you became possessed of these papers Mr Dobie Snitch must be too well acquainted with the law, not to be aware that the abstracting such documents exposes him to——

" And what will you do? exclaimed Snitch, interrupting the speaker " Expose me if you please I have a secret worth two of yours

' What those papers have revealed to you I know not,' returned Ronald " That you are ready to part with them to the highest bidder I see clearly Fluentleigh would either dupe or disappoint you if my offers are more modest, they are more sure

' I am not unreasonable ' observed Snitch

His companion considered a moment To gain possession of the papers, and secure the future silence of Dobie, was his object A scheme suggested itself and met the approbation of the clerk It was agreed that all papers in Dobie s possession relative to the Minhurst family should be delivered to Ronald, on his securing to Dobie Snitch an annuity of fifty pounds, so invested that the power of suspending it remained with Ronald in the event of any disclosure of the purport of such papers being made by the annuitant

To these terms Snitch consented, having, however, stipulated for the first half year s payment in advance and as soon as the requisite steps were taken, Ronald received the silent witnesses on which the honour of his family depended

They had been some time in his possession before he ventured to peruse them He turned with disgust from the details of a crime, no longer a matter of doubt or conjecture and a deep sense of duty alone induced him to undertake the terrible task To an indifferent person it would have been a curious employment to observe how documents, literally voluminous, collected at widely distant periods, and furnished by different hands, tended to confirm one leading fact the tediously minute law deed, and the hasty scrawl dictated by affection or desperate passion, strangely blending their cold and fervid testimony To Ronald, however, each paper gave a deeper wound and the torture produced by the tragic tale was strangely aggravated by the different styles of the writings that told it The legal documents, in the cold and stiff pomp of their phraseology, seemed a biting satire on the agitated and distressing story of which they formed a part

But the distressing employment left consolation to the reader, since it told him the worst, and accordingly enabled him to take measures that might put an end to his uncertainty, if they could not remove the poison, infused, for him, without remedy, in the cup of life

These measures were promptly taken

CHAPTER XXVII

Some days after the eventful night described in the preceding chapters, Mrs Bondell was very busy, arranging with the utmost diligence and invention her little apartments

' I really do think, soliloquised the old lady when the violence of her admiration had a little subsided, " I really do think, when the curtains are let down, and the fire burns up, and the two candles on the table, and the two on the chimney piece, and the two on the piano, are lighted, the room will look nery nice very nice indeed '

And Mrs Bondell seated herself on the sofa with the greatest possible satisfaction, smoothing down her silk dress, looking at the flames, and listening to the muffin bells in the street, until she was aroused from her state of repose by the chiming of a neighbouring clock

In reply to the friendly warning she made a common-place remark upon the flight of time, and summoning into her presence a smart looking maid of all work inquired with great anxiety about the safe arrival of sundry comestibles

' All s come, Ma am, ' said the girl

" I am very glad to hear it you may tell Miss Somers that the clock has struck six

In a very few minutes after the exit of the maid servant, Évine made her appearance

" Are you perfect, my love? asked Mrs Bondell, as they seated themselves on the sofa in the fire light

' I am quite prepared for the rehearsal, replied Evine, who having drawn crowded houses on eight or nine successive nights in the character of Juliet, was now busily employed in studying a leading part in a new play

" You are looking very nicely to night my dear a little fatigued, I think I will have the candles lit that I may look at you

' I recommend your having lights, or our guests will surprise us in the dark '

" I hope you will be satisfied with my arrangements, my dear Miss Somers but for my own part, I cannot excuse you for receiving company in this style '

" Am I not living magnificently, compared with my former mode of life ?

" Very true my love nevertheless, you do not, I must say it, Miss Somers, you do not support the rank in Society your talents and the patronage of the public have conferred upon you A first rate actress, in the receipt of your salary, Miss Somers, should live in the Squares, keep a set of servants, drive a close carriage, and—'

" Find myself a beggar the moment age or accident incapacitates me for the exercise of my profession no ' no ' Mrs Blondell, I must earn money to requite the services of Edward, to secure a competency for my poor father and yourself and then, perhaps, I may think of a little more outward splendour than I now deem it prudent to indulge in—but even then it would not increase my happiness

' You are a good girl and deserve all your success   No wonder the public take a liking to such a face as this

And as she spoke Mrs Bondell drew her companion opposite the mirror   The glass indeed reflected a lovely image

Her golden hair simply arranged in a knot at the back of the head displayed to the best advantage the graceful outline of head and neck a white muslin dress fell around her in white draperies, while her beau tiful features beamed with lovely intelligence   She was however, greatly altered   the change in her mode of life, rather than the interval of time, had driven from her features and figure the extreme youthful appearance, and although she still retained the freshness of early youth, the pensive ness of thought had crept over her placid brow and smiling cheek   Her mode of education might account for this change , while other females more fortunately situated are led by degrees to that maturity of thought, which makes the chief difference between childhood and womanhood, she unaccustomed to mental discipline till her mind had attained its vigour had passed with a bound from one state to the other, and the rapidity of the transition made it the more evident   Evine might have looked complacently on the figure the glass reflected without subjecting herself to the charge of vanity   as it was however other thoughts occu pied her, for gently disengaging herself from Mrs Bondell s embrace she advanced to the window and looked out into the street

It was a cold boisterous evening and the snow fell in large flakes, and as the young actress glanced first at the comfortable furniture of her sitting room looking warm and bright in the light of a cheerful fire, and then at the desolate street an involuntary sigh escaped her

" My warm, pleasant home, she thought   " how happy should I be if my poor father shared it with me !

Mrs Bondell was very sagacious in discovering the turn taken by her companion s thoughts especially when they assumed a gloomy hue, and she prided herself though not perhaps with very great reason, on pos sessing equal skill to enliven them

' And who is the young gentleman Mr Edward so very much wishes to introduce to you ?   inquired the good lady

' We shall not be kept much longer in suspense as to who the gentle man is   returned Evine   so, if you please, we will get ourselves in order

And accordingly she drew to the curtains, and taking her seat at the table began her embroidery with all the grace of a young lady who had studied the mystery of silks and worsteds for three complete lustres

Mrs Bondell also found something to do and when they were thus seated sewing and talking, and laughing they, or rather the fire and the room and the persons presented as truly domestic a scene as the most home loving heart could wish to look upon

Their gossip was soon interrupted by the appearance of Edward and Ronald

Before we proceed to relate what transpired, it will be as well to inform the reader what induced Ronald to wait on the actress in her home

He had gathered from the papers in Dobie s possession that the right heir to the title and estates enjoyed by his father was still living that he led a vagrant life, bore the name of Wilfred Welbourne, and had one daughter called Evine after his own mother the lawful Viscountess Minhurst The most recent of the papers was in Grasp's hand-writing, and proved to be the letter which had led Dobie Snitch to visit the mad house Guided by this document Ronald made immediate inquiries, and soon learnt the particulars of the fire As no doubt was entertained but that Wilfred and his mother had perished in the flames, Ronald at once perceived that Evine, the new and favourite actress, was in her own right Viscountess Minhurst

No sooner had he satisfied himself on this point than honour dictated immediate restitution of Minhurst with its title to the lawful owner But, alas ' with what sacrifice was that duty connected To abandon, at his age, and with his taste for the enjoyments of refined and elevated life, all claim to a high position in society and a fair fortune, was a task that Ronald s sense of honour would have enabled him to perform with cheer fulness he would even have felt reconciled to the shame of illegitimacy attendant on the disclosure, and preferred it as immeasurably more honourable than the enjoyment of name and fortune unlawfully his own but to reduce his father to poverty and shame, to give him a deep and perhaps a mortal wound, by revealing the dishonour of his mother was a task from which he shrunk, and if conscience would not allow him to renounce it entirely, affection postponed indefinitely the evil day At times he looked forward to the demise of his parent as to a period that would release him from the dreadful conflict between right and wrong to which he was now a daily prey and acting on this prospect, he took measures to preserve at least from waste and injury the property he felt it out of his power immediately to restore

This Ronald found a more easy task than he expected The expenses of his father, who, vexed to find his daughter make less happy than he hoped by her splendid alliance, had again sought seclusion at Minhurst, were too modest to require any retrenchment For himself, aware that he must one day lose his name, and endure privation, he found no diffi culty in shunning society and reducing his expenditure to the lowest sum compatible with his parliamentary duties

Of the whole family Lady Minhurst s expenditure was alone likely to prove, as indeed it had already done, detrimental to the estate but Ronald well knew that his fatal discovery had given him a power over that unhappy woman which could easily restrict her to the smallest income

One of his first cares was therefore to write to her His letter began with a touching description of the agony of mind into which he had been thrown by his recent discovery he dealt at length on the particulars which had come to his knowledge, and clearly set forth the alternative to which he was reduced, of inflicting a deathblow on his father s tran quillity, or of becoming an accomplice of crime by concealing it Warm tears of anguish saturated his paper as he attempted to detail the motives which induced him to adopt the latter course, and urged the necessity of mitigating the guilt of such a step by making every effort to leave the property in the state in which they had found it He would not, he said, dictate the plans she ought to adopt, but trusted she would feel the necessity of aiding him from her own handsome jointure to repair the injuries the Minhurst estate had received while in their hands

This epistle reached the Dowager Lady Minhurst soon after she received intelligence of the fire and the supposed death of Welbourne Though it gave her pleasure to know that only one person now stood in her way, she shrunk with horror from the dark temptation ambition suggested, and the conciliating letter of Ronald promising as it did to screen her from shame, induced her to abandon the plans she had formed to avoid it.

After a day s consideration she ventured to reply and Ronald ad every reason to be satisfied with her answer

She expressed the sincerest sorrow for her past errors and satisfactorily proved the truth of her penitence by the plans she proposed to adopt She assured him that heartily weary of the pleasures she had so dearly purchased, she no longer found a difficulty in reconciling herself to seclusion on the contrary, she looked forward to a modest retirement with pleasure, as the only way of cultivating the state of mind she found necessary to secure future peace Acting on these principles she had, she said taken measures for placing her expenses on so small a scale, that the surplus of her jointure accumulating for a few years would more than restore the property to the state in which the recent Viscount Minhurst had left it.

"To-morrow,' she concluded, "I leave London for ever You will spare me the pain of an interview—Ronald, I dare not see you again It would please me if you would accept from my jointure enough to secure you a humble maintenance but I know your honourable nature, and I dare not urge it Farewell ' May you live to obtain the honours I would have secured for you by your own merit and to enjoy them without a blush ! Ronald, my son adieu '

It will be difficult to describe the pleasure Ronald experienced on receiving this letter The dispositions of repentance which it so plainly betrayed, had a soothing influence upon his mind, and for a moment reconciled him to the equivocal station he was henceforth to hold in society

"Yes,' he soliloquised, ' I will save them both from dishonour and the retribution that awaits the author of our misfortune shall at least be so softened as to sanctify without embittering her last moments For my own part I am young and should possess energy to weather a worse storm In a few years Minhurst will be restored to the state in which its late lord left it, and freed from all encumbrances revolve to the lawful owner at my father s death, in a better state than we found it In the meantime I must relinquish, as soon as possible, my seat in the house, and obtain some honourable employment that will spare me the pain of living on the go'd of another

While these transactions were going forward, the intimacy that commenced between Edward and Ronald on the night of the fire increased rapidly This was a fortunate circumstance for the former: the very evident alteration in his circumstances he was constrained immediately to make would alone have been sufficient to leave him companionless had he not found in Edward a friend of better principles and higher capabilities than the bevy of butterflies that always flutter round the wealthy heir to a peerage

Both of the friends were however cautious and knew only as much of each other s history as accident brought to light in the round of their daily intercourse   The circumstances of his family made Ronald studi ously avoid mentioning the young actress when once he knew her to be connected with his new friend Edward however, had reasons for bringing Evine on the tapis almost as strong as those which urged Ronald to avoid the subject

Vivyan, in his anxiety for the welfare of his fortunate protegee, felt it his duty to provide her with society suited to her new station   He knew very well the impertinent intrusions to which a young and lovely female in her way of life would be exposed, and saw clearly that nothing would so effectually secure her from insult or danger as a circle of worthy

intelligent friends   In selecting Ronald for one of them, a young hand
some man of fashion with whom on their first meeting he had spent the
first night in a tavern may appear an unpardonable imprudence on the
part of Edward   it should, however, be recollected, on further acquaintance a congeniality of mind made them sworn friends, and friendship
never exists without the esteem which would induce us to confide our
dearest treasure to its keeping   To keep off the worthless Edward de
termined to surround Evine with the worthy, and for this purpose contrived the interview we are about to describe Ronald made the en
gagement   partly with a view to oblige his friend, and partly, perhaps,
to satisfy an incipient curiosity respecting the future Viscountess
Minhurst

A few minutes spent in her presence sufficed to satisfy Ronald that as
far as present gratification was concerned, he would not have to regret
his engagement never had he beheld a lovelier person never had he
met with sweeter simplicity of mind and manners

Very soon after the arrival of the friends the tea equipage was brought
in and that social meal itself, as it ever does, soon put each individual
of the little party at perfect ease

You are looking very well, Miss Somers ' observed Ronald   "you
have encountered bravely the anxiety of your late most extraordinary
efforts

"I had so much encouragement she replied, endeavouring at the
same time but without success to recal where she had heard the voice
that addressed her   "I shall never think it formidable to encounter a
hundred times the number of friendly faces I meet in Drury Lane

"Ay, ay ! said Mrs Bondell, 'that is a pretty speech , but it is not
quite so pleasant to think about the old men who criticise you, and the
young men who quarrel and fight for you "

"But Miss Somers has the advantage of being able to disarm the
critics,' observed Ronald

"It would be very well if she could pacify the young heads too '
continued Mrs Bondell, determined to support her position ; perhaps
you don t know, Sir, that Miss Somers was the cause of a duel the first
night she came out—I really read as much in the papers '

"Dear Mrs Bondell—' interrupted Evine,

"Nay, my love, persisted that worthy lady , "you must not be so
modest let the gentleman know your merits Yes, Sir there was a
duel, and both killed on the spot "

"Both ?' ejaculated Edward with a smile

'Couldn t they be both killed ? asked the lady, presuming she had
made a mistake 'Perhaps it was one then—I thought it was both—
but I am quite sure it was one then   Now allow me to ask if it is a
trifling matter to make your curtsey in public, if these are the conse
quences ?"

"If it will afford Miss Somers any consolation to know that no gentle
man was killed, I think I can satisfy her,' said Edward

"There was a duel then, exclaimed Mrs Bondell with an air of
triumph "I was sure of it '

" Not exactly a duel, interrupted Edward

" I always treated the report as ridiculous observed Evine

' It was not wholly without foundation ' continued Edward

"There ' exclaimed Mrs Bondell, recovering a little from her dis appointment ' I felt satisfied it was not without foundation

" A challenge was given   returned Vivyan, notwithstanding a sign or two from Ronald   but the meeting never took place   When the hour came, this gentleman and myself were the only persons on the ground

" Was it you then, Edward ? said Evine with more earnestness of manner than she was perhaps aware of   ' Why were you so rash ?

" You look so thankful, that I am almost sorry to undeceive you But I must not wear unmerited honours   I was not your champion To this gentleman your thanks are due   I must be satisfied with my humble share as his second

Evine's confusion at this intelligence concealed from the spectators what was passing in her heart   She was conscious of something like disappointment, and blushed deeper to think she should have wished Edward had given the challenge than at this sudden discovery of a de fender in a stranger   Ronald came in for his share of confusion   he felt awkward, he knew not why, but hoped it was owing to the rich car nation that, mantling over the cheek of the young lady, added greatly to the charm of her countenance

Edward and Mrs Bondell laughed heartily at this incident, the latter pronouncing it ' capital fun

In this way the evening passed lightly away and Ronald was sur prised when he found the hour arrived, at which the regular habits Evine found it necessary to observe in order to meet the exertion de manded by her profession, required the departure of the friends

' What a charming acquaintance you have here ' exclaimed Ronald, as he took Edward's arm, and they walked from the door ' I confess I have seldom seen such a union of beauty and simplicity '

" It gives me pleasure to hear you say so   although I anticipated your confession   During the evening the gloom habitual to your coun tenance disappeared, and I saw at once you were gratified   This visit has done you good, Ronald you must come again

Take care I may become your rival   observed Ronald, jestingly

There is no fear of that, returned the other with a deep sigh, that immediately attracted the attention of the listener

" How so ? said he, with an accent of commiseration

" Because my affections have been long and hopelessly set on another object

" You tempt me to catechise you

" Do not yield to the temptation your efforts will be vain   No rack will extort from me a confession of my love   I mean of its object '

' At least you will account to me for your intimacy with Miss Somers   I cannot understand it, since you say you have no serious in tentions towards her

" Ours is an intimacy of brother and sister   but to make you under
stand it, I must trouble you with her history

And Edward Vivyan detailed to Ronald Evine's history as we have
narrated it. The young man listened with attention, and that night a
new and strange plan occurred vaguely to his mind

CHAPTER XXVIII

In a very elegant drawing room in Harley Street at a table so laden
with pamphlets and books of all shapes and sizes, that but for their dis
order it might have passed for a bookseller s counter, in a morning
wrapper and slippers, sat Lady Inkenstand, intently engaged on the
fabrication of some romantic story

Her ladyship was so thoroughly of the sentimental school that she
not only adopted that particular style in her writings but her conversa
tion dress, gait, manners, attitudes, all partook, as far as dress, manners,
conversation, &c are capable of being endowed with such qualities very
largely of her sentalism   This was quite evident to all who knew her
ladyship, and especially to those who were admitted to behold her in her
inspired, or as she termed them in her " rapt moments

Her ladyship s peculiar forte however, was the romantically senti
mental, or the sentimentally romantic and any artist labouring to throw
on his canvass a personification of genius, would have been a fortunate
man indeed could he have been introduced to her presence as the reader
now is while immersed in the crisis, or *vulgariter*, the crack scene of
her romance

" Mr Vivyan, your ladyship,' said a smart little page, entering the
room

' Admit Mr Vivyan   Dear, obliging Vivyan, to come to me in such
a moment of perplexity   said the lady, advancing to receive her visitor

" I am indeed fortunate, if I come in time to assist your ladyship
replied Edward, to whom Lady Inkenstand had shown much real kind
ness,—for, to do her justice, notwithstanding great eccentricity, she
possessed an excellent heart, and liberally supported the pursuits she
loved

' Oh, I am in such a dilemma   quite at a stand still --a dead stop, I
assure you !

" Are you perplexed about concluding your plot," enquired Edward,
whose frequent visits and obliging patience had made him familiar with
her ladyship s daily task

" No I have settled that my heroine dies of a consumption her
seducer is to get rid of himself by a timely suicide, and the husband is to
die of grief   My denouement, you perceive, is of the quiet order

" Just so—since they all die,' remarked Vivyan, unable to resist the
joke

" It is what I call gently-tragic   But I want your assistance in one scene to help me in a description

" Of a character ?

' No—I would not loose your patience with so heavy a task

' To describe scenery, perhaps—a landscape, or sea view ? '

' No ! No ! I want you to give me an idea how to describe, simply and poetically, a tear trickling down a pillow   Have not you some pretty image now ?

" A dew drop, ' suggested Vivyan with a smile

' Hackneyed, lamentably hackened, my dear friend,' observed the authoress   " But bless me ! How singular—I have it ! The very thing —a ball of quicksilver ? Is not that good ? Striking and pretty '

' A very *lively* image ' observed Vivyan, with an emphasis that almost gained the attention of the lady, and would inevitably have excited her displeasure, as she was exceedingly tenacious like most of the sisterhood, of any jests at the expense of her favourite pursuits

And now, begae Lady Inkenstand, after a pause, " what are *you* doing my dear Vivyan ?"

" Keeping holiday, my lady '

That is wicked and unkind   the public are famishing for want of your poems   Without flattery you write divine verses   I consider them a kind of mental ambrosia

Edward bowed   he could do no more in return for a well meant, though ill conveyed compliment

" Do you know, ' continued her ladyship " a divine subject has occurred to me recently, but I don t know whether to make it a novel, a play, or a poem in cantos   I want your opinion

' May I hear the story ?

" Oh ! yes   the simplest and shortest imaginable   The sufferings of a wife is the subject—a young beautiful, clever, accomplished, virtuous wife—you understand—a paragon

' An interesting heroine

" Oh ! beyond all conception interesting   Then I intend having a tyrant husband—a capricious tyrant   One of those men who, possess ing all the attractions a husband can possibly have, love passionately as lovers, and hate as violently in their matrimonial capacity—you under stand ?

' Perfectly   your ladyship would contrast the independence and power of the betrothed with the bondage of the wife

' How completely you apprehend my design, my dear Vivyan   my work, you perceive, is not to be a mere work of interest and pathos, leaving no lesson deeply graven on the mind of the reader   No ! I in tend that idea shall pervade it—to invest it with a powerful moral scope—to make my heroine a warning to wives for ages to come '

A serious design for a novel '

' So I have thought   Would it do better as a play ?

" Has the subject sufficient *action* for a drama ?

' Oh, no subject can have more action   just consider it ?

" True ! thought Edward, " a quarrelsome husband and wife

I think a poem after all the most suitable There is a dignity about verse better calculated for works having an important moral design do you not think so ?'

I perfectly agree with your ladyship

" Throughout the whole I intend to adhere strictly to nature not a character will be fictitious or embellished not an incident invented

I fear you will find a difficulty in meeting with paragons in nature

You look on humanity with a stern eye Mr Vivian Our species presents many paragons I don t exaggerate when I say paragons lovely men and women so different from their race that you might imagine them fallen spirits doomed to expiate some error by a weary sojourn in our lamentably contagious world

Paragons of penance observed Edward

Ah you are severe I fear you are dreadfully sarcastic Mr Vivyan —a very bad quality in a poet Sarcasm is in my opinion an untuned string in the poet s lute—the curd in the rich milk of his verse But to resume my heroine gives me (to speak as the artists do) a sitting to day you shall see her and pronounce on the correctness of my portrait

The lady is not aware I presume of your purpose ?

'Poor creature no ' She has no one to sympathize with her unfor
tunate situation something congenial in our dispositions procured me
her confidence The opportunity is too valuable to let pass, without
making an attempt to benefit mankind

Here a servant announced the Countess of Wagmouth

It is the—the person I was speaking about said the literary lady,
with evident pleasure

" Allow me to withdraw,' implored Edward, with emotion, " I have
an engagement

' It is impossible I want you, Vivyan besides she is at the door,
and it will be rude to go now

Forced to remain with a beating heart Edward prepared to confront
Mira Adhering faithfully to his intention, he had not seen her since
the night on which his acquaintance had commenced with Ronald

Under any circumstances an interview with the Countess would have
given him pain but the description that prefaced it made it doubly
painful Lady Inkenstand s literary plans had put him in possession of
Mira s sad domestic history and the appearance of the young wife fully
confirmed it

Her cheeks of late always colourless seemed now more sadly pale
the habitually pensive expression of her eye had deepened and com
pressed lips betrayed the resignation of a broken spirit The enduring
character of her beautiful exquisitely moulded features was unchanged
but all the charm a gay unfettered noble heart had lent them was for
ever gone

Edward sighed as he returned her graceful salutation and though for
a poetical temperament his mind was well poised and could make allow
ance for the strange anomalies to be met with at every step in life his
spirit rose with indignation against society that like the deity of a
savage creed, required the repeated and renewed sacrifice of victims as
lovely and as innocent as the one before him

If her appearance gave him pain it was greatly aggravated during the
course of her visit Every word she uttered the slightest gesture she
made, betrayed to Edward s nice observation the dreadful conflict to
which she was a prey No expression of discontent escaped from her
a smile played upon her countenance but her silence and her smiles
like the fleeting sunshine and dull calm on the ocean told the passage
of the storm

Mira was the first to address Edward

I hope we have not offended you Mr Vivyan

' How very odd that you should be acquainted ' observed Lady
Inkenstand I was talking about you to Mr Vivyan as you came in

" It is not astonishing that you supposed us strangers to each other
rejoined Mira Mr Vivyan will not afford us the gratification of enter
taining him at —— Square

Edward pleaded a pressure of pursuits and engagements

' I hear of your movements, Mr Vivyan and am led sometimes to
think that the old fashioned plea of long standing acquaintance might
have obtained for me the preference

Edward was embarrassed and the appearance of Lady Inkenstand contributed to his confusion. That indefatigable authoress was very manifestly collecting from their interview the materials for a scene and though he had no very high opinion of her powers of observation he had a great wish to avoid furnishing that imaginative lady with a hint that had any connexion with the state of his heart. He accordingly stammered a reply, which most certainly required an explicit interpretation to render it intelligible to either lady

I will accept your apology if you will promise to behave better, resumed Mira 'let us not stand on ceremony, like absolute strangers. You were more friendly when I lived at Minhurst. And she blushed involuntarily as she recalled the brief but romantic intercourse that in happier days had subsisted between herself and the poet

Have they been so long acquainted'' thought Lady Inkenstand "how very mysterious!

Edward tried to speak, but the effort was impossible feelings the most contradictory contended in his bosom. He would have learnt with anguish that his ill fated attachment was shared by Mira Countess of Wagmouth and yet he felt vexed and even wounded, to find from the artless, and to say the truth unfashionable freedom with which she sought his society that her heart was a stranger to the emotions he proved

"At any rate, he thought, "there can be no danger in our intercourse if my unhappy feelings are neither shared nor suspected. She is unhappy in her home if I can quicken the passage of one bitter hour. I shall be repaid for the anguish I experience in her presence

"How very absent you seem Mr Vivyan remarked Lady Inkenstand

"I beg pardon—I was—considering my engagements—that is when I could safely promise to comply with your polite invitation said he, bowing to the countess

Do not perplex yourself on that subject returned Mira, "I am always at home we receive no company but a warm welcome will perhaps atone for a dull house

'No company! How very dull you must be my dear Countess, said Lady Inkenstand, in a tone of compassion and glancing significantly at Edward

"I do not regret what appears to be inevitable rejoined Mira with a slight smile. Lady Minhurst and the Viscount have returned to the country, and I am now quite alone

The Countess soon brought her visit to a close after once more reminding Vivyan of his promise. Edward remained a few minutes longer with the literary lady and when at length he took his way homeward through streets inundated with the crowd of a full season the words 'quite alone, and the sad music of the tones in which they were uttered still sounded in his ear

Lady Inkenstand in the mean time resumed her contemplative attitude and was soon inspired with the very bright and original idea of bestowing on her unhappy wife an unhappy lover and before the close of the day had audited five hundred lines of most mellifluous verse, descriptive of that gentleman s eye brows and had devised as many more, intended to convey to the reader an idea of his no less distinguished eye lashes

---

CHAPTER XXIX

WE resume the action of our story at an interval of some months from the occurrences described in the last chapter

During that time no change of importance happened to the characters we have introduced to the reader, unless the increasing intimacy between the younger personages can be considered in that light

In this respect their condition had undergone considerable alteration Though they were comparatively strangers to each other when we last noticed them the brief interval had sufficed to bring Evine and Ronald Mira and Edward, beneath that cementing influence which is the invariable prelude of friendship or love Their intercourse, in the first place the result of accident, had become to all parties the source of much enjoyment, and was indulged in without a fear of danger on either side Alone in her splendid solitude, the young Countess received with sincere pleasure the visits of Vivyan and they were encouraged by the foolish vanity of her husband while in her equally secluded though far happier home Ronald was welcomed as the only visitor that cheered the retirement of the youthful actress who nightly administered entertainment to thousands

It was now high summer London was thronged and the success of a protracted season still kept Evine in the metropolis The excitement of her profession the close habit of study she had been induced to adopt in order to satisfy the demands of the management upon her services and to secure the handsome emolument it held forth had materially affected her health To conceal her debility from the few kind friends that made her intimate circle was impossible yet even these, in her great desire to fulfil her remaining engagements were kept ignorant of the worst symptoms of over exertion from which she suffered

At their request however, she repaired to a pleasant lodging at Hampstead—charming cockney Hampstead and soon derived evident benefit from the change of air Here she spent the whole of her time with the exception of the nights on which she had to play, when she slept at her apartments in Town On the other evenings Ronald and Edward came to her retreat and after a short stroll in the summer twilight the little party beguiled the remaining hours till midnight with conversation and music

To the casual observer Evine s situation might appear perfectly happy Her early acquaintance with the distresses attendant upon poverty en abled her duly to appreciate the prospect of opulence great theatrical success presented. Her utter ignorance of the prejudices current in society might seem to place her beyond the mental trials peculiar to sensitive and well directed minds in her position and to palliate the wearying anxiety of a public career, she found in Mrs Bondell, Edward and Ronald the soothing influence of sincere and warm friendship Yet Evine was unhappy. It was not merely her extraordinary efforts of mind and body that had driven the colour from her cheek, and broken the light tones of her laugh she suffered from a rankling heart wound no success, no friendship could repair her father was not at hand to share her unexpected prosperity

Hitherto this circumstance had sufficed to embitter all her enjoy ment. The presence of her father, to whom she had been *all*, as he was *all* to her was the constant want, that attended her, like an oppressive shadow both in the social circle and the crowded theatre. For his well known fond regard, nowhere now to be met with, save in the recesses of her memory, she would have exchanged the tears, the smiles, the plaudits that formed the nightly homage of her crowded audience

Poor Evine! Languishing under one trial, she did not forget the other that awaited her more terrible in its consequences, because beyond the power of circumstance to avert or mitigate

They will not come this evening said Mrs Bondell to Evine, who was looking from a jessamine shaded window, in the hope of seeing her usual visitors approaching the house

I fear not. Can anything have happened to Edward?

Silly creature! you are growing nervous. He is quite as likely to be detained by amusement or business, as by any misfortune '

' Business might detain him. I do not think amusement would

"I do not know *that*. He has very many agreeable acquaintances I have heard him speak of a certain lady lately, in such warm terms that I should not be surprised if she furnished amusement fascinating enough to detain him

' I remember said Evine, blushing unconsciously ' The Countess of Wagmouth, I think

The very lady sister of Mr Ronald

They say she is very lovely

"You may be sure she is. Mr Vivyan has good taste, But we must not lose our walk because our beaux happen to be remiss Quick, my love on with your bonnet we may yet see the sun set

In a few minutes the old lady and her charge sallied forth from the little garden in front of their red brick dwelling, and were quietly taking their way under the large beech trees that threw a thick shade on an elevated walk or terrace not many yards from the house

Evine checked the speed of her companion

' Let us stop here a moment said she seating herself on a rude bench the cherished seat of many a delighted Londoner on his pilgrim age to Jack Straw s Castle This is my favourite halting place it is a pity it is so near home for when I pass it I confess I feel little inclination to extend my walk

"No one comes this way   observed Mrs Bondell, who in her ex treme sociability, preferred the society of the donkeys donkey men, nurse maids, and the diminutive gentry in their infantine vehicles who are to be seen on the frequented parts of the Heath to no company at all ' However, she continued, disposed on all occasions to humour the fancies of her young friend "I must say it is very pleasant to sit here and see the sun go down

This terrace (for though no result of art, its elevation regularity and broad, well shaded esplanade made it worthy of the name,) had a nor therly aspect nevertheless at sun set the glories of the western sky were reflected obliquely on the foliage of its leafy canopy, and on the ver dant carpet bordering the walk   This northern aspect, at such an hour, had its peculiar advantage, as the spectator could embrace, without changing his position, the magnificent dyes of the closing day on the left and the calm and pensive colours of coming right on the right   It also overlooked a charming landscape the miniature hill and dale of the heath the more picturesque from minuteness, with glimpses of the fertile,well wooded meadows beyond

As our friends seated themselves, the last segment of the sun disap peared from the horizon exhalations like the rising of waters floated in the tiny vale at their feet, and the new moon, like a crescent of brigi test silver shed upon them a benign influence from the depths of a dark blue heaven

' What scenery is this ! said Evine in accents of the most devout admiration breaking the protracted silence into which even Mrs Bon dell had been betrayed by the stillness around

" And what a stage ! rejoined her companion, who, incapable of seiz ing the poetry of her profession had nevertheless an enthusiasm for its matter of fact details   Fancy my dear here are the wings ' pointing to the sturdy trunks of two very fine trees that rose on either side of her at an interval of twenty paces 'and here we have the foot lights   and she indicated several tufts of daisies and primroses that grew luxuriantly on the borders of the terrace

' Pray, do not put such fancies into my head,   returned Evine, "or you will set me against wings and foot lights for ever

" I cannot understand you   If I had my days to go over again, and had to play the Juliets and Belvideras this is the very place I should choose to study in   Why the trees, and the mist and the stars, are al most as imposing as gas lights and crowded benches

' And when I look on scenes like these, returned Evine "nothing but necessity could induce me to continue another hour in the profession

" Mercy upon me ! Why so ? '

" To think that, with a glorious theatre like the world to play our part in we should debase our energies by consecrating them to a fictitious scene

" Stuff and nonsense! As if our energies were more nobly employea in plying a needle

Every stitch of my needle seems the result of an effort to relieve a natural want replied the actress thoughtfully

Well and did you not hear what fine things Mr Vivyan said the other evening in defence of the stage?

'Oh he *is* eloquent' As he spoke I felt a holy enthusiasm for my employment so successfully did he exhibit the extending penetrating influence of the drama But alas! the difference between the glorious object of the vast machinery and the degrading wear and tear of its component parts!

Component parts my dear? I can't make you out You are going beyond my depth

And I fear beyond my own replied Evine, 'for I only employ the language of others to convey sentiments that are very near my heart But I suppose I must be satisfied to grovel amongst my rouge and tinsel, much as I hate them *that* is the province of the actress rather than the grand design of her vocation Out upon its trumpery! I am sure Edward loathes it

My name associated with trumpery said a voice not far from the speaker who in the warmth of conversation had not heard the footsteps of the new comers 'You make me inquisitive Miss Somers

'Pray do not keep him in suspense added Ronald, who bore Edward company ' He is afraid you were criticising his last poem

Excuse me Sir the world would assure him the contrary he can fear no such judgment from me '

" I shall address myself to this quarter for the truth retorted Edward taking Mrs Bondell's arm 'Come mother I presume you have not had your walk so you and I will lead the way, and leave Miss Somers full liberty to defend herself or to plead guilty

And with these words he took the direction of a walk much admired by all the parties leaving Evine too far in the rear to remonstrate This may seem a circumstance of very little moment to the reader but he will doubtless excuse our naming it when he remembers on what extremely little hinges the great movements of life are made and is, moreover assured on our veracity that the tete a-tete with Ronald to which Evine found herself exposed was preconcerted and arranged by the young men, and that for the very purpose for which nine cases out of ten, tete a tetes between young persons of different sexes are contrived But our statement to this effect is superfluous, as the account we shall give of the scene that ensued will abundantly prove

The little party had not proceeded very far, before a sudden turn in the road placed the couple that went first out of sight of that which followed and by a very singular chance a cross road being at hand the four friends parted off in two different directions Evine and Ronald were thus left not only alone but quite secure from impertinent intrusion a circumstance which, as far as Ronald was concerned greatly influenced the tenour of their conversation

' Your professional duties are too much for you, Miss Somers! said Ronald with true concern it is evident you are suffering from over exertion

'The season draws towards its close in another week I shall be able to take a little es Your appearance warrants my making the same remark respecting yourself but that does not surprise me—political disputations must be very harassing much more so than the stage

' No duties can be so exciting as constant success Miss Somers I am a little wearied perhaps I have however, the prospect of a long holiday—in all probability an interminable one A speedy dissolution seems inevitable

' But you will put up again ?

' Not I ' I have done with Parliament my maiden session will be my last

I am sorry to hear you say so '

" May I ask wherefore ? inquired Ronald, who had a very important motive for wishing to ascertain the real nature of the interest Evine took in his proceedings

" A senator s career appears to me so glorious, she continued with enthusiasm " what employment can be more noble than to legislate ? Can there be a higher privilege than to have a voice in the enactment of laws by which the multitude are ruled and protected ?

Those who can make vibrate the heart s swee est chords have, I think a nobler vocation

' I perceive your allusion but to me our callings will not bear com parison Raise the histrion to a level with the senator ? Fie '

" Yet the former can boast the most extensive influence

" If you tempt me to talk on subjects beyond the compass of my understanding, I need hardly apologize for tiring you with my ignorance In my opinion no influence can exceed the legislator s Is he not the potent succour of the helpless ?

To grant that I must make a great admission and that granted it remains a question whether the actor, who holding the mirror up to nature gives the affections their proper tone rectifies and even sanctifies them—has not a wider influence than the senator whose prerogative at most can merely curb the lawless and protect the weak The one but puts a check on the bad propensities of humanity while the other has the nobler task—since in elevating humanity it removes the evil which the laws can restrain

' I am not convinced nevertheless it pleases me to hear arguments that would lead me to view with favour my present mode of life

' Is it possible that in the midst of success like yours you can require arguments to reconcile you to the theatre ?

" You would accuse me of affectation were I to tell you I dislike my profession ?

On the contrary it would give me great pleasure to hear you say so

And yet you advocate the player s cause with warmth

I trust I shall always do so but when called on to express my opinion with respect to yourself, I am urged by regard to acknowledge the pleasure it affords me to hear you express your dislike to the pro fession of an actress

' You then think it degrading inquired Evine mournfully

You mistake my meaning There have been, doubtless many whom it ennobled but for yourself, Miss Somers, I must confess I should rejoice to hear that a sudden change in your circumstances (a fortunate marriage for instance) enabled you to dispense with the emolument you derive from the stage

"Do I understand you aright? Would you have me prefer the captivity of a fortunate marriage to my present condition?

"It by no means follows that a fortunate marriage should be a state of captivity observed Ronald, musingly ' Can you not, he added after a pause, and with considerable warmth "on the contrary, imagine such a state accompanied with all the freedom the wife must ever experi ence, when united to the object of her love ?

"When we are loved rejoined Evine with a sigh that her companion was at a loss to interpret "it is not very difficult to resign oneself to any condition the first demand of life is then satisfied and its highest enjoyment secured Yet were I sure of being loved I should scruple to contract what you term a fortunate marriage

"May I ask your reasons, enquired Ronald, almost timidly

"They are reasons that would scarcely apply to any one but myself

'I am the more curious to hear them

"My birth and education unfit me for elevated rank ' returned Evine, unconscious of the pain she inflicted ' I am in the truest sense of the *people* Born and nursed in the midst of indigence I owe the short period of competence I have known, to a calling that alone would suffice for ever to injure my reception in society How then could I hope to find happiness in a fortunate match, that would place me in a sphere so different to that for which I am fitted by nature and habit? Not even love could make such a transition favourable '

"Your opinion seems plausible but trust me Miss Somers, it is founded on too favourable views of men Mankind are essentially weak their strongest prejudices nay their darling sentiments are often de stroyed by some sudden fascination You will not think I flatter, when I say that I recognize in you Miss Somers attraction that would not fail to gain you the esteem and friendship of the most exclusive of our aristocracy

"You will find some difficulty observed Evine with her happiest smile "in persuading me to undertake the seige of hearts so ably fortified

"I could, however say that which would at least convince you of my sincerity when I assert that you are qualified to shine in the highest circles of English society

"Whatever you may say, I need no words to convince me of your sincerity, Evine was about to observe but there was an earnestness in Ronald s manner that confused her, though she was far from conceiving the tendency of the remark and she remained silent

"You give me no encouragement to speak, observed Ronald, when a pause of some moments had ensued

"I need no proof of your sincerity observed Evine

'Forgive me then if I obtrude on you the best proof it is in my power to give rejoined the young man, with a warmth that alarmed his

No 29

companion " Accept, my dear Miss Somers, the declaration of my sincere and devoted attachment Whether you bless me with your favour, or banish me your presence, I shall ever remain your fond lover The moment of our union I should consider the happiest of my life "

' Sir ' do I hear—

' This is no unadvised step continued Ronald growing more energetic " I would not insult you by a rash declaration of sentiments I had not tried by the severest test My interest, my regard, I may say my love was excited, when first we met Not a day has passed since, but your image has been present to my mind ever presenting itself with new and more winning charms ever taking a firmer hold upon my heart Not a suggestion of fashion or prudence, but I have combated a thousand times, in the coolest moods, when passion was least inflamed, and my reason the strongest Need I say, that every struggle increased my love ? I need not, since I am brought at last to offer you the sincerest homage by placing myself at your disposal '

It will be sufficient to inform the reader, that this was the first decla ration Evine had received, to convince him that it gave her some alarm Though little versed in the ways of the world she however possessed both courage and tact and a great share of both was manifest in her reply.

Your notice honours me, she began ' I feel unworthy of it

" Say not so ' Were I the highest of the land had I the wealth of the world the boon I ask would be incomparably beyond my desert

These words were very far from producing the effect they were intended to do There was too much sincerity in the look and manner of the speaker to allow Evine to regard them as the language of exaggeration but this very conviction drew from her a reply that at once satisfied the suitor his case was hopeless she felt it necessary to avoid giving a passion she could not share the appearance of encouragement There was a firmness in her tone unusual in her manner, as she replied —

Let us waste no time in words, Sir they have little effect, when a decision is once made

Am I to consider—'

' Allow me to explain myself ' You have honoured me with an offer that my regard for you, more than its splendour, would induce me to appreciate as its deserves, had I been at liberty to do so You look surprised, Sir ' You may well do so for I am under no engagement and never listened till within the last few moments to a declaration of love Your offer, however, merits a sincere refusal I cannot accept it, because my heart is not as free as my hand and I will never give the one, when I cannot the other '

' And not engaged ? asked Ronald in a tone of astonishment

' I am engaged by no avowal by no human compact yet are my affections deeply and fondly engaged Is it taxing too severely your kindness as a lover, to entreat you to receive this avowal as a mark of my esteem ?

' Alas ' I hoped '

' If you love me you will spare me the pain of learning I distress you I see our friends you will excuse me if I join them '

The next minute Ronald was alone. He had attempted a plan which seemed to promise the attainment of objects, to him of paramount impor tance It had failed and the unfortunate condition appeared the worse, for the near prospect he had entertained of relief From his first inter view with Evine, he had become deeply enamoured of her person and the constant intercourse of a few months while it made him acquainted w th her character but served to deepen the impression Situated as he was divided between his affection for his father and his sense of honour, it will not appear surprising that he viewed with desire an union that promised to reconcile these conflicting sentiments His desire not to increase the injustice he was already guilty of towards Evine would have led him to abandon this idea, but for the deep regard, the love like affection he felt towards her Having subjected his passion to very reasonable tests for a few months he took as will be seen a more active step towards exlecuting his intention Ronald was unsuccessful, and relapsed into that dejected state of mind, which depriving life of an object makes it a toil and a burthen

When the little party met at supper there was an evident embarrass ment experienced by all present which checked the conversation and shortened the repast A full hour before the usual time of separating Evine and Mrs Bondell were left alone

The former sat for some time at the open casement looking upon the moon lit road by which the friends had departed while Mrs Bondell sat on the sofa waiting with inexpressible anxiety to know what had happened to her young charge during the short half hour she had spent away from her protection As the church clock struck eleven Evine drew down the sash and sighing slightly as she turned from the window, advanced with a very thoughtful countenance towards her companion

When seated side by side, both ladies indulged in a very different train of thought

" Perhaps I have made him unhappy ! said Evine to herself with that generous dread of giving pain which noble natures feel even when in self defence

" How serious she does look ! speculated the old lady " it is per fectly natural though—I remember myself in a similar situation— '

The remainder of the sentence was interrupted by a caress from Evine whose mind now occupied by novel and absorbing thoughts, felt a desire to be quite alone and she accordingly rose to bid her friend a good night The kiss exchanged she was about to turn away, when Mrs Bondell retaining her hand looked inquiringly in her face

' Your hand is feverish said she with solicitude

" I am not well returned Evine and a large tear trembled on her eyelashes as she spoke

' What oppresses you my love ? Did he—

Mrs Bondell was unable to finish the sentence for Evine falling on her neck wept bitterly

" Mercy on me how your poor heart beats ! What is there after all so very dreadful in a proposal from a rich, handsome young heir to a coronet ?

"Did Edward tell you it was his friend's intention to propose to me?" asked Evine with haste at the same time wiping away her tears, and regaining an appearance of composure

'Did I require to be told so? returned the other evasively "was it not very evident? Oh! I have observed the gentleman a long time I knew from his look, his manner that he had serious intentions Bless you! I was always sure you would be very fortunate'

"Fortunate! returned Evine, with a slight shudder "would that this circumstance had not happened'

"Do you mean to refuse him then? exclaimed Mrs Bondell, with mingled astonishment and displeasure

'First answer me I conjure you, returned Evine "did Edward Vivyan mention to you his friend's intention?

"We had a little conversation on the subject

"Ha!' cried Evine, while her bosom heaved violently with emotion she could not conceal

'Yes we talked about it I stated the conclusion to which my observations brought me'

'And what said Edward?

"What should he say, my love? Why, he rejoiced in your good fortune

" Did he call it good fortune ?

' That he did ' my heart lept for joy to hear him extol the young gentleman   The greatest amiability, the nicest honour   he said, nothing is wanting to make Miss Somers perfectly happy

" I am sorry to hear it,   observed Evine, taking up her taper, and making a step to retire   for I cannot listen to these flattering pro posals

" Do not be rash and silly Miss Somers,   expostulated Mrs Bondell there are titled heiresses who would jump at such an offer   Such an one does not occur every day, my dear

" It is uselees to reason with me, ' returned Evine, smilingfaintly   " my resolution is taken   I will not marry if I cannot love '   and she left the room

' Such a nice young man, too '   ejaculated Mrs Bondell, as the door closed after her friend.

On reaching her chamber Evine felt that she had never been so con summate an actress as within the last quarter of an hour   A few brief questions had given her information on the subject dearest to her heart and though the tidings destroyed her fondest hopes she had found cou rage to hear them with apparent composure   When alone, however, a reaction of feeling revealed to herself the violence she had done her heart by restraining its emotion   It was now that she experienced the dreadful and almost annihilating effect of mental anguish upon the frame and a weary time elapsed before she found in tears a relief from the throbbing heart and burning brow

She had received no slight blow   her affection for Edward had been conceived and strengthened under the most natural circumstances   Ad miration for his person, gratitude for protection, a deep and admiring acquaintance of his mental and moral worth, the long and daily inter change of every act of friendliness and engaging with him in all the trials, fears, hopes, and success, had given birth to a powerful passion in the bosom of the young actress   With all its intenseness, however, it had to contend with an inexperienced and spotless mind, unaware of the nature and consequently unsuspicious of the danger of the new and deep emotions that stole over it   Without loving Edward the slightest degree the less, her bosom might have remained long undisturbed by the fearful guest it had received had no fatal blow been given her by circumstance

The events of the evening had done irreparable mischief   Evine could no longer yield to the enjoyment of new and undefined feelings without speculating on their cause or their tendency , the felicity of ignorance was gone for ever—a declaration of love from a rejected suitor made her conscious of love   but the joy of the discovery was for ever destroyed by the too well founded conviction that her love was hopeless

Evine had the pride—the exquisite pride of her sex and she resolved her unrequited love should be dignified if it could not be happy   and determined to submit to any suffering rather than stoop to a humiliating confession of her passion

Adopting the resolution she attempted to rally against her debilitated state of body, and engaged with renewed ardour in the duties of the the atre   Her success, as the season drew to a close was wonderfully in creased the Town beheld with astonishment evident and rapid progress of an actress whose early efforts were pronounced the perfection of art Alas ! this progress was made at a cost the gold of London could not repay

Her assiduous zeal, encouraged by herself more with a view to staunch the wound of a bleeding heart than for the sake of flattering and golden recompense, undermined her constitution with fearful rapidity The energy of her efforts at night were invariably succeeded by a long day of pain and prostration In reply to the entreaties of Edward and Mrs Bondell, who conceived that exertions attended with such suffering ought to be given over at any sacrifice she urged her desire to fulfil her few remaining engagements and reconciled them to her resolution by promising to spend the recess in some pleasant retirement in the south of Europe, recommended by the physician

The interval wore quickly away and the crowds nightly charmed to enthusiasms with the acting of *the Somers*, little imagined that they derived their gratifications from the ebullitions of a broken heart

The last night of her performance and the last night of the season at length arrived Evine had been unable to rise from her sofa throughout the day, and would have despaired of going through the evening s task, had she not on previous occasions, proved how excitement supplied her with energy for the occasion Relying on this efficient but, alas ! destructive resource, she was pondering on her part over the coffee, while Mrs Bondell was superintending some improvements in the costume of the night It was a strange and melancholy study of the young actress as she went through the character of Juliet, from its gentle, delicate opening to its heart-rending close On that occasion she felt more than usually affected by the sorrows of the Italian The impossibility of forgetting her own, suggested a comparison and she felt that she could have joyfully welcomed sorrows intense as those of Juliet, and deemed them happiness, compared to the pangs of her own hopeless and unrequited passion

" I fear Edward will not join us this evening said Evine, throwing aside her book and looking anxiously at the time piece.

" You will not go to the theatre for an hour to come He can very well be here by that time returned Mrs Bondell

" Do you know where he is gone then ?

I was to keep it a secret but as the news may reach you from another quarter I almost think it would be advisable to tell you myself

" Pray tell me at once I feel unable to endure suspense

" Well, then you remember, I presume that we have not seen Mr Edward s friend, the Viscount s son, ever since the evening you walked with him at Hampstead

" His absence I very much regret but after what passed at that time, you cannot consider it surprising

' I am sorry to say it is but too natural continued Mrs Bondell assuming a very grave manner ' So nice a young man ! I shall never forgive you for throwing away such an opportunity

" I consulted my heart—the best guide in such a case Let us however, allow this subject to drop to me, it is not an agreeable topic

" You are not surely so cruel as not to wish to know what has become of the young gentleman ?"

' I shall always be glad to hear of his happiness

' I am very much afraid   added Mrs Bondell with something like severe solemnity, "you will be under the painful necessity of hearing something about him of a less agreeable nature

" Nothing happened, I hope—

" Oh no ! nothing has happened poor fellow ! He hasn t shot himself '

" I know you would not jest if you had anything serious to tell me, ' said Evine   yet I confess you make me anxious to hear what you have to say

' The unfortunate young gentleman, (I must call him so, for my *own personal* experience teaches me to consider it a great misfortune to be crossed in love at his age,) is only gone into voluntary exile, far, far away from his native land

' Voluntary exile ' What do you mean ?'

" I mean that the disappointment you caused has driven him abroad Parliament was dissolved last week   and he leaves London to day for a foreign part '

' To day ?'

" Yes ! Edward is gone to take leave of him   He is going out as secretary to the Duke of —— "

" As secretary ! thought Evine   How strange for a young man of his prospects and condition !

Evine was unconscious that Ronald had thus engaged in what to him was servitude in order that he might at some future day be enabled to present her with the estates of Minhurst in a more favourable state than they had been   Such however, was his design, when, tearing himself from every tie, he submitted to make one in the household of a noble man who purposed recruiting his fortunes by a few years residence on the Continent

While Evine was yet pondering on this piece of news Edward returned His countenance was pale, and even haggard   he compressed his colourless lips with violence, as if to restrain some powerful emotion , and in his restless eye the young actress read extreme anguish

" Let me give you some coffee ' she said, presenting him at the same time with a cup   " it will compose you

" I am very well perfectly so I want no composing said he but the quivering lips, and petulant tones with which he spoke, contradicted his assertion

He sank into a chair, faint with exhaustion, and, burying his face in his hands, he appeared overwhelmed with grief   At a signal from Evine, Mrs Bondell withdrew, and the affectionate girl advanced towards her protector

Let me beg of you to take this coffee, Edward ' it will do you good, said she, in an accent too kind to be disobeyed and he drank off the contents of the cup

" There, now you will be better stay, let me wipe the damp from your forehead   Edward is it the loss of your friend that brings these cold drops to your brow ?

PUBLISHER'S NOTE

pp 227-232 are missing / misnumbered

' Call no one my friend ' exclaimed the young man, with a violence that alarmed her "I am a wretch, and deserve none If any man calls himself my friend, he is a liar or a dupe I—a friend? No! no! There are no friends for such a wretch as I am!

'Check this excitement, Edward tis dreadful What can have brought you to this state of agony?

' Ask me not, if you would not spurn me from you with abhorrence I have done that it drives me mad to think of wretch, villain, that I am !

"I cannot believe it, exclaimed Evine, looking with alarm and pity on the features of her friend, now agitated almost to convulsions, and pa'e as death 'I cannot believe it"

Torrents of tears—tears of deep sympathy, streamed down her cheeks as she spoke

They were perceived by Edward in a moment he knelt at Evine's side and raising his eyes tenderly to her s

' And you, my kind and gentle friend, continued he "must I grieve you too, infuse a drop of bitterness into your cup make unhappy a moment of your existence which, to be equal to your worth, should be joyous as the sunshine? Do not shed tears for me I am unworthy of them Go my kind and good Miss Somers it is the hour the public wait for you Go, obtain their applause, and forget Edward Vivyan for ever '

"I do not leave you Edward till you are more composed '

"I am composed now, said he, seating himself sullenly in a chair "Leave me ! '

'Will you not go with us to the theatre, Edward ? '

"To the theatre! No! no! I dare not go to the theatre to night *she* will be there!

"Who, Edward? inquired Evine incautiously

"No one that yon know—one whom I |dare not meet—I cannot go to night '

"It is my last night,' said she, in a tone of entreaty

"I am glad of it nothing then need defer our visit to Italy

"You surprise me, Edward but last night you expressed a reluctance to leave London

"And now I dare not stop in it another four and twenty hours "

"Something very terrible must have happened to change so suddenly your intention

"You guess rightly, my kind friend—terrible indeed '

"I wish I could assist or comfort you '

"Bless you a thousand times ' Be not alarmed It appears terrible to me but there are many would consider lightly what has destroyed my peace for ever so be not anxious on my account, since a death blow to one is a jest with another

"I cannot be otherwise than anxious, when I see you so violently distressed '

"Then I will be distressed no longer said Edward, striving to assume an air of gaiety

As he paced the room, attempted to hum a lively air, adjusted his cravat in the glass, and made other manœuvres intended to conceal his agitation   Evine watched him closely, and saw easily through the deception he attempted to impose on her

' I would not be impertinent, said she, after a long pause, rising and coming towards him ' but I do wish you would treat me as your friend'

" Did I ever treat you otherwise, Evine ? '

" You do so now, she replied

" I am not aware of it   How may I rectify this unfriendliness you complain of ?

" Make me your confidant

This request, made in accents of the most importunate affection, was accompanied by a look that had a powerful effect on Edward

" Why should I not ? thought he and the next moment, " for what reason do you wish to be my confidant he inquired

" That I may enjoy the first prerogative of friendship, returned Evine " the privilege of sympathising with those we love

' If I were to comply, alas ' I should lower myself in your esteem

" I will answer that you shall not I may perhaps give you a better opinion of yourself

" I have been long unhappy, ' said the young man, almost won over to accede

' Oh I have known it—day after day for the past month if you would not grant me your confidence, I have perceived and grieved for your distress of mind '

" And you have speculated on the cause, perhaps?"

" I could not help doing so my wish to alleviate your pain made me curious '

" And may I ask the result of your conjectures ? ' inquired Edward, who had almost decided on making a confession, but wished to bring it about without making a formal prelude

" You will not be angry if I have chanced to conjecture aright ?

" Your sagacity will secure you a pardon so, my good natured physician, pronounce at once my disease

Blushing with deepest crimson, and with a beating heart Evine faltered—

' Love ' '

" Call it madness, infatuation, crime—by any other name than love,' exclaimed Vivyan, with violence   " Yes, he added, making an effort to be calm, and leading his companion to the sofa and taking a seat on it at her side —" you shall know it all—my bosom craves a confidant, Heaven knows it is laden with an intolerable burthen '

Alarmed at the agitation of his manners Evine implored him, if he felt the task too painful, to wait a calmer mood Edward, however, now seemed intent on revealing what a minute or two before he was unwilling to disclose, and immediately commenced his story

" I was very young said he ' a solitary diligent village student, when during a lonely ramble, my path was crossed by a beautiful young lady attired with simple elegance, and accompanied by a female attendant and livery servant   In our hamlet I had met many pretty faces, but never

No 30

before had I stood in the presence of high born beauty, adorned with the refinements of opulence and taste   She passed softly by me   but her passage remained impressed upon my mind like some exquisite visit of loveliness   Day nor night was she absent from my thoughts until the time of our next meeting   It was in the cottage of my mother that I next saw her   she had been drawn thither by some errand of mercy, for she was rich, and gave largely in the neighbourhood   I drew back when I perceived her   a strange feeling took possession of my breast, and though I longed to gaze upon her, and to catch the music tones of her voice   I dared not enter her presence   I listened to the conversation carried on between them   she questioned my mother about her comforts   the good old woman could not exclude her son from the catalogue   my mother named me, and the lovely visitor repeated the name   I thrilled at ecstacy that I have since smiled at as ridiculous, when I heard her pronounce the sound to which I had been taught to answer   My mother s affection made her proud of my acquirements   my little learning by juvenile rhymes—these were all mentioned   the maternal panegyric was listened to with patience   nay more with interest   and at last I heard   conceive my joy   my rhymes   my favourite piece   the piece in which I put confidence, read aloud by the fair stranger   Never shall I forget the music she imparted by her clear, well modulated intonation to my verses   My heart was enamoured before , but from that hour I lost all power over it   I became one overpoweringly in love—I the lowly sexton s son with the great peer s daughter   So enslaved was I by my hopeless passion   such was its pernicious tyrannising influence, that it consumed me like a malignant fever   my health failed rapidly, and I was obliged to seek a cure in the change and bustle of London   But you must long since have repented driving me to this long story

"Go on, go on ' said Evine, with the earnest tones that betray deep interest

The history of my success   resumed Edward, " since I arrived in London is known to you   but alas ' the good fortune which opened my way into society brought me again in conjunction with the lovely lady who had deprived my heart of its peace   When I next saw her, she was pale and pensive enduring with evident though uncomplaining torture the galling charms of a splendid marriage   It was at her own house, whither I had been invited by her husband   Our meeting renewed my unhappy passion   it raged in my bosom with redoubled ardour, and I again strove to shun the charming person whom honour as well as prudence now forbade me to cherish   Chance seemed strangely to oppose the attempts I made to expel her image from my mind   for we again met at the house of a common friend   This meeting was more dangerous to my peace than the preceding ones had been   She was now too plainly the drooping victim of domestic trials   unloved and deserted by her husband—separated from every friend she valued she pined away in solitary splendour   Had you seen her pale face and worn frame, Evine you would not wonder that I complied with her request, that I would visit her notwithstanding the danger of such intercourse to my own peace   I consented, where denial would have been cruel, and hoped to merge the lover in the friendly visitor bent on diverting a neglected wife from the ennui of her situation But why should I distress you with the sad details of this unfortunate attachment Trust me Evine we were neither of us so criminal as to seek it Unawares we became enslaved—we loved —we became necessary to each other yet both concealed the passion honour and duty required us to avoid While we were silent, we could yet confront each other without the blush of shame or the pangs of remorse but the fatal moment of avowal was destined to arrive—our hearts surprised our prudence—the irrevocable expression of what passed within us took place and this day—but this day, Evine we tore ourselves asunder—lovers never to meet again

" Poor Edward ' sighed Evine who had listened to his story with all the interest a tale so like that of her own heart was calculated to inspire ' you have been weak perhaps, but your decision to part is noble

I have acted vilely returned Edward have I not destroyed the peace of an innocent heart—dishonoured myself by confessing the unhal lowed secret of my breast ? I am miserable—deservedly miserable, Evine ' But you will keep them waiting at the theatre I cannot go with you *She* will be there with the earl her husband , it is an engage ment of some standing Go Evine and may you never prove the an guish of a passion opposed to duty '

The sigh which accompanied his last words was responded to by a deeper one from the bosom of his companion as she left the room

We will not attempt to represent to the reader all that Evine experi enced as she exerted herself for the amusement of the public an hour after the above interview Weak in body and oppressed in spirits she needed the flattering homage that greeted her appearance as the play proceeded excitement overcame debility and she infused into her per formance a pathos that produced a great sensation on the audience

Towards the close of the third act a slight circumstance powerfully affected the actress, and the sorrows of her own bosom identifying them selves with those of the character she represented, threw into her acting touches of nature that drew tears from the most indifferent spectators At this period of the play a party entered the stage box on the first tier Evine was standing near it and her attention was drawn towards the new comers by the noise their arrival occasioned Her hasty glance towards the box enabled her to catch the pale and pensive features of a laay A high forehead and regular features satisfied Evine that she be held Ronald s sister the countess of Wagmouth, the unhappy object of Vivyan s attachment and in reality her own rival

It was a dreadful task for the young and timid girl, a prey to the most violent and tormenting feelings the breast can prove, to struggle with her emotion in the presence of a multitude and to give all her energy to the business of the scene There are seasons, however, when the fever of conflicting feelings supply the place of self possession—when the mind rushes to duty and discharges it impetuously with the same effect as when under the influence of calm deliberation

Scarcely conscious of what she did the young actress gave the reply to her cue and fell in with the business of the scene as it occurred

The warmth with which she delivered the verses of the poet gave relief to her own heart at times they seemed strangely suited to her own case, the very interpretation of her passing thought   It was then that her voice rose loud and appalling with passion through the crowded area, or sunk into the deep whisper of oppressed tenderness then came the tran sition from wild elation to vacant despair then the loud laugh of phrenzy, with all the fearfulness of nature, subsided into the stifled sob of grief

The throng were spell bound, awe struck   and when they recovered from the emotion such passages produced, applause protracted and deafening rung through the house   These tremendous sounds scarcely suf ficed to bring the performer to a sense of her situation, so nearly did her excitement approach to idiotcy   If they checked for a moment the " whirlwind of her passion,' the unconscious gaze she turned on the au dience, mistaken for the perfection of art, drew down renewed plaudits Among the thousand faces, one only could be said to meet her vision the mournful countenance of Mira who, moved by deeper sympathy than the fiction of the scene could excite, watched the performance with breathless interest from her box

The public were that evening gratified at the expense of a broken heart   and when the curtain fell on Evine s last performance, she was borne senseless to her dressing room

---

CHAPTER XXX

As soon as the necessary preparations could be accomplished, Evine and Edward, accompanied by Mrs Bondell, started for Italy Edward having first paid a brief visit to his mother, who had long since derived every advantage from the good fortune of her son

In the brief space of a month, the invalid and her friend were comfortably established in a modest villa on the banks of the Arno   In this re treat we must leave them for a time, and bring before the reader some events that took place in the neighbourhood of Minhurst during their absence from England

It was a fine autumn noon, and two foot travellers, leaving the borough of P————, journeyed at a slow pace in the direction of Minhurst The female was old and decrepid, and almost too infirm to use the heavy staff on which she lent for support   Her companion, yet in the prime of life, affected the appearance of age and bearing on one arm a basket containing a stock of wares, varying in value from a farthing lace to a sixpenny razor, jogged on heavily at her side   They conversed but little exchanging a few words at rare intervals and then the wild random re marks of the woman often failed to disturb the meditations of her fellow traveller

' Tis a weary way,' she exclaimed, coming to a halt at the summit o a steep ascent

' Patience, mother ' another hour s walking and we rest for the night

" Why do you drag me about thus ? continued the old woman, pet
tishly   " Better have let my old limbs burn in the mad house, than trot
me about till they ache at every joint

" Another day and we shall have finished our search in the neighbourhood   then if I learn no tidings of my poor daughter——

" Poor thing !" muttered the woman   ' he can think of nothing but
his daughter   Well, well ! it is natural   I had a son once '

" And you have still, mother   a son who will never forsake you ' said
Welbourne with warmth   at the same time helping his mother as she
attempted to seat herself on a bank

" Ay ay ! you say so,' returned the crazed creature, looking vacantly
on him   " but how am I to know that ? you have nt got one feature of
my poor lost babe   No, no ! you are mad   I should not have believed
you when you told me so in the mad house

But Welbourne had relapsed into his reverie, and the mother mum
bled out her complaints without interruption for some time   They had
been reposing themselves a few minutes when a merry peal of bells from
Minhurst church rang through the air

MASON

The old woman started at the sound   it seemed to have revived some
powerful recollection, for her face beamed with a look of intelligence it
too rarely could boast, as starting from her seat, she ran towards a neighbouring style, from behind which the sounds appeared to proceed

Welbourne, astonished at this display of agility, hastened to the same spot It was the style on which Edward leant when he was overtaken by the mendicant and his daughter on the day when he started, a poor ad venturer, to seek for fame and fortune in London From that situation the spectator commanded, as the reader has been already informed an extensive prospect, embracing Minhurst park and mansion among its principal features

On these the poor old woman now gazed with intense interest a wild joy lighted up her countenance while the mendicant noticed it with sorrow—it so resembled the maniac looks of her most insane moments As she continued to look on the roof of the mansion glittering above the trees in the sunshine, her agitation increased, until the style over which she hung shook beneath her

" What affects you ? On what are you looking, mother ? inquired the mendicant hoping to divert her attention from objects that evidently caused too violent an emotion

In reply, she stretched out her ill covered withered arm in the direc tion of the house and exclaimed, in high shrill tones, with a frantic laugh that rent the air,—

' To my home' to my home ' A carriage to bear the lady of Min hurst to her home !

Welbourne looked astonished but his surprise was rather excited by hearing her call the place by its name, than by the title with which she chose to invest herself it being her habit as he conceived in common with insane persons to assume the dignity of a person of rank

You do not believe me, ' she continued ' No wonder It is as strange that I should be the lady of yonder mansion as that you should be my son But come,' added she, " let us go they may want me at the great house let us go "

Welbourne hesitated a moment, and then placing the staff in the hands of his mother followed her as she hobbled off in the direction of the principal entrance to the Park Although he humoured her by apparent compliance with her request, he was far from approving the course He secretly feared the issue of the visit of a vagrant and a maniac to the mansion, and while appearing to comply meant only to secure their more prompt arrival at the village where they intended to quarter for the night

As they drew nearer, however, he became apprehensive that it would be a difficult task to divert his companion from her intention Every step toward the lodge, which had for some time been in sight, her pur pose seemed to strengthen and Welbourne was about to remonstrate, when the rapid approach of a carriage brought them to a halt by the road side It was was a low phaeton, occupied by a lady and gentleman, and passing our friends on foot at a swift pace, drove through the lodge gates into the park

" The master, perhaps, said the mendicant, wishing to impress his companion with a respect that might restrain her from the execution of her plan

Precaution was, however, unnecessary for, with a voice and manner fearfully agitated, the old woman besought him to advance no further

" Shall we go into the village, then and seek a lodging ? he inquired, greatly relieved

' Any where but *there* ' she returned, pointing to the gates " Any where but there !

They turned towards the few cottages that formed the village of Min hurst and they pursued their way at a leisure pace

" *Alone*,—I must go there *alone !* muttered the old woman to her self

When they reached the humble lodging house Welbourne s surprise was again excited This time it was caused by the same demeanour of his companion Never had he known her so free from the sad symptoms of her unhappy state of mind With great composure she busied herself in making preparations for supper, a duty she had never before attempted during the course of their peregrinations Her style of conversation was also changed, the incoherent allusions she was in the habit of making to former grandeur were dropped and her whole deportment exhibited an alteration that cheered her companion

It had been a weary day with Welbourne who procured a scanty maintenance for himself and mother by the sale of wares and leaving her engaged with the mistress of the lodging house before a turf fire, sought at an early hour his wretched bed

An autumn evening shed soft shades over a rich harvest scene when the old woman stealing from the cottage in which the mendicant slumbered took her silent way with great caution towards Minhurst Park From time to time she paused and gazed with interest on an object she drew from her bosom and the bright steel of a rude but well sharpened blade reflected the moon beam that played upon it

Daft Mary had recognised an old acquaintance in the Dowager Lady Minhurst as that lady the same afternoon passed her in the phaeton

On reaching home after her drive, which she had taken that afternoon in company with her son, Lady Minhurst retired to her own apartment, and dined alone at an early hour alleging the demands of a corres pondence as an excuse for her unsociability

Although the Viscountess had other serious reasons for her retirement, there was some truth in this apology She was indeed engaged in inditing a long epistle—an epistle that had already occupied the leisure of many days It was addressed to Ronald, and she laboured to complete it with a zeal unaccountable to herself

The reader will perhaps remember that her ladyship, when first made acquainted with Ronald s discoveries respecting her previous life, and with the fact that the right heir of Minhurst was still living, at first decided on employing the most violent means to secure to herself and family the rank and fortune she had usurped Her subsequent compliance with Ronald s request was produced at the time, more by a dread of exposure than of any desire on her part to atone for the past Seclusion had how ever effected a great change in the opinions and feelings of the unfortunate woman Her retirement from circles where she had once been the chief attraction subjected her to neglect from persons she had considered as her best friends and thus stung by the world s ingratitude, she began to regret the heavy sacrifice of principle with which she had purchased its short lived favour The absence of occupations and amusements that at one period of life left her no leisure to heed the clamours of conscience also prepared the way for remorse and it now penetrated the proud and *sered* heart of Lady Minhurst, inflicting the utmost anguish of regret and terror

Among other painful effects produced by this alteration of feeling, was a constant dread of some terrible and sudden retribution and to prepare to meet the catastrophe she foreboded, was her first act

With this view she began to draw up a paper containing a narrative of the chief events of her life, that might be termed with no impropriety a confession, and addressed it to Ronald as the only person acquainted with her guilt who had not been either an accomplice or sufferer and chiefly as the only one whom she could hope would treat her memory with indulgence

Fortunately for erring men there is no degree of guilt and remorse that may not derive some alleviation from repentance The Viscountess found comfort in her task notwithstanding the black testimony she had to bear against herself, and the cruel memories it revived Though warm tears often bedewed the page and horror would thrill her frame till the pen could no longer trace the fatal record still she persisted, and towards the evening of the day we have before noticed, she brought her work to a close

Hitherto she had come to no decision as to how or when she ought to deliver the writing to Ronald and having placed it in an envelope, she sat down to consider in what way she had better dispose of a document so necessary to her peace As she sat in the twilight ruminating on this subject, she perceived a dark shadow pass the window of the apartment, a boudoir on the ground floor of the mansion, and opening on a handsome pleasure ground Unnerved by her employment for the first few moments, she felt considerable alarm conjecturing however, that it might be some of the servants, she resumed her reflections That evening her thoughts were mutually sombre indefinite forebodings of the most gloomy character overcast her mind and so materially influenced her, that she determined on forwarding immediately the papers drawn up, to meet the exigency of a future day

Having come to this decision, she rang for a light, and sealing the packet directed it to Ronald, at Florence, from whence his last advices bore date While she was thus engaged, her back turned towards the window, the form she had seen a short time before again drew near it and by the feeble light of a taper the worn features of Daft Mary might be seen observing with an expression of exultation the solitary occupant of the room

The Viscountess had scarcely scribbled the direction, before a servant entered as usual with a post bag to collect the letters for the evening mail A moments hesitation delayed Lady Minhurst before she could decide on placing the terrible secret beyond her own keeping in a minute, however, she allowed the letter to mingle with the others It was on the road to its destination in less than half an hour

The twilight was now almost gone and the large harvest moon illumin
ated the pleasure grounds with splendour   Lady Minhurst instinctively
opened the window and walked forth on the lawn   Her recent task had
given her mind more ease than she had experienced for years and the
moonlight had a soothing effect upon her spirits   She wandered on long
and thoughtfully through the grounds till she reached a sheet of orna
mental water at some distance from the house   At one end of it the
water fell in a cascade over artificial rocks into another basin situated about
twenty feet below   In this direction the Viscountess strolled allured
perhaps by a wish to see the dashing waters sparkle in the moonshine as
they fell over the diminutive cliff

No sooner had she reached the edge, than a long and loud shriek rang
through the air

'Merciful powers!   cried the Viscountess   that shriek—how well
I know it' No, no' impossible   It could not be real — it was my
fancy

These thoughts passed swiftly as lightning through her mind yet had
hardly occurred before the lady felt herself seized by an uncourteous
hand from behind

'Speak! Who are you?' shouted a shrill voice

"The Viscountess Minhurst   exclaimed her ladyship, striving to re
No 31

gain her self possession, and hoping to inspire the stranger with respect

" A lie—a cursed lie—death to the liar ! cried the same voice, while the speaker made an attempt to hurl the unfortunate lady from the pre cipice

Mercy ! mercy ' implored Lady Minhurst, saving herself from falling over by clinging to the garments of the frantic woman who stood near her

" You heeded not my cries, said the woman, 'nor will I heed yours away ! '

And, with a force that a death hold alone could withstand she at tempted to unclench the grasp of the wretch at her feet

A piercing shriek was the only reply Lady Minhurst returned and she clung to the other more firmly than before

The mendicant s mother now drew out a knife, and began to hack the wrists of the hands that clung to her The first cut succeeded in relax ing the convulsive grasp but the affrighted lady, making a last despe rate effort for safety, threw her arms violently round the neck of the mad woman The terrific thrust with which the latter endeavoured to push her off proved fatal to both they lost their footing, and, struggling in each other s hold fell into the deep basin beneath

The ill fated Viscountess received retribution from the hands of her victim

CHAPTER XXXI

AMIDST the confusion occasioned at Minhurst by the circumstance re corded in the last chapter the first care of the Viscount was to send his son tidings of the dreadful event

Ronald was then at Florence endeavouring to vanquish his dejection by assiduously attending to his duties as secretary, and by an enthusi astic study of the treasures to be found in that fairest of cities He was already restored to partial tranquillity, and if the image of Evine occa sionally disturbed the philosophical resignation he had almost succeeded in acquiring, he endeavoured to soothe the pang of disappointed love by encouraging an elevated friendship for its object —a poor substitute for the unutterable felicities of a reciprocal passion

Among the few acquaintances he cultivated during his stay was a Mr Osborne a young English physician of small fortune whose passion for the fine arts fixed him at Florence This gentleman united an excellent heart to an intelligent and well educated mind and in his society the presumed heir of Minhurst passed many pleasant hours

Ronald and Osborne were together when the post arrived from Eng land, that brought Lady Minhurst s packet, and with it the tidings of her death

" I have employment provided for the evening, you see, ' said Ronald, as he took the letters from the servant, unaware as yet of their con tents

' I am sorry for it,' returned the doctor   I wisded to introduce you this evening to some new acquaintances of mine,—a worthy English family whom I visited professionally, till they welcomed me as a friend

' Friends of yours, Osborne, would draw me from home at any time

" Then I must engage you for the first leisure evening   I am sure you will be delighted with the introduction   I have rarely met with more interesting companions than the young people '

" To morrow evening you may rely upon me

The friends now separated and Ronald sat down to peruse his dis patches   Alarmed at the signs of mourning they presented which had escaped notice on first receiving them   his heart beat violently as he ran over the contents of the first letter

It was from his father   and relieved him from painful anxiety, by an nouncing the real nature of his bereavement   As soon as he recovered from the shock the information produced   he proceeded to examine the other packet

It would be difficult to describe his feelings when he recognised the hand writing of his grandmother   and found that the paper was dated on the day that she had ceased to live   but his emotion knew no bounds when he ascertained the contents

After expressing at some length, sentiments of true penitence and re signation   Lady Minhurst gave a circumstantial account of the crime which had embittered the best part of her life

She dwelt long on the temptation that led to its commission   Her early life, it appeared, had been spent in obeying every impulse of a warm impetuous temper   Born in a low station   but endowed with many per sonal and mental advantages   she became at an early age   deeply ena moured with the father of the present Lord Minhurst   The attachment was reciprocal, and unknown to his family   He made her promises in an hour of youthful enthusiasm that he afterwards wanted courage to keep   l rom that moment she had set her heart on becoming Viscountess Minhurst   With indefatigable zeal she acquired accomplishments that were considered rare even in the highest circles   and to render more complete her expected change of caste, severed herself, without excep tion, from the friends of her humbler condition   Scarcely, however had she finished the process of education which she hoped would qualify her for the high alliance   than her hopes received a death blow by the marriage of her lover with a young lady   an orphan of rank and fortune The whole energy of her nature was now bent on the ruin of her success ful rival, Evine   Viscountess Minhurst   Circumstances favoured her project   the new couple lived unhappily together   and the birth of a son failed to appease their mutual aversion   This dissatisfaction was increased on the part of the husband by discovering that his lady had previously to hre marriage   entertained a passion for another   Finding no pleasure in her society, the Viscount renewed his intimacy with his former mistress, and, in a moment of confidence, made her acquainted with his domestic misery The same night a plan was conceived by the ambitious woman, which held out in the event of success, prospects equal to her proudest hopes   At this juncture she became acquainted with Grasp, in whom she found an efficient aid   At first they proposed to make the then Viscountess the instrument of her own ruin   being, however, baffled in this design by that lady s prucence, it was next resolved to strike a surer and more desperate blow   The Viscount, exasperated against his lady confined her to the seclusion of Minhurst, where she beguiled the tedious hours by nursing her sickly son

The servants of the place, all taught to hate their powerless mistress, were easily bribed to carelessness and neglect   and one evening, while they were engaged at a village festival got up for the occasion the soli tude of the unfortunate Viscountess was invaded by her implacable foes The wife was then desired to give place to her rival and on her attempt ing to remonstrate, was given to understand by the worst of proofs, that she was wholly in the power of a desperate and incensed woman   To wring from the Viscountess some writing that might criminate herself, while it accounted for her sudden absence was part of their scheme This request, however, she resisted with heroism until she saw her child s life was endangered by her refusal   The mother then prevailed over the woman and with a trembling hand she scrawled a few words dictated by her rival, that sufficed to condemn her for ever in the Vis count s estimation

This done, the young wife was carried by force from her home   and separated from her son, she languished for a whole life in captivity with the desperate and insane   and, as we have seen on her restoration to liberty, differed in no respect from the unhappy society she had so long been compelled to keep

The writer further then described the effect produced on the Viscount by the sudden disappearance of his wife, and the note in her hand writing found after her departure   Prejudiced enough to form the most unfavourable opinion of what he willingly believed to be a voluntary step he at first determined on making her flight public and thereby expose her to the censure of the world   There were, however, those near him whose interest was opposed to this course   and one of them had sufficient power over his lordship to induce him to adopt measures more compatible with her ambitious schemes

We will spare the reader the long arguments by which Lord Min hurst was won over to comply with her views and which were fully detailed in her letter to Ronald   It will suffice to inform him, that a fortnight after the supposed flight of Lady Minhurst, a splendid funeral issued from the mansion which was understood to convey to their last abode the remains of the Viscountess

Before the usual period of mourning had elapsed the mistress of the Viscount became his wife, and exulted in the state and influence due to the Lady of Minhurst   It appeared also that his lordship had been assured his lawful wife would never again trouble his repose when he consented to the feigned interment but it was not till a few days before heir marriage that he ascertained the true particulars of the case   At

hat time however, he laboured under the infatuating influence of pas
sion, and became, in some sense, an accomplice to the crime he would
in his latter days gladly have avoided, had his courage or circumstances
permitted

An earnest request that her grandson would adopt no rash steps to
reinstate the lawful heir of Minhurst in his possessions, with an assu
rance that every measure as far as the writer had influence should be
taken to improve the estate, concluded this long confession of early
crime

CHAPTER XXXII

RONALD read the epistle, the substance of which has been given in the
preceding chapter, with mingled feelings of emotion and surprise With
this if a sense of a gratification was blended when he reflected that the
last hours of his relative s existence were softened by repentance, his
meditations will be easily understood Giving way to an expression of
regret at the fate of one with whose fortunes he had been so closely
interwoven, Ronald sat down to write a note to his medical friend for
the purpose of cancelling the engagement made between them, alleging
that the intelligence he had received from England incapacitated him
from enjoying the pleasure he would otherwise have experienced in join
ing the party of the evening

Thinking that a stroll in the open air might contribute to revive him,
Ronald quitted his apartments for the *Piazza del Cano,* where the lateness of the hour and the absence of intruders contributed to render the
scene peculiarly adapted for one disposed, like him, to meditation The
sky was without a cloud, and of that clear blue colour that can be met
with alone in Italy A general warmth pervaded the atmosphere, and
gentle zephyrs impregnated with odours from the sweetest plants that
the gardens around Florence could boast of came floating towards him,
laden with an exuberance of perfume that soothed, as much as it re
freshed, the mind of the wanderer He was absorbed in a reverie of
the past when his attention was aroused by the sound of footsteps that,
approaching slowly towards the spot where he stood, seemed from the
regularity with which the footfall fell upon the pavement those of per
sons who like himself were attracted thither by the beauty of the night,
and the tranquillity of the place Selecting one of the most secluded
of the porticos for the purpose of concealing himself from the sight of
those passing Ronald stepped behind a pillar, as he did not choose to be
disturbed by the officious, although perhaps well meant, remarks of any
casual stranger he might meet He had scarcely carried his designs
into execution before he found, to his surprise, that the voices were fami

liar to him and soon after recognised in the speakers the persons of Ed
ward and Evine

Edward, said the maiden, as if in reply to some former question
" in obedience to your wishes I quitted for a time the country of my birth
to roam over the plains of Italy To you I owe not only the restoratio
of my health but the peace of mind attendant on it You have taugl
me to subdue a passion which I had no right to encourage to control
temperament that had nearly wrought my ruin If gratitude warme
into love at first, the same feeling now impels me to allow my love 1
subside into gratitude With a woman s heart I have cherished the pa
sion—but with a woman s pride I here discard it Henceforth beho
me not your betrothed wife, but your sister—your *own* s ster Evine '

And as she said this her countenance became even more beautiful tht
before as the energy of a wise and firm determination reflected its infli
ence upon her features, to which her recent illness had imparted a pal
and more thoughtful cast

' Thanks thanks my dear sister Evine, responded her companion
' for such you now are your acknowledgments of the past love you bo1
me I appreciate as it deserves and my unabated interest in your welfa1
for the future, will prove to you that with the salutary change in your ow
sentiments, my affection—brotherly affection I mean—remains as stro1
as ever '

' Then I shall end my days in happiness, as well as in seclusion,
smiled Evine

" In seclusion? What mean you?

' In me you behold a self elected candidate for the veil I inten
becoming an inmate of the adjacent convent, and resigning the glitterin
robes of the London actress for the plainer and more congenial habits (
the F orence nun My mind has been dwelling on this for some time
and I am now determined

' Evine I beg, I entreat you———

" It would be of little use There was one indeed who, next to your
self possessed an influence over my heart but he is far, far away, fro1
here perhaps we may never meet again '

" You allude to my friend Ronald? said Edward " Would indee
that he were here to second my entreaties, that you might alter your d€
termination, and that the pure and ardent affection he has so long born
in secret towards you, might meet its reward by a response in your ow
breast

" Then behold him here' cried Ronald having been unintentionally
listener to the latter part of the conversation, and stepping from behin(
the pillar, continued, ' he is here, Evine here to throw himself at you
feet and own for the mistress of his devotions her claims to a title whic!
too long has been withheld from her In you, Evine, I behold the Vis
countess Minhurst

Edward! Ronald! by turns exclaimed the doubting girl " is thi
some dream in which I am indulging, some frightful phantasy from whic!
it were happiness to wake? Or is it true? quick, relieve me from m
suspense

"It is indeed true, pursued Ronald "and the only reason that on our last interview prevented my explaining the circumstances then was that by retrenchment and my exertions here I might present the estates to you as ample and as rich as when they first fell into the possession of our—I beg pardon—of your family

"Ronald my friend can this be so ? exclaimed Edward Vivyan "this is then, indeed a day of joy—but let us lose no more time in idle conversation in the street come with us to our hotel and we will there discourse further of these matters

"Evine Countess of Minhurst ? he thought to himself "then the once forlorn beggar girl now is really a peeress ' the open heath is exchanged for the marbled hall—the floral carpet that nature spread in profusion at her feet, bartered for one of art s most costly productions and the blue vault of heaven yielded in return for a tapestried roof Well ! Evine wherever she may be will yet remain an ornament to her station, and in whatever exalted position of society she may be placed in will reflect lustre on herself and all around her

Returning to the hotel where Vivyan and his fair charge stayed the events of the last few months were briefly recapitulated and explained Ronald related at length the details that had reached him of the fate of his relative the late Viscountess Minhurst, and pressed once more his suit to Evine who urged by her own heart and still further by the persuasions of Vivyan, gave way to the torrent of eloquence with which Ronald enforced his appeal and sinking into his arms proclaimed herself *his* The joy of the two friends on receiving this manifestation of her regard and love became almost too great for utterance and they were compelled to read in each other s looks the pleasure that they individually felt could not be expressed

When the first ebullitions of joy had in some degree subsided, Edward inquired anxiously after the health of his first love Mira the sister of his friend and was surprised to learn that Ronald had not received letters from London for some time past, the cause however he attributed to the uncertainty of a continental transmission of letters, and not to any neglect at home

The night having now become deserving rather of another appellation Ronald, his heart bursting with emotions of joy and pleasure at this unexpected meeting retraced his steps homeward but not without receiving from both Vivyan and Evine a strict injunction that he would call with his medical acquaintance, Mr Osborne who by the way turned out to be one of their daily visitors, at an early hour on the following day

We shall not dilate upon what followed The nuptials between Ronald and Evine were speedily solemnised and the four—for it must be remembered that the good old lady, Mrs Bondell was one of the party—set out very soon after on their return to England Evine s health had now become completely re established and, as if with the assumption of the title, her form had likewise undergone an alteration her gestures were more stately and majestic than before and her features more commanding The papers which Ronald had placed in her pos session proved beyond a doubt the validity of her claims and the only drawback upon her happiness was the hope that her parent he whom she had too much reason to believe was dead, would still be able to share her brighter prospects as he had done her more cloudy ones   Arriving at length once more in the metropolis, her heart beat with a quicker pulse as she reflected on the triumph she had here made, and the new world it had opened to her   Edward too who had as they approached their journey s end become more and more depressed seemed to feel with Evine the influence of the bustling scene into which they were now plunged and became more cheerful as the carriage advanced over the stony tho roughfares that led to one of the Squares

The conductor had received his directions, and now pulling up his vehicle at the door of a mansion the massive architectural beauty of which gave warrant of the opulence of the owner the footman descended and on the noisy summons that he made to the domestics being attended to inquired if the Countess of Wagmouth was in town?   To the sur prise of Edward who had watched with feelings of great anxiety the conversation that had just taken place the whole of the household were in black whilst an escutcheon before unnoticed by him, suspended its black border over the upper portion of the building

Good heavens ' he exclaimed involuntarily   surely Mira is not dead !

But his fears on that score were soon set at rest by the porter who had opened the door, returning with an anxious message from the Countess, that her brother and his friends should be admitted imme diately

On reaching the drawing room Ronald beheld his sister in widow s weeds with looks, however, considerably improved in the interval that had elapsed since he last saw her   In answer to his interrogations Ronald learned that the unfortunate Earl of Wagmouth had, during the hunting season of the preceding year the misfortune to fall from his horse which, dislocating his collar bone caused mortification to ensue and death soon followed   His companion in the chase, the Honourable Francis Fraser Fluentleigh rode over without picking him up and to this his death may be immediately attributed, as, had medical aid been instantly procured, the consequences would not have been so serious   That person, however met with his punishment soon after for returning late from P————— one dark night at the conclusion of an election dinner where the wine had been circulating rather too freely his horse slipped from under him and the rider was thrown with considerable vio lence upon the ground inflicting bruises from the effects of which he never afterwards recovered

Ere her narrative had entirely ceased the figure of Edward struck her attention and discovering that it really was Vivyan she advanced with all the first impulses of a fond heart to greet the object of her early affection   We will not prolong the scene imagination must supply what the pen would fail to do, even if it attempted it and the only resource we have left is to ask the reader to place himself in Edward's situation and imagine what ensued   The thoughts of early days and times when her highest ambition was to receive the first fond out pour ings in verse from the hands of her humble lover, came gushing back to Mira's heart like a newly found spring bubbling up its gladdening re miniscences, and scattering its hopes around like liquid drops of chrystal, freshening and revivifying the barren soil around it   Nor were the feelings of Edward less striking and acute   He thought of the period when he the poor sexton's son the world despised village usher, proffer ed his earliest lays to her whose beauty had inspired them and he re membered the wild throb of joy he felt when the blushing cheek and downcast eye of her he loved whispered to him they were accepted The portrait she had sketched and which he had preserved with a jea lous care was once more present to his imagination, as clear and distinct as when fresh from the pencil of the limner it lay upon his mother's table Since then years had come and gone   time had blanched the locks of his playmates and furrowed his own cheek with the signs of maturity but Love—that incarnation of the elixir of life—had outlived it all, and now came swelling up in his breast with the vigor of earlier years and the ardor of a first attachment   From that day Edward became Mira's constant visitor   Ronald and Evine too were likewise present upon these occasions   and the long winter evenings were generally passed in the recital of circumstances attending the struggles each had had pre viously to encounter   Thus had flown some weeks   and as soon as the rules of decorum permitted the following paragraph made its appearance in the columns of the fashionable newspaper of that day —

" We are happy to state that Mr Edward Vivyan, whose poems and novels created so much interest in the literary world some months since, is about to lead to the Hymeneal altar the beautiful and accomplished Countess of Wagmouth, who by the accidental death of her husband some time since had become a widow   The union is reported to be one of af fection alone   arising out of circumstances that we cannot, without intru ding upon the mysteries of private life   lay before our readers   The happy couple, it is stated   will immediately upon their marriage proceed to P—— the scene of the Countess's early life   We can only add that our fervent wishes for their happiness attend them thither

The announcement was in every respect correct   Edward and Mira were united   and learning that Ronald and Evine were making prepar ations to visit Minhurst they agreed to accompany them thither   Ac cordingly the carriage was soon in readiness at the door, and before long the brick lined streets and smoky atmosphere of London were exchanged for the green fields and clear blue sky of the country

It was towards the decline of one of those days in Spring when the earth, released from the icy chains of Winter, seems revelling once more in the sunny beams and glowing warmth that the sun darts down upon it that the carriage in which our two happy couples were seated arrived at the entrance to the borough of Stanstead   situated at about eighteen miles dis tance from their destination   It had been market day and farmers ped lars and idlers of all denominations were gathered into groups in the mar

ket place, listlessly detailing the news of the day, and emitting clouds of
smoke from their long clay pipes as unconcerned as if the intelligence
they had just heard of war having broken out was as unsubstantial as the
vapour that floated in circling eddies around them   The stalls had with
one or two exceptions been removed and the miscellaneous articles that
had a short time before been exposed on them for sale were now begin
ning to be packed up for the evening, and there kept until the next op
portunity occurred of their attracting the attention of the passers by
Suffering the carriage to proceed at a slower pace down the High street,
than it had previously been driven, Evine, throwing herself back in the
carriage gave herself up to reflection and watched with feelings of min
gled gladness and regret the well known objects on which she had gazed
with so much awe and veneration when she had passed through the same
town but a few years previously as a houseless wanderer   There was
the old church clock that had before appeared to frown in awful solem
nity as she passed beneath the Gothic portal of the sacred edifice now
seemingly smoothing its time worn features into a harsh attempt at wel
come   The post office too where the letters ranged in one monotonous
line against the window impressed her formerly with a high veneration
for its station now seemed a low obscure building where a peasant him
self might disdain to enter and lastly the inn—the one head inn, where
she had been driven like a criminal away on her asking for food at a time
when her father and herself had only shared a pennyworth of bread be
tween them for forty eight hours—at that very house the landlord, who
had treated her so ungraciously and accompanied his refusal with a ribald
jest and a bitter sneer—this very landlord was now eyeing the carriage
with a wistful glance at the custom he hoped to obtain, and to that end
was muttering to himself the cringing compliments and unmeaning ser
vilities that before long he hoped to practise on his visitors

Whilst she was thus occupied, she observed an apparently worn and
infirm old man slowly approaching the carriage for the purpose as it
seemed of asking alms   His patched and ragged attire plainly bespoke
the wretched poverty of the wearer and the few ribbons and laces that
dangled from his arm seemed placed there more for the purpose of
evading the charge of vagrancy than for obtaining any sum that might
be procured by their sale

The rich folks here may purchase something of me   muttered the
old man to himself   nothing to eat for two days ' I shall die yet without
finding my poor child—but who knows ? who knows ?

Concluding his speech with his usual vain interrogatory he approached
the window of the carriage at which Evine was seated and who remem
bering her own unfortunate condition was the first to extend her arm
for the purpose of bestowing a small donation on the mendicant A few
yards yet separated the beggar and the peeress when Evine who had
been for some moments hastily scanning the old man s features, burst
into a wild cry of joy and throwing open the carriage door both father
and daughter were in one instant locked in each other s arms

The old man was, indeed, Wilfred Welbourne   On the death of his mother, whose fate he had conjectured from finding her cap and shawl floating down the stream where she was drowned he continued his pil rimage from town to town still supported by the hope of again seeing his daughter, but expecting however to find her the same young guile less and poorly clad girl she was when he left her—entirely forgetting the alteration that time works in all   The manner of their meeting we have already detailed, but the power of the pen is inadequate to describe the scene that followed   Evine in the sudden extremity of her joy had fainted and the party therefore availed themselves of the accommodation the neighbouring hostelry afforded them of preserving this demon stration of filial attachment from the eyes of the vulgar crowds that had already begun to assemble

As soon as Evine recovered, the recital of her history since they had last met was narrated to her father by Vivyan, who was at intervals interrupted by Evine either to place Edwards generous conduct in a stronger light than his own modesty would allow him to do or explain away some passing remark   Thus was spent the evening and it was with strange comminglings of joy and gratitude that Evine that night sought her chamber   nor was a prayer to Him who had brought about thus a meeting between her father and herself and who had conducted her in safety through her trials forgotten by the unostentatiously pious girl   She wept long and loud in secret but her tears, instead of being the indicators of sorrow, were those of joy

On the following day they pursued their journey towards Minhurst, at which place they arrived the same evening and finding Lord Minhurst absent from home having after the decease of the Viscountess gone for a time to another part of the country Ronald insisted upon his friends making that mansion their home until Mira had fixed her place of abode as she intended in the neighbourhood

As Ronald traversed the tapestried apartments of the building and viewed the room in which the Viscountess spent nearly her last minutes upon earth he could not repress a shudder, when he reflected on the career of guilt that his unhappy relative had been drawn into by the indulgence of her wayward passions   Mira, too participated in the sentiments to which her brother gave utterance, and gazed on each well known ornament, each well remembered article of furniture with a feeling that partook of a more sombre character than she was willing to confess even to herself   With Edward Mira revisited each spot that memory hallowed by recollection of their early loves and endeared to them with its associations   It was on one of these rambling excursions that Mira found concealed in the bower already introduced to the reader as the repository for Edwards poetical productions a packet that had evidently escaped her observation before   It was placed in the centre of a bouquet of roses   the flowers had faded long since and the stems were withered and dried up but the writing was as fresh as if the words had been written the same day

The lines were as follow, and Mira smiled as she remembered that

the author then unknown and friendless was now standing, wealthy and
renowned listening to her recital of them, at her side —

"To ——

> While the busy crowds adore thee
> Far from thee I'll take my flight
> But when sorrow darkens o'er thee
> And thy beauty now so bright
> Shall fade like these fair flowers and die,
> I will return my love once more,
> To dry thy tears to check thy sigh,
> And love thee better nan before

These lines have at least verified themselves Edward said Mira
as Vivyan recalling the circumstances under which they were written
remained thoughtfully leaning on the trellis work of the arbour

I trusted they would have done so when they were penned and
viewed them in that light answered Vivyan but see your brother
wondering at our long delay is hastening to meet us and remember
that I have a filial duty at the same time to perform this afternoon
namely to settle on my mother the increased annuity she is henceforth
to receive

Resigning Mira to the support of her brother s arm Edward proceeded
in the direction of his mother s cottage which although considerably
improved in its internal and external arrangements reminded him of the
period when he had crossed the threshold for the first time to seek his
fortune in the metropolis

The old lady who had seen her son but twice since his return to
P——— welcomed him as cordially as of yore and it was not until he
had earnestly and repeatedly urged his solicitations that she could be
induced to accept the stipend that Vivyan proposed to settle on her
Leaving her in the cottage which no persuasion upon his part could
induce her to leave he set out on his return to Minhurst and was
threading the mazy avenue that led to the grand entrance when he saw
before him a figure that he fancied he had seen in his wanderings some
where before Overtaking the passenger he encountered much to his
pleasure and surprise the well known features of Mr Share the mana
ger of the strolling company, under whose auspices he first made his
debut in the theatrical world The worthy manager who at that mo
ment appeared to be lost in the perusal of some most voluminous bill
of fare drawn up as illustrative of the performances of the evening
stopped sudde ly short on hearing somebody behind him and surmis
ing from Vivvan s bearing and demeanor that he was connected with
the *chateau* solicited his interest in obtaining him a bespeak from the
proprietor of the noble domain of Minhurst This Edward willingly
undertook to do and still keeping his name and person a secret from
his companion conducted Mi Share into the presence of Evine

The scene that followed was far more ludicrous than any that it had

fallen to the manager s lot to represent upon the stage Share alter
nately opened and closed his eyes as if doubting whether he was awake
or not and at last, finding from Evine s manner that she was really
the young actress whose fame had extended from his boards to those of
a metropolitan theatre could scarcely be restrained from throwing him
self into the arms of his *protegee*

The recognition of Vivyan was productive of the same effect, and he
gazed by turns on each with the air of a person who suddenly wakes
and finds one of his wildest dreams realized The result was that the
whole party honoured his barn—we beg pardon—theatre with their pre
sence that evening and aided by sundry substantial testimonies of their
esteem, the manager left P———— considerably the gainer by his
visit

Mrs Bondell whom Edward had, before his departure seen comfort
ably settled in London was a frequent visitor to Minhurst and from
her Vivyan learned that Mr Dobie Snitch Grasp s shrewd man of all
work had taken unto himself a wife and had thereto added the respon
sibility of a public house

The last accounts of him stated that in conjunction with his fair con
sort, the late Mr Grasp s housekeeper he had been seen occasionally
with a certain ominous colour on his nose and an occasional unsteadiness
in his gait that gave rise to certain reports not calculated to enhance his
reputation for sobriety Rumour added that Mrs Dobie Snitch was also
guilty of indulging in certain matinal potations a trifle stronger than tea
but whatever may have been the causes, certain it is that in the list of
bankrupts shortly after appeared the name of Mr Dobie Snitch, occupy
ing a very prominent situation in the Gazette, and shining in all the
lustre of newspaper capitals

Ronald of course on his arrival had lost no time in communicating
with his father and from him received a letter in reply stating that Min
hurst recalling scenes and images to his mind that he would rather banish
he had determined on quitting that part of the country for ever He
approved of the choice his son had made and congratulated Mira on her
happy union—consigning to them both the care of the estate

Evine finding that her father s health was severely injured by the
severe shocks it had recently undergone recommended a change of air
to the sea side but the fatigue of the journey and the lateness of the
season probably contributed to hasten the poor old man s death—for a
few months had scarcely elapsed when a green mound circled by a rude
iron pailing in B———— churchyard, covered all that was mortal of
Wilfred Welbourne Happily when his life was taken it had become
a burden to him and his demise was therefore viewed by the only rela
tive he had remaining as the result of an unerring Providence

If Edward and Evine ever looked back upon the attachment that bound
them previously together it was with a pleasurable rather than a painful
emotion Time had softened the more tender feelings of love into the
purest ebullition of friendship and this threw a halo around their social
intercourse that influenced not only their happiness but that of those

around them Thus through the most severe trials through the most
adverse circumstances, and under every change of fortune did the self
relying power of a woman's heart make its way to rank and opulence, to
wealth and happiness   If it has been shown in the course of our narra
tive (and it is only fictitious as regards the names), that to control the
passions, to support hope, and to persevere in the path we have chosen
to conduct us through life are the only ways to ensure true happiness in
this world and pave the way for that in another it will not be said that
we have failed to attach a moral to the history of

THE PEER AND BEGGAR

THOMAS WHITE
Printe 59 \ ych t cet Strand